"I've heard yo

Molly might h

he hadn't used her mother's word.

"I don't chart love spells or cast hexes, Day." She'd had no intention of using his name. "I practice herbal healing and I read character from the lines in your hand."

"But not the future?" His face showed no challenge, but a spark of it heated his voice.

"Sometimes."

It was enough to make him sit submissively on the red velvet couch.

Molly set the candle alight. In a lowering of her hips beside his, she felt the tranquil focus which accompanied a true reading.

Hastily consulting the lines, she droned through a recitation. He was ambitious, but not prideful. He had courage, but not cruelty. He would reap riches, but not from the earth. They all wanted to know about money. It took no witch to predict his next request.

"What about love?"

PRAISE FOR TESS FARRADAY'S
Tumbleweed Heart:

[Farraday's] delightful sense of humor is in evidence here, along with a tantalizing romance."   —*Reno Gazette Journal*

"A delightful portrayal of Western life through the eyes of a widowed woman."   —*Rendezvous*

Jove Titles by Tess Farraday

TUMBLEWEED HEART
SHADOWS IN THE FLAME

SHADOWS
IN THE
FLAME

TESS FARRADAY

JOVE BOOKS, NEW YORK

If you purchased this book without a cover, you should be aware that this book is stolen property. It was reported as "unsold and destroyed" to the publisher, and neither the author nor the publisher has received any payment for this "stripped book."

HAUNTING HEARTS is a registered trademark of Berkley Publishing Corporation.

SHADOWS IN THE FLAME

A Jove Book / published by arrangement with
the author

PRINTING HISTORY
Jove edition / September 1997

All rights reserved
Copyright © 1997 by Terri Sprenger.
This book may not be reproduced in whole
or in part, by mimeograph or any other means,
without permission. For information address:
The Berkley Publishing Group, 200 Madison Avenue,
New York, New York 10016, a member of Penguin Putnam Inc.

The Putnam Berkley World Wide Web site address is
http://www.berkley.com

ISBN: 0-515-12140-1

A JOVE BOOK®
Jove Books are published by The Berkley Publishing Group,
200 Madison Avenue, New York, New York 10016, a member of
Penguin Putnam Inc.
JOVE and the "J" design are trademarks
belonging to Jove Publications, Inc.

PRINTED IN THE UNITED STATES OF AMERICA

10 9 8 7 6 5 4 3 2 1

Acknowledgments

Walking down the streets of Virginia City in the October dusk, I saw a curtain twitch at an upstairs window. On closer inspection, there was no curtain and likely no one watching, but I had the good luck to be strolling with Diane Howard, Charlotte Voitoff and JoAnn Burnett, women of great imagination who encouraged my fantasies and Molly Gallagher's birth.

On a later research trip to the Gold Hill Hotel, I met front desk clerk Viki Miller, who blanched as I chattered about the book I was writing. She grew whiter with every detail, then confided that the room I'd originally reserved had suffered storm damage. She'd moved me to a room rumored to be haunted by a prostitute named Rose. Thanks, Viki, for showing me I was on the right track.

For help designing Molly's wardrobe, I'm indebted to Jan Loverin, curator of clothing for the Nevada State Museum. To understand Molly's psyche, I turned to Deborah Fredricks, R.N., B.S.N., and very nearly Ph.D.

My warmest thanks go to Dr. Ron James, state historic preservationist, piper and a quick hand with a Comstock census, who's shared his rich brain-vault of Celtic lore time and again.

Thanks, again, to my parents, whose faith never falters.

Cory, Kate and Matt: There'd be no love stories without you.

Prologue

Virginia City, Nevada
January 1862

He arrived too late to shoot the groom.

Rose Gallagher fumed at such luck. No doubt the guests figured it was a blessing for the newlyweds, for the gunman standing spraddle-legged in the saloon doors might have taken the bride for himself and given Rose the groom as her escort back to the hereafter.

Of course, it mightn't have worked that way.

Ghosthood was a wry riddle, indeed. For instance, Rose wondered why, after months of haunting only her own cottage, she now stood in the middle of the Black Dog saloon, barefoot and clad in a white night-gown, watching renegade Lightfoot O'Deigh break up her daughter's wedding party.

Lightfoot's smile might make her Molly's heart flip like a

flapjack under her bridal gown, but he was proving himself as useless as a milk bucket under a bull.

Once, Rose might have fancied Lightfoot for herself. With his Cornish blue eyes, black hair, leather chaps and hard rider's body, he made quite a picture. Murdering the groom might earn him what he deserved—a short drop, a stiff neck and a honeymoon in Hell. With her.

But her darling Molly loved the rogue, even though he'd stolen her horse, heart and decency before spurring out of town. And Rose, brazen trollop in life, now a shameless matchmaker in death, blamed herself for her daughter's downfall.

With only a wee bit of ghostly meddling, she'd taught up-pity Moll, God love her, how hard it was to be good, when a handsome lad took you in his arms.

Now, the barroom fiddle faded to a cat's yowl and the piano's *clink-tink* hung amid cards flicking down. One last glass slammed on the bar and Rose knew she'd barter her soul—what remained of it—for a sip of throat-stinging whiskey.

With every eye in the place following, Lightfoot crossed the saloon, spurs ringing, chaps slapping. Following just behind him, riding the breeze of his wake, Rose heard the whispers.

"Right down cocky—"

"—he'd fight a rattler and give him the first bite—"

Lightfoot heeded nothing but Molly.

"What are you doing here?" Molly, furious and trembling, stood firm beside her legally bound husband.

Lightfoot stopped. His arms rose past his holsters and lifted above his gun belt. His fists opened and closed. Would he fight Molly's husband? Or run his rope-rough hands over Moll's satin gown from her nape to her crinoline's flare?

Though she had eternity to fill, Rose felt even less patient in death than she had in life. If the men planned to sling fists, she wished they'd get after it.

Rose hovered behind the gunman, but only Molly, wide-eyed and exasperated, noticed her. Lightfoot took full advantage of Moll's distraction and squared off with Richard

Griffin. Candlelight glittered on Griffin's diamond shirt studs, marking him far more gambler than husband.

"Here now, Richard." Lightfoot flashed a joker's grin and reached for the gambler's beer, abandoned on the bar. "I only came to drink a wedding toast to my best girl."

Get on with it. Rose gave the gunman a thump between the shoulder blades. *Enough of your jawing.*

Lightfoot's arm stopped short of the glass.

Are you a jester or a man? Rose swatted his backside, enjoying the chore, though her fingers slipped right past him. *Take Molly back, or take to the hills, boyo.*

Suddenly Lightfoot caught the bride to him, bending her backward with a branding sort of kiss.

Fluttering commenced where Rose's own heart had been. Full of herself and the blessed whiskey fumes floating above the bar, Rose celebrated the passion she'd set in motion.

Her jubilation stopped short.

No! Rose wished for a voice to scream that Richard Griffin had dug a pearl-handled derringer out of his fancy gambler's vest. *No!* She wished for a fleshed finger to point at Griffin, coolly aiming at the couple lost in embrace.

Lord, no. Had they held off love so long to lose it now, in a belch of fire and lead?

Shadows swirled through the saloon, candles flared and flagged as Rose's silent howls bemoaned the cold autumn morn when Lightfoot O'Deigh first rode into town and saw green-eyed Molly Gallagher, the Witch of Six Mile Canyon.

Chapter
One

Widow's weeds streamed behind her, riding the wind like a flag of warning. Beneath the signs of mourning, her hair burned bright as the autumn leaves skittering down the boardwalk. She stopped before a rough-looking freighter and pushed her shawl away from a cheek like an ivory madonna's.

Certain that she'd speak with the tongue of an angel, Lightfoot eavesdropped from behind Abner, his vicious mule.

"Your choice, Mr. McCabe," she said to the hulking driver. "Trade the milk cow or I'll offer no remedy for that gut pain. What did you say of it last time? It could split an iron bucket?"

The madonna shrugged and the giant stood, dumbstruck.

Ah, well. Mam had railed at his "poet's imagination," demanding to know how such fancies profited the son of Cornish fisherfolk and why he'd leave the sea and strike off for a land filled with heathens—red, white and yellow—who'd lead a poor boy astray.

Mam'd had *that* right enough.

But he'd wager she couldn't explain away this plainspoken angel with a voice sweet as midsummer pipes over meadows. The beauty was a flesh-and-blood omen, proof that he'd chosen well in selecting these mountains to hide in.

Lightfoot cinched down Abner's tie rope on the steep-pitched rail behind the general store. He tugged the knot, testing, before sneaking another look. They'd passed beyond view, the freighter McCabe storming after the widow as shushing leaves parted for her slippers.

Alert for her voice, Lightfoot heard only the pounding stamp mill down the hill and the slam of hooves hauling loads of rock along the town's main street. Beneath both sounds, his caged cats mewed complaints.

"Well, hell, Molly—" The freighter's growl broke over the smack of the coiled bullwhip he slapped against his boot top.

Molly. The villain addressed her rudely, but the widow let him talk as she smoothed wrinkles from the cloth covering the basket she carried.

"I'm not saying that I have a milk cow. But if I did, if I *did*—" The freighter bellowed as if increased volume would make her attentive. "I could lead a cow down to Persia's, stake it in trade and have myself a ha-reem—"

"And your belly would still hurt." The widow's veil fluttered with her nod. "Good day, Mr. McCabe."

Lightfoot slipped his index finger through the wire cage. He let the calico she-cat give it a bite and hoped the widow would toss a reprimand over her shoulder.

Wind gusted, bringing a whiff of fresh bread mingled with pine. Warm bread then, nestled in that basket over her arm. Retrieving his finger from the cat, Lightfoot leaned around the corner of the store for a last glimpse, and rammed heads with the freighter.

Big as a bull and almost as smart, judging by the matchstick space between his eyes, McCabe stood undazed.

"What in hell're you lookin' at?" He spat. "Cussed witch and her potions." The behemoth's forearm guarded his stomach as he shoulder-butted past.

Before his left hand could drop, Lightfoot clenched it into a fist. *No gun on your hip and no call to use one. Settle, man.* He would not look after the blustering giant. He would not consider the nasty glob beside his boot. *Roarin' pride is a luxury just a bit out of pocket-range.* He breathed deliberately and rubbed his brow. *Settle.*

The aroma of bread and pine lingered on the high desert air.

No reason he couldn't look after her, though he'd gain nothing *settling.* Sweet Mother, no.

A widow's hips, swathed in layers of black, shouldn't sway like one of McCabe's imagined harem girls. Shouldn't, but there she went, proceeding down the boards like Cleopatra of the Nile.

A viper in ambush moved no quicker than Eleanor Van-Brunt.

Molly still held the skirts she'd raised clear of mud puddles as she dodged across the street between ore wagons, when Eleanor, prim in a white-collared blue gown, emerged from her store's shadowed doorway to snatch Molly's wrist.

"Miss Gallagher, I know how you've tried to overcome your circumstances—your mother's frailties—"

Molly stiffened. Eleanor wasted no time on small talk. Born a man, Eleanor might have heeded a call to the ministry, instead of dry goods. But Molly refused to let Eleanor poison this flawless morning. Not when she had escaped the suffocating shroud of visions that had clung to her all night long. Not when she knew that McCabe would appear at her door, holding his stomach and towing a cow, within hours of succumbing to Deborah Green's fried-dumpling and cabbage soup. Not when Eleanor hurled emotional darts so old and dulled.

"—and I can't help thinking it would be un-Christian not

to offer my advice." The finest seamstress in Virginia City,
Eleanor preened. She fingered the edges of her white collar,
awaiting encouragement. Lack of it slowed her but an instant. "Talking to that common wagon driver?" Eleanor's
fingertips flicked after McCabe. "Letting him speak so fa-
miliarly? I can't fancy what you expect decent folks to
think."

Molly's eyelids drooped and she escaped into silence. The
refuge was the only decent inheritance Mother had left her.

If you don't like what other children say, don't listen.

In her mind's eye, she saw Rose Gallagher—*silly fortune-
teller, drunken slut . . .*—advise seven-year-old Molly—
whore's spawn, who's-your-daddy . . .—after scrubbing dirt
from her abraded cheeks and knees and a ripped green
jumper.

Don't listen. For Molly, Rose's advice lit the world like
lightning. Molly had mastered the skill at once. Childish
practice led to adolescent skill. Now, at twenty-two, she
could release the thick languor at will. It spread over her
scalp, down her neck, until her body drowsed and the person
before her, to her ears, turned mute.

Now, Eleanor's tirade faded to a distant hum. Molly's
wrist sagged limp in the shopkeeper's fingers and Eleanor
released it.

" . . . Bess mentioned how you *will* converse with that
gambler Richard Griffin, who's leading her husband down a
wicked road . . ."

Names. So often names snatched her back. Now her
trance snagged on Richard. Molly bristled as the woman
chattered. What a pity Eleanor didn't possess a normal person's need for air.

"Mrs. VanBrunt, even 'common wagon drivers' deserve
help for their ailments." Molly shifted the basket and
thought how she wanted to shake her sister Poppy for cud-
dling back into warm blankets instead of getting this bread
baked on time.

Frosty autumn mornings tempted them both to slug abed,
but an hour of comfort couldn't compensate for Eleanor's
sermons.

"Ailments! Men like McCabe and Griffin will find themselves as healthy as horses when Virginia City gets a real
doctor instead of a pretty fortune-teller." Duty done, Eleanor
tilted her head to one side. "Is one of those loaves for me,
dear?"

Eleanor plucked at the flour sacking wound around the
bread. A tendril of steam curled free.

"All for Mrs. Green, I'm afraid." Molly retucked the cloth
and prepared to walk on. "But Poppy will have an extra
batch soon, tomorrow being Sunday."

"Poppy?" As if summoned by the name, Hans VanBrunt,
broad and booming, his hair lank as moldy hay, emerged
through the door of the mercantile.

Molly nodded a greeting and the man vanished back into
his cavern of pickle barrels, shovels and iron pots.

Movement, and a cracked voice shouting, made Molly
turn. After hailing her with an arm that flopped like a
drunken pendulum, Stag began crossing the street.

"Wait." Molly raised her palm and looked quickly up and
down the street.

A frequent patient, the freckled miner had earned his
nickname, "Stagger," from beer binges rendering him too
unsteady to dig.

"Stag, stay there." Her voice faded under the approaching
thunder of a double-teamed ore wagon.

Holding a breath tight within her lungs, Molly hoped
Stag's unsteady progress wouldn't prove the wisdom of
Sheriff Merrick's ban against crossing C Street during day-
light hours.

He might make it. Most able-bodied Virginians flouted
the law, though they knew full well it made sense. Ore-
wagon drivers, paid by the load, whipped their horses into
frenzied gallops.

One lead horse shied, eyes rolling white, legs spread, trying to stop before reaching Stag, but both wheel horses
stumbled, pushing the leaders on. The wagon tongue
groaned as wood screws wrenched and chain clanked, running tight, then straining link against link.

Stag recoiled as a splattering clot of foam flew from the

horse's mouth. Bone snapped under a hoof, then Stag skidded to Molly's feet, a blood-flecked bundle of canvas and flannel. Some fool, some *second* fool, had sent Stag flying before the wagon finished him.

"Molly." Stag shuddered with tight-closed eyes. "Get Red Molly! I want—"

"Hush that, I'm here." Skirts pooling, she knelt. Gravel spat from hooves and Molly glanced up to guarantee that she'd escape trampling, here at street's edge.

The other idiot, a stranger, stood tall enough to grab the beasts' bits. He looked too lean to restrain them, but the rearing horses didn't lift him off his feet. He quelled them with some gurgling Cornish nonsense.

"I want Red Molly!" Stag trembled, face ashen, eyes hidden in a squinting web of wrinkles. Across his trousers spread an alarming stain of red.

"Stag, open your eyes. I'm here." Molly grabbed his jaw and squeezed. "Open, I say."

"Mol-ly." Her name fluttered out on a sigh and Stag relaxed, only to twist his face away. "My head!"

Molly froze in her move to examine his leg. Something was wrong. Something had been wrong all morning. Last night she'd smelled her mother's perfume, strong as if Rose hadn't died ten years ago. Well, Rose wouldn't have this man.

Molly gentled her voice, hoping Stag wouldn't further injure himself.

"Your head? Where, Stag?" She set her fingertips on his dirt-streaked brow, walking them to his hairline.

"The horse—" His nose wrinkled and she understood. Stag shuddered in disgust, not pain. The horse's panicky froth still clung in Stag's hair.

"Oh, for Heaven's sake." She used her sleeve to wipe his hair. "There. That has it. Lie still while I see to your leg."

Molly scooted down, positioning herself near the miner's knee. She picked the edges of hoof-ripped cloth free of the wound. No white bone jutted through. That smacking impact between horse and man should have done worse damage. Puzzled, she resolved to wind on a bandage and thank the Lord for sparing Stag a fracture and the attentions of Cutting Jack Slocum.

At the sight of bone, Jack Slocum, Virginia's surgeon-barber, decreed amputation, deeming it "kind" to cut before putrification set in. More than once, Molly's parlor had turned hospital to delay Cutting Jack's mercy.

Someone touched her. Most people in town knew better. Molly shrank away before glancing over her shoulder.

"Robin, good boy," she greeted the suspendered boy who'd elbowed through bystanders to fidget behind her. "Take these loaves to Deborah, can you?"

She slipped the flour sack, a satisfactory bandage, loose from the bread, and handed the basket to the boy before turning back to her restive patient.

"Quiet your moaning." Courting cleanliness, she flipped the flour sack over her shoulder. "Did I imagine your suffering increased when I 'neglected' you for little Robin?"

Taking the bait of her teasing, Stag shook his head in denial as she probed the wound. He gasped when she edged a shred of cloth aside.

"Sorry." She stopped, letting his pain fade. "That shouldn't have stuck yet, but it's all to the good. Stag, truly, if you'd open your eyes, you'd see things aren't so bad. It's a cut, yes, and that hoof took a fair chunk of flesh, but no larger than this . . ."

She let her voice trail, holding her fingers in a dollar-sized circle before his eyelids. Curiosity should lure him to look.

"There you are!" Molly congratulated his opened eyes.

"Never seen you smile like that before, Moll."

"Uh-huh!" Behind them, Eleanor VanBrunt sniffed.

"I told you to hush, Stag." Reminded that an audience pressed close to witness her every move, Molly weighed the quickest end to this roadside drama.

The fact that Stag's blood had already thickened probably meant she could safely rip the pant leg for a better view. Besides, she'd grown tired of humoring him.

Molly gripped the tear's edges, preparing to expose the wound, when she felt Robin behind her, again. She'd sent him to Deborah, away from this bloody mess. Why had he lingered?

"Could you use some scissors, now, ma'am?"

It wasn't Robin.

The stranger who'd ejected Stag from the street, then caught the rearing horses, squatted so close that Molly tucked her chin against her neck to keep from brushing faces. Black hair, blue eyes, square jaw showing morning whiskers. All intolerably close.

"Scissors?" He placed them in her palm as if assisting a field surgeon.

Molly accepted them and snipped. Why in Heaven didn't he move farther off? He sat practically on the hem of her gown. Molly grabbed a handful of material to twitch her skirt loose. At her peevish jerk, he moved.

"Thank you for fetching the scissors."

"Molly, it's here." Stag patted his inner thigh, above the wound.

Molly shook her head. Stag confirmed her conviction that grown men turned into babies when injured. Each time he thought her attention wandered, Stag complained more loudly.

Still, she snipped where he'd pointed.

"Holy Mother!" The stranger at Molly's elbow shouted, dodging the same blood spray misting her face. Snatching the flour sack from her shoulder, Molly wadded it into a pad and leaned against the blood.

A hole. For an instant, she'd seen a pinprick in the pulsing red vein.

"Get the sheriff!" VanBrunt yelled, so near she smelled onions on his breath. "Send for Cuttin' Jack!"

Stag jerked as if to sit and the stranger grabbed him. Molly resented the violence of the restraint, even though gentle hands couldn't keep Stag still. A summons for Jack the barber sounded as leaden as a death knell.

"Don't worry, lad." She leaned over Stag's ear, inhaling scents of whiskey and soap. "I'll keep Jack from you."

She sent for rope and bound it above the wound, then

called for help lifting Stag from the street into the Van-Brunts' dark store.

"Eight o'clock on a beautiful fall morning and this store's so dark you'd think it December midnight in the bowels of the earth!" Molly pressed her back against the door, holding it wide as the men squeezed past, then deposited Stag on the yardage table. "Get me a lantern."

Bolts of calico scattered as they rushed to obey.

Molly took a deep breath, blocking out the press of bodies, the hot gold light and the risk of what she must do.

As if she sat overhead, astride one of the rafters, Molly watched Hans VanBrunt dose Stag with whiskey. She had better pain-killers and mind-dulling herbs in her stillroom, but no time to fetch them.

A man lit a cigar and she whirled on him.

"Get that out of here! Are you mad?"

"No ma'am, but I ain't too sure about you!" Abashed and afraid, he backed from the store.

Stag coughed and the flesh above the tourniquet bulged. That rope must come off. And the pinprick hole must be sewn. Now.

"Tell me what you need."

Without turning, she knew the stranger's voice. The blue-eyed fool had appointed himself her assistant. Minutes ago, she'd sent him to fetch silk thread, needles and Eleanor Van-Brunt, Virginia City's best seamstress.

"I won't touch him!" Eleanor crossed her arms. "This is a job for a surgeon, not a God-fearing woman, or a—"

"Witch."

Molly didn't count how many voices uttered it. She only wondered how Eleanor could watch Stag die. How she could turn him over to Cutting Jack. Even now, the barber excused himself past one shoulder, by another, edging nearer Stag.

Molly's breath came too fast. For all that her needle took clumsy stitches, her fingers inflicted less harm than Jack Slocum's hacksaw.

The stranger touched her elbow again, reminding her he'd asked what she needed. Molly jerked away, but considered.

The Cornishman's arms had held rearing horses in place.

"Don't let that . . . butcher . . . near him." Her widely spaced words made such poor sense, she underlined them with an unwilling glance.

Did he understand? His eyes flared like a watchdog's. He nodded and straightened, rising to face Jack. Even then she wasn't certain.

"Naw, man. She doesn't need you, just now. Don't you see?"

The stranger's movements had foretold a fight. Instead, his accent thickened and his tone jollied as he drew Jack outside.

Then the crowd parted before Deborah Green, muttering that she wouldn't host Stag's laying out until she knew the reason why.

Molly ignored the warmth of deliverance. Deborah's sure stitches could replace her clumsy ones. Instead of giving in to the rush of thanksgiving, Molly explained what she required.

Deborah's brown eyes peered from beneath her crown of braids. "Make two small overhand stitches, three if I can, to tie it off, then sew the skin closed?" Deborah repeated.

"Yes. Can you do it?"

"If I can't, will you try?" Deborah frowned at Molly's tattered buttonholes and uneven collar.

"I won't leave him to Jack."

"You don't ask much, do you?" Deborah rolled her cuffs and scooped up a spool. "This will cost you a week's worth of bread."

"Gladly."

"And stay right there." Deborah nodded at a spot beside the table and bit off a length of thread. "This isn't quite the same as hemming a petticoat."

Moll's fingers fisted against the nerviness of watching her friend do the work for her. Truth to tell, she was in no hurry to go home. Her fanciful fortune-telling had finally turned on her. Looming superstition made her flesh crawl, though she concentrated on the task at hand.

Lantern light glinted off Deborah's gold scissors. Stitches

tied off, she used her wrist to push a swatch of hair back from her eyes.

Molly loosened the rope tourniquet and waited, trying not to remember this morning. She'd coiled her hair high and pinned it before stoking the stove. Kindling in hand, she'd bent, then jerked around, certain a breeze had slipped between the wallboards, causing a scurry of cobwebs to graze her nape. But her rafters were clean-swept. The second time she felt it, Molly stripped off her dress and shook it, just in case a spider had dropped into her hair.

"Well?" Deborah poised her needle in midair, ready to finish the operation.

"It looks like your stitches will hold." Molly focused on Stag's bruised and swelling flesh. The hoof had battered a basin into the leg and ripped up a flap of skin as big as her palm. "Connect whichever edges match best. I don't think he'll complain about a scar."

Hypnotic and smooth, the needle flashed in and out of Stag's flesh, making the wound ever smaller. With half her mind, Molly swore she heard the mad Cornishman selling Cutting Jack Slocum a cat.

Even that didn't amuse her. She couldn't stop thinking of the morning. As if skin had a memory, her bare neck had recognized the touch. Her flesh had warmed with melancholy, then shivered with fear, recalling the fingertips of Rose, her dying mother, as she'd reached out and stroked her daughter for the very last time. Ten years ago.

Chapter Two

Rose jolted from sleep as black as the foot of a mine shaft. What yanked her up, up, heart frantic, mind scrambling for intelligence? Ordinary sleep had never left behind confusion so profound. Had one of the babes cried "Mama!" in the dark? Had the hearth fire gone unbanked and flared into her room, slashing midnight with its heat?

No. A clock ticked in the parlor.

No. Cats bumped the floorboards, jostling for space and warmth beneath the porch.

All the ordinary sounds of home attended her as she passed the calico curtain, into the kitchen. And yet . . .

The old walls exhaled the tang of timber freshly cut. The iron skillet and the broom with its leather-wrapped handle hung side-by-side from nails *she'd* never pounded. Silly. She *must* have, and then been so gone with drink she'd forgotten.

But the crock sat out of place. Why? Thick and round, the color of milky tea, the guardian of washday rice—Faith, what a long time since she'd boiled and steamed rice and poured off the starchy water to stiffen muslins. The girls loved washday rice with sugar and cream and raisins so hot and winy-sweet you didn't care if they burned your tongue.

This dull dizziness struck her as an odd sort of headache. Disorienting. Well, it was late enough to be early. Kitchen shadows glimmered gray, not black. Coffee would put some starch into *her*, if she hurried and brewed it before the girls woke.

There now, the kettle was in its accustomed spot. Tent-shaped with its upthrust spout standing proud as any lad's—

Dear Jesus, her hand had slipped right past it. Again.

And there, where the wall belonged, glass glimmered. A glass window where there should be wood.

Where am I? Rose's cry echoed in her mind, even as she saw a reflection—not her own—in the glass window. Without turning, Rose watched the image of a strange woman move closer, bustling as if it were *her* kitchen. Sweeping past as if Rose were nothing. Oh, but she'd felt that jab before.

See here, miss—

Oh God. My Molly. Older! My Molly all grown up. A fresh beauty in—her teens? A wavering wing of madness shadowed Rose's mind. How long had she lain sleeping? How long since her gangling girl with blue-black smears beneath her eyes, with spidery cracks from water and work marring her hands, how long since she'd whispered and pleaded at her feverish mother's bedside?

Pretty, pretty Moll. Rose formed the words, but could not say them out loud. *I feel so much better! Sit, child. Let me stoke that fire and brush that pretty hair up off your nape.*

Oh, what was this nightmare? She could see her child, smell lavender from the clothes chest clinging to her dress, yet—? Her hand slipped right through Molly.

And the baby. Where was the baby? *Molly, where is the baby?*

Molly turned and Rose felt relief, then a drenching cold, like river water that paralyzes and weakens. Molly's eyes stared past her as a sudden fog clouded the kitchen.

Yes, Molly love, I'm here. Here! Look at me, girl! Leave off brushing at your hair and dress. But oh! Rose saw her girl had hair glorious as sunrise. Even through this cursed fog, that fiery hair shone, touched by the morning light—

Chapter Three

"I've no room for a boarder, unless she's a well-behaved maiden lady." Mrs. Deborah Green, delicate wielder of needles, shot the Cornishman a glance that said, flat-out, he did not qualify.

He looked pointedly at Stag, washed, stitched and still, lying in a bed that must be the lady's own.

"You heard what I told Miss Gallagher." Deborah Green creased a white sheet across Stag's chest before sweeping from the room. The Cornishman followed quickly enough to catch her words. "This arrangement is temporary."

Black-and-tan-figured carpets graced the parlor floor below. The Cornishman grew almost dizzy peering over the upstairs rail as he pursued the house's gray-frocked mistress.

"I took Stag in because it's proper. I'm married. Molly is not. I have the child and two other boarders. My husband, Mr. Michael Green, is searching out gold in California."

When Mrs. Green faltered before him, the Cornishman knew Mr. Michael Green wouldn't soon materialize to crown his lady with riches. Gold sang a siren's song many men couldn't resist.

"Keep up, sir, I've dinner to serve in half an hour." Mrs. Green's tapping heels punctuated her words with renewed vigor as they descended. "Molly and her sister are women alone. Stag's presence would be unseemly."

She paused so suddenly in the kitchen doorway that he almost collided with her. "Smell that broth! Scorched beyond—"

"Mrs. Green, I would not be saying a single slur against that soup." He savored the aroma of chicken and onions as they entered the kitchen, but she ignored him, dipping pieces of fowl from a cauldron of golden broth. "It's the best thing I've smelled in days."

"High praise, indeed, from a man traveling with a wagonload of cats." She tightened her apron strings before facing the cabbage, abandoned on a cutting board beside a wide-bladed knife.

"I shouldn't be in your kitchen. That's the truth." He ducked his head and shoved his hands behind him. What had possessed him—coated with trail dust, smeared with blood, reeking of cats and three nights without a scrub—to follow her? "And you so polite not to mention it." He backed toward the door.

"So polite, I ordered you to help McCabe haul Stag's slack carcass down here—"

"Requested, ma'am. You never ordered—"

"—and carry him upstairs." Brown eyes assessed him again, and for all that Deborah Green claimed to be married, he wished that green-eyed Molly would regard him in such a measuring fashion. "So polite, I didn't ask your name before setting you at tasks. At least I'll serve you a bowl of soup . . ."

He'd known from the instant he galloped away from Lake's Crossing that this moment would come. She wanted his name. The request lay in her tone. He avoided her eyes, knowing he couldn't use his own name, or the alias he'd earned with a gun.

Deborah Green ladled broth into a bowl, sliced off a quarter loaf of fresh bread and nodded toward the table.

"You can wash up in the back." She grimaced as he turned his filthy hands palms up. "Though you wouldn't be the dirtiest—what? Not a miner? Drover?—"

"Cat peddler, ma'am."

"Cat merchant, then, who ever sat at my table." She went back to chopping cabbage. "All the same, I won't seat you without a name." She tossed the words over her shoulder, loud enough that he couldn't pretend not to hear over the creaking pump.

Daywell. Mark Owen Daywell. His tongue knotted at pronouncing the name his mother had given a pure babe who'd grown into a man accused of murder.

He splashed water over his face and slicked his hair back. He'd raised both hands to tame his beard before the smooth jutting jaw reminded him he'd doffed the beard with his name. Hating the deception, he walked back inside, holding his hat.

"Well, Mr.—?" She held the soup bowl above the table-top.

"Day—"

"Mr. Day." She nodded, left the soup, then set upon a bowl of dough, rolling balls that she cast into sizzling grease.

Day. Far enough from what Rankin's boys had called him. *Day.* With poetic simplicity, the name signaled a new start.

He seated himself and rubbed his thumb across the cream-colored tablecloth.

"Clean sheets on your beds and pressed linen on your table, Mrs. Green."

"And why not?" She put the knife down. "I take my business serious."

"That I can see, but I've slept places where they whip the very sheet off a man to set the table under mornin' flapjacks." He gave her a mournful grin before raising the spoon to his lips.

Deborah Green shook her head and tightened her apron

strings once more, suppressing a smile. "And how is the soup, Mr. Day?"

"Excellent, ma'am. And it's just 'Day,' no 'mister,' if you please."

Deborah Green couldn't work in silence. By the time he finished eating, she'd multiplied tenfold his knowledge of Virginia City. If Day remained, he could share a shack with one of hundreds of men drawn to Virginia's capricious veins of silver and gold. Of course, he could build his own shelter. Or, he had one more choice.

"You could call on Brown Bess," Deborah mouthed the words as if they were tainted. "She'd have room. And rent includes board as well as bed, but only the unluckiest take their meals from her. A bad cook and stingy, I've been told."

Discussion of Brown Bess gave Day an opportunity to ask how many ladies the boomtown had attracted. Lone men might put up with rats chewing their biscuits, but ladies would not. His cat-peddler disguise wouldn't last if he couldn't sell his felines.

At the new year, Sheriff Merrick had counted one hundred women in Virginia City. Deborah couldn't say if he'd included the soiled doves at Persia's joyhouse, or those wretched souls in the cribs of Chinatown, but he'd numbered housewives, laundresses, Brown Bess, Eleanor Van-Brunt, Molly and Poppy Gallagher, the minister's wife and the two sisters of Christ.

At this, Deborah's eyes had lifted toward the stairs.

"You board sisters here?" Day asked.

"Two nuns, but no priests. Shall I tell them they've an addition to their flock?"

"I wouldn't be getting their hopes up. Mam was an Irish Catholic, my dad a Wesleyan convert." He savored his soup and pretended not to notice her scrutiny. No need to say he'd spent his youth yanked between Cornwall's shores and Ireland's Bere Peninsula. Easier to hide a background that remained secret.

Determined to parry all inquiries with jokes, he downed his last sip of water and winked. "Best solution to religion is to swear and swill like a Catholic, sing and shout like a Methodist."

Her laugh brought Robin, the boy he'd seen in the street, to her side. Together they stood framed in the doorway, the boy clinging to Deborah's apron pocket as he whispered toward her ear. She brushed dark bangs from Robin's forehead and sent Day a look that arrested his move to replace his hat.

"Robin thinks we should have one of your cats."

"Even the Queen keeps a mouser or two." Day bent to meet Robin's eyes. "Was there one you fancied?"

The boy twisted his finger in Deborah's apron until it bundled his entire hand. "The white one."

Day shook his head, settling into a crouch at the boy's level. "Ah, but you know white cats are often deaf? He might not hear vermin hiding in the walls. I only took him out of kindness. To keep him from being drowned."

"The white one."

"You get that table set, Robin." Deborah turned the child and dusted the seat of his pants with a swat. "You." She shook a finger at Day. "Come see me, tomorrow."

Feeling the humor in her dismissal, Day opened the door to leave and saw a straggling line of men awaiting Deborah's dinner summons. He glanced back and caught her smile.

"And, Day? You better bring two of your fine felines."

Cinnamon and wood smoke welcomed Molly. Not sulphur, not dank decay, just the familiar scents of home.

"Molly? I have your tea," Poppy called from the kitchen.

Molly leaned against the door, closing out the clamor of hooves and the slamming stamp mill. Drawn parlor curtains blocked the sunlight and she heard Poppy strike a wooden spoon against a pot edge. Then Cinder's tail thumped from his cave beneath the kitchen table.

She should scold Poppy for not coming to the door, but her sister's answer would be the same as always: Cinder would bark a warning at anyone other than Molly.

Instead of wasting her breath in a reprimand, Molly blew it on chilled hands.

"Molly?" Head cocked to one side, Poppy stood silhouetted against sunlight from the second room.

Molly moved through the dimness and took the teacup Poppy offered before turning back to the stove.

"I'm sorry there's no cream." One hand draped in a fold of her apron, Poppy dumped a loaf from its hot pan. "I used the last of it. What will I do for icing, now that the Van-Brunts' cow's gone dry?"

"I'm working on that." Molly sipped and mused. McCabe should be slurping Deborah's cabbage soup now, and Molly had ample sage tea and dill to soothe his belly when he presented it and the cow.

"You were gone so long." Poppy dusted her hands together, then bent to check the stove's fuelbox.

"There was an accident. Stag wandered across the street in front of an ore wagon."

"Oh no!" Poppy snatched back a burned finger.

"It's nothing to hurt yourself over." As Molly watched Poppy suck the burned finger, she hoped her sister's distress was for the burn, not Stag.

"Did you help him, Molly? Where is he?"

"He's fine. He only collided with a horse. Some fool—" Molly tapped her fingernails against her teacup, irritated for no reason by the Cornishman's print on her mind. "—pushed Stag out of the street before the wagon could crush him."

Molly gulped the tea impatiently and burned her tongue. Poppy shook out her apron, hung it on its hook, then whisked the broom over the floor. She took up the basket Molly had returned and arranged loaves and sweet rolls inside. Then her routine faltered. Biting her lip, she looked back at Molly.

"And what happened? After he got pushed?"

"The horse's hoof had struck his leg. I held off the bleeding and kept Cutting Jack away until Deborah stitched Stag up and took him to one of her rooms." Molly pressed her index finger on the cutting board scattered with cinnamon, sugar and pastry scraps.

"I was about to tidy that, when I heard you." Poppy

frowned. "No. I thought I did. I thought you'd sat down on the red couch." She shook her head. "Then you did come, and I hoped as soon as you had tea, you'd tie my ribbon. I can't get it."

Poppy fluttered a scrap of ribbon and the tassel end of her braid. Cutting board forgotten, Poppy turned her spine to Molly, just like an obedient child.

Which she was. Though Poppy looked every minute of her seventeen years, her mind worked like a sweet five-year-old's. Molly licked sugar from her finger and tied Poppy's yellow ribbon into a bow at the end of her braid.

"Did you give him medicine?" Poppy took up the basket.

"No." Molly scanned the herb pots and labeled jars on the dry sink, then studied the bottles casting shadows of amber, lavender, blue. Some contained herbal infusions or steeping teas. Others held only water, but the play of sunlight lit the kitchen like a kaleidoscope.

"I'll walk down later and see to him." Molly refused to fret over the delay. If McCabe weren't due, she'd go tend Stag now. Poppy stood waiting, both hands on the basket handle. "After you're done at the store, you could walk down to Deborah's, couldn't you?"

Poppy's braid lashed as she nodded her head.

"But nowhere else."

"And I won't talk to men."

From another seventeen-year-old, the vow would sound facetious, but not from Poppy. Molly wrote rules, helped Poppy sound the letters, puzzle out words, and Poppy obeyed.

Molly had long since abandoned guilt. A grown beauty with a child's mind, living in a town full of reckless, rootless men, could live no different life.

Molly ground comfrey into powder, twisted it in paper and tied mint leaves in a square of calico. She tucked both in the basket.

"Tell Deborah he's to have the comfrey." She touched the paper. "In the mint tea." Molly tapped the calico bag. "He won't drink it otherwise. It's too bitter. If she's too busy—

I—he needs that soon, to repair some of the damage . . . Oh, I'll go!"

"Molly, I can make tea."

"Of course you can. Just tell Deborah I'll be down later." She walked Poppy to the open door. "And send for me, if he's having too much pain!"

Poppy left, holding her skirts down against the wind, and Molly's throat tightened with reluctance. She shouldn't worry. Six mornings each week, Poppy delivered her wares. Molly scanned the road. No one.

"Poppy!" Molly saw Poppy turn, shading her eyes. "Where are the cats?"

Poppy shrugged in an exaggerated move. "Only Ginger—" Wind caught her words and Molly waved again. Why did the cats' absence make her edgy?

Their house, the last structure before the stamp mill, sat where even the poorest miner refused to build. Liam Gallagher had hammered the house together years ago in Johnstown. Only Molly's shrewd bargaining had gotten it moved to this bit of shovel-ravaged earth. In spite of the din, the isolated house suited her.

From behind the screen of firethorn bushes, she could see anyone approaching the house. Few did. The ore wagons rumbled by, a few miners shuttled between Virginia City and Gold Hill or Carson, and once or twice each year, a bandit galloped past.

That's it then, you've moved my house! Your poor mum was in such a muddle! Rose forced herself to show. Not that it hurt. Not quite; it was more like laboring with a babe, forcing all her energy to outline the form that had once been hers. She tried . . .

Hand on the door, Molly felt pinpricks at her temples, then the tingling dizziness she hated. *Mama, is that how it felt for you?* From the corner of her eye, Molly saw Rose, as vivid as life. When she turned, nothing was there. Molly slammed the door.

Drunken slut. Gypsy whore. She'd heard her mother called that and more.

See here, young woman! Rose found that she meant it in

fact. She saw the fingers on her right hand. *Molly, look at me!*

Molly fumed. Oh, Rose had made a fine teacher—of what *not* to do! As a paragon of virtues, she served as well dead as she had alive. So why did she long for Rose and imagine her sweet perfume?

The instant Stag had called from across the street, Molly's pulse had throbbed in her temple. As some patients felt impending seizures, she sensed the onset of what Mama had called "the Sight."

Molly splashed boiling water from the kettle into her cup. Her mother was dead. She called "it" nothing, now. Besides, the reflecting pool she'd used to conjure images had, toward the end, been a cup of whiskey. If her spirit guides had held up a red-lettered sign, Rose's bleary eyes would have missed it.

Molly shivered and glanced over her shoulder. The door hadn't fit its frame since last winter. She blamed the lingering chill on another chore neglected, but what of that odd glimmering? Molly blinked. It faded, leaving an afterimage of sunset orange.

Spirits, indeed. She had no time for weak-minded imagination.

Molly settled into the kitchen chair with Cinder's muzzle trapping her toes. Closing her hands around the cup, Molly blew across the tea's surface. Steam wisps danced in crazy swirls. Sunlight, patchworked and prismed by the bottles, warmed her back as her eyelids drooped. Through her lashes she saw the steam whirling like a snowstorm slashed with crosswinds.

A horseman all in white, on a white steed, rocked closer, closer . . . Rubbish! Molly forced her eyes open and blew a spurt of breath at the vapor. She gulped the tea, yelped at its heat and stared at the ceiling, refusing to let her eyes lose focus.

She must keep the dream at bay. The fancy had occurred a dozen times of late. Each time, her heartbeat quickened, her windpipe constricted. Molly knew that if she allowed the image closer, she'd strike out at—nothing.

A tap at the window triggered Cinder's scrabbling claws. Molly winced as his head rapped the table's underside.

The smooth-coated black dog lurched barking toward the window where a marmalade cat butted her nose against the glass. Ginger, the last of Rose's cats, wanted in. Another thump, and a gray tom, his coat thick as a squirrel's pelt, landed beside her. Not all the cats had scattered, and a good thing, too. She'd be a sorry witch without "familiars," and Molly knew she owed her privacy to her eerie reputation.

Cinder woofed. Ginger rubbed against the pane.

"They're not afraid of you, Cinder. Of me, either." The dog's pricked ears fell limp as he plopped a graying muzzle across Molly's knees, then scrubbed his chin across her skirt.

Before she took another sip of tea, the dog bolted, nearly upsetting her chair, and stood barking at the front door.

Molly passed into the other room, closing the curtain across the kitchen doorway. She straightened her spine and twitched her skirt into place. Probably a customer, come to have his palm read or his illness dosed. If so, he'd be lucky. Trance webs still trailed across her mind, leaving her sensitive and eager to work.

A demanding *moo* rolled through the door, overriding Cinder's bark. The dog turned, giving his tail an uncertain wag.

"Mr. McCabe," Molly greeted loudly. Let him hear her voice from outside, before she saw him, and her darkling powers would swell in his mind. Oh yes, she could tell the future right enough, when it came to cabbage soup and digestive complaints.

Molly opened the door to the freighter, who held his stomach with one hand and the rope of a milk cow in the other.

Chapter Four

Lye strong enough to singe a man's nostrils foamed under Eleanor VanBrunt's scouring brush. Day figured if the bone-deep mountain cold didn't freeze him and the brain-skewering cat cries didn't strike him deaf, sure this smell, harsh on eyes, nose and throat, would slay him this Sabbath dawn.

Still, Day knew he'd inhale it like perfume to get inside by that glowing potbellied stove, now that he was awake.

An odd wakening it had been, shivering in the bed of his wagon, struggling to part ice-crusted eyelashes because a voice flavored with Cornwall had pierced his restless sleep.

"A shot of the Black Dog, that's what you need, cousin." The voice had come from one of two miners, arms wrapped around their ribs to hold themselves upright.

"Aye?" he'd croaked at them, though his throat was frozen and the cold had sunk so deep that he believed his feet would shatter as he swung from the back of the wagon.

"The Black Dog, over C Street way." Day thought the darker one had spoken. "Madam Persia has everything for man and beast, or the beast in every man!" Elbowing his companion, the dark one lost his balance and clutched the wagon side.

A whorehouse, then. Drink must have struck the boys blind if they could look at him, aching from a night spent with scrawny cats and two blankets for warmth, and think he wanted a woman.

Then Day's mind conjured a beauty with hair like hellfire and eyes like emerald smoke. Her touch might make him thaw. But Widow Molly was nowhere in sight.

Now, Day stood on the boardwalk, raked back his hair and settled his hat. Once the miners had staggered off, the sleepy boomtown had stretched away from him, silent except for the rasping brush in the mercantile. Day edged the door open an inch.

In a blue dress and linen collar, the shopkeeper glanced up. "We're closed." Startled but diligent, she recommended scrubbing the table Molly had labored over, saving the drunkard's life.

"Begging your pardon, Mrs. VanBrunt?" Day inhaled the heavenly scent of coffee and blessed his knack for names. His stiff fingers swept off the hat, which stayed velvet-black no matter how he abused it. "We weren't introduced yesterday, after the accident. My name is Day." All without chattering teeth.

"Day—?"

"Yes, ma'am. I'm seeking advice." He edged a step closer to the stove. Blissful warmth caressed the seat of his pants. "And thought to save myself asking half-a-dozen citizens by asking you, a businesswoman, first."

Turning her head on the side like a bird, the woman studied him with piercing eyes. And kept scrubbing.

"Not that I'd be asking free advice." He forced his eyes away from the tin coffeepot, dancing as it boiled. "In return, I'll protect the fancy goods your store's famous for." Day stood firm against a rill of shivers. "Like champagne, tinned fruits, pearl-handled pistols for them who strike it rich."

When his flattery softened the quill-sharp lines between her eyes, Day pressed on. "Thick yellow honey and silver buckles, fine-ground cornmeal without one grain of grit, and leather goods." He took up a belt, smoothing its length before replacing it. "What a shame if you lost any merchandise to rats . . ."

"Mice." Mrs. VanBrunt stopped her brush and raised one brow.

" . . . infesting so many civilized towns. In San Francisco, for instance." He touched a parchment square identifying burgundy wine. "The rats developed a particular taste . . ."

"Mice." This time, her correction came more softly.

" . . . for the mucilage on labels, leaving shopkeepers baffled as to the contents of bottles and tins!" He gestured wide, sidling nearer the stove.

That he kept his hands from trembling owed no thanks to her. Most women would have sized up a fellow with ice in his eyebrows, felt a twinge of pity and offered coffee laced with a bit of whiskey. Still, he'd hooked her attention. Lord knew, he could have made a fortune selling cats, hats or anvils years ago, if he'd discovered this talent for spinning folks silly with talk.

Today, his profit came in words. In twenty flank-warming minutes, Mrs. VanBrunt confirmed that the miners' Persia, proprietress of the Black Dog saloon, was "a hoor." Though unsure why he craved the information, Day had learned to follow his brain's peculiar demands. And when he offered Mrs. VanBrunt a brown tabby for her time, she accepted, so satisfied with the bargain that she asked if he needed anything more.

"I might, at that, with the cold nights coming on." He chafed his arms, hinting more broadly than a gentleman should, but the witless woman had a porcupine hide for a heart. "I wonder if you'd know where I might keep my cats until they're sold?"

Mrs. VanBrunt resumed scrubbing, frowning in thought.

"I thought to stay with Brown Bess." Before he detailed the difficulties of keeping two dozen cats in a boardinghouse, footsteps on the wooden walk outside intruded. And why should he think them Molly's? Why should he imagine

high-buttoned boots and clinging black stockings, when
Mrs. VanBrunt was scolding him?

"Elizabeth Thomas is her name. A good God-fearing
woman—not 'Brown Bess'!" She dropped the brush. "I
know who you've been gossiping with to hear such slander.
Still, you're right. No inn would allow such 'merchandise'
inside. Your only hope is the witch."

Molly. *The witch.* He'd heard that accusation, but it wasn't
his hair that was standing on end when his mind conjured
her.

"The one you helped yesterday." Mrs. VanBrunt flattened
her palms on the scrubbed pine table and glanced over with
strained understanding, as if she'd insulted him.

"The widow?"

"Is that what she told you?" Mrs. VanBrunt cut off a
laugh. "I mean Red Molly. The Witch of Six Mile Canyon.
She wears black, but she's no widow. A reader of palms, a
healer—but no widow. Pity she's your only hope." Mrs.
VanBrunt leaned nearer, lowering her voice. "The girl's a
man-hater, never met one she liked. With that and the burden of her sister . . ." Mrs. VanBrunt covered her lips, suppressing a secret. "It's not likely she'll ever be a widow, Mr.
Day."

"But she does keep cats?"

"Hundreds! Howling and yowling under her porch."

A man-hater. The words tempted him like a dare. Clearly,
she hadn't met the right fellow, let alone one who'd lured the
Death Bitch to hand. He'd tell sweet Molly that tale some
rainy night as they twined together before her fire.

Forget it, man. A week more and you'll hit the back road
to Carson, with no time to wait for rain or coaxing or yielding, no time to touch wet red hair raising a halo of steam before the fire. No, a few days more and he'd go. Even the
laziest sheriff could ride from Lake's Crossing to Virginia
and order him hanged.

A man-hater? It hadn't been hate glimmering in Molly's
glen-dark eyes when she turned to him for help. *Don't let
that butcher near him.* Aye, she'd hated needing his assistance, but she'd recognized a man who'd give what she

needed. He'd been so hot to protect her; he'd craved his gun and a chance to drill the "butcher" who'd scared her. That impulse alone was reason enough to leave town.

Warmer than he'd been all morn, Day swallowed and stepped away from the stove.

"Run along and meet Elizabeth. And do have yourself a meal. You look hungry, Mr. Day." Mrs. VanBrunt shooed him, as if he were a boy. "When you return with my tabby, I've no doubt Poppy, Red Molly's sister, will be here. You'd best approach *her* about the cats. She's a simple girl, but if anyone can turn the witch in your favor, it's Poppy."

Run along he had, but not far. Just outside the store, Day was struck stone-still by the sight of a tall, fox-featured man, neat and glittering as a bar of silver as he chatted with Molly.

Her black dress was a queen's train held by the autumn wind. Attentive, she neither fluttered nor coyly lowered her head. She looked directly at the man.

"Miss Molly." The man bowed where her hand would be if he'd held it for a kiss. "Since your kindness has been known to attract strays"—his voice held a slight Southern accent and Day had no doubt its timbre would carry under the clink of coins and slapping of cards— "I hope you'll heed a friendly warning to keep your door barred. I've just heard of a murderer on the run, a lady-killer named Light-foot O'Deigh."

Day dodged around the corner of the store, startling Abner to braying. The mule quieted as Day snagged his gun belt from beneath the buckboard seat. He freed his pistol. It settled in his palm, natural as a lover's hand.

Alone in the alley between buildings, Day flattened his back against the mercantile's outside wall. Gun raised shoulder-high, hammer cocked, he squinted in concentration.

Just yesterday, he'd stopped here, listening to her banter with the freighter. Now he waited in silence, waiting for words that might make him kill again.

By afternoon, Molly stood on her kitchen table, hanging herbs from the rafters to dry. Recalling Richard Griffin's

warning, she thought his words typified all that was right
with him and wrong with other men.

Richard had known her mother in Johnstown, known
what she was and what Molly feared becoming. So he spoke
delicately. Rumor said that an Irish gunman, hired by a
rancher named Rankin, had run amok, not caring who got in
his way.

"And someone *did* get in his way, one Shawnee Sue,
an . . . unprotected woman." The name clearly belonged to a
saloon girl, but Richard hadn't snickered. He'd merely adjusted a diamond cuff link and pulled his coat sleeve to
cover it. "Rankin hired this new Pinkerton Agency to track
Lightfoot. The detective is in Carson, and he'll head up Virginia way, next.

"Suspicious sorts, those detectives." Richard's thumbs
had skimmed the ruffles of his shirtfront. "Especially of a
too-successful gambler."

Richard had ducked his head modestly, then hinted he
might leave town in a hurry. Without saying it outright,
Richard told her that he worried when he couldn't watch her
hilltop home. Countless times, she'd seen him leave a saloon and glance reflexively toward her cabin. And his protection came without strings. He always let her walk home
alone.

"Hush, Cinder." Molly tied the last bundle and balanced,
hands on hips, listening. The dog growled, then wagged his
tail, hearing a male voice mixed with Poppy's approaching
laughter.

" . . . and so I asked Miz Bliss, being the parson's wife, why
she'd use a contraption of wood and iron to—*smack!*—"

A sharp crack of clapped hands sent Poppy giggling anew.

"—kill one of the Lord's creatures, when cats, God's own
mousetraps, could benefit from them?"

Poppy parted the curtain between the rooms. She looked
up, and up some more, gaping as if she faced an avenging
angel.

Molly couldn't have recognized his voice. Still, when the
stranger advanced through the parlor, into the kitchen sanc-
tuary behind, holding Poppy's hand between his, Molly was

not surprised. Had *that* set Poppy tittering? Male hands trapping hers like a helpless rodent?

"Poppy, explain, please." After all the rules, all the lectures and warnings, Molly could say no more.

Poppy's hands tugged free and cut in front of her as if erasing the scene.

"Molly, he's not a stranger. His name is Day and he needs a place to keep his cats. Eleanor—Mrs. VanBrunt"—she explained in an aside—"told me to bring him about his cats. A funny idea, a boardinghouse for cats . . . a sort of cathouse."

Poppy's eyes rounded. Her fingers plucked her skirt pocket and her voice caught.

"Honey." Molly sighed, but before she offered a word of comfort, the man's arm circled Poppy's shoulders.

The mad Cornishman. Now that he'd looked up, with set jaw and blue eyes reproving her, Molly knew him. Where on earth had he found the audacity to reprimand her? She'd judged right, calling him an idiot for braving the frenzied horses. He was equally insane to invade her home and confuse Poppy's loyalties.

As Molly clambered down from the table, his glance flicked to her ankles. Oh, she wanted to slap him.

"Who do you think you are?" Molly kept her voice low, her feelings shuttered. "To come into my kitchen, when no one, *no one*, walks farther than my parlor?" She drew breath for more, but he turned on his heel.

He leaving *her*? Enraged, Molly couldn't even shout after him. She waited for the front door to open. It didn't. Somewhere in her parlor, he waited.

Very well. She hadn't lived among cats without learning to be a patient puss, herself. Molly breathed deliberately. She smoothed one hand down her red plait, turned it into a flat bun and listened. The arrogant Cornishman thought wrong if he believed she'd humble herself by trailing after him.

"Molly, really." Poppy leaned forward, seeking an embrace, then hugged her arms around her own waist. "He sells cats. He needs to keep them warm. They al-almost froze last night."

"He made them sleep out? With no shelter?"

"He slept with them."

At least he wasn't cruel. As Poppy fumbled with her pocket, Molly harkened to a creaking board, but it was only Cinder, straining to follow. Would the Cornishman never open that door?

Poppy fished a folded sheet from her pocket and extended it. Molly jammed the letter into her own pocket. Had she ever received a note that didn't vibrate with outrage? Anonymous letters, complaining of her thronging cats or stomachaches unhealed by her "potions," were as common as rocks.

One letter, however, had offered threats. Molly hoped this wasn't another such. She looked to Poppy and swallowed hard.

"Eleanor said to—" Poppy pointed at the letter. "But, Moll, the most wonderful thing about Day? He's Cornish!"

"Unlike nearly half the men in Virginia."

"Listen." Poppy recognized sarcasm, but rarely bit its lure. "He says with all the Cornishmen in town, we could be rich if we made pasties."

"You've already tried, honey, remember? After the first few, they went back to cooking their own."

Did the stranger plan to stand in her parlor till nightfall?

"I know, but Day says if we could get milk—" Poppy gestured toward the field where McCabe's heifer—no, their new heifer—grazed. "He'd teach me a recipe that would have men sleeping in the snow for a chance to buy one!"

"Miss Gallagher?"

Ah, the intruder spoke. Satisfied that he'd weakened first, Molly walked halfway into the other room. When the faded green curtain draped her shoulders, she was forced to slip away and stop a step closer to him than she'd intended.

"Are you still in my house, Mr. Day?"

"Day, ma'am. No 'mister.'" He corrected her, making it clear he'd no intention of apologizing. Fine. He could thank his pride for canceling any hope that she would shelter his woeful cats.

"Miss Gallagher, I'm sorry for stepping through to the private part of your cottage."

It was only a shack, nothing so fine as a cottage, but she didn't object. She merely nodded.

"I'll be leaving you to yourselves, but first I have three things to say." His hand rubbed the slant of his jaw.

She'd wager that a closer look would show that clean-shaven jaw a lighter tan than the rest of his face. Not that she'd waste time on such an inspection.

Cinder growled from the kitchen and Molly pictured Poppy restraining him with gentle arms.

"She could let the dog in. It's been too long since I've rumpled a pup's ears."

"Cinder's far from a pup. He bites." Molly smiled.

"Your sister is right that I need a place to board my cats. The creatures all but froze last night. For a bit of shelter, I'd gladly pay a percentage of the price they fetch."

As he waited, watching, Molly felt a flicker of wariness.

Fiddle! His narrow-eyed study only meant he was haggling for a bargain, and though they always needed money, having this man's cats would mean having him underfoot as well. Day had already proven himself unpredictable and reckless. She'd simply refuse.

"I think not. You've only to cover the cats' cages with blankets and they'll be fine."

"You might think on it, all the same." He grinned as if he'd already arranged it. "Now, about those pasties. They need a countryman's hand, to start, but I could teach young Poppy the knack. She tells me baking is your business."

"Her business." Molly reminded herself of his slyness. "And the cost of your recipe, Mr. Day? I heard you spinning your web over Mrs. VanBrunt." She *tsk*ed as if to shame him, when, truth be told, she'd love to see Eleanor and a few other pinch-nosed snobs hoodwinked. "I suppose you're thinking to get your cats fed free in exchange for a few scribbled lines of cooking advice?"

The Cornishman's laugh made his eyes wink shut. They

opened on indecent gaiety and she might have shoved him
out the door if he hadn't confused her. Why had he laughed?
She'd said nothing amusing. The fool bloomed under her
cynicism.

"No, I'm not sure I could write the way of it. Y'see, I
learned 'a handful of this,' 'a blob of that,' and mix until the
dough feels 'this way.' I'd stake repayment on having me
pasties cooked in a real stove"—he nodded toward the
kitchen—"instead of pitched into a campfire. I'd ask the
right to filch one or two a day, long as the cats last."

Molly found her perceptions in a muddle. In dark canvas
trousers and loose shirt, he looked like a windblown scarecrow, incapable of halting running horses with strength. And
yet he had. The man must have a way with animals.

But what of the flash of violence she'd sensed when he'd
agreed to hold off Cutting Jack Slocum? Molly tapped her
fingers against her skirt, dismissing that jolt of danger as no
more than imagination, heated by anxiety over Stag's
wound.

A low growl erupted into barks. Poppy had released Cinder out the back door and now the dog snuffled at the front
step. Cinder's snarling fanned Day's amusement rather than
damping it. He was a fine idiot, really, to relish savaging.

"You said three things?"

"Aye." He drew the word out, hands turning his hat,
avoiding her eyes, suddenly self-conscious. "I've heard you
have the Sight."

Molly might have gloried in the man's superstitious
weakness if he hadn't used her mother's word.

"It's nothing, sure, but I've been hilla-ridden lately. Bad
dreams and the like, and I hoped you might put them to
rest."

"I don't chart love spells or cast hexes, Day." She'd had
no intention of using his name. "I practice herbal healing
and I read character from the lines in your hand."

"But not the future?" His face showed no challenge, but a
spark of it heated his voice.

"Sometimes."

It was enough to make him settle submissively on the red

velvet couch. A souvenir of Rosie's spells and seductions, the fusty thing should have been burned long ago, but the raucous cat salesman looked suddenly tame, sitting there.

"My medicine comes cheap, but my readings are quite dear."

He brushed away caution, and the gesture drew her. Yesterday, she'd kept her eyes from his hands. Now, she looked. Blocky, capable, but tapered—not the sort to need her guidance.

"Are you sure a paper of chamomile tea might not soothe your dreams as well?"

He shook his head and proffered a gold dollar. *Wretch*.

Molly set the candle alight. In the lowering of her hips beside his, she felt the tranquil focus that accompanied a true reading.

Candle wax. The stamp mill's far-off rhythm. The stranger's stillness. All these drained off division. She was one with the flickering candle flame, a safe distance away from this couch, this parlor, this shack. A warm hand was her only anchor.

Careful. No need to fall headlong into it. Molly forced her lids to blink. A simple reading for a simple man.

Hastily consulting the lines, she droned through a recitation. He was ambitious, but not prideful. He had courage, but not cruelty. He would reap riches, but not from the earth. They all wanted to know about money.

"And many sea voyages." She'd never seen so many of those threads. "Not just the one to get here, but hundreds, going back to your birth!"

Molly wished he'd speak, wished he'd interrupt this flow of revelations. When he didn't, when his hand stirred in verification, she lost control, like a child rolling down a grassy hill.

"Oh, they almost lost you, did they?" Without direction, her fingers hovered above his breastbone, where the threat had lodged. "Many childhood illnesses, but this one . . ."

Molly sucked in a breath, touching a fingertip to the gaping links of his early lifeline. It was then she noticed an etching she'd never seen before.

"Where do you see it?" He jerked forward, his shoulder striking hers.

Molly recoiled from the contact. Startled from concentration on that singular line, she snapped at him. "What would I sell if I taught you my trade?"

She braced for the bawdy rejoinder she'd expect from any man. It didn't come. Still, her cheeks heated with humiliation. It took no witch to predict his next request.

"What about love, Miss Gallagher?"

"Oh, you've a fair amount of swelling in the mount of Venus." Her fingers grazed the flesh at the base of his thumb. "Not uncommon for men alone in this town."

"I'd wager not." His words shivered between amusement and chagrin. "And marriage?"

He'd received his money's worth. She could puzzle over that odd marking later. She skimmed the love lines, as she would a well-known page.

"One-and-a-half marriages. A broken engagement in your home village, I'd say." Because the last a guess, Molly raised her lashes to gauge his reaction.

And caught him watching her. Candlelight leached the color from his eyes, turning them the feral gray of a wolf's. Firmly replacing Day's hand on his own lap, Molly stood.

"Nothing uncommon, then?" His voice taunted her.

Suddenly, as if the dusk filtering into the room had given her insight, she knew how to fling back his teasing.

"Yes, something quite uncommon." Molly linked her hands behind her back and smiled up at him. "Two lifelines."

There! She'd struck him speechless. Day started to put on his hat, and stopped, but his abashment was sadly temporary.

"You'll consider taking the cats, then?"

He opened the door onto sunset skies overlaced with red and green firethorn. Molly felt anger lance through her like pain.

"Man, are you deaf?" Realizing that she'd shouted when Poppy peered into the parlor, Molly closed the door behind her. Reason returned as she followed him outside. "No. I will not house your cats."

"I think you will."

Molly gripped her hips with tight fingers, then leaned forward to whisper, so Poppy would not hear.

"When Hell freezes over, *Mister* Day!"

The Cornishman replaced his black hat. He drew a deep breath and spoke without looking back. "Ah, but there's a decided chill in the air, Miss Gallagher, a decided chill."

Chapter
Five

With sunset came the light. As if a dingy blanket had lifted from a statue of purest gold, Rose understood her predicament and her power.

All day, since daybreak lit the cottage, Rose had been confined, caged tightly as if bars held her beneath the red velvet settee. In time—if that element still existed for her—she'd grasped it: She was a ghost. She had died—long since, to judge by her beauteous daughters—and returned as a phantom.

She had neither hand nor foot, nor skin, bone, voice. After so long, she ached to touch her girls, to smooth the frown from Molly's brow and stroke the sunshine glory of Poppy's hair. *Poppy*—the babe so sleepy and slow to suckle, so late to speak and toddle—Poppy had grown into a beauty. But Rose couldn't touch Poppy's golden hair, nor push back her sleeve, which trailed so dangerously near the lantern's flame.

But now, she'd begun touching their feelings. As the

blithe, bonnie Cornishman left the house and the sun sank, Rose focused on Molly's emotions, and the girl's feelings flared.

Accidentally, Rose had spurred Molly to taunt the Cornishman. Then, testing her power, Rose magnified Moll's anger, making her bait the rogue. What fine sport for a ghostly busybody!

But now, with the girls asleep, Rose had no company except Ginger. With wide yellow eyes the cat watched Rose, then arched her back in languorous anticipation of her mistress's touch. The dog called Cinder kept his distance.

Rose swirled toward the girls' room and hovered beside Poppy, who slept with a brow smooth as cream. *Baby, ah my babe.*

When Poppy's lips formed *mama*, then *mama* yet again, Rose's heart squeezed small, as though wrung by a miser's hand. She stood guard over her girls the whole night through.

Suspended outside Deborah's upstairs window, a brown bird no bigger than a bay leaf beat its wings against the wind. Molly shook her head. For the progress made, the bird might have fought ocean currents instead of shoving his beak against the wind.

" . . . *sick* of . . . infero*blk*!" Deb's muffled outburst drew Molly's attention in time to balance against a hem tug that nearly toppled her from the stool. Deborah crouched below, plucking dressmaker's pins from between clamped lips.

"VanBrunts have a russet cotton," Deborah's mumble turned intelligible as she stabbed pins into a velvet pad. "Brown, Molly, I'm speaking of dull reddish brown, and there's the length of sage green I bought just to set off your eyes."

"Which you knew I'd never wear."

"I thought you'd take one look and change your mind." Deb motioned Molly to step forward. "Go on and get down. But I'll remind you, black's hard to work on and your mother's been dead for . . . Mind the pins at the waist."

She steadied Molly's elbow, then listened as bedclothes rustled beyond the screen dividing the room.

"Stag?" Molly let her question hang, then ducked out of the dress.

"You've snagged your bun loose." Deborah collected the shower of hairpins as Molly shed them.

"No matter. I'm taking it down." Molly shivered into the old dress. "Shall I read this to you downstairs? After I check him?"

"I'm expecting Persia."

"Perhaps I'll go." Molly heard her own stuffiness, folded the letter she'd been holding and scanned the floor for her reticule and medicine box.

"Oh, stop it." Deborah peered around the screen, satisfying herself that Stag still slept. "It's Monday. She comes each Monday. She has a right to see Robin once a week, don't you think?

"You knew she might be here, Moll, and decided the letter was important enough to risk seeing her." With the black dress draped over her arm, Deborah waited.

Molly rubbed a chill from her palms, considering. Should she tremble with cold upstairs, trusting Stag to sleep as she read out Eleanor VanBrunt's letter? Or should she sprawl on cushions by Deborah's parlor fire, knowing any minute might bring Persia wafting through the door, embracing Robin against a bosom heavy with scents of her hurdy house?

The upstairs chill was no worse than the cold that mantled Molly whenever she remembered.

January: Persia shivering in lilac silk, leading a cortege lurching over crusted snow, which gave beneath each footfall . . . Persia's silver beads clanking as hollowly as the runners of the sled bearing Rose's coffin toward burial . . . Persia's hand, the day's only warmth, towing a wan child whose rage-chopped hair made her look like an angry red squirrel.

Molly banished the memory. "All right," she snapped, unfolding the letter. "'Dear Miss Gallagher,

"'It has been Determined by the Mothers of Virginia City

that the Time Has Come to employ a suitable Teacher for
our Young Ladies—'"

"Our young men being too half-witted to appreciate the
advantage of education," Deborah mimicked. "Sorry, go
on."

"'—since you are appointed keeper of your sister, we
Know you will contribute the $20 hiring fee—'"

"Twenty dollars! The Ophir's not paying charge-setters
twenty dollars a week!"

"Deborah, you'll wake Stag."

"And is there more?" Deborah flicked her fingers at the
inscrutable page. "About the special school in Sacramento?
And threats, like before? About 'maternal fitness'?"

"Moll?" Stag sounded adrift.

A scrape, bang and thud sounded below stairs, and a
moan rolled from the bed behind the screen.

"Sounds more like an earthquake than Persia." Deborah
eluded Molly's glare. "We'll have Robin in that school. Persia can afford it, and another pupil reduces your cost."

Deborah paused, face shadowed by the hall, arms crossed.
"You know, she'd pay Poppy's fee as well."

"Never." Molly grabbed her medicine box from the floor.
"I'd leave the territory first. Poppy is seventeen years old.
She doesn't need a school."

"Mol-ly!" Stag whimpered.

"I agree the 'tuition' is blackmail"—Deborah made no
pretense of whispering— "but mighty cheap blackmail, if
they take twenty dollars to leave you be."

"My leg!"

Molly swallowed the guilt churned by neglecting her patient and let Deb leave. Stag's hair lay lank across his forehead. Pale freckles spattered his cheeks. In a white
nightgown instead of his red miner's shirt, Stag looked no
older than Robin.

"I'll pay, Miss Molly. See if I don't! Before long I'll be
back to minin', and I've family in Sacramento City—"

"Hush." Molly felt his face for fever. Working himself
into a state over money wouldn't heal him. "I'm not here to
gossip, Stag. At home, I've a horse and dog to feed, a cow

to milk and cats to tend." Molly drew the sheets down to his waist.

"But I heard you sayin' about money—"

Flurried movement beneath the sheet convinced Molly that Stag's worries were physical as well as financial. Why hadn't he asked for the chamber pot?

"I need help with the stock. Pay me back that way." Molly unbuttoned her cuffs, wincing at the chill. "Or bring in water, chop firewood. The shack could be yours, too, now Harold's gone."

None but the gouty old man had offered menial work in exchange for shelter. Why should they, when the mines promised treasure tomorrow, the next day, certainly by next week? Molly's offer roused no word from Stag.

She flipped the sheet back. Stag's hands tented his privates, blocking her view of the wound and his other discomfort. Molly placed one chilled hand against his bare thigh, staring into eyes that sprang wide above his gasping lips.

"Forgive my cold hands, lad." All signs of the boy's impersonal arousal wilted.

Deborah's stitches held and Moll felt no inflammation.

"Whose gown is this, Stag?" Molly indicated his nightshirt, calculating her chatter to distract him from her prodding for lumps and tenderness. "I'd have noticed if you'd worn it crossing the street."

"Some Cornishman, Miz Green said—Ow!"

"Sorry." Molly cursed the start that had nicked her fingertips against his stitches.

"Miz Green said some blessed Cornishman—They're nabbing all the jobs with their square timberin' and pumps. They make the owners' eyes sparkle, and then it's, 'Oh aye, and me cousin Jack just arrived! Would you be havin' room to take him on, sir?'"

"You're sure you're not mocking an Irishman?"

"What's the difference?" Stag's color waned as blood beaded the bottom two stitches and she blotted him with a linen square.

"God's own truth, Miss Molly," he said through gritted teeth, "I'd trade shares in any mine for a bottle of whiskey."

"Not with me." Molly swirled a bottle before his eyes. "A little of this in hot water is what you'll be getting. And, about that Cornishman—?" Molly stared out the window, wondering if the bird had flown or dropped dead trying.

"A stranger, Miz Green said, looking for a place to stay, probably taken my shack as well," Stag mourned. "Serve me right, wanderin' off skunked, the way I did."

Why feel honor-bound to defend the brash cat salesman when the gown might not be his?

"That 'Cousin Jack' saved your neck, Stag. Walkin' along, full of bug juice and stumbling out into C Street, you were, when he pushed you clear of the horses." Moll grimaced as if she'd swallowed a pinch of peppers. "And carried you up here, too."

"I've got strong legs . . ." Stag's protest wavered, then rekindled. " . . . and stronger fists." He extended a shaking hand.

"I'll send someone to check your shack." Molly stood and smoothed her black skirt. "Now, rest. I'll be saving you plenty of chores."

Gathering her things and girding for a collision with Persia, Molly glanced back. The tiny pinpricks of blood meant nothing. And his trembling hands might signal nothing more than weakness. Still, drunks suddenly off the bottle could have horrible fancies, with no cure but keeping them tied in bed.

"Tell Deborah or one of the sisters if you need me . . . Stag?"

She pulled the door softly to and let the boy sleep.

Day snatched his hand from under Deborah's tea-green settee. Let Robin take the blame for this ruckus.

"Come back, Soapy." Robin crawled over a hillock of ornamental pillows. "Catch him, Day!"

A white furball ricocheted off the fireplace poker, then shot straight up, hissing. Day's test of the kitten's hearing had turned full tussle, sending the three of them over tables and under couches. Deborah, summoned by the noise, had departed in mock disgust.

"He's in my clothes! Look!" Robin rolled on his back, his spine a rocker as he caressed the mound undulating beneath his shirt. "It tickles, sort of, and then—Look, Molly!"

Red Molly peered under the couch. A braid thick as Day's wrist swung free, catching the firelight and flaring it back in sparks of red, amber and flame.

Properly, he should stand to greet her, but Lord, he'd lie on the carpet all night for the prize of watching her. What if she sank down beside him, here, as she had on that tawdry couch in her parlor?

The planes of his hand heated as if she still touched him. A man might weep at the beauty of Red Molly, catching the tail of her braid and winding it at her nape.

"'Soapy,' is it? Can you bring him to me, Robin?" Molly eyed Day as if he'd corrupted the child.

"He's Day-the-cat-man," Robin explained.

Just Day-the-cat-man, drownin' in love on a stranger's floor. Twice, his calf muscles tightened, but he couldn't stand.

Half-a-hundred men had drawn down on him. Each had tried to hold his eyes, unblinking, and failed. They'd all looked away. Now this willow switch of a girl looked, stared and judged.

As if she'd lifted her spell, Day's boots found the floor. He stood, smoothing one hand over his absent beard.

Gunshot!

Moving faster than reason, Day's palm slapped his holsterless thigh before the pine sap finished popping.

"Watch for those sparks." Had Molly recognized the instinctive grab for his gun? She stroked the knuckle of an index finger over her lips, falling thoughtful.

How many signs did he need to leave town before she bewitched him?

"Robin, my treasure! Deborah says you learned your alphabet, in cursive! A new kitten, too? Come show Persia!" Voice gurgling like whiskey poured with a liberal hand, a woman in purple satin and tinkling beads rustled into the parlor.

Robin polished thin hands over his bangs and hitched up a suspender before cradling the kitten and standing.

The fair but frail, Westerners called this sort of woman. When she dipped to Robin's level, her skirts puffed a powdery scent that felt grainy on Day's tongue and clogged the back of his throat. Loose and sheared at the shoulder, streaked an unnatural gold, her hair flared like a lion's mane. Persia assaulted every sense, looking not one bit frail.

"So you are the cat man I've heard about."

The madam extended nails so curved that Day hesitated; she caught his shirtsleeve as if testing the fabric. Her eyes measured him, from his hair waving free of its civilizing douse of water to his scuffed boots.

"Why haven't you visited Lady Persia?"

"Persia." Deborah's brusque voice sounded from the doorway as she dried her hands on her apron. "I didn't hear you come in."

Rippling purple satin, the madam picked through a huge reticule. The withdrawal of her gaze made Day feel as if he'd tripped. He took a deep breath, catching the aroma of licorice that had Robin dancing on his toes.

For the first time since the madam entered the room, Day looked to Molly.

Teeth locked so tendons knotted at the turn of her jaw, Molly clutched a black box against her like a shield. Beneath Molly's black-banded collar, her throat bumped with a swallow.

Yet the madam opened her arms, inviting an embrace. She swirled close, purple skirts twining with Molly's black ones.

"Molly." Persia's voice reminded Day of a vaquero who'd downed two mescals to each of his red-eyes last week in Green Diggings. "I'm sorry you lost Harold." Persia traced a cross above her breast. "But you made his last days happy. He worshiped you for keeping him useful."

Molly's eyelids dipped drowsily and tension flowed from her in waves. Her sudden limpness made Persia whisper a curse.

"I'll buy four cats if you'll deliver them . . ." Persia turned to smother Day with attention. " . . . and me as well, since your buckboard is outside. I'll tour you around the Black Dog and Shambles if you like, too."

Day's exploration had shown him Persia's Black Dog saloon. The establishment faced C Street, opposite the Van-Brunts' store. A man sober enough to locate the Black Dog's back door might navigate down a wooden staircase and away from respectability, into a brothel whose gilt scrolling spelled out "Shambles."

Day fidgeted, watching Persia and Moll wage some sort of battle, with him in the middle.

Though Shambles squatted like a white hen hemmed in by lime-washed cottages, he hadn't mistaken the place for a village of laundresses. Each dwelling boasted a hitching rail, a caged lantern swinging from the porch post and ripe women with elbows propped on window frames. Virgin's Alley, Sporting Row, Maiden Street—whatever Virginia City's bawdy district was called, a blind man could recognize the sour musk of whoring.

Should he visit Shambles? Before he considered Persia's invitation, Deborah bristled. Persia stopped stroking Robin's hair, but didn't lift her hand as she aimed her index finger.

"I honor our agreement, Mrs. Green. I planned to offer employment, after he sold his cats. That's all. Each man I hire to tend bar or protect my girls, gets greedy. Silver, gold, shares and profits! The men talk of nothing else. Endless babbling of blue clay and then they're off!" Persia considered him. "What's in your face, Day, that says you might be dependable?"

Picturing Lightfoot O'Deigh, gunman and wild rider—who'd once spurred his stallion straight into a saloon after a man—as a sedate salary-drawing fellow bred laughter in Day's throat.

"Would you read the truth of his hand, little one? Say if he would labor diligently for Persia?"

He hadn't imagined it. Persia goaded Molly. Interlocking her fingers, the madam began a slow, suggestive sliding.

Molly shrugged, but a flicker of green showed beneath

her lashes. Day felt a hair-on-end force surround him. It crackled from Molly like the aftermath of lightning.

This is a test, her mind shouted over the silent storm. But her eyes only idled on a seam at the top of his shoulder.

"My mam raised no sporting man, Miss Persia. I've a poor head for numbers, makin' me a donkey when it comes to catching card cheats. As for protection"—Day closed his fist and rubbed his knuckles— "I'd as soon not hit a man. Rather talk him to death, y'see?"

"A bartender!" Persia diagnosed. "You're perfect."

"Maybe, but soon as the cats are gone, so am I." Day imagined that he sounded as self-righteous as a bishop.

"There's money to be made." Persia dangled the offer until Deborah interrupted.

"Better still, there's dried-apple pie with cider, if you'll wash it down before my supper rush."

Day steadied Persia's whalebone-braced waist as she tipped out of the buckboard. The carnal interest she'd feigned remained behind at Deborah's. Now, she left him at the door like a servant, with orders to give the cats to Luba Washington.

He took a single step inside the brothel—dark hall, huge unlighted chandelier creaking overhead, a sense of silken rustling and secrets whispered from other rooms—and then a gap-toothed Negress embraced the crate of mewing cats.

Lord, the woman might snap the spine of an Irish brawler and call it practice for Christmas-tree harvesting. Day stepped back onto the porch. Before he could provide care-of-the-cat guidelines, Luba Washington disappeared on a waft of roast goose.

If sisters in sin dined so well every night—Day dodged Abner's hind hoof and climbed back into the wagon—he wished he'd considered Persia's offer.

Pretending to gaze at the brothel's draped windows, Day slid his hand beneath the buckboard seat. His fingers traced the metal ridges and hollows of his Colt. He had plenty of ammunition, but it cost no more to buy before he ran low.

He slapped the reins on the mule's back and decided that

none would watch his stockpiling. Not Molly, summoned
before her first bite of pie, by a miner whose pregnant wife
had sprung a leak. Not the hinge-tongued barber, Cuttin'
Jack, who nodded and went on talking to a fellow outside
the store.

Day tethered Abner and peered inside the mercantile.
Even Mrs. VanBrunt, spearing a sorry supper of pickles for
a half-dozen dirt-caked miners, wouldn't care a lick for his
business.

"Excuse me." Day waved to attract the hulking shopkeeper. "Mr. VanBrunt?"

The man reminded him of a loaf of something unwhole-
some. Day couldn't say what. Bread gone moldy? Cheese
awash with slime? Yet there was no stench to him, not compared to the lads who'd been underground all day. VanBrunt
bore only a faint whiff of boiled cabbage as he deepened his
frown toward the block of light marking the doorway.

"Might there be the chance—" Day bit off all reference to
ammunition when he saw the target of VanBrunt's frown.

Molly stood in the doorway, a folded paper in her hand.

"—for you to weigh out a quarter pound of coffee?" Day
amended his request.

He needed bullets, not coffee, but if the watery brew he'd
sipped at Brown Bess's signified, he'd boil his own on a
campfire in the street, and thank Red Molly for the inspira-
tion.

He wouldn't thank her for turning him back into a gangling boy. Silent as a coyote's shadow, he'd skulked and
stalked dangerous men when he worked for Rankin. Now
she appeared and he'd regrown kneecaps so wide they
jammed together, tripping him as he eavesdropped on her
conversation with Eleanor VanBrunt.

Day collided with a table and toppled a pyramid of silk
thread. He fumbled to set the spools back in order—blues on
the bottom, yellow in the middle, scarlet on top—and
missed Molly's soft question.

"—why speak of it to me?" Eleanor VanBrunt adjusted
the brine barrel's cover.

Moll glanced at the sheet she held, then elevated her chin

and creased the paper into thirds. "I assumed the families would give you the money for safekeeping until a bank draft could be sent to the teachers' school in—" Molly broke off, unsure.

"Chicago." Eleanor VanBrunt missed Moll's small smile. "And did you want to pay it all now?"

"Twenty dollars," Molly separated the syllables.

What the hell kind of lessons could she be buying? He had only one more spool to replace, blood-crimson to crest the display, when Molly lowered the black shawl from her hair to her shoulders and called him by name.

"Day?"

He closed his fist around the spool. "Miss Gallagher?"

Moll's hands clutched her medicine box, showing each bone. "You asked after boarding your cats, but we didn't discuss a price."

The other day, on these same wooden floorboards, she'd fastened him with that same look, trusting him but hating to.

"Whatever you think reasonable, Miss Gallagher."

"Twenty dollars." Her chin jerked even higher, clearing her stovepipe collar by three inches. "Not reasonable, by any standards, but that's what it will cost you."

His pocket wrinkled and bound his fingers, protesting his insanity, but Day touched the twenty-dollar gold piece. Was he buying shelter for the cats or another chance to touch her, a week's worth of excuses to climb the hill to her cottage?

Before the coin fell to the hollow of his hand, Moll snatched it, breathing as if she'd run to him. She flattened it on the counter before Eleanor VanBrunt.

"That concludes our business, Eleanor. I've animals to tend, so I won't wait for a receipt. Mr. Day?"

Just Day, but he couldn't correct her when she looked this way: white around the mouth, upper lip beaded with perspiration, snatching shallow breaths to keep her upright.

"Mr. Day, bring the beasts when you please. And my receipt. I have, as I said, livestock to tend—" Her hand fluttered as if caught in the wind outside; then she left.

"You see what I mean." Eleanor VanBrunt lifted the coin with two fingers. "It near killed her to take your money! She hates men." The coin dropped out of sight. "Didn't I tell you?"

"You told me, Mrs. VanBrunt." Day wondered if he had the steadiness to replace the last spool of crimson thread. "Aye, you told me."

Chapter Six

"Mama has a man in the parlor." Rose read the words and recoiled as if the letters were snakes, launched wide-fanged at her face. A ghost shouldn't feel such outrage, but she'd waited all day for freedom and now she must face her sordid past.

After dinner, Molly had fished the book from beneath her bed. Now, Molly fought down choking breaths as she read the childish letters she'd formed. Rose forced herself to read, too.

"Since Papa died, they come. Papas friends like Sam want te leaves read all the time."

A child couldn't understand. In the early days, this hard-scrabble town offered women without capital two occupations: laundress and whore. Damn Liam for stranding her with two babes to feed! Damn pride, which forbade scrubbing strangers' long johns, but let her read tea leaves as a prelude to—Rose smothered her shame. Why hadn't feelings fled with her flesh?

"Why don't you let Moll bring te, Sam told Mama, but she said No, she is reading. Tot her self to read. Mama relly showd me. She does not tell foks she was going to teach in Sanfrisco when Papa decided to get some gold insted of fixing shoes like they planed. When she came for the te, she asked wouldn't I like to read outside, where the air was fresh from thundr showers? She petted my face like she does and looked so beging in her eyes. She says Sam brought nice fresh trout. Better than salt pork and beans and won't the cats be hapy with the scraps?"

Death granted Rose another revelation. Ghosts moaned because they saw the errors of their lives. They saw all and could mend nothing. Rose tried to look away from the text, but couldn't.

"It's almost to dark to read, so I'm doing 25 lines writting in my copy book. The clothes look like ghosts flaping we had to hang them late because of the storm. But the sage smells good. The cats are cudling up wanting dinner.

"I wish Mama and Sam would come out. I went in but the house was dark and still, then I heard Sam say Rose, Rose, let me see thos other rosy cheeks of yours and Mama cried a yip and when I started to open the curtin to see if she was hurt she said Molly honey, no, she could hardly breeth Molly go on back. I hear cyots in the hills and I wish Mama would come out."

Rose hurled against the cabin wall. If she shattered into one hundred dust motes, if she went straight to Hell, it would be sweet relief. But she only glanced off one ceiling beam, then another, until Molly slammed the journal closed.

Molly shuddered. A more superstitious sort would claim a goose had crossed over her grave, but Moll Gallagher knew better. She shivered because she'd had a close call. Her childish writings reminded her that no good came from trusting men. For a moment, in VanBrunts' store, she'd almost forgotten.

Water splattered out the back door as Poppy emptied the dishpan. Plaintive meows spiraled up from beneath the house.

"Move, silly things. Molly will bring your dinner. Smokey, you can't come in. Only Ginger, because she's old. Lily, get back. Keep the new ones company." Poppy closed the door. "We slept late this morning. Why am I tired?"

"We chopped wood and milked. Without getting kicked, I might add." Molly matched her sister's yawn. "Makes me miss Harold."

"He got down with that broken hip, and just never could get up again," Poppy recited the words she'd heard so often.

Molly combed fingers through hair still bumpy from the day's braid, and watched Poppy. Her sister removed her yellow calico, hung it, then brushed it, as she did every night. Next, Poppy would wash her face, pour the water on one of Molly's potted herbs, pull on her nightgown, unravel her own braid and burrow into their bed. Curled to the cabin wall, Poppy would doze before Molly walked her rounds and slipped in beside her.

Molly set the copybook beneath the bed and mused that she didn't deserve scolding. Not really. She'd had no choice but trusting him. *Day*. Hardly his real name. The fast-talking charlatan hadn't blinked before handing over the gold piece, yet he'd hardly spoken as he unloaded his cats.

"Believe it when I see it." Molly pictured a proper schoolmarm alighting from the Geiger Grade stagecoach.

"Hmm?" Already drowsy, Poppy raised herself on her elbow, looking like a wild pony, blond mane tumbling over her eyes.

"Nothing, honey. You go to sleep. I'll just check things."

Molly doused the lantern, left a candle to light her return and stepped out back. Lifting the knob so the warped door closed, she tasted ice on the peak-chilled wind. The Sierra snowmelt had frozen silver and hard already, though September lingered.

Cinder bounded from the brush, feinting a nip at her heels.

"No hamstringing your mistress. Who'd feed you, then?"

The old dog jumped back, turning his head on the side and snapping his teeth joyfully. He growled at a gray tom who wound too close. If the felines paraded behind or dodged from rock to rock, Cinder tolerated them, but he claimed duty at her side.

Tonight the cats hissed and twisted, wild from wind and the new cats hidden under the porch. Tomorrow, there'd be some spats. Molly hadn't warned Day. A cat salesman should expect such territorial disputes, a few shredded ears and bent whiskers.

The stamp mill stood silent. Night wind swept Sun Mountain, shaking the piñon pines. Molly flexed her neck, rolling stiff tendons and naming the stars. Alone and safe, she lured the cats with a hum and strode the boundaries of her land.

Down thin grass to the road, she crossed behind the Red Rovers, a row of reddish boulders, then struck uphill over gullies and ground-squirrel burrows. Glory's nicker floated from a copse of juniper and Moll's steps followed the grindgrass rhythm of Hannah the cow. Then Molly returned home, to Poppy.

He hadn't meant to spy on her, but when Brown Bess's fare fulfilled its foul billing, Day escaped. He'd bowed away from a table set with boiled beef, tan beans and yellow turnips, accepted by the bleakest men he'd met outside a boneyard.

Wandering the streets seemed a reward. He hunted for the mannerly Southern gambler who'd warned Molly of Lightfoot O'Deigh. The gambler must have offered a piss-poor description if a lass so canny hadn't recognized him.

Day jammed his hat low against the wind chasing him down the dark street. No posters yet, thank the Lord. Molly had served him a full measure of distrust, but none of the hatred due a killer.

Damn. As he stepped off the walk to cross the street, tightness knotted beneath his breastbone. God strike him if he'd killed Sue. He hadn't. Had *not*. And yet, if a decent woman like Moll asked him to swear it wasn't possible—amid rearing horses, cattle and shouting men—could he? Damn.

Settle yourself. By the time wanted posters appear, you'll be gone. Mark Owen Daywell will never meet Molly Gallagher.

Torches flared outside D Street's saloons, only three of which featured solid roofs, bars a man could stand to and cards.

Daddy Slim's had a fiddle player and a bartender who invited him to "lay the dust and play a hand." After one beer and a glance around the dim interior, he knew the smooth Southerner wouldn't ply his skills among this lot.

Day only stuck his head in the second place. The Shaft smelled like a privy. Its patrons competed in a belching contest, then howled as a man towed a jaded female toward a partition at the back. Not that silver-and-lace gambler's sort of place.

Day hesitated outside the Black Dog saloon, certain old Fox-Face waited inside. He hesitated for one reason: the heat between Persia and Molly. And Persia owned this place.

"Ah! There he is now!"

With his fingers deliberately stiffened away from his holsterless thigh, Day turned.

"What kind of countrymen would we be, not to buy you a drink?" The two Cornish miners who'd staggered out of yesterday's dawn pelted Day with back slaps and steered him toward a canvas-walled saloon packed with miners. After a round of gut-warmers, they promised Day the best entertainment in town.

"But only if you can keep silent," warned the dark one, who swore his name was Arthur Pendragon. "Thayer will kill you, else. I've seen him sit on a man's chest, pound his head on the ground and choke him, for no more than clearing his throat."

"Witch opera, we calls it." The shorter one, Geordie, had led them away from the saloons, the shops and the noise.

Now Day crouched in darkness, along with several others. The natural ridge and deserted diggings across from Moll's cottage afforded balcony seats. The moon provided footlights.

Thayer, whoever he was, had disciplined the miners well.

Squatting in brush that pricked through their canvas pants, they waited, silently. Day focused on the shadows crossing inside her house, then reexamined his companions. Seven men saw Moll's door open for a shower of water. Even when the door emitted a shaft of light and Molly, there was churchly quiet and a mere quaking in the air, as if each man's shoulders tightened.

Trailed by a court of cats, attended by the old dog, Molly surveyed her domain, humming something like Chinamen's music. Darkness buoyed her down the hill, back up. A horse neighed.

The old dog jumped up on Molly, whining from pain in his arthritic joints, but staying, until she rewarded him with a hug. Then Molly vanished.

Moonlight or age grayed the hair of the man who rose first. Then the others stood and drifted back toward town.

Twice tonight he'd felt the knot in his chest. Day turned to Pendragon. "Every night?" It was despicable, unjustifiable.

"Aye," Geordie answered with a sigh. "Ain't it lovely?"

Molly walked into town, alone. Indian summer had crested overnight. Sweat stung in the creases of her black gown. With each step she blamed her stubbornness.

She'd moved the milk bucket from table to floor, then scoured a skillet free of fried cornmeal. Before she turned back, Poppy tripped through the doorway, overturning the bucket.

She'd already skimmed the cream, too. Though she'd been the careless one, leaving a bucket by the door, Molly felt martyred as she dropped to her knees to soak up the milky pool.

"Oh, Moll! I'm sorry, but Day is back for some cats!" Poppy rejoiced, as if the thumping and banging weren't evidence of the Cornishman's arrival. "He'll give us a ride to town in his wagon if we come now. And bring me back and teach me to make pasties!"

By then Poppy had stood poised with a basket of bread. No mystery in why he'd offered Poppy transport. He'd beg one of those currant buns for breakfast. Why did Poppy assume she'd allow this ride? And why, Moll wondered, peering outside to see Poppy's calicoed shoulders dwarfed by Day's, why *had* she agreed?

Molly hefted her medicine box higher and lengthened her stride. And since she'd allowed Poppy to go, why hadn't she chaperoned? Why refuse a gift, even if she despised the giver?

Not that she despised Day. She felt only annoyance. He'd charmed Poppy, then followed her home like a tramp dog. He'd invaded their cabin and made Molly a liar over the matter of his cats. His cocksure smile taunted her.

Moll stepped back onto the road's shoulder as an ore wagon thundered past. The dust drifted, dispersed, settled and Molly yawned. More than the heat made her sleepy.

The white horseman had stormed her dreams, pursuing her endlessly, bearing closer, wheeling the horse right, left, blocking, trapping and cornering her.

Well, she refused to fall into a trance at the roadside! A bit of hard work would shake out her foolishness. After checking Stag and Jenny, she and Poppy could scour the lonely straggle of juniper by Chinatown. They'd pick until both were too tired to dream, then pray she wasn't called for an emergency.

No one had called last night, but she feared Deborah had slept through Stag's feverish tossing, or that the sisters had heard his ravings and substituted prayer for treatment.

And Ike-the-miner's wife, Jenny? Molly had ordered her to bed, certain all the same that dawn would see Jenny working their Happy Days mine. With only a few days left on their claim, they'd labor, even if it cost them a babe. Patiently, Molly had explained that Jenny's "leak" had drained the bubble of water protecting the child from dirt and disease. They'd only stared.

The stamp mill's pounding matched Molly's pulse as she descended the slope toward town, praying for Jenny and the babe.

*   *   *

"Two Cornishmen, having done a day's work before the Irish eased on down the shaft, settled themselves to unwrap their dinner pasties."

Day spun words over the miners' moans and denials. He left his legs hanging and blue shirt sleeves rolled up, seated on the buckboard tailgate, back against a crate full of cats.

A crowd of about twenty surrounded him. Among the miners stood the VanBrunts, Brown Bess, Persia and three hurdy girls. Twenty souls come to hear him sell cats, but not Moll.

Just as well she'd stayed home. "My Bright," he'd call her if she came to be his. *Idiot thought, Daywell.* Bright-haired and bright-minded, Molly would be on to him, arms crossed and foot tapping as he snared customers with simple storytelling. Aye, he'd do better without her watching.

"Not bein' much for talking, these two lads—" Day broke off.

Contrary wench. He leaned forward, pretending to urge his audience closer. In fact, he'd spotted her. Moll's walk, skirts swinging, hips swaying, strangled the words right out of him.

Molly smiled, head tilted to hear Deborah Green, but her content faded when she saw him at the crowd's center.

"Not the talkative sort, as I said, the two Cornishmen chomped their pasties, until . . . they heard . . . a sound.

"*Knock-knock* on a timber?" He let his knuckles graze the wooden wagon side. "*Tap-tap* on hard rock? It came from the tunnel behind them." Day let chills tickle his listeners' spines.

He would not look toward Molly, though her red hair blazed at the edge of his vision.

"'Y'did not be forgettin' to leave a crumb o'dinner for the wee ones, did y'now?' Ned asked Ted, breaking a bit of crust and casting it into the dark. ''Course not,' answered Ted, flinging a chunk big as his fist. The tapping went on."

Day had every man's attention.

"Now it could have been the spirit of some brother miner, buried in a rockfall. Or it could have been *buccas*—tommy-knockers, you say. Those tommies put a man in a quandary.

Y'see, sometimes they warn of steam, about to blast through the hole a man's chipping, past his hands, to peel loose his face. Sometimes buccas feel earth shift, timbers slip, and warn ye to get above, so ye'r mother gets no letter, saying y'was crushed 'neath a mountain of black rock, and ye ain't never coming home."

All but leaning on Day's knees, Hans VanBrunt worked his lips. Behind him, two miners stoutly denied they'd ever been scared as those fools Ned and Ted. The only smile in the crowd was Molly's, knowing just what he was playing. Day drew a shuddering breath.

"Then again, buccas are tricksters. Ned and Ted followed the tapping, and viewed a ghastly sight. There, at the cross of two tunnels, lighted by a lantern on the wall—" Day coughed. He covered his mouth, protesting with his expression, that he'd continue when he could.

"What?" VanBrunt pounded the wagon side. "In the name of God, what did they see?"

"A shoe."

"A shoe?" The chorus came back, as if on a crashing tide. Even Molly's forehead creased in confusion.

"Aye, a shoe. Dancing all alone, sashayin', minuet-in' and whirlin' a wild mazurka, there in the tunnel.

"Now, Ned and Ted were brave men, but no fools. They banged on the cage to be taken above, then told their foreman what they'd seen. Ridiculin' them all the way, the foreman ignored the wise lads, who warned him not to go.

"Sure, they'd pray for Ned and Ted, if that was all they could do, but they cursed the bullheaded foreman, who had all three lowered, once again."

Day paused, and not for suspense. Molly pulled the black shawl from her shoulders and knotted it around her waist. Soon as her hands left, it slipped, slanting from one hip down to the other. He'd lose the thread of this story, if he took that thought further. Day let his breath hiss out past his teeth.

"Just as before, there pranced the shoe, hornpipin' away as if it didn't never want to stop. Stranger still, the pastie crumbs were gone.

"The foreman drew a beefsteak from his pocket—foremen, as y'know, can well afford keepin' such things about—and threw it on the floor of the tunnel. The shoe shifted into a schottische, for all the world like it was sizin' up the meat. The foreman threw down an apple—his pockets were commodious big—and the shoe slowed to a waltz, and two-stepped near for a peek. Then the foreman cast down cheddar cheese, ripe and orange as a pumpkin squash. The shoe stopped.

"And out of that shoe, out of the black tunnel, crept a tiny, wee mousie, who'd terrified three brave men in the darkness, and a dozen more up top in the sun. And if only the fellows had taken with them their *mine cats*," —Day drew a black-spotted tom onto his knees— "There would never . . . have been nothing . . . to fear."

The crowd erupted into self-mocking guffaws, into back-slapping and elbow-jabbing. VanBrunt paid cash for six cats. For a quarter hour, Day took money as fast as his hands could grab. Each time he looked up for Moll, he saw the fiery glint of her hair.

As the gathering dispersed, Persia's girls bickered about housing cats when each caged a canary in her room. Between him and Moll glowed Poppy's flaxen hair, the leaf-shaped bonnet of Deborah Green and, a head taller, the gambler. Damn, didn't he let himself stand good and close to Molly?

Twelve cats lighter and twenty-four dollars richer, Day bolted the wagon's tailgate and walked toward Poppy. He owed her a ride home, after all.

Molly saw him coming. For the first time since he'd crouched beside her in the blood-soaked street, she refused to meet his eyes. Day's stomach went cold. Does she know?

" . . . Chinatown. Some injury to one of the girls," Molly explained to the gambler as Day approached.

"I don't like to see you go alone, Miss Molly."

Over the gambler's voice, Day heard Persia interrupt.

"Those are Favor's whores, down there. You watch your back, Moll Gallagher."

Brown Bess sidled in front of Day, hefting a bag of something flesh-pink and smelly.

"Chickens!" A grim smile tightened Bess's face. "Ten for a dollar, plucked! Enough meat to make soup and stew for a week."

Day cursed the distraction and edged past Bess in time to see Molly's skirts flap her departure. Trust him to arrive one minute too late!

"Molly had to help in Chinatown." Innocently shameless, Poppy clung to his gun arm and he hadn't a chance to stop Molly.

Behind him, Bess sniffed. What could he ask with the landlady standing there, rubbing her belly and eavesdropping?

"Did you know the girls are slaves?" Poppy rushed on. "They can't leave, even if they want to. The masters give them bad medicine to keep them there. Moll hates to go, but Mr. Slocum won't. They've no one else to ease their troubles."

"Your *sister* is trouble." Bess spat for punctuation.

Though Moll wasn't there to defend and wouldn't welcome his protection if she were, Day couldn't stop. Unfurling his tongue came more natural than reaching for his gun.

"Isn't it strange, now?" Day bumped back his hat brim. "It seems to me, folks are always bringin' their troubles to *her*."

Shoulders to knees, Bess trembled with outrage and Day wondered whether anyone would notice if he wrung Bess's neck, just like one of her bare-assed chickens.

Chapter Seven

"Our healer has another young gallant to defend her. Miss Poppy, perhaps you'd introduce us." Warning surged beneath the gambler's honeyed politeness.

Day didn't miss the threat, but Poppy swept between them, and he hoped the man's sarcasm would wane.

"Richard Griffin, meet Day. We're boarding his cats, until he sells them all."

"Which shouldn't be long, if this is typical of your showmanship." Deborah Green nodded her approval.

"I know what you need, Day." To the visible relief of three foot-dragging prostitutes, Persia slowed to talk. "A top hat and a fancy gambler's vest." Persia's glance ran over Day as if she inspected a stallion. "Mrs. Green's a fine seamstress. I trust she could measure you."

"Oh, couldn't she, just," giggled a prostitute with corkscrew curls and a red velvet gown. "Teach me to sew, quick!"

"Claret," Persia took the girl's arm. "Pigeon-brained

66

chit'd starve if she earned her bread with anything above her—"

"—nose!" sputtered the girl with unlikely yellow hair.

Deborah blushed redder than the hurdy girl's gown and seemed to grope for another line of conversation.

Day-the-raucous-cat-salesman or Lightfoot O'Deigh would have joined the bawdy wordplay, but Mark Owen Daywell presided over a respectable bit of his mind. By right, Day should have shyly studied his boots, but Griffin still wouldn't break his stare.

"Michael always admired Moll's idea of running a medicine wagon between here and Carson City," Deborah blurted. "Hidden treasure, why wouldn't he?" Embarrassment had left her feelings unguarded. Day glanced her way, hoping for another clue to the ever-absent Michael Green, but Deborah only straightened Poppy's collar. "You remember, don't you, Richard?"

Griffin's stare never faltered as he nodded in answer.

"She wouldn't use a tambourine, but it's a pity she won't learn a speech from Day. Moll could pay for Poppy's teacher in an afternoon."

Day's hand twitched to smooth his beard before remembering his jaw was bare. He itched to hang a thumb in his gun belt, too, but he wore none. It took all his concentration to remain still and fixed on Griffin.

"Miss Gallagher and I arranged payment for Poppy's schoolin', yesterday." Day figured he'd only been neighborly. Griffin apparently thought it sounded too blamed cozy.

"How's that?" Griffin's lazy voice held an accusation.

"The cats." Damned if things weren't headed toward a fight. Just what he bloody needed, and with a man primed and ready.

Only madmen and trophy hunters preferred their victims wary. Working for Rankin, Lightfoot O'Deigh had learned to wait until the men he tracked turned drunk or angry. The gambler was neither. A derringer probably nested inside the brocade vest, and that bump in his trousers seam would be a stiletto.

"Neither of you gentlemen appears to be a cur dog, so put your hackles down." Deborah divided a superior gaze between them. "Poppy's coming home with me, to occupy Stag's mind. He's been babbling about bugs, and I assure you there are none." She glared when they didn't disperse. "Just go." Her hands dismissed them.

Two whiskeys sat sentry between Day and Griffin when the gambler finally spoke. "I've seen you twice up at Moll's place."

"Aye?" Day wondered when, but the gambler gave nothing away.

"Indeed. And I saw you heft Stag's drunken carcass all the way up to Deborah Green's."

"Now, he was not so very drunk. Stampedin' horses have a way of soberin' a man up, I'm thinkin'."

"You needn't pull that simple-minded Irish bullcorn with me." Griffin shoved back from the table.

"Sweet Mother." Day felt his heartbeat swell his neck, then his temples. "I can do Irish, Griffin, but that wasn't it. And since you're a plainspoken man, mayhap you'll just say what you're itchin' to, and y'won't have to die of lead poisoning."

Griffin's short bark of laughter didn't change his dire expression. "What do you want with Moll Gallagher?"

A chill night in a hayloft without that cursed black dress? May noon with wind in her hair and daffodils bowing her past? A walk down the sunset beach of home, wet sand turning purple and Mam on the cliffs above, hailing them for fried chips and haddie?

"Nothing." Day held his hands palm out. "I haven't said two dozen words to the girl and she's had less to say to me."

"You were in her house a good hour." Griffin rolled the glass between his hands and squinted at it.

"I'm a bit superstitious. She told my hand."

Their stares lasted long enough that Day wondered why Griffin cared, why he hadn't mentioned Shawnee Sue, shot dead in Lake's Crossing, and why Griffin had let Molly leave for Chinatown.

Griffin's chair, tilted on its back legs, slammed down.

"Moll has no one to look out for her." Griffin stared over Day's shoulder. "And I knew her mother. Not carnally. And I'm not old enough to be her father. Don't conjure any romantic notions about my motives."

"Cat peddlers have few romantic notions or anything else." Day rubbed his bare jaw. "If I *were* interested, I'd have nothing to offer a woman like her."

"She wouldn't take it if you did." Griffin shook his head.

Ah, yes, Moll was a man-hater. Day drained his whiskey.

"Not knowing Virginia City, I wonder if she's safe, down in Chinatown?"

"Safe enough." Griffin's thumb traced the faceting on his glass. "Poppy's right about no one helping those folks. The whorelords want Moll healthy. She protects their investment—bandaging cut wrists, making girls vomit laudanum overdoses, cleaning up messy self-doctoring of the female kind."

Griffin's grip threatened to crush crystal shards into the whiskey. "Molly will spin some cock-and-bull story about slavery"—the Southerner lowered his voice. Only talk of religion or a man's capacity for drink stirred debate as fast as slavery, these days—"but most of those women bring on their own miseries. Still, some of the girls can't be more than twelve."

Griffin shuddered with the first involuntary movement Day had seen him make. Even tough men had soft spots.

Like the desire to save your own hide, Day recalled.

Griffin'd take Day for a twitchy old woman if he asked the questions he wanted answered. So he'd wait. Or try to, but if he'd inherited a fisherman's patience, he'd still be home.

Action seduced a man. Day had learned that as soon as he'd hugged Mum good-bye to tramp across Ireland, soon as he'd found Gaelic murmurs soothed "unbreakable" horses and sailed off for American racetracks, as soon as he'd learned that a Colt's revolver felt more natural than oars and nets.

Action urged the short route to satisfaction. Grab Griffin's ruffles and shake the truth off his slow Southern tongue. Steal a hot-blooded stallion. Jerk the red-haired witch up before him and kiss her silly a hundred miles from this pissant village.

Aye, and action'll get you killed before you have a chance to touch lips to her hand.

Day turned a button on his shirt cuff five times, six, until it fell off in his fingers.

"And Persia?" Day tucked the button inside his pocket. "She said something about 'favored whores'?"

"'Favor's whores,'" Griffin corrected. "'Favor' is an alias he likes. Persia calls the man a whore's nightmare." The flesh over Griffin's cheekbones went white.

Two soft spots, then. Griffin's molasses eyes turned feral, then carefully blank.

"He owns the Chinatown cribs and rents them to whorelords who bring girls in from Frisco. Favor owns Daddy Slim's, too, but he doesn't visit. Most often sends one of his donkeys to collect rent, now he's decided to get respectable."

Just like Rankin. If Rankin had his way, he'd turn senator the week Nevada went from territory to state. But senators couldn't weather accusations of land grabs and cattle rustling, so Rankin's toadies made folks with accusations disappear.

Day pictured the green kid he'd been, thankful to Rankin for marking his talent with horse and gun, thankful for being named a range detective. A hero, puffed up and proud, he'd tracked wrongdoers and surrendered them to "the law."

Hired killers, more like! Men like Antonio, Rankin's right-hand man, had managed a naïve Cornish boy as if he were a puppet. An accident had melted the flesh on one side of Antonio's comely face. Innocent Mark Owen Daywell had blamed his own uneasiness on the deformity. And felt ashamed. If Day had listened to his instinct, Shawnee Sue might still be pounding the goose feathers.

Day squeezed his temples to dispel the memory of Antonio squinting down his gun barrel across the corral, of Sue wide-mouthed and spinning, of a bodice with blood spreading like a crimson spider.

Day straightened and a wave of Griffin's whiskey slopped onto the table.

"I'll take a drive down that way, toward Chinatown. I owe you one." Day nodded at the spilled drink. Griffin dismissed the promise and called to the bartender for a deck of cards.

Day jammed through the doors. Two miners adjusting each other's suspenders in the middle of the boardwalk parted as he stormed past. And he still had ammunition to buy.

Abner, haltered and tied in front of VanBrunts', rolled his eyes white and kicked the buckboard when he saw Day coming. How had he managed to buy the only equine immune to his charms?

Before he reached Abner, Poppy emerged from VanBrunt's and addressed the mule, wiggling her fingers as she bent over the hitching rail. When Hans VanBrunt followed and stood admiring Poppy's backside, Day itched to shoot him.

Settle yourself, man. You saw her that way, too, first time she swished down the street before you. It's only bein' stirred over those China girls. It's only a chestful of panic over Moll, who can by God take care of her nerveless self. Right?

No.

VanBrunt leaned forward as if he'd join Poppy in petting the mule. Then, his left hand pretended to steady Poppy's waist. A guilty look up and down the street and the bastard cupped Poppy's skirts, just where the girl's bottom curved.

Day broke into a trot as Poppy wheeled, wide-eyed, to face VanBrunt.

Talk. Don't strike. Talk, even if the knuckles pop off the tops of your fists!

"VanBrunt, I need bullets for a Navy Colt. I need 'em now, God love ye." Day forced his snarl into a genial chuckle and judged himself an awful actor. Still, VanBrunt disappeared back into the store. After all, who feared a peddler?

"Poppy, could you go back to Mrs. Green's and wait for me?"

"But didn't you say to come here? I thought . . ." Poppy's voice trembled and tears gathered in her eyes.

"That's right, dearie. You're right. I've just changed *my* plans, see?" Day stifled the urge to stroke her hair. "You can wait for me and Molly, can't you? I'll give her a ride back from Chinatown. We'll all go to your cottage for tea. Would you be having any more of those currant buns at your house, now?"

"I might." Poppy brightened at his smile.

"Off with you, then!" Day whisked his hands at her, as if shooing a child out of doors. The girl went.

How, in the name of Heaven, had it happened? Two weeks ago he'd shaved his beard, bought cats and set off for Virginia City, set on hiding among a hundred empty-pock-eted Cornishmen. Three days after he arrived, he'd put on the feelings of Poppy Gallagher's protective dad. He wanted to kick VanBrunt's lecherous ass.

The Chinese woman wore a ragged camisole and brandished a knife. Her voice rose keening, faltered to a groan, and on every slide down she flicked the knife across her stomach. Hellish bright with honing, the knife trailed knotted red silk cords.

Dodging past vegetable vines and a tethered pig, Day had passed a row of tidy houses before finding the shack. When a sob choked inside, he'd squinted through a crack until dust grated his eyeballs. Blinking, Day rounded the splintered wall and a portrait of misery remained in his mind.

The woman didn't feel the blade. Lit by ragged streaks of sun, her face oiled with sweat, she didn't flinch or gasp as the blade slashed her belly.

Out front, a man in canvas trousers and pressed shirt, probably the whorelord, paced. Women in faded wrappers fanned away heat and gnawed their nails, sighing words that told despair in any language. One rawboned female smoked a clay pipe. She cuffed a youngster aside and motioned Day closer.

Purgatory couldn't be murkier. Dark and hay-strewn as a stall, the shack's roof leaked sunlight. Movement stirred smells of worse things than a man wanted to think on and dust motes frenzied as a shadow tilted toward the woman. The shadow was Molly.

"Tell her again. Tell her it's just the opium." Moll's words flowed as a squeaky voice in the darkness translated. Molly halted for a blazing chatter of questions. "She will feel like herself—" Moll amended, but the questions rattled on.

"Oh, merciful Heavens! She won't want to hurt herself soon as she's had food and a bit of rest."

The knife flicked forward, tore back.

Moll leaned into a sun slash and Day saw her eyes bleached pale as green water, forehead drawn in concentration.

"She's asking, can you get her sleep?" The piping voice queried. "She don't have to work overnight?"

The woman's head lolled on her neck, the knife stilled and Day knew what had to be done. Rush her! Now. Shoulder through the crowd, snatch her wrist and twist that knife free!

Too late. The blade jerked, borne on a question and a sob.

"She's stupid, Molly. She knows you, but asks again."

"Tell her I'm just a woman from town. I have tea to make her feel better. I'll rub salve on that cut, if she wants me to."

Bulling in would have been a mistake. He saw it as the woman's shoulder blades met the shack wall. Moll's words had soothed her like fingers smoothing cat's fur. Her twitching eyelids sagged and a sigh rushed out as the knife thudded down.

"Leave it," Moll cautioned as slippers scuffed forward. "Leave it be, Lin. It's all right.

"No stove in here, so just take this out and heat it. Get some honey if you can." Moll waited as the woman slid down the wall. "You're cold, now, aren't you?"

God, in this stifling heat? Moll must be mad.

"Here, try this." Molly settled in the filth and raised her shawl like a protective wing.

Day swallowed. Sifted sun crowned Moll with dust

motes. "My Bright," he mused, wishing he could stroke that sorrel hair as she accepted the shelter of *his* arm. Molly appeared every bit the angel he'd taken her for that first day.

"Lin, keep that bastard outside." Molly arranged the shawl as her eyes flashed at the interpreter. "Just keep Kee away from her. And me."

He sat in the buckboard for an hour, scrutinizing a sky dull as a lead lid and crucifying himself over who "Kee" might be. When Molly emerged from the shack, blotting her forehead with a handkerchief, she saw him, pushed back her hair with one wrist and nodded. The gesture yanked him off the seat as the whorelord, in a newly donned blue satin coat, approached, hands full of money.

Like a scrawny bird, Lin hopped at Moll's elbow.

Arms crossed and lips set, Moll defied the man. "Tell him I insist on having my fee applied to her passage."

"Kee says, you have this fight before. You understand Favor say the answer is no."

"I won't take money. He can give it to Favor against the girl's price, or be a dishonest snake and cheat me."

Lin moaned in frustration before translating. Day hoped to God she had the sense to pretty it up.

Moll, though she didn't move, gave the impression of having stamped her foot. Clearly, she hoped Kee would bow to her will instead of dishonoring himself. One glance told Day that Moll would lose.

Kee mirrored Moll's position, crossing his arms, inclining his black skullcap to the exact degree of her head before stepping in to gain eye level.

Day strode nearer, too. His shadow grayed the man's features and Moll twitched in irritation. Very well, but he stood close enough to grab her if he must.

"Kee's not afraid of you, Molly." Lin rolled her eyes. "He says he will take your money and buy another whore with it."

Blood sprang up in Moll's cheeks. A duck quacked three times in ascending harshness. Nearby, children played a hand-clapping game. Molly waited, and Day figured

Griffin'd miss a sure thing if he didn't teach Moll Gallagher to play poker.

The whorelord laughed and settled his hands on his hips before addressing Lin and walking away.

"Molly, you are too stupid to live long. This is Kee's deal: he keep the money, you get two donkey loads firewood gathered by her boy." Lin wagged her head toward the shack. "And for *you*, she get the night off."

"Not good enough," Molly muttered, then shouted after him. "Not good enough, Kee!"

The man turned, hands on hips, once more.

"Four nights off!" Molly straight-armed four fingers his way.

Kee's smile faded. His lash-thin mustache outlined his lips' grim set before the blue satin arm copied Moll's movement.

"Three!" Kee yelled and vanished inside a cabin.

For the barest breath of a moment, Day imagined Molly leaned back against his arm.

Her hands shook so badly by the time she climbed into the buckboard that Day figured Moll'd scold him, to prove her mettle. He didn't give her a chance, only peppered her with questions.

"What were you tryin' to do, there, about the money?"

Moll glanced back, watching Chinatown recede. "The girls are sold into slavery by their parents, in China." She ticked off her index finger, as if other atrocities would follow. "When they reach San Francisco, they're sold again, to a man like Kee, who pays six hundred dollars for their ship passage."

Moll touched a second finger, her hands shaking a bit less. "The girls are promised a wage, usually a dollar a week, and told they can pay back their slave price and ship fare in a year. But every time they're sick or 'indisposed' they lose their pay.

"I've heard of girls set free by men who marry them." Moll squinted off between the mule's ears. "But I've never met one."

"And so you were trying—"

"What were you doing?" Moll's tone said she'd been held off long enough.

Day gave himself a minute, studying the buckboard bench, smooth and bare between them. If he stretched, his fingers could touch her, but she'd left no chance that it could happen by accident.

"Just backing you up, Miss Gallagher, in case there was trouble." Day slapped the reins. At a grudging trot, Abner turned onto C Street. "I've been called a good man to have behind ye in a fight. I was just backing you up, like friends do."

Until now, Day had never seen a person slack-jawed with disbelief. Moll's incredulity said this lowly cat salesman had skipped a few steps on the way to friendship, and left her far behind.

Chapter
Eight

This cat man named Day hadn't learned Eve's lessons. He thought he might purchase her good nature with an apple.

Molly stood in her dooryard, offering an apple core to Day's mule. After collecting Poppy from Deborah and the fruit from a freighter off-loading at VanBrunts', Day had driven them home.

"Cinder, stay." The black dog wanted a piece of the Cornishman. Cinder stalked, stiff-legged from arthritis as well as warning, baring his teeth toward the house and the intruder who'd accompanied Poppy inside.

Ignoring Molly's prediction that the lowering skies threatened a thunderstorm, Day had bowed to Poppy's pleading. Presumptuously, he'd tied the mule, slipping its bit and unbuckling the harness as if he'd stay all afternoon to teach Poppy the art of Cornish pasties.

Cinder's ears lifted and growls rumbled in his throat at the sound of wood being split behind the house. Inside, Poppy stacked wood Molly had cut into the stove's firebox. She'd stacked ample kindling. Why must he heft their ax? Day was a show-off. Still and all, if he saved her labor, she wouldn't stop him.

"Flour and lard and salt." Day's voice carried between ax blows. "And a bit of meat, whatever you have."

"Venison?" Poppy called out the back door. "It's dried."

"That's fine, though we'll set about getting you some beef. Now, what about potatoes? Onions?" The door clunked into place.

Molly released two buttons at the back of her high collar. Merciful Mother, he'd keep her from going inside her own house to wash up, and her smelling no better than the mule, after praying and sweating inside that crib half the day.

And payment? Two donkey loads of wood. Dear stuff, wood, when lumber went for mine timbers. Wood, Kee had promised, and he'd best not send sagebrush. If it stayed warm, which it wouldn't, two loads would last two weeks.

She'd needed that money, and Kee had been willing to pay. Next time, she'd harden her heart and take the gold to pay Stag's board. Deborah couldn't afford charity any more than she could.

Molly clucked Cinder to her side. She kneaded the dog's hackles. "I'll slip you some venison before they use it all."

Cinder turned brown eyes to hers, as if a dog of higher principles would reject bribery, then followed at Moll's heels.

This infernal switching of places—Day for Cinder, inside and out—wouldn't work for long. Molly knew the dog would win because the man refused to believe Cinder hated him.

"Roll the dough into circles, while I soften the jerky."

Molly marveled at how easily Day had invaded Poppy's domain. Tightening her apron strings, Poppy leaned to her floury work. Day claimed a table corner, with cutting board and knife.

One of his shirt cuffs gaped open and he unbuttoned the other. Oft-washed blue sleeves folded neatly as he made one quick turn, then two more. Faint veins pulsed at the inner crease of his elbow. His forearms curved taut, not the bulging musculature of a miner, but molded by other work. Browned almost cinnamon against the blue cotton, they flexed while he chopped the venison. The fingers of his left hand steadied the blade. His right hand lifted the haft and stopped. Poised.

In the instant their eyes met, Molly thought his matched the weathered blue of his shirt. Before her stomach constricted, before fear closed her throat, he turned, raked meat into the black skillet and watched it sputter.

Why had she allowed him into her house? She had no reputation to save, but Poppy did. And Day had lied.

Molly clenched her hands into fists, hiding them behind her. She'd thought him thin, compared him to a scarecrow. But she'd been wrong. His clothes fluttered and sagged against his ribs, as if worn in by someone else, but Day was no weakling. Those muscled forearms, the spread of shoulders beneath fresh-cut black hair baring a too-white nape— all testified that Day had earned that twenty-dollar gold piece as something more than a peddler.

"Why is it they don't buy cats from *you*, seeing you have so many?" Day's voice rose over the hiss of cooking onions. Did he keep his back turned because he'd seen the knowledge in her face?

"Molly's cats won't stay in town," Poppy answered. "Every one comes prancing home with its tail straight up in the air."

"A bit territorial? Even if the pickings are better in town?" Day met Poppy's nod, then turned again to the skillet.

In spite of his belt, Day's secondhand breeches slanted down his hip. He shifted his weight to one leg, relaxed. Moll thought she'd like to kick that foot out from under him.

"Talk to your landlady. She'll give you a different story." Molly cursed the approaching storm for her irritability.

"Aye?" Day poked a wooden spoon at the mixture and reached for the carrots mounded on the table.

"She'll say I *charm* the cats home. She'll tell you how I saved a child from a raging creek, and didn't have the decency to drown! Witches float, you know."

A low rumble underlined her gibe. It might be Poppy's rolling pin or thunder. Rain on the roof joined in. Day slowed his movements, narrowing his eyes to watch her. The kitchen walls seemed to hunch closer as Molly prepared to tell him—before others did—about the death of Moses Franks, the freighter she'd "cursed and killed."

Poppy began rubbing her eyes and the dough lay forgotten. Flour dusted Poppy's face from cheekbones to hairline. No tears cut paths through the flour. Yet.

"Tell you what—" Molly tweaked her sister's braid. "I'll go out front and watch the rain. You put those to bake, then introduce Day to Hannah and Glory." Molly escaped through the curtain, into the dark parlor.

"Stop, child. You've no need to scare him off. Let him care for you. He's got helping hands I can't offer."

A draft buffeted Molly's arm and she pulled away as if the breeze were a detaining hand. Anyone would think her mad if they knew how often she heard her dead mother's summons.

Hands over her ears, Molly rushed onto the porch. Raindrops shook the erratic lattice of firethorn.

Since her skirts already needed washing, Molly collapsed on the dusty step, glad she'd removed her crinoline and stays. She crossed her arms around her knees. She stared past the shelf of black fabric, through a thorny frame, down the slumped hillside, beyond the Red Rovers. She counted raindrops, letting them cover the voices inside her house.

One, two, threefour . . . one, two, threefourfivesix . . . Drops spattered so fast she lost count. They pelted down, blurring into a vision, into a mist of snow.

She didn't resist. This time she followed willingly, because the flurries cooled her and a gentle voice hinted that she might understand. This time, the dancing flakes parted like curtains and the horseman cantered. This time she distinguished a head inside the helm, and almost, a face.

"Molly," Rose's voice scolded, as if her daughter had been silly and slow with a lesson.

No. Molly shook her head, banishing the daydream.

"Molly, pay attention."

No. Here, Cinder stood barking. Here, rain blew damp on Molly's stockings, sneaking under her wind-puffed skirts. The door opened behind her and Cinder's warning barks grew shrill. Slivers stabbed real pain as Molly dug finger-nails into the porch boards, but Rose's voice was insistent.

"Molly, honey, look at him." In the snow, hooves hunted after her, shaking the ground as the white horse pivoted.

"Back, boy. I'm not hurtin' her. Down—" Day's voice had no place in her vision in her terrible winter realm. Her mind brushed it aside.

In the snow, the horse huffed vapor from hot nostrils. He gathered himself and charged.

Nothing else was real, nothing but Mama's voice screaming, *"Heartsblood!"* Scarlet flared, arced like a rainbow and splattered on the snow. *"Heartsblood."*

Feet, real feet, stumbled beside Molly. A flesh-and-bone head slammed against the house wall.

"Bloody hell, Molly! Gi' me a bit of help, here!"

Coffee splattered, burning her. Poppy wailed and Day's knee bumped her shoulder. Snarling lips raised over wolfish fangs, head leveled for launching, Cinder attacked. His jaws gripped Day above the elbow, grinding for a deeper hold.

"Cinder, down!" Molly's voice clashed with Cinder's snarls. She smelled sulphur-harsh lightning as she lurched to her feet.

The dog loosened his teeth enough to growl and Molly crowded against Day's front, shielding him. She rapped Cinder's muzzle, still trying to reach Day. With a yelp, Cinder dropped to the porch and limped away. He collapsed next to the tethered mule.

"Lovely, just lovely, m'Bright." Day's lips touched her ear and she recoiled. "Just what was it," he whispered, "What fool thing did I do . . . Christ, were you *letting* him chew on me?"

Shocked at the intimacy of his lips, Molly's head half turned to refute him and shake off his arm. But Day stood so near that his arm had to reach across her to clutch the wound. As he did, his spread black pupils signaled a faint.

"Sit down." Molly pressed his shoulder. "Do as I say, now."

"Yes, lass."

In spite of the faint growth of beard peppering his jaw, he looked mild, perhaps frightened. Cinder's attack had been wholehearted, but the dog was frail and old.

"Poppy, hush." Molly quieted her sister's weeping. "Day's all right. Cinder didn't hurt him."

"The bloody hell he didn't." Day laughed before his forehead fell against her shoulder.

Squatting beside him, skirts tangled above her knees and between his, Moll exerted her authority. "Let's see it, then. Bites need to be washed, so I'll want you inside."

"I'll wash it at Bess's." Weaving, he plucked the blue sleeve to display its rips and grimaced as a thread stuck to the wound. "I won't stay for pasties, ladies, if it's all the same to you."

He edged through the firethorn, down the steps. Poppy ran ahead, jerking her hair ribbon loose and knotting it around Cinder's neck for a leash.

"I'm so sorry, Day. I thought he'd get used to you." Poppy's other hand sheltered her hair from the rain.

"Don't worry yourself, dearie. And don't let the pasties burn." He rebridled the mule as Poppy ran back to the house.

Moll watched Day lean against the buckboard, cupping his hand over the wound as he gathered nerve to mount the bench.

"Could you step a mite closer, Miss Gallagher?" Day stared toward town, oblivious to the rain slicking his hair and cheeks.

Underfoot, the thin film of mud shifted and tan dust reappeared. The storm had ended before accomplishing a thing.

"Don't leave Poppy alone with VanBrunt."

Molly wrung a few drops from her chignon as rain plopped from the eaves. He might have the decency to look down after issuing such a commandment.

Then she understood. A man who blanched at a little pain must regain his manliness. Ordering her about might do the trick.

Strangely disappointed, she considered how little it would cost her to help him recover. Molly nodded consolingly.

He grabbed her wrist, then loosened his grip, so quickly she might have imagined it. More startling than his touch was the slight smile and focused flatness on the surface of his blue eyes. Warnings as small as sparks burned down her spine and out each finger.

"Molly, m'Bright." No trick of cloud-strained light painted his wolfish expression. He pulled her closer. "I am not a poor wight, confused by your dog's attack. Look in my eyes. Do you see I've quite got my wits about me?"

Molly nodded. He dropped her wrist.

"VanBrunt means ill toward Poppy and it's not my imagining. I saw him touch her and I did not like the look of it."

The sparks of warning burned out, leaving her as stiff as a blackened stick.

Awkwardly, his lips pressed tight together, Day climbed into the wagon and took up the reins. He frowned toward the house, but Molly caught nothing but the glimmer of window glass through the firethorn. She turned back to Day as he slapped his black hat against his thigh and settled it with his left hand.

"Take care of me cats, now. I'll be back."

Rose swayed at the window. As the storm grayed into dusk and she watched Molly study the Cornishman as he drove out of sight, Rose remembered the clinging weight of rain-wet skirts and the chill of a breeze over dampened sleeves. Then she looked after the man.

Oh, Molly. Foolish girl to drive that one away. He'll go if you force him. They all do.

Moll came into the house. She leaned her back against the closed door and Rose surged to the space before her. What would she give to take Molly's face in her hands and make her listen? Rose mourned. Why hadn't someone told her that sinking into sin, into selfishness and sloth meant giving up her girls?

Though Rose knew she had no claim on her daughter's heart, she tried to reach her.

He's the one who'll save you, from whatever storm is brewing out there. He's the white knight in your dreams. He doesn't mean to hurt you. Not that he won't. He'll wring blood from your dear heart, Molly lamb, but it's worth it. The joy surpasses the pain. Take it! Take what he offers, for the days he's here. After all this—Rose swirled away, and Molly squinted, as if a dust devil swept through the room—*after pasties and poverty and propriety all are gone, only love remains.*

Chapter
Nine

Coyotes yipped and chorused, working up for a night of hunting, and he'd ridden only halfway to Carson.

Head back, assessing the twilight sky, Day took long swallows from his canteen. Three things he'd do before returning to Virginia City. Shoot, to keep his aim in spite of the dog's bite. Ease through Carson to check for posters bearing his portrait. Last, he'd stay gone until he'd broken Red Molly's enchantment.

Day slung the canteen from the saddle horn and let out the livery horse's cinched belly. White spots patched the roan's eyes, making him look like an Indian pony, but he beat Abner for companionship and folks in Carson would notice the loud-marked horse, not the rider.

On horseback, Day could breathe again. Riding tight as a burr in a mustang's mane was one thing he did better than drawing a gun. If he'd followed Da's wishes, he never would have known. He'd never have left the sea, never have walked halfway to London, and never have heard old

Trelawny cackle, "Yon Markie has a horseman's hands and seat. Aye, any animal between his legs moves better for it."

If only Moll could see him ride.

He'd uncoiled his gun belt from his saddlebags and lifted a handful of cartridges before he heard his mind circling back, under her spell.

Bewitched or not, work couldn't wait. A stranger, even in a town full of strangers, caused suspicion; Griffin probably hadn't been the only one watching as Day prepared to leave town.

"You don't wear a gun." Griffin, atop a steeldust mare, had eyed Day's rented horse and the bullets from Van-Brunts'.

"Sometimes I do." Day had kept filling his saddlebags.

"Hit what you aim at?" Griffin's drawl had teased Day into answering.

"Almost every time."

The gambler had nodded before cantering north, leaving town. Day knew he'd better limber up his arm before Griffin or some drunken miner forced him to back up that boast.

Day fed the well-oiled leather, supple as a snake, through the buckle, then yanked it hard enough that the dog's teeth burned again. Still, once the Colt slid into its holster, once the ammunition loops glittered full and the belt clung an inch below his hipbone, Day felt settled, able to examine what he'd blurted to Griffin during their saloon talk.

"I'd have nothing to offer a woman like her," he'd told the gambler, but something in Moll Gallagher beckoned. He couldn't put name or reason to the yearning. Beautiful witch, cold businesswoman, healer—it didn't matter which form she assumed; her blood called out to his.

Day slipped brass cartridges into the revolver, concentrating on their coolness rather than Moll's warmth.

He tied the horse in the shade of a granite cliff and kept the rock wall on guard behind him. Lifeless sagebrush targets made poor substitutes for cautious prey, but they'd serve. Half blocking the approach from Virginia, the rock would deter unwanted company. Hearing hidden gunfire, most men would think twice, then step careful.

He'd stepped right into that old dog's ambush. Regardless of Moll's diagnosis, Cinder had bitten badly enough that Day's belly still felt cold-pitted, his head muzzy and fevered. But, truth be told, pain hadn't made him grab the wound, his arm barring Moll's chest. He'd wanted her to stay.

Day closed his eyes and the inside of his forearm recalled her breasts. He hadn't meant to touch her like that, but once he had, he couldn't draw back. Skin had spilled soft over the top of her underpinnings. Through the damp dress he'd felt it.

Fire the gun, you blessed idiot. Day waited for the skip between heartbeats, then pulled back the hammer and shot in a single, opposing motion.

Jesus, Mary and Joseph! Accursed dog had ripped him good. And he was nothing near as stiff as he'd be by dawn.

Moll had looked capable of ripping him herself, when she'd thought he was groping her. Soon as she'd seen his pain, though, her vixen face turned sweet. And when Moll, so close they breathed each other's breath, had said she wanted him inside, his randy brain had bucked with glee.

Sinful thoughts to have as Moll crouched next to him, showing petticoats and stockings as she doctored. When he'd slumped against her shoulder, a shred of sanity kept him from kissing the white skin above a loosened button.

Day shot the Colt's cylinder empty, grinding his teeth as each kick of the gun tore at his shoulder. Pitiful. Three shots had hit home! A child's score. He should have let Molly clean the bite. He'd merely sluiced off the blood, changed shirts and snatched provisions from Bess's kitchen before renting the roan. If he'd stopped to think, he might have gone back to her.

Day poured out the spent shells, clamping one between his teeth while reloading. Biting down against the pain, he shot. *Better*. Again. *Ah, yes.*

He had the skill and instincts to face sheriffs, U.S. marshals or bounty hunters. But did he have the right? Was he a killer who should be brought to justice? Until he knew, he had no time for Moll Gallagher.

He decided to forget her, feeding his agitation with biscuits and ham, occupying his hands by graining and hobbling the roan. Might as well risk a fire, too, try warming the arm, so it wouldn't kink later.

Eleanor VanBrunt had called Moll "the Witch of Six Mile Canyon," and sure her sorcery preyed on his weak mind. Even his saddle blanket, slung over a bush and fluttering against the ink-blue sky, conjured memories of her windsnatched skirts.

Day stacked twigs and struck a match, glancing up to see if moisture haloed the stars. What else but a spell painted Moll's face on the remote ivory moon?

When the fire blew ruby-gold sparks, enchantment murmured that Moll's hair was just that hue, and all her black coverings could not hide its flame.

Hell! A man set on acting the bloody poet should have stayed home and become a bard of the moors, with weeds in his hair and sand in his eyes, instead of traveling to this far wasteland.

Day snapped a branch and muttered. Everything about Molly and everything kindling inside him mimicked this reckless fire, burning hot red against the black. Even surrounded by hundreds of miles of night, it couldn't be hidden.

Day fed the flames a twig of sage. *The drawing together keeps getting stronger; the space between us gets smaller each time we're alone.*

You can't hide it, can't help it, he consoled himself. Gathering strength, the fire flared, gushing heat, but Day's practical mind shamed him.

A man couldn't hide a fire in the dark, but he could—if he were stronger than a frightened boy—decide not to let a campfire burn out of control and consume him.

Aye, a smart man stepped in before the fire got too hot. He kicked dirt over it, smothered it and watched it die.

Miss Margaret Bride, of Chicago's Lane-Sylvester Normal School, had arrived. Molly and Poppy Gallagher stood on the boardwalk as the stagecoach creaked to a halt.

"The schoolmarm!" A dozen tongues passed the news before Margaret Bride set foot on rutted C Street, grabbing the coach door to avert a fall.

Milk-pale and trembling, the teacher sagged under brown tweed garments, a hat like a white plate, and spectacles. This frail rabbit of a woman didn't belong in the West.

Leaf points clattered on bare cottonwood branches as the teacher clutched her reticule and greeted the VanBrunts, Brown Bess and Reverend Bliss. Waving hands no wider than the brittle leaves, Margaret Bride directed the unloading of her trunks.

"They're dreadfully heavy, mostly books and slates."

Molly added bad lungs to the woman's failings. Her wheezing voice presaged a single Virginia City winter. Such lungs couldn't tolerate more. A band of off-duty miners, watching left and right for ore wagons, marched in to assist. Their rowdy help covered Eleanor's monologue.

Mostly books and slates. If Poppy got more practice in writing, if she learned to enjoy reading instead of facing books with the same resignation she did laundry, the teacher would have earned her outrageous salary.

Another wagon stampeded past, causing the stage to shudder and the teacher to flatten a hand on her wind-winging hat.

Without provocation, as if she were a beast and some scent came borne on the Indian-summer wind, Molly's mind flared with a memory of Day, eyelids lowered, jaw tense.

That look of—lust, she supposed, had shadowed Day's blue eyes, twice. In the buckboard, when he'd claimed to be her friend, and in the yard, before he disappeared, she'd seen it.

In those shameful moments, her body had understood what her mind would not. Her pulse had urged her to stroke that sun-browned jaw, before her brain said to slap it.

Molly's face tightened with embarrassment and she glanced about her. Had anyone had noticed her vile preoccupation?

"Truly, I prefer 'Miss Margaret.'"

The schoolteacher's words snared Molly's attention. The pale woman twitched a smile to soften her stridency.

"Out of respect—" Eleanor protested.

"Honestly—" The schoolteacher coughed and another trunk slammed the road. "—'Miss Bride,' at my age, seems rather a cruel joke." Her embarrassed words fell into a pool of quiet.

Molly wanted to applaud the trembling woman or, like a man, give her a congratulatory smack on the back. Purple humiliation soaked Margaret Bride's cheeks, telling the cost of her honesty.

"Oh, we have no old maids in Virginia City!" Hans Van-Brunt belched with laughter. "These boys have been so long without a good woman, you don't have to worry!"

As if to prove Hans right, the men rushed to finish Margaret Bride's schoolhouse. In three days, it stood nearly complete.

Poppy walked beside Molly as they climbed the hill toward the banging hammers.

"Do you think she's pretty? Miss Margaret?" Poppy asked.

"She looks kind."

"Her hair is a nice color, sort of like sarsaparilla."

Molly tried not to smile.

Half a mile down the hill, across the road and midway between the stamp mill and town, sat the donated strip of ore-leeched land. A handful of men squatted on the roof, pounding.

"When she blushes—remember, when I forgot to call her Miss Margaret—her cheeks get blotchy. Do you think she had the smallpox?"

"No, no," Molly hushed her, raising her voice as the blacksmith pounded door hinges. "Not everyone has a fine complexion, Poppy, and you must pretend not to notice."

When Poppy looked down, Molly's heart twinged. Over Poppy's hair, she saw Hans VanBrunt pause in lifting school desks from a wagon. As he watched them, Molly felt the barb of Day's warning.

Far down the hill, Poppy and she had seen the men notice their approach. Red flannel shirts had flown like flags as the men, working shirtless in the October sun, covered themselves from the sisters' eyes.

Only Hans VanBrunt hadn't dressed. Meaty and pink, his breast sweat-shined, he propped a boot on one of the desks.

Molly linked her arm with Poppy's and her sister nestled close as they climbed against the wind.

Most men nodded. Two on the roof made quick salutes. Hans stretched, scratched, but didn't wave or smile.

"Pardon, Miss Molly, but how's Stag doin'?" asked a voice muffled by a mouthful of nails.

"Better," she called. "If I can keep him off the drink, he'll be back to work before long."

A chorus of laughs, raucous but kind, followed.

"Aw, Miss Molly, the bosses like a man who drinks! First hired, last fired. A hard-rock man who goes on a binge will pick out his penance for days, workin' twice as hard!"

"Beggin' your pardon, Miss Poppy," sang out Geordie, who'd been in town over a year. "Would you be makin' more pasties, tomorrow? I'll be working me own bit of tribute mine, after shift, and I'd wrap one of your pasties to carry down w'me . . .?"

Poppy giggled, promised Geordie a pastie, and skipped up to the brow of the hill. With corn-silk hair and snapping blue sashes, Molly thought Poppy seemed a fairy to these men who labored underground. When she glanced back to wave farewell, the miners had begun shucking their shirts. Only Hans stared after them.

When Hans presented himself for a reading an hour later, Molly stood waiting. Against such a possibility, she'd sent Poppy and Cinder to the stream for willow slips.

Not that she credited Day's accusation.

Molly lighted the candle. She tried to wipe her mind clear as one of Miss Margaret's new slates as Hans dried his sweaty palms on his trousers, then looked about, probing corners, examining the ceiling, searching for Poppy or witch's treasure.

Mama had told fortunes from teacups, swirling the leaf dregs left, then right, three turns each way. She'd sold hex bags tied with strands of her own red hair. Molly would have practiced either bit of fakery rather than touch Hans Van-Brunt's hand.

As before, Molly couldn't ignore his thumbs. She tried to joke off her foreboding. It was no curse to possess thumbs that looked like large toes. Still, his hands' stiffness and the turgid, immovable mounts of Mars and Venus underlined old superstitions. Molly couldn't imagine where she'd learned it, but she knew what to call thumbs like Hans's: murderer's thumbs.

She told what truth she could. Instead of pointing up a smoldering temper, Molly said that Hans exerted control over his feelings. Instead of examining emotional breaks and reunions, she said he'd soon renew a friendship.

Then a chill settled over them both, a chill Molly had learned to ignore.

This one's got a seat reserved in Hell. Murderer's thumbs and a cruel streak. Rose read Hans's palm over Molly's shoulder. And he smelled like old stew. The idea that beautiful Moll must waste a pinch of hours on this Hans—big in the middle and ugly on both ends—provoked Rose. So, maybe she'd provoke him.

Rose faded a few feet off. Hans could see her; Moll could not. Soon, Rose would meet her girls, and talk with them, but it was devilish tricky to show her whole body and project thoughts, all at once. Half measures would only frighten them.

I'll practice on you, Ugly Hans! Who on earth cares if you're frightened? As if she'd slapped him, Hans's head bumped back against her settee. *Lovely, we're communicating. You can quit trying to make spit. You came to see a witch, didn't you, Hans? Let's see if Mad Rose can't show you at least part of one!*

Rose's will pressed outward, tightening, forcing the foggy form of her right arm afloat in the dim parlor. *Fingernails, knuckles and all! Not too shabby for a new specter!*

Hans licked his lips and stared at the disturbing display.

You're all googgly-eyed and swollen up like a toad in a butter churn! Rose wished for a cackle to fan his fear.

Hans's sputter made Molly turn. Rose vanished. Simple enough. She blinked off her energy and disappeared. *Be proud, Rose Gallagher! You've unlooked-for talent as a ghost!*

No Hans, don't be getting comfy and studying my Moll's knee beneath your ham-hand. I haven't finished with you, quite yet.

Rose's cheeks puffed forth and then her entire head! Sakes, such splendid terror spewed from Hans's face that Rose tried once more, letting her ghostly eyes roll back in her sockets.

Hans jumped to his feet, scanning the room, but Rose had vanished. Touching his pocket, he began bumbling over Moll's fee.

"Y-You'll take store credit for payment?"

A s-s-stutter, is it, clever Hans, and still searching for a bargain? Rose concentrated on her right hand.

"For my herbs and medicines, yes." Moll's lips made a careful smile. "But not for readings, Hans, remember?"

Molly released a breath in tiny increments and stared at the curtains, mullioned with firethorn shadows. Rose watched her daughter deny Hans access to her eyes as she worried over Poppy.

Stay away, honey. Skip another stone. Rose focused more energy. *Find a shred of velvet from a buck's antlers, Poppy love, or follow a family of quail—this next part might be nasty!*

That's when it happened.

Enjoy your encore, jelly jowls!

With a silent shout of glee, Rose waved a single spectral finger. Lecherous Hans understood, for he bolted past Molly, squawking loud as a goose in a funeral parlor.

What had possessed the man? Molly prescribed basil and borage tea for her nerves and let Hans's silver coins lie as she scrubbed her hands and contemplated a visit to Stag. Chamomile tea no longer soothed him, but an infusion of catnip might.

As Molly swirled the jar, her hand wobbled. Outside, a

hoof struck rock. With a flour-sack towel, she wiped her hands, then scooped up Hans's coins in passing and lifted the parlor curtain.

Day. Standing next to a roan horse, he moved in painful jerks, using his left hand to pull a shirt from his saddlebags. The clumsy tug jerked the bags off, onto the ground. He leaned sideways to reach them, snagged the shirt with a hooked index finger and held it in his teeth while his left hand unbuttoned the shirt he still wore. Stubborn fool.

Surprise tightened her throat as she noticed Day's wide, muscular shoulders. Uncovered, his skin was dark.

The shirt between his teeth escaped. He left it in the dirt, regarding the sky with lips that muttered prayers or curses. She needed no magic to predict the course of Cinder's bite. Festering and hot, red streaks running away from the punctures . . . Her fault for not forcing Day to accept her care.

Molly dropped the curtain. She needed to air the parlor. She needed to brew tea. Molly hurried back to the kitchen, folded the towel and listened for his boots on the porch.

Her heart still pounded from the sight of Hans's misshapen thumbs. That must be it.

Molly counted orderly rows of bottles arranged against the window. She touched her fingers to the surging vein in her throat. The bad reading. The bicker over money. That must be it.

She closed her eyes, but sun slanting through the bottles painted her eyelids rose-gold. This runaway pulse did not rampage at Day's return. She simply would not allow it.

Chapter
Ten

"Miss Gallagher, good afternoon."

Miss Gallagher, again? What a confounding man. Thank the Lord his health and money were her only concerns.

"Good afternoon, Mr. Day. Have you come to gather up your cats?" Molly examined him in a glance and offered him another chance to lie.

Day's grip crimped the brim of his black hat. His whiskers had been scraped unevenly, left-handed. His eyes glinted hostile gray. He hurt. Whoever "Day" really was, wherever he'd been, he needed care. "How *are* my cats?"

"Growing braver, ranging farther and learning to dodge coyotes." She returned his faint smile and corrected her first evaluation. His eyes were feverish, not hostile. She would need willow bark and catnip for him, too, if she lanced Cinder's bite.

Day's shirt collar moved as he swallowed and he grimaced at even that faint disturbance of his wound.

"How long will you wait on my step, before asking me to examine that bite, Mr. Day?" Molly crossed her arms.

"How long before you learn there's no 'mister' before that 'Day,' Miss Gallagher?" He taunted her with the same cocksure smile he'd worn the day she refused to board his cats, but he stepped inside, all the same.

"No." She stopped him from settling on the couch. "I want you in the kitchen. This will be a bit messy for the parlor."

As she drew him away from the love seat, a voice—dear, but decadent—snuggled among her own thoughts.

"Flustered? Skin feelin' a bit tight, sweet Molly?"

Heavenly powers, it was her mother's voice. Molly stood transfixed and wondered why Day couldn't hear it!

"You're a good girl and I'd have y'stay so, but give your long-lonely mother a peek at the man's fair flesh, can't—"

"'A bit messy for the parlor,'" Day muttered. "Words you'd never hear from a surgeon."

"Cutting Jack Slocum will offer more manly conversation." Molly shook her head, dispelled the buzz clustering in her temples and resolved to get more sleep. "And a male solution to your malady." She indicated a chair, but Day didn't sit.

"None of this mucking about with plants and flowers for Cuttin' Jack, eh?" Day glanced at the green-cluttered niche, more stillroom than kitchen.

Molly tied on her bibbed apron. "Jack's manly solution calls for taking that brawny arm off at the joint."

"I don't recall meetin' a more gruesome woman." Day eased into the chair. Closing his eyes, he suppressed a weary smile.

Satisfied that he'd be a compliant patient, she dipped water for tea into a pan, splashed a jar of sage water into a kettle and set both to boil. When she turned back, Molly found she'd been mistaken about the smile.

"Let's get it over with, can we?"

"I am sorry about the bite—Day. There's been no rabies since last summer, though, so that shouldn't be a concern."

Still he glowered.

"You had fair warning about that dog!" As soon as the words erupted, her hands slid off her hips and Molly resumed a mild countenance. Let Day be angry if it stemmed his fear.

Her stomach tipped in a bottomless slope as she remembered the clamp of his fingers pulling her close. Molly stepped back.

"I had warning. Did I say I hadn't? No! I said I'd appreciate a bit o' alacrity!"

Alacrity! Molly stacked the clean rags she would use for compresses. An educated cat salesman, was he?

"Strip to the waist." Molly gloated at the surprised widening of Day's eyes.

But he obeyed, pressing one metal button through its hole, fighting with the next. When he had worked each button loose, Day shook the sleeve from his left arm and drew a chest-filling breath. His teeth grated as he set upon the right sleeve.

Stubborn Cornishman. Molly squatted, braced her elbow against his knee and unbuttoned the cuff before he protested.

"Lean forward." She eased the shirt off, shook it and folded it. She noted a flush of sunburn, not serious enough to treat, over his shoulders. Why? More important, why did this peddler carry scents of leather and gunpowder?

"I wouldn't normally worry—"

"You'd best worry about this one." Lord, why hadn't she tied Cinder?

Purple, black and blue, the bruise from the dog's crushing grip spread from Day's elbow to his shoulder. Five red-black rips slashed the mound of infection. Thready lines of blood poisoning crawled away from them.

He'd need the catnip for sure. Molly poured a glass. No time to heat it. The sooner he swallowed, the sooner she could work.

"Drink this, please."

"What is it?" Day didn't wrinkle his nose, nor did he drink.

"A relaxing tea."

"I don't need relaxing!" Day slammed the cup down.

Then his arm crossed his chest, fingers rubbing the hollow beneath his collarbone. "Just get on with it!"

A flush raged up from his neck. He looked gravely fevered. Molly stroked Day's disordered hair, seeking his brow, testing for temperature. If she flooded him with too many herbs, he'd vomit them all. Should she use the willow bark for fever, or catnip for pain?

When Day shifted away from her touch, she caught his head, holding him still by forking her fingers under the Indian-black hair at the base of his skull. She pressed her cheek against his brow to sense its heat.

"Jesus Christ, woman!" His cursing intensified when he jarred the wound against the chair.

"Sorry." Molly scooped a bowl of boiling water to steam the compresses. "I don't like handling, myself."

She'd never noticed Day's aversion to touch before. Just the contrary, judging from the fatherly pats he'd awarded Poppy. Such sensitivity must be part of his affliction.

Molly sympathized. She felt cornered and angry, even sick, when touched in the most innocent ways. A friendly handshake crushed like a fur trap.

She knew what had planted her fear, and had no interest in uprooting it. Handshakes and hugs were not necessary. Fortune had given her a different mission: her hands healed those in need.

As Day most definitely was. His fury simmered in vicious whispers. With her back turned, Molly listened and washed her hands again.

"Will I be able to use the bloody arm when you're done? Or will I be a cripple?" He glared through the sweat-damp hair she'd tried to smooth.

He's sick. Take a breath. Give him a choice and he won't feel cornered and weak. "You can still seek Slocum's advice."

As suddenly as he'd exploded, Day calmed. "All right, lass. I'll let you do what you do best. Just tell me how and why."

Day's left hand pushed the wild black tangle from his

eyes and he cocked one eyebrow. As a current of pain seized him, Day set his jaw.

"Fair enough. First, I'll give you catnip tea for pain or—something for fever. Just now, I'm inclined to tend your fever." Day nodded and she pressed on. "I'll soak the rips open, and when I see what I've got—" His frowning intensity said he'd catch any half-truths.

"No, what I've got, Day, what *you've* got, is blood poisoning. I'll spread the rips." She almost flinched, herself, at the expanding pincer motion of her index finger and thumb. "Then, I'll clean out the corruption and rinse them with sage water before bandaging."

"Is that all?" His voice crooked stiff as the fingers forming a claw-shield over the wound.

"I'll give you rose-hip tea to drink, three times a day."

"Is *that* all?"

Molly gazed toward the rafters, considering precautions. "And probably thyme or juniper tea, too. You can choose which."

He stared at her, still waiting, as she unbuckled the strap of her instrument case.

"That's all—except that I'd ask you to stay clear of my poor old dog!"

Day laughed, his eyes flashing blue. Molly kept the image as she worked, because he had no cause to smile again, that day.

Poppy's footsteps scuffed at the back door, but Molly didn't stand to greet her. Molly sipped her sour rose-hip tea, across the table from Day. For half an hour they'd sat so. Pain excused his silence. Her excuse was shame.

Molly's imagination played the scenes through again, forcing herself to decide whether she'd loved this last hour or hated it.

She'd hated his knuckles going gray, grabbing the table's edge when she lanced the swelling. She'd loved the long, deflating breath rushing through his lips as the corruption drained and he sighed, "Better."

The deep tooth slashes had been devilish to irrigate, even

with the tip of a sheepherder's drinking skin, and she'd
hated each painful attempt. Day talked her through that
sweaty, stomach-clenched surgery, telling her of long-
legged horses he'd galloped across misty moors, of purple
heather, yellow gorse, wild black seas, shipwrecks and
buried skeletons glimmering through the sands on moonlit
nights. His stories stilled her shaking hands. Only once did
he ask, "Has that got it, then?"

She'd loved the silk-over-sinew ridge from the base of his
neck to his shoulder. After lancing each slash, she allowed
him a few pain-free breaths. Resting after the fourth cut, she
allowed him a few pain-free breaths. Resting after the fourth
cut, she laid her fingers on that muscle, calming him as she
would an animal.

Only later had satisfaction fired into hot shame.

Molly had tied off the last bandage and begun brewing
rose-hip tea. Pleased and talkative, she'd faced him, thinking she'd accept the friendship Day had offered driving
home from Chinatown.

"You've a way with horses, then, learned in Ireland?"

She reviewed the conversation syllable by syllable. After
that last sentence, she'd twisted her braid into a tighter coil,
repinned it as the tea seeped, then asked his help with Glory.

"She's a Kentucky thoroughbred, according to the man
who left her after I dosed his son's whooping cough. I
haven't an idea how to train her to carry me."

"I'll be gone before we could catch her, and that's the
Lord's truth. I swear it on my mother's head."

That harsh and final, and just moments before, as she'd
nursed him, his eyes had been wide and filled with her. As
soon as she reached for his friendship, they went shuttered
and dark.

Now Poppy fluttered around Day, serving him a slab of
meat pie intended for their dinner, assuring him she'd tied
Cinder.

Molly's throat closed in disgust. Wouldn't any man feel
revolted when she carved up his arm, then fondled him? Any
man who wasn't as twisted and lewd as a whore's daughter?

A gasp rushed through the room, but whose? Fingers

shaking as they hadn't even in cutting him, Molly closed off thoughts of her mother, sparing but one instant for a lesson Rose had taught her.

Touch was a trap. Venture close to the edge, and you were guaranteed naught but the sandy slide downward. She understood this much: her touch had turned a warming friendship cold.

Poppy eased Day into his shirt and he left without paying. Still, Molly thanked God for His mercy. She hadn't allowed Day to touch *her*.

Godforsaken cheap-ass boardinghouse didn't even have a wall a man could pound his head against! Day glared at the muslin, tacked floor to ceiling, that divided him from his neighbor. He slung his saddlebags to the floor, wanting a pitcher and basin to wash up for dinner. Instead, he'd use the trough out back. Day pulled a hunk of soap from the saddlebags. Brown Bess furnished her rooms with a sagging bunk—never more than two nails to a crosspiece—and a henskin army blanket.

Nothing else. Not even a thunder mug, for a man to ease himself. No, for that, a man pulled on boots and hiked to the outhouse, where rumor said black widows lurked.

By the smell of things, his neighbor had decided to forgo the eight-legged hazards by peeing on the floor.

Day wedged the soap into his pocket. Just why was it he'd scorned Persia's offer of room and board where a man breathed roast goose and scented talc? Ah yes, he'd been watching Moll's eyes, sunning in her delight.

Day buried his face in his hands. This room could teach a man to despise Moll Gallagher. Brooding by his campfire, before he reached Carson, he'd resolved to ignore her. He'd held to it; during Moll's doctoring, he'd said nary a civil word.

What a bloody strange thing to be proud of!

It had been a harsh test, all the same. When her hand slid up his neck, under his hair and pressed his face to hers, checking for fever, his hands had nearly outrun his brain. Even now, his imagination had convinced his palms that they held the memory of slipping up her ribs, to cup and hold her breasts.

His mind understood fantasy, but his body learned slow. It laughed at the danger posed by Moll's incisive mind, and reveled in the pads of her fingers resting on his shoulder, gentling him.

If he didn't leave tomorrow, he'd do something stupid.

Blood and phlegm splattered Day's boot as Bess's husband washed up. Rawboned and nervous, Pierre choked out the boardinghouse rules to a newcomer in greasy buckskins.

"No pocketing at meals. That is first and most important. Plenty is served, but it is eaten at the table, yes?"

Stepping beyond range of Pierre's next cough, the newcomer's leather pants rustled with paper.

Day held the water cupped in his hands, then plunged his face in. He blinked the water from his lashes and glanced back, beneath his arm.

"My Elizabeth, she keeps all guns. There is no fighting at the table. You wash out of doors, and no sleeping in bed with boots on." Pierre's hand fidgeted toward the man's leggings.

Laced and fringed like Indian gear, the leggings were grimier than a red man would tolerate. That paper in the stranger's waistband was no prized clipping from home, either.

"We take no quartz, nor notes, for payment, and the cost of a new day's lodging begins at first light."

Scorn twisted the stranger's lips, hinting that he rose early, rode long and prided himself on it. His hand dropped past a lighter swath of leather, to touch a beaded knife sheath.

Day's eyes veered back to the lighter leather, certain it had been covered by a gun belt. The paper . . .

Hell and be damned, a bounty hunter stood two steps off, and Day hadn't a gun, a blade or arm strength to fight.

"The man I'm trackin' was in Carson yesterday. I'll be gone long before six."

Who'd seen him? Day gathered more water to cover his

face. He'd seen no posters in Carson and he'd searched everywhere.

Bess's bell rang dinnertime. Pierre picked at the skin over his knuckles and regarded Day.

Sweet Madonna, don't let him call me by name. Day and O'Deigh. Why had he allowed the similarity? But Pierre ushered both men ahead of him, without a word.

Except for the black oilcloth tacked to her table, and the paltry number of platters, Bess's dining room looked as fine as Deborah Green's. Oil lanterns lit a corner hutch sheltering china painted with blue roses. Day imagined bullet-shattered shards rocking on the floor. A bad omen, since his own Colt hid in the saddlebags upstairs.

He'd pay for his fastidiousness. Nine men flanked the table headed by Bess and Pierre; the only seat open to Day placed him beside the bounty hunter, his back to the door.

Bess ladled out puddles of lamb-shank stew. Conversation ran in fits and starts. Day waited for the bounty to flash a poster.

"Tommy gambled away his last nugget—Thanks, ma'am, I will have some." Sean, a talkative man with bushy blond brows, acted as town crier at Bess's board.

"To who?"

"Peck, I heard, but Joelle played, too. Thanks, don't mind a bit of lard, myself, makes the vittles stick to your ribs."

Day snatched a piece of gritty, thin-sliced bread, then watched his plate, chin tucked to his collar. If only he could tuck in his nose. The bounty smelled like a muskrat trapper.

"Down below—" Grady, an Irishman known for intolerance, licked his teeth. "—train headed for Mormon Station got sick oxen. Just sittin' there, now, wonderin' what to do." Nose almost skimming the surface of his stew, trolling for more lamb, Grady peered through his eyebrows at Day.

Day's legs hummed with the energy to escape. If revealed, he'd dump his dinner in the bounty's lap and run.

Grady squinted his way. "A gent like you, with a buckboard, could make a pretty piece of change ferryin' folks from their dead oxen to—wherever they want."

Day grunted agreement. "Might try it."

"And did they not send for the witch?" Pierre asked. "She might help even the animals."

Did Day imagine that the men leaned closer to listen?

"No." Grady's eyes targeted a plate of white sugar cookies before catching Bess's frown. "No money, I expect."

"A mistake." Pierre focused on the front window and waited for the miners' agreement to die down. "I know, *chérie*" —Pierre soothed his glowering wife as the bounty came alert—"but if one cannot pay the medical doctor, one is better off owing the witch—"

The bounty interrupted, snaring all attention.

"This 'witch,' is she a young female? A sassy sort?"

A chorus of reaction covered Bess's outrage over such conversation at her table. Day's hackles prickled like a hound's.

"This killer I'm tracking has a weak spot for mean females."

Be damned if he did! Day reached amiably for the poster the bounty brandished, but Sean grabbed quicker. It traveled from hand to hand, but the bounty's mention of women, not the poster, held the men's attention.

"Mean females, eh?" The miner on the bounty's left elbowed him hard enough that Day felt the jostle.

"Yeah. Now, look at him good. He mighta passed through on his way to Carson. Mighta been alone, or with his gang."

His gang? Day halted the spoon he'd finally lifted.

"He's a fighter, will hammer on a fellow until his knuckles get numb."

Oh, aye, a gunman always beats his prey before shooting it! As for numb knuckles, any man who'd launched a punch knew his knuckles better go numb or he'd spend his time sucking 'em.

"But it's ladies will be the death of Lightfoot O'Deigh. That's why he left Ireland."

"Is it now?" Sean urged.

"Way I hear it"—the bounty slurped a limp tomato from his spoon—"he knocked up—"

Bess's screech would have scorched a more sensitive man.

"—he got too friendly, I should say, with a red-haired countess named Sheila."

Countess Sheila, was it? In Ireland? Day dared not laugh.

"Then, back East, he took up with a circus lady, tattooed, wearing pink tights, and got caught—" The bounty considered Bess's plum-flushed cheeks. "Well, he had to outrun her husband, the ringmaster, and that's what earned him the name Lightfoot."

The first true word the man had spoken, and so wrapped in lies that not a soul would remember Day leaping into the street and snatching Stag from the horses' hooves.

"What else, now?" Sean coaxed.

"Oh, he took up with Madam Silver in Jamesville. She killed her husband and brothers to run off with him. She opened a saloon in Carson, too, and smokes them little brown cigars—"

Close enough, though Silver had started as a pioneer wife whose menfolk had been massacred. Afterward, she'd found living easier, leaving tiny Jamesville, bleaching her honey hair and playing cards as Madam Silver. As for smoking? Lord, he'd tasted nothing but bitter tears and sherry on Abby Fletcher's lips.

Blackness rippled behind Day. The tail of his eye warned of someone in the doorway. Day gained his feet before Pierre bowed, scraped his chair back from the table and bowed again.

Molly. He could make himself sit down, but he couldn't look away. Lantern light cast a bronze glitter on her skirts and picked out threads of copper hair beneath her raised shawl.

A sassy woman? Cleaving to the doorframe, back straight, neck stiff, Moll kept her face turned from the table. The heat of all that male curiosity didn't cow her. Moll waited in the foyer, certain she'd be unwelcome.

Pierre's gut-wrenching cough explained why she'd come. He snatched a packet from her.

As the bounty cleared his throat, Day imagined slamming a forearm across the man's chest, striking him to the floor and holding a boot on him, so he'd not tax Moll with his questions.

"Get out of my house." Brown Bess skirted the table as she advanced. "I won't have my guests shamed by a harlot."

"I'm no harlot." The wanted poster fluttered to the floor as sweet Molly faced Bess.

Day felt as if a hand grabbed his heart and yanked it to his knees. A countryman of King Arthur, native of a land where Celtic knights spread honor and their seed far and wide, yet he refused to shield her.

Pierre did it for him, stepping between Moll and his wife. Day didn't hear what was said. Every screaming inch of him focused on Moll. Her smoky green eyes passed him, one brow cocked high with the conviction that she'd expected no better.

She's nothing to me. She can merge back into the twilight, damning me, but I will not go after her.

As Moll turned to go, gusting wind wrapped a curl of skirt around the doorframe, beckoning, giving him one last chance.

Day looked away. The wind caught the poster and sent it skidding across the floor. He grabbed his tin spoon and gripped until his shoulder ached.

With that bounty on the prowl, just knowing Lightfoot O'Deigh could get her killed. Day scooped up a mouthful of congealing stew, chewed and swallowed.

Chapter
Eleven

Rustling in the parlor brought Molly from sleep to drowsiness. She rolled onto her side, listening with eyes closed. On her return from delivering Pierre's medicine, she'd barred the door. So the movement must be cats, jostling for space beneath the porch. Still, it sounded like the hiss of skirts.

A blast of cold made Poppy scuttle down in bed, drawing the blankets with her.

Molly blinked and saw nothing but dark. Discomfited by Bess's tirade and Day's apathy, could she have forgotten the door? Did that explain the chill and the stirring of cats seeking the warmth of the stove? She'd best check.

She edged one arm from beneath the warm bedclothes, reaching for the matches beside the lantern at her bedside. A match was placed in her hand.

"Mercy!" Molly started upright. She croaked, swallowed, but could not speak again. In the dark, someone had touched her.

Outside, Cinder barked, warning against booted steps coming up the hillside.

Moll's fingers clenched, snapping the match in two. Gathering all her bravery, Molly swung her naked feet to the wooden floor. Nothing.

"Hey there! Jen's birthing!" Ike Mabrey shouted over Cinder's barks. "Can you hear me?"

Sleeping, she must have heard Ike's approach. She must have reached, half awake, for the match. No other explanation fit.

Six hours later, Sun Mountain joined Molly's celebration, its peak glinting calico sparks as she emerged from the shack. With her hands bracing the small of her back, she smiled.

In spite of Jenny's stubborn insistence on swinging a pick until labor twisted her double, she'd stumbled from the mine in time to bear a baby girl. Squirming with such energy that she almost bucked free of Molly's hands, the birth-slick newborn had howled, pink fists beating the air, protesting her name: Happy Days Mabrey. Had a babe ever before been named for a mine?

A blast of wind reminded Molly that dawn's sunlight was all golden artifice. She pulled on a pair of black gloves as the door slammed behind her, sucked closed by the wind.

Ike and Jenny's delight over their babe had gulled her into a mistake. Molly's foolishness bumped along in her pocket as she navigated the deer trail downhill, toward C Street.

As a businesswoman, she refused to take ore as payment. She had no assayer's eye and no scales. But her good sense had softened under Ike and Jenny's faith in the mine, then melted completely as she washed and wrapped little Happy Days.

Molly took the safe birth as an omen. She ignored Ike's silent insinuation of witchcraft. She focused past head and hands sore from massaging Jenny through the night, dismissed the dizziness of a wakeful night without a single cup of tea. But she couldn't ignore the nighttime presence in her cabin, or Day's second disappearance.

Molly squeezed her temples, squinted up C Street and marked Day off as stupid. Trusting her ears over the murky light, she hurried across the street, toward Deborah's boardinghouse.

Baby Happy Days shone as the second star of good fortune. When fire had belched from a mine shaft, deserted and unused for months, the explosion ignited the miners' superstition and packed her parlor with men wanting their hands analyzed.

For two days, Molly had sat in her lamplit parlor, lips interpreting each palm's etching, while her mind floated in a far sea of liquid amber. Not once had she seen the white charger.

She'd surfaced yesterday morning, drained, famished, but calm. Tallying her earnings as she devoured bread, honey and thick slabs of bacon, she'd found coin enough to pay their grocery bill and stock the pantry. Even though she'd be broke again after she paid Stag's board, it didn't matter. Poppy started school today. Although it was only Wednesday, Miss Margaret had moved into the completed schoolhouse, erected maps, set out books and decreed class would commence immediately.

Molly didn't knock before entering the boardinghouse. With boarders to feed and Robin to dress for school, Deborah wouldn't sleep late. Since her boarders might, Molly closed the door softly. A board creaked overhead as Molly climbed the stairs.

She might have gained Stag's room in silence, if Robin's kitten hadn't slumbered on the top stair. Bounding straight up with arched back and broom-flared tail, Soapy feinted pinprick claws at Molly's toes, then tumbled down the steps.

Molly sighed, composing her apology. No reason now, not to rap on Stag's door. It swung open before she could.

Gloating with a shaky smile, his body canted sharply toward his uninjured leg, Stag greeted her with hands held wide.

"Don't let's get cocky," Molly cautioned him.

"Now, Molly—" Stag's freckled face refused to fall.

"You're up and moving around, I see, but don't go ripping out Mrs. Green's stitching."

"I won't."

"I'd just as soon do that neatly, myself."

"I'm ready to go, Molly. I'd like to burn this infernal nightgown." He frowned toward the ceiling.

"We'll see how you feel after the stitches are out."

Molly watched him search for the spiders that had plagued his imagination during his withdrawal from drink. She'd kept him drowsy with herbs, instead of supplying the frequent drams of whiskey doctors advised. Mostly, he appeared better for it.

"I know they weren't really there." Stag guarded his neck with one hand. "But I still feel those hairy legs."

"I'm not about to be preaching, Stag." She set her bag on the bed. "But remember the spiders next time you crave a drink."

Stag chafed his hands up and down his arms. "Sister Amelia says I should count that runaway wagon a blessing."

"That's as it may be." Unwilling to speculate on ill-used horses and greedy drovers as divine instruments, Molly took the scissors from her bag.

Molly hurried downstairs. She deserved the names Stag had called her, but it was for his own good. Stitches pulled, Stag had asked for drink. She'd refused. He'd asked to come downstairs for coffee. Only when he could descend unassisted, she'd said. And then she'd left him, sighing, pale, head in hands, calling names after her as he tried to sit upright on the bed corner.

It was for the best. He'd reached that weak, cranky stage preceding full recovery. The payment in her black bag would be the last that Stag owed Deborah. She wouldn't let him see her pay.

Cornmeal mush sputtered on an iron griddle and Deborah offered Molly a cup of coffee as she entered the kitchen.

"Mmm, you've been busy."

"Stirred it up last night. I knew I'd be rushed this morning." Deborah pulled a gallon tin of sorghum molasses from under her table. "Robin! Come eat!"

Molly formed her hands around the warm cup and wished she could drain a vial of Deb's excess energy for her own use.

"Oh, Moll, your dress is finished. Glory be, you look tired! Have some of this mush."

"No—" Molly protested, as Deborah reached for a plate.

"It will perk you up. Between customers and patients, you're a haggard-looking wench."

"*Flush* and haggard." Molly accepted the plate, with a freshened appetite. "I've paid every creditor and still have enough for my friend." She placed a stack of silver coins on the table and took a forkful of the crisp-fried cornmeal. "I'm thinking I'll ask Stag to take Harold's shack, and job."

"Put the coin back in your bag. I told you extra bread was payment enough." Deborah peered stairward for Robin. "Stag is getting feisty, but I'll be charging you for the dress, so it all evens out."

What did Deborah mean by "feisty"? Her friend was tolerant of male behavior, but was house-proud beyond reason. A biscuit crumb couldn't fall to the floor before Deborah caught it. Molly scooted her chair a bit closer to the table.

"You'll love how I used the silk braid. Thank Heaven my diners left early last night! Although, they were full of gossip. No, wait." Deborah wagged her head. "It's *news*, isn't it, when men tell it? At any rate, a bounty hunter's sniffing around the saloons after that murdering Irishman from Lake's Crossing.

"And what else . . . oh, remember Day, that handsome Cornishman?" Deborah mimed an ecstatic shiver. "He's gone for good, paid Brown Bess and moved on."

Moved on? Molly held a breath until black dots crowded her vision. Now, she could resist that inhuman urging to remember him. Last night, before sleeping, something had recalled each of his movements, each of his words. A quaking had surrounded her, as if the very air inside her cottage recalled him.

Gone for good.

Hair slicked with water that still dripped down his cheek, Robin, in new knee breeches, rounded the kitchen door and plopped into a chair.

"You look fine, Robin." When he didn't look up, Deborah rubbed his pale cheek. "This is an important morning, you know."

Robin clutched his fork, though his plate sat on the stove. His fingertips turned white and his elbows hugged his ribs. Molly understood. School had offered no joy for her, either.

Perplexed, Deborah dropped a kiss on Robin's hair, placed a plate before him, then centered the skillet on the stove.

Bastard. Whore's spawn . . . Years later, the words still vibrated in her skull. Robin had a fierce guardian in Deborah, but she'd never be there when the taunts were chanted.

Poppy's school days would be sunny and satisfying. Molly would make sure of it.

"Breakfast was wonderful, Deborah. Let me take Robin to school with me." She smiled at Robin, hefting the molasses tin unaided. "I've got to hurry home to Poppy."

"I'll take him. I've plenty of time before the sisters come down." Deborah blinked toward the doorway. "Stag, should you—"

In the time it took Deborah to glance back at Molly, Stag lurched through the doorway and into the wooden table. It shuddered under the tin's weight as it slipped from Robin's grip and rolled, trailing a sticky ribbon of syrup. Molly gasped as the molasses drizzled onto her skirts.

Clamor froze into silence.

"Since you're feeling so lively, you can clean my table, Stag." Deborah took Robin's hand. With the fascination she'd award a serpent swallowing a hare, Deborah watched the molasses drip. "And my floor."

She turned her back on Stag, gestured Molly upstairs, snagged the silver pieces and slipped them into her pocket.

"How long, Molly, before you can ready Harold's shack?"

Minutes later, Molly strode toward Margaret Bride's schoolhouse. She held Robin's hand and wore Deborah's creation, which looked more ball gown than work dress.

Even Robin, fidgeting in a corner of Deborah's room, had approved. "That's pretty, Molly."

"Too pretty." She'd found herself unable to look away from the glass.

"You've no choice but to wear it home." Deborah had sounded smug as she dusted her fingers over the three rows of glossy braid ringing the high collar. "I'm washing today. I'll add your old gown to the batch. What *do* you do with your elbows, Moll?"

Shrugging, Molly had looked at her reflection and despaired. Single strands of braid swooped down from each peaked shoulder, forming the bottom half of a heart. They joined in a point between her breasts.

"Molly, look!" Robin tugged her hand and pointed as Poppy stepped away from the knot of children outside the schoolhouse.

Why did her throat tighten when she saw Poppy tower above the other children? Why did her heart puff full, seeing that Poppy had ironed the white pinafore to perfection before tying it over her blue work dress? How should she feel when Poppy scurried forward, beaming that she'd arrived early for school, without help?

"Did you get the bread delivered?"

"I did." Poppy's hands linked together and seesawed.

"And you milked?"

"Everything, everything!"

"Wonderful." Relief spiraled through Molly, as if someone had flipped off coils of rope that had wrapped her tight.

"Good morning, Miss Margaret!" Several children, some tittering, some sober, responded to their mothers' prodding.

"I hope you're always so punctual, class." Margaret Bride stood in the schoolhouse door, holding a polished brass bell. Her smile rewarded each child who surged closer.

Flipping a wave, Poppy followed the teacher. Robin's grip loosened finger by finger. Molly squatted before him, cursing a lack of sleep for her trembling voice.

"Have a good time, Robin. After class, I want you to give Poppy a message for me. Can you do that? Tell her the best thing you learned all day?"

Robin nodded.

"Master Green, I hope you'll be joining us inside." Margaret Bride reappeared, and Robin went to her.

Molly hurried off, hoarding her delight. Poppy had milked, fed the animals and delivered her baked goods. Stag and the baby had been tended. Barring a cave-in, she had the heart of the day to herself.

She'd have a deep bath, a glass of brandy and a nap, before folding yesterday's laundry. She'd begun indulging her fancy even further when Poppy leaned from the schoolhouse window.

"Molly, *that's* what I forgot! The coyotes ate Day's cats. I *kitty-kittyed* and put out milk, but they didn't come. And I think Smokey's gone. It's sad, but I guess he can take some of ours!"

As Poppy's head vanished back inside, Molly's headache returned. Miss Margaret's voice soared out the window. Laughter followed it. What would it be like to throw her troubles out the window for someone else to tend, and go back to having fun?

An hour and a half later, Molly's nape rested on the edge of her cramped metal laundry tub. Her damp hair streamed to the floor, near the crystal cup of brandy. Warm water lapped her throat and her knees angled above the surface, touching the tub's sides.

Searching for Day's cats had been sweaty work. The scratches on her brush-raked hands stung. Molly raised her head to drain a last scorching sip of brandy, then let the cup roll.

Day's cats must be dead.

"Not that anyone will ever know the difference." Molly addressed a chair draped with the blue shirt Day had left the afternoon he'd departed, bandaged and dosed.

She'd washed the shirt with grudging care, but refused to hang it from her line. A curious soul *might* examine her wash, and such a detail could light Eleanor's fuse and set her shrieking, again, that Red Molly was no fit guardian.

"Go and be damned," she told the shirt, sliding down so the water covered her lips.

Probing a cleft rock with a stick, half afraid a snake lay coiled in the shade, she'd recalled the glib story of the tommyknockers that Day had told in the street. She remembered how the sun had set bronze glints dancing in his black hair, how he'd blushed at the whores' taunting and how fine he'd seemed.

Calling futilely to feline ears, she thought how he'd sat in her kitchen and coaxed her calm, though he'd been the one having flesh lanced. During his tales of Cornwall, he'd gazed up as she looked down. Their eyes had held and his had seemed remarkably blue. The sun lines rayed around them had looked kind.

Searching the brush beside Howard's shack, she'd thought of Day's grace. A horseman's grace, she'd assumed, until he'd mentioned life as a fisherman. Then she'd imagined the fluid strength of men moving poles and nets in a wave-tossed boat.

Thinking of him, she'd smiled. Accursed Day made her smile even when she fought it.

When a hoarded chunk of smoked fish brought all *her* cats except Smokey, and none of his, Molly knew the truth. Day's cats were gone as far past her call as their master.

Gone for good. She pressed the words deeper, making them cut, instead of ache. She licked the last brandy from her lips.

Cinder's chain jingled in the yard. He barked once: an announcement, not a warning.

"Mercy." Molly sat up, glad she'd drawn the curtains.

Her flesh contracted at the thought of donning her soiled clothes. She deserved that punishment for not taking in the wash. Deb had kept her everyday dress and the rest hung outside on the line. All but an old brown skirt of Rosie's and the new dress she just couldn't wear.

Brandy and relaxation made her drag, heavy-limbed, from the tub. She swept her hair back, tied it with one of Poppy's ribbons and tugged up Rosie's old skirt.

Boots rasped on the porch. Boots meant a man with money.

Chapter
Twelve

A chalk shadow of moon hung in the blue sky above Molly's roof as Day approached. What in God's name pulled him back to her, in spite of the danger?

He didn't mean the dog. Cinder greeted him by ambling to the end of his chain and giving three restrained woofs.

"Didn't like the taste of me, is that it, me 'andsome?"

The white-muzzled cur swung his tail in a lazy arc, letting Day shoulder past the thorn screen and mount the porch.

"Came back for my cats." The dog didn't heed the explanation, merely spun twice before settling with a grunt. When Day turned to knock, the door stood open.

She wore his shirt.

Day focused on Moll's soapy smell, reveled in her smile and followed a wet tendril of hair looping down her neck. He saw the dark parlor behind her and knew they were alone. He smelled fresh bread and brandy. *Brandy* before the sun had half-crossed the sky. Nothing changed the fact that Molly wore his shirt.

A dozen cats thronged around her, twining in her skirts, showing him Molly's bare feet and girlish ankles.

She stifled the smile. When her quick tongue wet her lips, he knew she delved for something sarcastic to say, and failed.

"Molly."

She flinched, but didn't move away. The space between their bodies—narrow where her flame-colored hair tilted toward his hat brim, where her breasts swelled toward his shirtfront, widening where her waist fell away from him, almost closed where his thigh advanced one boot ahead of the other—that space vibrated with energy so tangible, Day thought he could cut it out, like saddle leather, and stand it up beside them.

If he reached across that space, would he shatter her stillness, or bridge it?

A bounty hunter could shoot you in the back tomorrow, man.

His arm wrapped around her. Through the blue flannel he felt no underpinnings, only yielding flesh. Quick as he felt her, she dodged away and he touched only the blue shirttail.

She reached up, tipping his hat away. "Fever?"

"Aye."

"I'd best check that wound. No doubt you've neglected it."

If he'd plummeted off a cliff after her, he'd feel no different! Should he grab her, kiss her weak and trust she'd thank him, later?

Day watched the proud set of her shoulders as she turned, expecting him to follow. The arrogant bastard who tried forcing Moll Gallagher wouldn't be him. Just yet.

He slapped his dusty hat against his pant leg before entering the house. Widow or virgin, Moll should learn what she was playing at. He refused to let her off this easy.

"Just sit down, while I wash up."

She pushed up her sleeves—*his* sleeves—then drew a dipper of water from the rain barrel. Hand-washing was her obsession. Even in the VanBrunts' store, she'd demanded soap and water before tending Stag's wound.

"Can you take off your shirt?"

"You're *wearing* my shirt."

"I mean your—I—so I am." Molly's fingers fluttered at her exposed throat, then touched the top button. "I—"

He missed her stumbling words about laundry and bathing, only marked the flush flowing from the shirt's open collar to her cheeks.

"I'd like to be taking it with me when I go." He indicated the shirt with a nod.

"Of course! I'll take it off now, I'll—"

Molly snatched a dress, stiff and new-looking, from a hook. Her unbound breasts bobbed as she hurried and he cursed himself for speaking before she'd hovered over him, tending the bite.

She stared, beseeching, for an instant, then marched through the parlor curtain.

He heard his shirt hit the red love seat. Skidding feet made him wonder if she'd tripped, shucking off the brown skirt in fury. Perhaps the brandy had made her clumsy.

Day's eyes closed to listen, imagining her breath fanned by passion, not anger. Not bloody likely. He'd be less surprised if she knotted the shirt sleeves around his gullet. Day eased his shirt down to expose the wound, aiming to look pitiful.

Moll didn't notice. She flipped the shirt to his lap and only the instinctive closing of his knees saved it. None too gently, Moll prodded the wound. He answered her questions with grunts and nods, taking pain as fair exchange for her touch.

Come on, beauty, like me. If she did, Moll hid it well. Whatever'd triggered her smile, outside, it hadn't been his young hide. She inspected him as she might a joint of beef.

"A damned fine job of doctoring." Moll stepped back with crossed arms.

If she chose her language to provoke, Red Molly failed. Her new dress, however, did the job.

He pictured his brown hands peeling the midnight black to her waist, pictured his lips kissing the ivory skin beneath. Day vowed to sit on his hands, if need be, to keep them from tracing the braids' shiny paths to the junction between her breasts.

"You can button up."

A cat mewed and butted its head against the window. Moll responded eagerly, flinging the door open. An orange cat slipped inside before Moll frowned and slammed the door. As she whirled away in a huff, Day rose to block her path.

"Are you really a witch, then, Moll?" The dark centers of her eyes widened. She grew as watchful as prey. "A Circe, enchanting men and turning them to cats instead of swine?"

"Get back from me." Moll's arms straightened, but didn't reach his chest.

In for a dime, in for a dollar, O'Deigh. He bridged the gap, sliding his hands beneath her forearms.

"Molly, can I kiss you?"

Damn. He'd meant to say, "I'm *going* to kiss you," leave her no choice, then do it.

Her gaze level, her body closing on itself, Moll backed away. Had he frightened her? No. As she edged around the table, keeping it between them, she sounded amused.

"No, you can't, but I'll give you a glass of brandy. Mercy!" She laughed as he bolted the drink. "Have another. Then, sit down, Day, I have some bad news."

As if laughing at a man's amorous intent wasn't bad news?

In a sentence, Day discovered he'd lost his grubstake. He was seven cats poorer. Molly wrung her hands, sipped nervously and offered to atone for her sin.

Day hid his face. He scrubbed his knuckles over his brow, as if distraught. A nicer fellow wouldn't have masked a grin as he mulled over the sweet concessions he could wring from her. Day's finger circled the rim of the empty cup.

Moll's eyes dimmed, misty-soft, as she rested her elbow on the tabletop and pillowed her head in her palm. She freed her hair from its ribbon, twisted and coiled it, then recalled she had no hairpins and tied the satin back in place. He wanted to snatch the ribbon, fling it into the dark parlor and fill his hands with Moll's heavy red mane.

"There's nothing for it but to name your price for my carelessness." Molly yawned, covering her mouth with one hand while she pushed her glass away with the other.

"The same amount you asked for boarding them."

"Have mercy, Day. *I* asked for a good cause." She yawned, again. "Poppy's at school, even now."

"Bless me, it *was* for a good cause." Paying for this secluded hour was a bargain well met.

As wind battered her cabin, Moll dozed in the glass-strained sunlight. He knew he'd have her. She held her maidenhead dear; just his gaze on her hand made her snatch it into her lap. But he'd never resisted a dare.

As if he'd spoken, Moll's eyes snapped open. "How much?"

A bottle glittered turquoise in the window behind her. Day, son of a patient fisherman, smiled. He'd cast his lure, wait, play Moll gently along, then snatch her into his lap.

Later, as Moll lit the candle, Day tried to gloat. They'd agreed to turn his buckboard into a medicine wagon, hawk her wares from Virginia to Carson, then divide her profits to pay for the cats. She'd also hired him to train her filly.

The bargain meant rattling into Carson, where a bounty hunter waited, instead of hightailing it for Mexico. And if he went and survived Carson, he'd be daft to return, filly or no. Any marshal with imagination could add a beard and gun-belt attitude to cat salesman Day and come up lucky.

With Moll settled beside him, cradling his hand in hers, Day banished good sense. He watched her absorb the flame. As the teardrop of fire stretched, flickered, reddened, then wavered clear gold, Moll went afar.

"You've a poor mount of Saturn for a peddler. Not level-headed enough. This waviness, see?" Molly's finger trailed across the center of his palm. "Sorry, did that tickle?"

"Not exactly, m'Bright."

Moll didn't glance up. Her words lazed on, vague and languid. "Mars is strong. One might cast you as a soldier or mercenary, but not a businessman."

Moll's magic veered bloody close to the truth, but by the

dismissing shake of her head, she didn't put much stock in
it. Her finger grazed a line higher up.

"Fancy *you* believing fairy stories of love. No link between your head and heart. That'll lead you astray, tempt
you to make bad choices."

Suddenly brisk, she shook herself a little, then hazarded a
smile. "You have an unbroken girdle of Venus, Mr. Day. A
rarity in Virginia City, but a blessing to the woman you
marry."

"And why is that?" He cleared his throat.

"It means you're"—Moll's breath feathered over his
wrist—"kind. You care about others' needs. Love for you is
an affair of the mind." She tapped her temple. "Not the
body."

Pulling her across his thighs would scatter that fantasy,
but he only returned her stare. His thoughts slid through her
pupils, as if a magnifying glass funneled them. *Gypsy fortune-teller, are you, lass? Well, your reading's run awry.
This "love" is in my body, Bright, rolling 'gainst my breast
like thunder.*

Black cloth moved against the white of her throat. She
swallowed and looked down, but her crisp manner mocked
him.

"Combined with this—" Her finger glided down the slide
between his finger and thumb, then tested the center of his
hand. "—and the flexibility—"

*Molly, Molly, don't look up, now. What you've started—
it'll be raging in my eyes and if you chance a look—*

She did, released his hand and stood. She cleared her
throat and swatted imaginary dust from her skirts.

"Consider the reading part payment for the cats." She
brushed away his coin. "Keep it and go. I have Poppy to
think of, you know." She glanced toward the porch, where
he'd embraced her. "Eleanor'd relish proving me unfit."

"Then you'd best take the silver, m'Bright."

"There's duplicity in your hand, too." Her chin hiked up.
"Don't think I'm not warned. Share the shack with Stag,
while you're training Glory, so I know you won't slip off
again."

"No." Wait. If he wanted to bed the wench, why not court
her with water hauled and livestock fed? "Then again, I've
had a bellyful of Brown Bess's cooking."

The brandy mist hadn't cleared. He saw a trace of pleasure lift Molly's lips as he conceded.

"We'll talk, Miss Gallagher, we'll talk."

Rose Gallagher's spirit perked like a hot pot of coffee.
Hell-bent or Heaven-sent, she'd got the way of making
those two quiver, one for the other. Now she'd figure how to
hone havoc sharp enough to cut Moll free of distrust. And
that book!

*"Mama is sik all the time. She is trying to hide it but she
spits blood up lots of it."* Rose hovered behind Moll, trying
to waft the pages closed, trying to ban the sour copper taste
of blood. *"She says if she goes I hav to tak care of Popy and
I dont know if I can. She crys all the time and I cant cook
good and nightimes when the cats com making nois to get in
Im afrad . . ."*

*Shut the damned book, Moll, and be thinking of your
man!*

When Molly closed her journal and kept the page with her
finger as she fell asleep, Rose knew it was time. Molly must
be confronted now. Otherwise, the strong-willed girl would
balk at her destiny and Rose Gallagher would have failed
again.

Molly rose from bed to investigate the unearthly blast of
cold wind. Nothing in this house could harm her. And she
had barred both the back and front doors as she always did.
Yet something rustled in her parlor.

Molly's hair blew back from her face as she advanced toward the parlor. As she remembered, the door stood closed.
Only the flick of a cat's tail made her look at the love seat
and Rose.

Her mother, pale as a rain-washed watercolor, sat with
Ginger on her lap. *"Molly!"*

No, Ginger wasn't quite on Rose's lap. Molly credited her

imagination with rare good sense for noticing. The cat, corporeal and real, sat on the love seat, surrounded by Rose.

"Molly girl, you can see me! Talk to me!"

In life, her mother's red hair had curled in a mass of messy ringlets, as if she'd slept with her hair still done up from a party. It looked the same. And Rose wore a high-necked white nightgown, very like the one she'd been buried in.

"Have a care, child. Sit or you'll faint, all pasty like you are." The vision floated, as if she'd come forward, dragging her shroud of cold.

"Stop! Stay there." Molly's hand shot out, flat-palmed.

"Molly, don't. I'm your own mama, come back to you."

"My mama is dead." Molly's dread fascination broke. For a moment, she'd sounded like the petulant child she'd been. At least she hadn't addressed the hallucination directly. She'd nearly said, "You're dead."

"That I am, child. But I came back some weeks ago. To help you." Ginger shifted, stretched, then kneaded the love seat with pointed peevishness before resettling.

Some weeks ago. Molly thought of the dozen times she'd sensed movement in another room. She thought of the cabin's draftiness and Ginger's unusual insistence on entering the house at night. Last, she remembered the night she'd been summoned for Happy Days's birth. Waking, she'd been so sure that someone had set the block of matches in her hand.

"Molly girl, come closer. Sit with me."

"No!" Enough. Her imagination had run amok.

Molly turned away. Before she could leave her weird fancy behind, Rose wafted in front of her. Cold clamped around Molly like a fist.

"Don't touch me!"

"Molly, I can't. My everlasting damnation is that I can't touch either of you girls." The specter's face dipped in profound disappointment, then, just as quickly, turned merry. *"Enough, as you said."*

Except she hadn't, Moll realized. She'd only thought it.

Gooseflesh pricked Molly's arms. Her throat and scalp tightened in fearful belief.

"I never dwelt on the sad times, did I now? I'm back from my 'eternal' rest and I've a slice of time awarded to me. I don't know how long." The creature stared off, musing as if time were a tool lost to her. *"It's enough that I've been smelling your coffee, seeing your sweetness with your sister and feasting my eyes on young Day. If his charmin' shoulders and dare-the-Devil smile aren't worth coming back for, I don't know what is!"*

Molly's hands fisted. Her mother had bumped an old wound, but Molly stayed as still as a child who knew she'd suffer if she spoke out. "So, you're a ghost."

"Yes, Moll, so far as I can tell."

"You don't *know*?" Heavens above, her mother was no more adept at death than life.

"The occupation don't come with an explanation, with a list of rules and duties, child."

Rose looked so fresh and young. Twenty, maybe, not the drab, failing female she'd been at the end.

"I woke hurtling head-over-heels through darkness and landed in my own parlor. That's all I know for certain. But I believe the Lord's given me a chance—"

The face within the red ringlets faded, then came back, brighter than before, as Rose reappeared on the love seat.

"—to fulfill my dying wish to be a better mother."

"How?" Molly chafed her arms against the chill. "What can you do?" Excitement fluttered in Molly's chest. What if Rose could conjure a house with rich saffron drapes and cherrywood furniture? Or materialize gold coins with a wafture of her hand?

"I can . . ." The ghost shrugged, overlooking Moll's thoughts this time. Rose's features, chagrined and pale, withdrew inside the frame of curls. Lifting a transparent hand, Rose moved to stroke the cat. Her hand fell through, and Ginger yawned.

"I can . . ."

"Move things?" Molly pictured the infernal dust that billowed in from the road. She pictured a broom, moving alone, sweeping the cabin clean.

"Only once. Usually I pass right through them. At first, I thought it was an annoyance, being deprived of touch and taste. Because I can see and smell and hear, well enough." Rose's wry smile brought to mind a girl who'd stubbed her toe after being warned to wear shoes. *"I thought I'd learn the way of it. Now, I see it's my punishment for—"* Rose broke off, unaccustomed to her daughter's maturity. *"—indulging my senses a wee bit too much, in life."*

"Can you do magic, then? Make the cat into a canary?" If Rose turned Favor into a snake, Molly thought she might lift a hoe to hack his head off.

Not really, she was a healer. Besides, the ghost had shaken her head. "Turn bread into cake?" Poppy could sleep later . . . another shake. "Keep my pump handle from sticking?"

A sigh like autumn wind shook Rose's words. *"You're thinking of angels, Moll. It's not like that for me."*

"What in Heaven's name is it like?"

"It's like every night, between dusk and dawn—and once or twice by daylight, if I work very hard—I've the pleasure of watching you and mucking about in your mind. Oh, I've said it all wrong." Rose's form dwindled to a wavering shadow.

"You invade my house *and* my mind?"

"My house, young miss, but that's not it exactly." Rose flared back, clear, if pastel. *"It's more that I attract your feelings. Then, I can act as a sort of magnifying glass."*

A magnifying glass. Molly thought of children using a glass to burn ants. Dreadful brats, focusing the sun's power to a bright point, leaving behind tiny crisped corpses and a wisp of smoke that blew away in the blink of an eye.

"You! You've made me think of Day like, like *you* would!" Day's gentlemanly conduct as she'd told his palm, right there on the love seat . . . Day's teasing on her doorstep . . . Day's warm shoulder, submitting to her stitching and her touch . . . None of it was real. Relief and disappointment warred in Molly's breast.

"I can't intensify it, unless it's there, Moll." A dullness crossed Rose's form, from her shoulders on down.

Molly didn't care. When Day adored her with his eyes, as he had today over her kitchen table, it had been Rose, her lusty mother, who'd responded to his warmth. And something—Rose!—had made Molly laugh at Day's lewd desire for a kiss. What might happen on the way to Carson?

"I'm bound to this house, remember."

Still. With two such hellions working against her, did decency stand a chance?

"Fie, Molly girl. You like the lad. In time, you'll love him."

"Oh no. That's your fantasy, Mother. Not mine." Her voice shook with sarcasm. "You wanted to believe every man loved you."

"Oh, for a bar of pine-tar soap and hands to jam it in your spiteful mouth!" Rose lurched off the love seat, arms waving. Ginger jumped to the floor, cleaned her shoulder with a vehement lick and stalked from the room. *"You're cold, girl. You do need a bit of me in you! If I loved more than my share of men—at least I lived! You've nothing but snowmelt in your veins!"* Rose's form paled to desert gray. Only her hair glimmered pink. *"Couched here in your dark house, cynical and alone. You'll have darkness aplenty, soon!"*

"Is that the gift you returned to give me? If it's your curse, you're too late. If I am that way, you're to blame. After all, I'm Mad Rose's girl, the hexmaker's daughter. The way men look at me—from the time I was ten—would you like to know how men look at me, Mother?"

"I would not." Rose turned transparent as water.

If she could have drawn breath, Molly would have told her. Men looked at her as they did a spittoon, a convenient receptacle for vice.

Sunlight bleached the last of Rose away.

Moll lingered, standing alone in the parlor, staring at the well-swept wooden floor, wondering if her mother's ghost would ever return, and wondering if she cared.

*　　　*　　　*

The kitchen water barrel wore a skim of ice when Moll finally doffed her nightgown and dressed. She anchored her hair in a windproof knot and packed her bottles in a wooden box.

Life seemed absurdly normal, with light flooding every corner of the parlor. Back from her bread run, Poppy hummed. She dressed for school while Molly fought down excitement.

Away from the house, away from her mother's eerie presence, she'd test her emotions. Telling his palm, yesterday, she'd caught Day wearing a look any sensible woman would flee. Yet, before she wakened to Rose, in her dreams, she'd missed him.

She wanted to blame her mother. She wanted to believe that if she trusted him, he'd beguile her with lies, pretend to care, use her body, then gut her like a deer. She'd seen it all, with men Mama had tried to love. If she blunted pain with drink, like Mama had, what would become of Poppy?

With deliberate steps, Molly returned to her room and found the journal. *You like the lad. In time, you'll love him.*

"I want to trust you, Mama," Molly whispered. "But every time I do, you disappoint me." Molly rubbed her thumb over fingernail dents cut into the journal's leather cover, then forced herself to open it.

"Im in Lubas room. I found the knif under her bed and if he coms in Luba said she'd make everthing right if I had to becaus a little girl shouldnt have thing like that done to her. Im glad Pop is to little to. They call him Favor . . ."

She could not trust Rose, who trusted men.

"Molly!" Poppy flung a buttonhook to the floor. "I can't fix my boots and I'll be late for school! Can you help me? Molly?"

Molly snapped the journal closed.

"Of course I'll help you, baby. There's nothing your big sister can't fix, is there?"

Chapter
Thirteen

"Hello, handsome."

Day blinked, focusing on the burgundy-colored pipe curls atop a freckled face that peered over his wagon side.

"I hope you haven't slept out here all night with *comfort*"—her words swayed like a hurdy girl's hips—"right next door."

He had. Day pulled himself to sit with knees cocked up as perches for his elbows. Lord, his head ached. No question what had caused it: too much cold, too little sleep and Moll's accursed brandy. He grabbed his hat and winced at the crick in his back.

Randy as a ram, he'd driven down D Street yesterday, taking the corner on two wheels. And then sat.

Music had streamed from Shambles's doors, and he'd told himself to go inside where the beds were warm as the women. Back-slapping hordes of miners, smelling of weekly baths and pressed shirts, had strutted past, and he'd known the girls would fancy him as much as any of them.

"I know you." The girl watched him settle his hat to shade his eyes. "You're Day, the cat man. Now, ain't I right?"

"Aye." He recognized her as one of Persia's girls. "Aye, dovey." He lowered his voice, hoping to quiet her head-spiking shrillness.

"Come down, so I can take a look at you." She tugged Day's wrist, until he allowed himself to be hauled out for inspection. She sashayed around him in cheap red velvet and a cloud of lilac scent.

Damn. Why should he care about Moll Gallagher's prissiness at being touched, with a girl like this before him?

"Listen, Miss Claret, I've left Brown Bess's and I need a meal before heading out for Carson. Would you know where I could find breakfast this side of Mrs. Green's?" He couldn't muster energy enough to face Deborah Green this morning.

"I would." She took his arm and drew him toward Shambles. "Poppy just delivered bread, and cinnamon twisty things."

" 'Twisty things'?"

Claret nodded, suppressing a yawn. "Yeah. She comes so early, sometimes I oversleep and miss her. Her sister won't let Poppy come inside for deliveries, so one of us has to come out."

Sunlight glossed Claret's curls as she led him down the side and around the back. Glass crunched beneath his boots and Day questioned his motives for having breakfast in a whorehouse.

"Hot rolls," Claret tempted, as if she'd heard his hesitation. "And Luba's coffee. She roasts beans on Saturdays and uses Truckee River water Persia has hauled up." Claret pressed a hand to her décolletage, leaning close to whisper. "And after breakfast, you might like a hot bath." Claret's rouged lips scratched his neck, promising more than cleanliness.

Moll Gallagher, you're to blame. Your tempting and turning away has driven me to it. But I'm only going in for breakfast. And maybe a bath.

*   *   *

Persia pushed aside cipher-covered papers, slid off her spectacles and hid them under taloned nails. Her breasts shimmied in a purple dressing gown as she tossed her brown-gold lion's mane in welcome.

"Day." Her greeting throbbed so warm and personal, Day bet she was richer than any man on the Comstock.

"Ma'am." Day held his black hat as she extended a bare amber leg from the overlap of her gown, using a foot to shove a chair his way.

After two of Poppy's rolls and a half-dozen cups of coffee poured by the formidable Luba Washington, Day wanted to leave. Before he could, Persia drew the discarded papers back, steepled her fingers and tapped them against the sheets.

"Do you have any idea what it costs to replace a broken window in this town?"

Fate being what it was, she'd surely tell him, since he should have drawn rein in front of Moll's an hour ago. Day's belly spun top over bottom thinking of Moll, waiting. He popped a last flake of crust into his mouth, shook his head as if agreeing that costs were blamed awful and started to rise.

"Day's driving to Carson City today. I could ride along and visit my sister." Claret's voice squeaked across the silence, surprising him, irritating Persia.

"Window glass costs too damn much, costs every time some drunk decides it would be amusing to fling his amigo through one. You could help." Persia's tone forced him back into his chair. "I want you to tend bar for me, Day."

"You mentioned it before, ma'am."

Claret leaned her head to the side, trying to catch Persia's eye for permission. The madam ignored her.

"Men don't 'ma'am' a whore, Day." Persia's voice rose smooth as her plucked and penciled brows. "This is a solid offer. You're out of cats. You haven't seen fit to head for Lake's Crossing or Carson, so you must need a job, or the appearance of one."

Or the appearance of one. Day's pulse jumped.

"A salary, free room and board . . . You shake your head, but not long ago I could have changed your mind—"

Claret, sucking the tip of her index finger, nodded.

"—but that was before I outweighed you by the bulk of a good-sized pony." Persia fingered the lapel of her robe.

"Sure, you must be fishing for compliments, Persia. I've always admired women with curve." Day crossed his forearms on the table, warming to the game. "It guarantees, don't you know, that her appetite for other things will be strong as that for good food."

Persia lifted the locks of hair around her face high on each side, then let them rush around her shoulders.

"Didn't I tell you, after we watched him in the street?" Persia glanced at Claret. "Clever, a good talker and devilish good-looking—

"I won't keep the girls away from you." Persia shuffled her papers into a stack. "*After* business hours. Breaks the boredom, having fun with men of their own choosing."

Day fidgeted. For what she offered, he ought to kiss the hem of Persia's purple robe. He couldn't. What had Moll done to him?

"Go gather your things, Claret, but don't wake the others." Persia pointed a dagger-sharp finger. "And you'll do a night's work every night you're gone. I'll have my percent the minute you return."

Hell. Would Moll tolerate a soiled dove as a traveling companion?

Watery sunlight spilled between the heavy draperies. Off to such a late start, they'd have to return in darkness. The idea made his blood sing.

"That girl needs bringing to her senses." Persia shook her head as Day glanced after Claret. "Not her. Moll Gallagher. And don't bother thinking you'll tame her."

"No?" Two thoughts warred in his mind. Why had Persia mentioned Moll, and why the hell couldn't he "tame" her?

"If she's the reason you're refusing my job, you're a fool. Moll doesn't want a man. Any man."

Luba Washington splattered more coffee into his cup, but

it was Persia's stare, direct as any gunman's, that tantalized him.

"Why not?" He watched for a brow crease, an eye shift, the biting of a lip, anything to refute her words.

"She had a bad scare, but she should've gotten over it." Persia shot Luba a dismissing glance and set her jaw.

There. Day closed on that flicker of guilt.

"A scare that put her off men?"

"It doesn't matter. A kind man could have eased past that. Moll's fear has hardened into something else. You've seen how she is around me. Stone cold. The thanks I get."

"Why is she like that? What did you do to her?" He grabbed for Persia's wrist, but missed. She read men and their intentions that easily.

"Get your answer from her, if you can. Truth is, though, you don't have that kind of time."

Five minutes ago he would have laughed. How much time could it take when he'd already had Moll in his arms? In a week she'd be gentled. In two, he could kiss her whenever he wanted. Inside a month, she'd be his.

But Persia implied—what? That Moll had worked for her? Impossible. Eleanor VanBrunt would have snatched Poppy away in a trice. That Moll hated men? No. Lingering wonder had wreathed her face as she worked on his blessed dog bite. In spite of herself, Moll felt the pull between them.

"You need to shave, Day." Persia slipped a sheet of paper from the stack before her. "This made the rounds at the Black Dog." She bumped the dirty, creased paper to him. "The hombre carrying it got distracted while I topped off his drink." Persia smirked as she unfolded the paper. "He dropped it. I retrieved it. Later, he didn't ask for it back."

Had she taken that stinking, buckskinned bounty for a ride just to get the poster? Day's confusion thickened as Persia ran her hand lovingly down her own throat.

The poster showed a man bearded and glowering, but it looked like him. Day held it by both edges and considered Persia.

"How long'd he show it around, before he 'dropped' it?"

"Ten minutes, but he'd been in the Shaft and Slim's first."

If Sheriff Merrick could read, Day figured the text below the picture could get him hanged.

"$500 Reward for the arrest of Lightfoot O'Deigh for the crime of Murder. Said O'Deigh is 6 feet 1 inch in height, is 27 years old, has black hair and beard, blue eyes, no scars and a threatening look; 180 pounds, horse trainer and shootist by profession. Any person . . ."

Day shook his head. Here, the bounty had ripped the poster so no one he showed it to could apply for the reward.

"You missed your chance to run, Day."

Why? So far, he'd stayed alive by intuition and wits.

"The best thing you can do is work for me, and hope no one else recognizes your handsome face."

Standing at a bar day in and day out where all could scrutinize his face . . . "Hide in plain sight, y'mean?"

"Exactly."

Day bristled at her smugness. What stake did Persia have in this? Blackmail? Or would she turn him over for the reward?

The madam's clock bonged seven. The best part of the morning gone, and he'd arrive an hour late to meet Moll.

"A salary and free room and board, y'said."

"You'll work from sundown 'til closing." Persia stretched like a sated feline, pleased with the finale of this farce.

"Throw in free livery for the mule and I'm yours."

"*Ay, guapo.*" She shook on the bargain. "That it could be so."

Molly winced at Claret's choking-strong lilac cologne as the buckboard stopped just outside Virginia City.

"He ain't no salesman, honey." Claret leaned close and her dress gaped to show the powder caked inside her neckline. "That's for double-damned sure."

Claret craned her neck to spy on Day, who'd dropped the reins and wandered off into the sagebrush. Hidden on the shovel-plundered hillside, a lone cicada chirred.

"I don't know how you can say that." Molly fought down

irritation at the harlot's interest. "You saw the man's performance selling those cats in the street. He's a buffoon!"

"You may have the Sight, but you ain't lookin' hard enough at him!" Claret shook her head. "When he comes back, watch the way he walks. And in Carson? Look how other men give him space. Not on account of he can sell cats, no sir. They don't dare crowd him. He don't look like he'd ever turn down a fight."

Even without Claret's admonition, Molly would have watched Day's return, because of the gun.

Her heels had grazed a rifle tucked under the buckboard seat when she'd accepted his red-faced apology and climbed up beside Claret. She'd thought the weapon a mark of good sense, but now a pistol slung low on his hip, its holster tied down by leather strings knotted around his thigh.

Day met her stare and clapped his hand against the gun.

"In case I have to break up a stampede for your wares." His blue eyes narrowed, intent on separating her from Claret. She wanted to believe he'd offered Claret passage to her sister's out of kindness, not from stupidity bred of seamy sheets.

They'd passed the rock-faced hotel in Gold Hill when a rear wheel struck a rut, setting Molly's bottles ringing.

"Sorry." Day spoke briskly, sick of apologies. "Do you need me to stop?"

"No." Molly clambered into the wagon bed to set things right. "Go ahead. Only one broke." Molly poured a stream of green liquid over the side.

"What is it?" Claret twisted to face Molly.

Moll gentled her tongue before answering. Only a jealous shrew would think Claret meant her torso to bounce against Day's. "Parsley tea, for arthritis."

"I thought nothin' could cure artha-ritis! I wish my mama weren't in St. Joseph. Could I send her some, do you think?"

"It's not a cure, really." Molly wiped the other jars clean. "It just relieves the pain."

"You can't sell nothing telling folks *that*." Claret's eyes rolled to Day for confirmation.

He shook his head in dismayed agreement.

"I won't lie—"

"*You* won't have to. What about the rest of that?"

Molly pointed out alfalfa tea for quieting belly acid, chamomile for nerves, clove oil to calm toothache, laxative sassafras and dandelion tea for purifying overused livers.

"Folks don't want to be buying plant tea." Claret rummaged in her tatty orange carpetbag. "Even"— She held up a cautioning hand—"if that's what it is. Think of fancier names. Like 'Dr. Strongheart's Muscle Magnifier' or 'Zanzibar Sheik's Balm, for restoring manhood!' Now, that would work!"

"I wouldn't—" Still crouched in the back, Molly tried to avoid Day's eyes as he glanced over his shoulder.

"If you had some liniment, m'Bright, I tell ye the girl's right. Men would buy it, and what could it hurt?"

Molly felt herself blush as she grappled for an answer.

"*What* did you call her?" Claret asked.

Day mustn't answer. He'd never said the name in front of anyone else, nor explained it to her.

"I have red-pepper pads." Moll proffered a packet, for distraction. "They warm the skin like a poultice. Not as well, really, but miners like them on sore muscles."

Claret took the pads and turned toward Day. He frowned, raised his brow, then broke into a grin.

"Dragon's Breath, it's called, in some parts of Asia."

The man had a wizard's tongue. Molly looked away from the two, forcing her fingernails against her palms.

"Oh! Here it is! You've got to wear this, Miss Molly. No excuses." Claret quit her digging and withdrew a red sash edged with tiny gold bells.

"No."

The wagon lurched again as Molly climbed from the wagon bed back to the bench. She shot Day a poisonous look, and though his eyes remained fixed on the space between Abner's ears, his jaw might be set against a laugh.

"I'm not wearing that."

"You have to, see?" Claret took a pair of scissors from her bag and slashed the belt in two.

Molly gasped. Monstrosity or not, the sash—undoubtedly fetched from San Francisco—had cost someone dearly.

"Now, we'll let down your hair, of course," Claret tilted her own head to one side.

"Of course." She wanted to shake Day for his murmur.

"And we'll bind it like this, so the little bells tinkle across your brow. Sit still!" Claret's laugh verged on vexation. "Didn't you ever play dress-up in your mother's clothes?"

"No."

"About time you did, then. And this piece, we'll wrap around your waist. There's no chance, I suppose, that you'd switch dresses with me?"

"Why?" Molly folded her arms, hard.

"All that black's not real inspirin'," Claret admitted.

"We'll rechristen you." Day's voice curled like smoke below Claret's chatter. "Genevieve of Gold Hill. Serena, Seeress of Virginia City. Lucy Lightskirt—"

Just like a boy with a rag, teasing a dog to make it snap! Well, he'd made out poorly with her dog, and he'd do just as poorly with her.

"No."

"What about the *Good* Witch of Six Mile Canyon?" Claret's fingers teased the bone pins from Molly's hair.

"I could endure that, but not the clothes."

"Just the hair, then."

When Claret's nails snagged in their enterprise, Molly grimly unpinned her hair, telling herself that she'd only imagined the prostitute giving Day a self-satisfied wink.

Chapter
Fourteen

Aye, he was a patient man. A tolerant man.

Day rolled the Colt's cylinder with his thumb. An impulsive man would've shot Moll's first customers.

Backs bent to work a dead streambed near Devil's Gate, the miners stopped, dropped their tools and came running when Claret hailed them.

The trollop had fashioned a tambourine from a tin dinner plate, and Day thought the sound might incite the mule to bolt, scattering women and potions from here to Mexico. So, he stood down and held the animal's bit, while Claret sat astraddle the bench, blocking Moll from view, and commenced a yodeling moan.

"Oh, ooohhh, help me, gentlemen, please," she quavered skyward, then let her chin fall to her chest.

Dirty, sweat-stained and by-golly determined to help such a provocatively clad damsel, the miners crowded close. One reached for her and Claret's head snapped back. The men retreated.

"That's what I woulda said, how I woulda begged," Claret's hushed baby talk drew the men. "If I hadn'ta been cured."

Best that Moll couldn't see that the most convincing part of Claret's performance took place within the neck of her faded red dress.

"I had the whoopin' cough!" Claret's pitiful choking shook her shoulders. As she tapped her chest, the men's eyes followed.

Though sweat-beaded and none too clean, cleavage was cleavage. At Claret's theatrical gasps, her fingers curled into the edges of her neckline. She bent forward and flared the old velvet in and out, as if for ventilation.

"Ohhh, gentlemen, sometimes the cough does come back upon me, and I have to seek succor once again."

Sure as hell, they didn't have a clue what "succor" meant, but they watched Claret throw back her head and swallow one of Moll's green potions.

Claret shuddered. Stood. Her arms shot overhead and her neck arched until those fat purple curls brushed her tailbone. Her hips rotated and one leg slid up the other, then kicked toward her audience, baring her to the knees.

Moll still faced the other way, her back a black backdrop to Claret's cavorting.

"Artha-ritis cured! Whooping cough cured! I'm a new woman after a sip of Emerald Energizer and a rubdown"— Claret hiked her skirt high to massage her knee—"with Baghdad Breast Balm."

The men would have bought sagebrush and nibbled it out of Claret's hand. In a cartwheel of red skirts and black petticoats, she jumped from the buckboard. Her eyes cued Day to take over.

"Ah men, d'ye see what wonders a bit of elixir can do a poor sickly girl?"

They *did*, the miners chorused, practically pawing the ground with sincerity.

"And I know y'never thought you'd be so lucky, so blessed of Dame Fortune that you'd meet *her*." Day closed his mouth, turned to look at Moll's back and stood counting to ten . . . fifteen . . .

"She goes by many names. Scarletress." He gestured toward Moll's braid-rippled hair, wending red sunstreams down her back. "Priscilla, princess of the Pyrenees, heiress to the sorceress Bathsheba. Her secrets are sought by wizards from Trinidad to Tasmania, viziers in Araby and Abyssinia, even exiled magicians, couched beneath the streets of Paris, France."

His words faded as the miners stared at Moll's sword-straight spine and glistening hair. Her shoulders trembled in laughter or outrage. Clinging bells told Day his moment.

"Turn, m'Bright. It's time."

She obeyed.

A goddess in black and red, Moll Gallagher faced them. Flames of hair licked over her shoulders. When she tossed them back, the bells at her brow tinkled. Those on her waist echoed. No matter that her eyes skewered him, threatening to end the charade with bloodletting. She looked haughty, otherworldly.

"Our lady does not speak." Be damned if he'd let Moll tear the mystery he'd spun around her.

The men nodded in downcast understanding and Claret's tight-lipped "ah-hem" told Day to ressurect their excitement.

"For all the worldly temptations the Virgin Enchantress resists—" Heads jerked up. Trust the scent of a virgin to incite any man! "—there's one temptation she cannot refuse."

Two men worked their hands low in their pockets. One slammed a grimy fist into his other hand. Lust blasted from their loutish faces. It didn't matter that he'd kindled and fanned it. He wanted to wipe those faces clean with gunfire.

"The Enchantress cannot resist healing the sick."

The men sighed. Moll graced them with a smile. Claret hauled out an armload of medicine.

The miners rubbed sore backs, yanked up sleeves and rolled pant legs to show yellowed bruises. Moll's wide-eyed disbelief didn't stop Day from demanding two gold dollars for each bottle.

*   *   *

"Eighteen dollars, even."

"And two bits." Claret fished a last coin from her bodice.

"Keep it!" Moll pushed Claret's hands away. "Take half, at least! You and Day earned it!"

Like the afternoon sun painting Carson's main street, Molly's laughter warmed him. Head thrown back, hair plucked by the autumn wind—God, she looked good.

The sun had made her open buttons at her cuffs and nape. Now, cream-smooth skin beckoned him to let his fingers trace the notch below her ears to follow those curves described by her dress.

Bullets. Think of bullets hammering between your shoulder bones, Daywell. Carson is no haven to you; the bounty is here.

As they drove the first city block, Day planned the ride home. He'd banish Claret to the wagon bed, hold Moll's hand and settle for nothing less than a kiss.

Then he saw her. Didn't the Devil let a man rejoice before he set the hook to snag him? Two hard blinks verified Day's fear. Abigail Fletcher, alias Madam Silver, stood on the sidewalk, about to snip the lifeline Moll Gallagher had found so fascinating.

Day hunched low, shedding all trace of menace. Lightfoot O'Deigh, strutting-tough gunman on a red stud horse, shared nothing with Day-the-cat-man, who drove a mule and proved his mettle by conning simple miners.

Cotton-blond hair, nipped-in gray suit and a white blouse too lavish with lace decorated her. Was she a rich man's courtesan or had the bounty been right? Did Abby run a prosperous Carson cathouse?

She shared a street corner with two other women, one in bustled ocher, the other in much-washed pink. Abby's hands topped her trademark walking stick. Abby claimed to carry the stick for protection, but Day knew better. He'd shared a loving cup of sherry sipped from the engraved head of it.

She knew him. One hand left the stick to perch on her hip. She squinted disbelief at his rustic trappings and then laughed.

Cynical and cutting, Silver's laughter forged an armor that men ached to breach. He'd taken the challenge, and the rare tremble in her smile kept him going back, certain he'd slay her demons. It never happened.

Claret's elbow all but ejected Day from the wagon.

"She knows you, Day."

Molly busied herself, ranging bottles upright as Day slapped the reins into Claret's hands.

"Hold him." He vaulted from the wagon before Abby called him "Lightfoot."

He had every intention of locking his hands behind him, where Moll could see, but the mocking lure of Abby's lips made him hug her shoulders with quick affection.

Day jerked his arm away and glanced back. Moll stiffened so much her height increased a couple of inches.

"Your wife?" Like a well-honed knife, Abby's tongue drew blood before a man noticed its cut.

"I haven't married, dearie." Day stopped as, heads together, the other chits poised for gossip. "There's been some trouble."

Abby would understand, and keep his secrets, but he couldn't reveal them on the street.

"When isn't there trouble, with a man like you? But you didn't lose that big red horse, Samson, did you?" Abby shot Abner a look that should have shriveled his ears.

"Sam was part of the trouble." Trading that stallion for a buckboard full of cats might have been the worst sin of his life.

Squealing and dropping the reins, Claret jumped from the wagon as the pink-gowned woman minced forward. The very sister Claret had come to see had not recognized her until now.

Braying a warning, the mule stumbled into a trot. Moll grabbed for the reins, ensnaring herself in their unwieldy length before Day grabbed the mule's cheekpiece.

Black, white, red. Moll's face shone pale, blanched by fear or anger.

"Sorry. I thought Claret had him." Day swung up beside her.

"We need to get back." She jerked off the scarlet head-band. "I do, anyway."

If Moll wouldn't look at him, there was bloody small chance she'd swoon in his arms before sundown.

Moll strained to untie the belled red sash knotted at the small of her back. She arched in a way that'd provoke a man who didn't have a blond madam and a purple-haired whore to juggle. And a bounty hunter on his tail.

Cooking smells wafted on a breeze that warned the sun would soon drop into the mountains.

"Let's have dinner before we start back."

"I don't have time." Her eyes shone pale green and deso-late.

If they left now, they'd reach Virginia near midnight. He wouldn't fight her, but he would have a decent feed before starting back.

Day wheeled the mule in a tight turn toward the women. Abby had gone. Claret and her sister clung together.

"Velvet asked me to stay the night, Day!"

Claret and Velvet. What had possessed their parents? And the other one's hair an even darker purple.

Day nodded, asked directions to the best dinner house in town and hardened himself against Moll's effect on his re-solve.

Lightfoot O'Deigh had shot off the tip of a man's cigar to keep his attention. He'd scattered five hundred sheep like sea-foam, ignoring the shepherd's plea that Rankin had leased him the pastureland. As an unprincipled newcomer to San Francisco, he'd broken a crusty old tart's hand. She *had* wedged a knife in his ribs as a shortcut to his two gold coins. Nonetheless, he'd proven his harsh nature.

So why, when Moll's fingers knit together in her lap, did he worry? She'd start home when he bloody well said. She was at his mercy. Why didn't that thought calm him? Why did such power feel like a rope tightening round his chest?

"Poppy will be fine, Moll." Day clucked the mule along.

"She's never been alone after dark."

"Never?"

Moll continued facing forward, but shook her head once.

"Never? But, you knew how long it would take—"

"You were late! And I've never been here before."

"But it's a half-day's drive! Never?"

"Don't keep saying that!" Moll slammed both palms to the bench and turned on him. "Why would I come here? I walk everywhere I go, remember?"

He opened his mouth to speak, then exhaled heavily. Abner wandered toward a hitching rail where saddle horses stood outside a saloon. Rinky-tink music heralded a player piano and beer. In a town this size, with an icehouse, he might even get a *cold* beer. Day drove on.

"I'll break that filly to saddle and you can ride wherever you want." Aw, wasn't he just a regular Saint Nicholas?

Day squinted past her. The sun's beams, slanted above the far mountains, crisscrossed in frenzied radiance.

An hour passed before he really spoke to her again, and then he snapped in irritation.

"Oh leave it, can't you!" Day's voice exploded as Moll tried to braid her fluttering hair. He'd not let her rob him of this sole pleasure.

Moll's cheeks were sunburned. Her lips shone red and a bit glossy from the fried chicken he'd bullied the dinner-house waiter into packing like a picnic. Her breath was sweet from the wine they'd divided.

And the mule stank from exertion. He and the wretched mule had given over everything Moll wanted, today, and she could let him watch her hair toss as they hurried her home!

Moll's brow wrinkled, battling this small concession. He watched her wait for some logic she could bow to.

He wouldn't offer any. He'd have no mistakes about his intentions. He wanted her. That was a beginning, middle and end on it. Day kneaded his temples before remembering the grease on his fingers. Moll remained at far end of the bench, but left her hair down.

Scattered fires, sage-scented and smoky, marked miners' camps. Swallows dipped and cut the twilight sky for bugs. Lazy fingers of steam rose from hot springs. Creaking wood. Tanned harness leather. And Moll's hair. Strange, what soothed a man.

He hadn't been caught. Neither Abby nor Velvet nor the twitchy waiter had studied him with suspicion. The bounty had done a poor job raking the city. He had time.

No sense plunging headlong into Moll's gentling. He'd coax her like he would her filly. He wouldn't break her, wouldn't force the final joining. The coming together that would ruin her.

Ruin, hell! He was no gentleman and Moll was no lady. She sold colored water and fortune-telling. He was a gunman on the run with no time for scruples.

"Oh! Look!" Moll stood, grabbing Day's shoulder for balance, then snatched her hand away, pointing after a knot of mustangs.

A cream-colored stallion, fairy-pale by the rising moon, wheeled away, dark mares reaching for his heels.

"In Six Mile Canyon, when I harvest, sometimes I see them."

Twilight and the mustangs' spell nudged her closer to him. As Day's hands tightened on the reins, she wished he wouldn't shatter dusk's sweet melancholy with words.

"Y'look beautiful, just now, m'Bright. What is it that keeps you from smiling? What makes you so afraid?"

The mule's hooves crunched several steps. She couldn't answer. Day put his arm soft and light around her shoulders. The giddy thrill of it made her shiver. She stared into the night, trying to believe that he threatened her.

"They'll take Poppy. If I do one thing wrong. If they think I'm—like Rose."

"That's your mum." He nodded, weighing the information.

She watched, daring him to respect her once he knew the truth. Rose's ghost was bound to the cabin, but the spirit still haunted Molly, here.

"My mother fed us by taking venison, trout and rabbits from miners. She paid with her body."

He'd make as fine a cardplayer as Richard.

She shrank from his arm and he took it away, returning both hands to the reins.

"You think the VanBrunts would take Poppy? What would they do with her?"

"Send her to school in Carson."

"Be sensible, Moll. She's near grown." Day's hand dashed black hair back, baring harsh lines between his brows. "Send her to school. Oh, aye, and who'll pay for lodging and teachers, books and dresses? That skinflint Eleanor, y'think? Or philanthropic Brown Bess?"

Reluctant to encourage his performance, but helpless to stop, Molly laughed.

A bat sailed through lavender sky, cookie-cutter wings slicing, plummeting and soaring, unafraid in the darkness.

How could Day make her mock Eleanor and Bess? How could he make her confident she'd beat them both?

The bat plummeted after a bug. Molly looked at Day, and her heart went tumbling free through the night sky.

Moonrise saw them through Gold Hill. They'd almost reached Virginia City when Day surrendered to his boyish craving.

He let his fingertips touch her back, but he didn't flatten his hand. He held his chest away as he touched his lips on hers. He felt her breath come quick, too quick, and his mind chanted, *I won't hurt you, won't hurt you, won't hurt you, Moll.*

She didn't pull away. She waited. Day closed his eyes so there was only black. Black that was Molly's dress, as his fingertips stroked the fabric covering her back. Black night air that hid them as he pressed close enough to feel her breasts.

His lips opened against her mouth, but he kept his hand free from winding in her hair, pulling her head back so he could plunder her neck.

"No!" Moll wrenched away.

He needed to see her face. Let it be his poised hand that she feared. *No, lad, she hasn't been beaten. That would be too easy. You know bloody well what it was.*

She shoved his shoulder with both hands. "Why do you keep trying to kiss me?"

"It's a mystery to me, Moll."

"You just couldn't—" Moll's voice dropped low and heavy with sarcasm, but she didn't finish.

Day didn't ask her to. Moll jumped down from the wagon, stumbled and righted herself.

"Moll, get back in the wagon."

"Don't be using your smooth Cornish tongue with me! I'm not one of your cats that'll come purring under your hand!"

"I'm only saying—"

"I'm not some simple miner you can hoodwink into believing you, either!"

"Just get back in the wagon and quit acting like a child!"

"Oh, I'm no child, Mr. Day. I'm quite strong enough to walk home on my own. My only childish mistake was trusting *you*, when I've been smart enough never to trust another man in my life!"

She stumbled, swore inexpertly and trudged on. Fine. *Let the flower-cuttin', herb-brewin', cross-my-palm-with-silver gypsy queen* walk *the two miles home!*

Day watched for lantern light from the cottage windows. He'd followed Molly's striding silhouette for a half hour, and the dark hump of her house surprised him. No light. Something was amiss.

Jumping and yipping, Cinder met her. Moll plodded on as if sleepwalking, then stopped.

"She's not here."

Moll ran up the hillside. Day heard her foot slip on a rock, heard her fling the door so wide it hit the house. He followed.

"Poppy!" Her call held a forced steadiness.

No candle glow relieved the darkness inside, but he heard her move confidently from room to room.

"Poppy!"

This time Moll's voice was so anguished, he ran to join her.

Chapter
Fifteen

Poppy lay in complete darkness on the bed that had held Stag. Even sleeping, she nuzzled against Molly, who'd sat beside her, upstairs at Deborah's, all night long.

The door moved. Not Robin, who'd come twice in the night, tugging Molly's skirt, talking of the stranger, begging Molly to believe him. The man had leaned down to grab Poppy; no matter if the adults had seen no more than another runaway wagon.

Dazed by emotions that rained upon her like blows from a rifle, Molly couldn't decide what to believe. Certainly not what she'd seen in the empty cabin. Because the reflection she'd caught, passing the mirror with a candle, had looked like a wide-lipped, fiery-maned vision of her mother, screaming, *"Where?"*

Molly searched the room's dark corners. The ghostly demand still ricocheted inside her skull, yet Day had heard nothing. Except Molly's scream.

Thank God Deborah had brought Poppy here. Still, Molly

had spent the night fearing phantoms. She deserved punishment for failing her sister, but she'd never expected a banshee.

Molly shifted the shawl to cover her shoulders, rose and met Deborah in the doorway.

"Come out in the hall, so you won't wake her." Deborah's hoarseness said that she, at least, had slept.

"No." Molly smothered her yawn and took the coffee her friend offered.

"For pity's sake, she won't vanish if you walk three steps."

Molly followed, sinking on the top step, beside Deborah.

"She almost died." Molly bowed her face into her hands.

"No. Now get that out of your head! She's not even bruised. You're far more glum than she was."

"Of course I am! She has no idea—"

"Give Poppy her due, Moll. She knows she might have been hurt, but she wasn't. That's all."

That wasn't all.

Even if she'd imagined—the other—the black and empty house had freed Molly's worst nightmares. Poppy lost, long hours past, with no one searching for her. Poppy dead in the dark house, victim of her own error. Poppy abducted, finally, by *him*.

Day's rapid-fire questions—What time did Poppy leave school? Could Poppy have stayed with Miss Bride? Or Deborah?—had helped Molly think, until Stag limped from the shack.

"Miss Molly, Poppy's over at Mrs. Green's. A freight wagon driven by a crazy man hit her. He didn't even stop!"

Day had steadied Molly as he urged Stag to keep talking. "And use a touch of good sense, man. She's raw worried. Help her out, can't ye?"

"Freight wagon almost ran her down, but she's fine." Stag had rubbed his injured leg. "Not even scared, really, but Mrs. Green took her off, since you weren't here."

Guilt had crashed through her careful calm, then, trailed by the banshee's screeching echo.

"—almost had to fight Miz VanBrunt for her, but Miz Green doesn't take much guff from anyone, you know?"

Now, sitting on the step in Deborah's house, Molly knew Eleanor and Brown Bess weren't finished. But Day would help. Molly's stomach dropped as she remembered his kiss. Out of the darkness, his hand had pressed hot against her back. The kiss in front, the hand behind. She should have fought him.

No matter. Just this moment, her concern was for Deborah.

"What will you do without bread?"

"Molly, your mind's soft, dear. I'll make do with yesterday's or fry flapjacks."

"And the others—" The VanBrunts counted on Poppy's bread. So did the nuns who tended a ragtag Virginia City flock, and even Persia's girls.

"Yes! They'll complain when Poppy doesn't make deliveries. So what? Quit thinking you can do it. It's six o'clock. Too late, and you're no better baker than you are seamstress."

"You're right."

"Of course, I am. Besides, didn't you say you earned a potload of money, yesterday?"

"*I* didn't, Day and Claret—"

"It was your medicine, Moll. You keep the money. Lord, better for Day if he'd left town, like everyone thought. Each time you speak that poor man's name you make a fist."

"Poor man, indeed," Molly scoffed. "That son of a—"

"Molly! What did he do?"

He took me away from here. He made me laugh. He served me a picnic and worried my worries with me. Then he kissed me.

Molly drained her coffee, then circled back to words lodged in her mind from the night before. "A man tried to grab her?"

Deborah clutched her head as if Molly's switch in topic dizzied her. "I don't think so, not really."

"Last night, Robin said the man grabbed for Poppy's arm.

He said Poppy froze when the wagon came at her, the team swerved and the man leaned out to grab her."

Deborah's hand wavered in the air, considering. "I was standing right there."

"Talking."

"Yes, talking," Deborah admitted, "but I saw nothing like that. Now, no more coffee for you." Deborah addressed her as she might a cranky child. "You've a bitter enough tongue without it." Deborah whisked the cup away. "You're thinking it was Favor."

"Robin said the man was a stranger."

"Like half the town, love." Deborah touched Molly's arm. "Don't go intriguing, just because you weren't here."

Molly glanced back, into the dark bedroom. Poppy's form lay still, while dawn's gray drizzle pattered at the window, beckoning Molly toward a trance. After last night, she wanted none of her mother's occult legacy.

The Sight hadn't planted her worries. She blamed Day for resurrecting old fears, for warning her about VanBrunt, for firing her nightmares with Favor's evil.

Molly's eyelids drooped. *You'll be sorry,* Favor had threatened. *Watch out for your precious sister. Better tell her about the real boogeyman.*

But that was years ago. Molly blinked away the memories, for they were nothing more. Not omens, nor premonitions. Then she realized that Deborah beckoned her to follow, downstairs.

"Can you keep Poppy here, today? The rain—" Molly knew it for a feeble excuse and knew Deb wouldn't care. "It might be my last chance to gather rose hips in the canyon."

Deborah raised her eyes to the rain's pattering on the roof before she asked, "You don't want her to go to school?"

Favor's fingers, soft as maggots, might have touched Molly's neck. She shuddered that hard.

In the kitchen, Deb fed wood into her stove's firebox and looked back over her shoulder, frowning. "She'll be fine, Moll."

"Don't leave her—"

"The sisters will walk Robin to school." Deborah rubbed

a bit of sap from her finger. "Poppy can sit here and laugh at my bread-making. Or teach me to make those pasties the men crave."

"Slimy, awful things!" Molly turned in a tangle of skirts, hardly knowing if she spoke of the pasties. "Loan me a basket?"

"By the cupboard." Deborah pointed. "Have a lovely day in the canyon, Moll."

Snow waited in the white-bellied clouds, but Molly didn't care. Their icy breath kept her awake.

Last night's horror had fractured into the sweaty aftermath of a dream she still felt. This time she'd surrendered to the white rider's lance. And died.

Wind blasted through her clothes, chilling her legs and flaring her skirts before her. Indian summer yesterday, winter today. "Welcome to Nevada Territory, Mr. Day," she might have told him if he'd walked beside her.

She blinked back drowsiness. He wasn't there, of course. About now, he'd be slogging through snow-dusted mud to Deborah's, if he came as promised, to check on Poppy. And her, he'd added, last night, underlining the words with his blue stare.

She'd be gone.

And yet she felt a grudging reassurance. Day could protect Poppy. He'd almost shot Stag when the miner lurched out of the darkness last night. Day had an awful facility with that gun, a fluid suddenness she'd noticed through her anxiety.

About a mile into the canyon, Molly squatted, plucking rose hips, some ruby, some shaded with ivory or gold.

Like soap shavings, stray snowflakes touched her eyelashes and cheeks. She set down the basket and scrubbed black-mitted palms over her cheeks, assessing the sky. If she settled for the rose hips she'd already picked, she could be sipping tea at Deborah's hearth when the storm closed in. And Day arrived.

No. Serious snow would hold off a while. Early storms

rarely brought more than bluster. Molly hurried down the canyon, where wild roses bloomed in profusion.

Molly squinted behind her. Snow sifted into the dark footprints she'd left, obliterating them. She should have brought her cloak, not this thin shawl. Time to start wearing full gloves, too, instead of mitts that left her fingers exposed. Molly shifted the basket from hand to hand, breathing on each.

The west wind fled, pursued by gusts from all directions. Molly held the black shawl back from her eyes, trying to make sense of snow shafts dancing, shifting, cutting and blurring, dissolving and reforming, wrapping close enough to smother her.

Time to go. Sheltered by a cove of three pines, Molly peered skyward, searching for Sun Mountain, her infallible guide home.

Where was it?

For that matter, where was the sun? Molly's mind registered twilight, not noon. She looked up through flakes that whirled and fused. A faint disk, less substantial than communion wafers carried by a traveling priest, glimmered, then disappeared.

She knew this mountaintop. She'd harvested this canyon for seven years. She could walk out of it as confidently as she'd walked in, landmarks or no.

Some time later, Moll steadied herself against the wind. Grabbing a tree trunk, she recognized the pine as one of three set in a wagon wheel–sized crescent. She'd walked in a circle.

More than once, Cinder had led her home, sniffing and listening, ignoring weather, nightfall and the undependable sense of sight.

Molly closed her eyes, knowing the futility of trusting her blunt human senses. She smelled wet wool and cold. She heard rose branches scratch, rose hips bob. Wind moaned like a haunted owl in the pine tops, but she heard no voices, no iron-rimmed wheels, not even the slamming stamp mill.

A horse. A gust of wind made her trip, but she'd heard the neigh of an irate horse. Through the slashing storm she saw it, head tossing against a mad rider who spurred into the white.

Nonsense—her mind had only served up the dream rider. Blowing clots of snow, like tea leaves, could be imagined into any pattern. But he looked so real.

" 'Roany-good-pony,' my arse!"

Day wrenched the gelding's head toward the canyon. Snorting and crow-hopping, the animal fought to go home.

Day had asked Riley, the liveryman, if the roan would behave in a blizzard. Whiskey-blind bastard! He'd practically kissed the nag, blubbering that Roany-good-pony would go anywhere!

This morning, snow had swarmed like gnats, not deep enough to stomp out a footing, just slippery frosting over the mud from Shambles to Deborah Green's boardinghouse. He'd sweetened each step by envisioning breakfast. Fresh biscuits. With gravy. Redeye gravy with chunks of ham. All served on a white china dish. And Moll. By the time he reached Deborah's, he'd pictured Moll, sweet and contrite, beaming at him across the table.

Instead, he'd found Poppy braced in the doorway, stammering that Moll had hiked into the storm, seeking herbs. Deborah's noncommittal fidgeting made his stomach cramp. There'd been nothing for it but to cross the street, buy jerky and hardtack, then hire this rebellious jade so he could go find her.

"Fall on yer face if y'like." Day let the roan lunge, skid and thrust its jaw, trying to lock the bit. "But ye see how 'tis with me?" Day sat hard into the saddle, firming his legs on the beast. "I'm not fixing to go down with ye!"

Riley claimed a single path led in and out of the canyon. Even with the tireless stride Moll had used to match the wagon's pace last night—damn, he would *not* feel guilty over one kiss!—how far could she have gone in a few hours? Wouldn't she have started home before the storm broke? Could he have passed her?

One thing for sure, it would be suicide to try riding back to town before the weather eased. Cold clamped over his leather gloves and coat. Lord help that girl if she hadn't bundled up over her funereal black dress.

Despite his contortions, the roan turned white from clinging flakes. His chin bristled with ice whiskers where his breath had melted the snow, before the cold refroze it. Day's jaw grated and stuck when he tried to part his teeth. It had cooled off a bit.

Another half mile and he'd conclude he'd missed her.

Blowing and snorting, the roan settled into a jog. Day patted its neck. Not the animal's fault if he mistook his rider for a complacent cat salesman and a piss-poor excuse for a man!

He'd had Moll beside him and driven past the only inn in this forsaken territory!

Day drew rein. Flakes tapped the brim of his hat. Lightfoot O'Deigh's black hat. He'd had done with that mealy-mouthed merchant who clucked requests at the backside of a mule. It was past time to resurrect the gunman. Lightfoot rode. He preferred girls intoxicated by adventure. Lightfoot would give Moll one taste of loving. If she refused, he'd away. To hell with coldhearted virgins.

Coldhearted, -headed, -handed, and about everything else, if she had a nerve in her body, because there she was.

Without a coat, black skirts blowing between her legs, Moll followed an avenue of tattered roses, moving away from the canyon's mouth.

Ah, Moll. You're stepping out in exactly the wrong direction.

The wind stopped. Silence. Whiteness fell straight and solid as a curtain and he lost her. The gelding's ears tipped forward and Day too, caught the sound of snow piling up, quiet as a fingertip leaving an ice-sweated glass of beer.

He saw her again, blinking against the flurries, then walking away.

"Moll!"

She stopped, shuddered, then walked on.

"Molly!"

Roany bolted at his bellow and Day all but rode her down

before Moll turned, eyes terror-wide above the muffling shawl.

Jesus! Her lips worked like a madwoman's. She watched the plumes snorting from Roany's nostrils as if she believed him a dragon! Day swept off the hat and smacked it free of snow. Couldn't she see it was him?

Blanching, Moll backed away, stiff-legged.

"No, m'Bright, stay. Let me rest this horse a minute. Then, I'll haul ye up where it's warm, and we'll go."

Moll cast a look over the horse, frowned and regained her senses. Perhaps he'd looked like a ghost, all covered in white. All the same, Day considered he'd be lackin' sense to mention they'd go *after* the storm abated.

Day slid off, gripping a rein. Only a fool took a chance on being stranded afoot. He reached to take her bare fingers, to chafe them between his gloves, but she pulled away. Could she still be prickly from last night?

Day's pulse tripped, then beat steady. He ached to hold her again. With another chance, he could remedy yesterday's errors.

Why not drop Roany's reins and let him run home? Stranding would be no tragedy if he convinced Moll that only body warmth would keep them alive.

Day searched Moll's face for a hint it could happen. With her hair plastered dark beneath the shawl, Moll's green eyes sparked like a cat's, the only color in a landscape turned black and white.

"I can walk." She refused his offer and flounced away.

She'd had a scare and wouldn't admit it. Fair enough, but he wouldn't leave her to freeze. She tripped on her skirt, bundled it high enough to show thick black stockings and staggered on. Be damn, she was willful. Just now he didn't find it charming.

"Then be good enough to walk that way." Day didn't fret that his order had been stern enough to make her head snap around. "Help me build a shelter, and I might be prevailed upon to let y'warm up with me."

Oh yes, spittin'-cat green were his Moll's eyes, now.

Day pointed toward three trees clustered trunk-to-trunk

like sisters. Riding in, he hadn't seen a single cave, rock or overhang, but those trees would serve as a skeleton for a snow hut.

"I'm walking out, now." Moll articulated syllables as if he were simple.

"Now y'know cats."

Her brow furrowed, puzzling over his wind-blurred words.

"Y'know beasts, aye? Look at that horse, and tell me it's safe to go walking out."

Tail clamped down, head lowered and facing away from the wind, Roany edged toward the trees, eyes closed, settling in.

For an instant Moll appeared resigned; then she chafed her arms, circled her palms over her cheeks, and raised her chin for a visible swallow. What had her so scared? He wanted to fold her against his chest, brush his lips over her hair, her temples . . .

"I'm walking out."

"Nonsense." He balled both fists to keep from grabbing her. She'd bolt if he made a move, and a good shaking would drive her away for good. And he couldn't have her freezing to death. Poppy had sent him to the rescue.

Day assumed a scholarly pose, drawing diagrams in the air as he explained how they'd use the tree trunks as spines, lower branches as racks for crossbars and fill in gaps to create a hut. Then he put her to work gathering branches. It worked.

"Faster." He fit a branch into position as she dragged in her first contribution. "Keep them coming."

"But—"

"No excuses, unless you want to freeze, m'Bright. Look." He pointed upward at the thickening storm.

Moll stared at the black underside of the branches and staggered a step as if dizzy.

"Get about it now!"

Thunder rolled, stopped, battered and cracked. Day had the bare bones of the shelter assembled and the main joints lashed when he noticed Moll shaking her head.

"Pine needles."

"They're all under the snow." *You stupid ass,* implied his testy angel. Moll sore tried his patience, but that flicker of spirit made him smile.

"Aye, Bright, and I'd be pleased if you'd hustle your lily hands into digging them out. Packed amid these branches, they'll keep out the wind."

"If you insist on staying, shouldn't we build a fire?"

"Later, but a fire'll do no good when the wind comes up and snuffs it with snow. We need cover."

His hip bumped her and she scuttled off to do his bidding. God love her, what had happened at Persia's to make her so scared?

"I won't let you freeze, m'Bright. You understand that?"

Moll looked as if he'd thrown her a line in high seas and she'd missed. As if she wanted to believe, but knew better.

"I understand." She raised fingers to her mouth; perspiration ringed it as if she'd been shot.

If she'd only keep her eyes on his, she'd be fine. *There, Moll.* He soothed her with his thoughts. A hell of a lot more got understood between them when neither spoke.

In perhaps twenty minutes, the shelter had become a rough dome. Day glanced up to see that Roany hadn't tested his tether, and noticed Moll's teeth chattering. Time for some heat.

"You get inside while I build the fire." Day kicked a dirt patch clear of snow and glanced back up at her. "Go on."

As if entering a crypt, Moll edged in, crouching as far from him as she could. All this over a single stolen kiss? He'd be taking it to heart, if he weren't gloating over the sawdust he'd picked up by Deborah's woodpile and tied inside a sock.

Lads from wet coastlands learned a thing or two about making fire in damp weather. Sawdust kindled with a *whoosh*. Day blew to keep it building and thought that was all he heard. Then he turned and saw Moll, trembling in the hut's opening.

Could she truly have the Sight? If so, what did she see?

Roany snorted a warning. Wind screamed through Day's

clothes and the fire raged in its dirt circle, turned back by a margin of snow.

"This could have been bad." He lowered his voice, hoping talk of the weather would lure her. She edged closer, wrapping her arms around her waist. "Think if we hadn't built the shelter." He stood, stamping his feet against the cold.

Moll swayed in a sudden gust. When he reached to steady her, the slim dip of her waist begged his arms to circle it, to cross behind her and tug her close.

"Shh, now." If only she'd see how safe he'd made her. Instead she struggled. The top of her head slammed his jaw before she shoved past him.

A man would be twenty different kinds of fool to hitch up with her. His teeth ached as though he'd been in a brawl.

"Moll, you have to stay in."

She whirled on him, looking fierce enough to bite.

"Stay in, dearie." Could she even hear him over the wind? "Your clothes are wet."

"It doesn't matter. I'm going." She wiped windblown strands of hair from her mouth.

"You'll take a chill," he yelled over the gale. "Poppy has to be cared for, don't forget. And who else'll be doin' the doctorin' but Jack Slocum. Y've no—Watch the fire for God's sake, Molly!"

Fuel-starved, the flames licked her hem as she ran from him.

Lightfoot O'Deigh, oh bloody *Lightfoot* was he, who couldn't catch a girl before she burned?

He lifted his knees, felt his thigh muscles stretch and reach, felt his legs' singing power, and caught her.

All elbows and skirts, she went down beneath him. He doused the flame by rolling. Char smell told him it must be out, but he couldn't see past her flailing arms. Her snow-clumped hair whipped him as she struggled.

"Stop it!" Fear roughened his voice. He pinned her wrists and slammed them against the dirt.

She bit him. Day released her, holding pressure against the crown of blood ebbing from his hand. He watched Moll stumble through drifts. He saw the blowing black scarf blind her and he was up and running when she slammed her forehead into the tree.

"Sweet Mother of God."

Day worked one arm beneath her knees and cradled her head against his shoulder. Finally, he held Molly Gallagher, quiet in his arms, but there was no joy in it.

Chapter
Sixteen

"Mama?"

Molly felt the hand on her face withdraw. Someone had touched her eyelid. And sung as she slept. She fought to rouse, but her head's leaden weight held her down.

"It's only the wind. Rest, Moll."

Mama had baked cherry pie with the new stove. She'd heard the kettle's song and pretended to slumber, like a good girl, so Mama would let her stay up late for the New Year.

Molly yawned, rolled over and plunged into a whirlpool of nausea. Trapped in a small dim place, she smelled something sodden and acrid beneath the blaring, clear scent of wet pine. Fire burned a few feet away. In the darkness behind her, he moved.

"No!" She'd meant to shout, but the word was mere breath, setting off another pitch of sickness.

"It's better to lie still. Each time you move, it happens this way."

Twice she raised her head by knotted neck muscles alone.

Twice she fell back, retching, then surrendered to the weakness.

"It'll ease if you close your eyes. Nothing to see, anyway."

The low voice made it easy to sink. Molly let the fire hypnotize her. The warmth behind her shifted.

Pain slammed like a log against her skull. An angular pressure lodged in her throat, blocking her tears.

"I'm so tired . . . I can't . . ."

"Close your eyes. There's nothing to do, Moll. No place to go, no one to care for." The voice rippled, amber water over stream stones. The sunlight warming its passage was fingertips gliding on her brow.

She should pull away, but it would hurt. Was it raining? Yes, the fire hissed and lagged. She would move away. In a minute. His fingers stroked between her brows. Again. A sigh lightened the crush inside her chest.

"Aye, close your eyes, sweet vixen. Just have yourself a bit of a nap."

It was so easy to do as he said.

"Samson was a strapping big horse. Red chestnut, thick-muscled, deep-chested with long fine legs. He could run forever, Samson, with those muscles and that heart. He'd have run himself to death if I'd asked. And I thought he was grand. But then, I'd never had a pet before."

When a jolt of orange firelight dodged between her lashes, Molly shut them. She pretended to sleep, knees pulled halfway to her chin. She lay in the branch hut they'd built together. Steeped in cold, she caught faint currents from the fire, outside. A saddle blanket draped her limbs.

His warmth molded her from behind, mirroring her position, heating the softness behind her knees. When she'd shaken with a teeth-clacking shiver, he'd drawn nearer still and his breath fanned her neck, soothing her back to sleep.

"Cold, lass?"

Don't move. Don't answer. You're asleep. You're not lying in darkness with a stranger. Not with Day. Who almost shot a man. Who tried to kiss you. Don't move.

He rose on one elbow, head cocked into his palm. Her shawl, turned dry side out, had been crushed into a birds'-nest pillow and tucked against the wall of his chest.

"Moll?"

In silence broken by the rasp of his trousers against cold ground, he shivered and moved closer. His hand sought the tender welt on her brow, fingering what darkness hid.

Then he sought her hairpins. He separated the strands of her braid, spreading them to cover her ears and neck, pushing locks over her shoulder, to warm her front.

He didn't touch her there, but she shuddered as if he had.

"You'll be a bit warmer." He moved apart, his denim-clad hips scratching the dirt and pine needles. "Fire needs stoking."

His form eclipsed the firelight. Her eyelids screwed shut.

"I did have a dog once."

Leather and straps, probably snow-crusted saddlebags, fell as he returned. He slid back to the ground, leaving a slice of frigid air between them.

Logic told her Day's pity should have become wariness after seeing Mad Molly nearly bash her brains out against a tree.

No man could understand the crushing panic of walls closing in, of males looming, filling doorways, cutting off escape. He could take her head between his hands and squeeze until it happened again. That crack, that liquid . . .

"Moll, would you like to hear about me dog or not? You're not with me, lass, and that's the truth on it." A lilting tease ranged in his voice. He waited.

Molly gave a nod small enough to sidestep pain.

"I didn't keep her as a pet, one to sleep at my bedside, so I could drop me hand over and stroke her. No, she came when she would, took food and followed when I was alone.

"I was about fourteen, that terrible age, when you're torn up with awful, rippin' longing. You can't look at a twilight beach or your mam when she's weary, 'cause it makes you cry. The other half of the time, you want to fight any bloody thing that moves—your da, his friends for givin' you knowing looks, the ocean itself, striking with your arms, swim-min' out far and farther, knowing it's killin' stupid."

Behind her eyelids she saw him, a boy wild as the rocky beach, barefoot, moody and handsome beyond reckoning.

She opened her eyes. Faint firelight painted a narrow strip of his face, cast his hair gold instead of black, caught the shadow of his eyelashes and gilded his lips, open and boy-ish above that hard slant of jaw.

Molly jammed her eyes shut. Why should it beckon so? His jaw! The lower half of this man's mouth. He chewed with it, talked with it. Had he been a horse, he'd wear a bit in it! Mercy, *what* was there to admire in a man's jaw? In spite of her vigilance, she'd inherited lechery from her mother. His skin drew her fingers. It took no seer to know if he looked down and saw her gawking at his lips, he'd kiss her.

"She might have come off a sunken ship. That's what I told myself, since it suited her nature, and my imagination.

"She was no beauty. Ungainly tall, tawny eyes high up on a shelf in her bony head, a stiff coat of yellow-gray. I tried finding her in a book of animals, once. She looked a bit like an Irish wolfhound, but more like those Turkish deer hunters, so light and hollow-boned, I swear, when I lifted her—"

She'd fallen into a trance, if she could read him thus. Without tracing the lines in his hand, she read misery.

"They called her an awful name. I wouldn't utter it to ye, except—"

She shifted in impatience and accidentally opened her eyes.

"Hello."

His *h* was almost missing, and he swallowed the second half of the word. Benign and friendly, lying behind her, canted up on his elbow, he smiled down on her.

"Fisherfolk called her the Death Bitch. She'd never killed a soul, but she'd be on the beach at dawn, bolting down things washed up overnight. Coming back into port, you'd see her, skulking, darting from rock to rock.

"She missed companionship, is what I think, but for some reason, she couldn't risk it.'

"So, I took her on—dared to by a girl who'd been darin' me since we were born. She bet me I couldn't tame the Death Bitch, and if I won the bet—Ah, what a stupid cub! Fourteen and thinking with nothing but—Just not thinking."

Jealousy clenched Molly's stomach. She wanted the wench's name and hair color, wanted to know how she dared him and what she'd promised, this girl he still shook his head over.

"It took weeks, months, but I won. Whenever I could sneak off from mending nets and gutting fish, I'd hunt her. Mostly after dark, since I never told Mam. She would 'a feared for me. But that way, she just thought I was off to Kathleen."

Kathleen. The name washed up and receded, returning amid his words. As he told of the shy dog, feinting near, scaring back, she heard the name "Kathleen." As he recalled offerings of fish heads and scones adding flesh to the dog's bowed ribs, Moll heard the waves crash "Kathleen."

"One day Kathleen and her friend—a freckled girl named Jenny—They called the dog to them, then they'd run, squealing like they were scared. A bad game to play with dogs . . .

"I never called her to me after that. I whistled, so she'd know it was me, hoping she'd go to no one else. But I had her trust. And when you gentle a beast to men, everything changes.

"I've seen it, with the worst horses. Once they're gentled, they trust men not to hurt them. I should 'a left her wild."

Regret framed the words against the wind. It made an odd ending to his tale. Outside, the horse stomped and whickered.

"The storm might 'a passed." Day crawled to the opening, fed sticks to the tendrils of fire. "It's still a few hours until dawn. We'll wait a bit.

"Now, then. What'll it be? Jerky and hard biscuits is what I'm offerin' in the way of digestibles." Day dumped a shower of paper-wrapped packets from the saddlebags.

"I *am* hungry." The jerky smelled festive as smoked Thanksgiving turkey. "Do you think I can sit up?"

Why had she asked *him*?

Day's eyes flashed back the same question, then he dropped the saddlebags and squatted. "Can I help you up?"

His question was no courtesy. He asked permission to touch her. Molly felt her face fill with blood. She curved her hand over the wound, shading her eyes from him.

"I'm not fond of small places."

"Aye, I noticed that."

"And when you—" Molly used her arms to make a gathering motion. "When anyone—"

He let her flounder, but intent creased between his brows.

"When I feel confined, I can't stand it." Idly, she sorted the pine needles within reach, grouping them by color. Rust-yellow needles dominated. Others were green, some nearly white.

A glance told her that he wanted to ask what had started her fear. He craved an answer so badly he fidgeted. Resigned to her silence, he offered his forearm.

"If I hold it still, like a bar, you can pull up on it."

"I think that would be fine." She grabbed his forearm, clawing her fingers tight until she sat up, cross-legged, covering her eyes against the fire's brightness. She released his arm, awarding it a final pat.

Day gave a short chuckle before turning back to the food.

One biscuit, one piece of jerky and she slumped back to the floor, letting her fingers touch her abrasion for the first time. She yawned, drifted, then started awake. She forked a mass of red hair from her eyes and stared at him.

"I won't hurt you," he said, quite clearly.

And for some insane reason, Molly slept.

"Sun's almost up."

He'd cleared away the food, saddlebags and blanket. He'd stripped the dwelling of their presence. It looked as if they'd never stopped here.

"Another hour, and the decent folk will be stirring." Hat

pulled low, Day offered his forearm once more, lending his support as impersonally as a bench or table.

Except he wasn't. If he'd moved close enough to match her strides, they might have progressed like two halves, but he did it her way. Clumsy and apart.

Snow had drifted into smooth humps and trees kept icy guard. She felt strong, sitting on the road as Day led, seeking paths that weren't too deep. Piñon pines showed blue against dawn-purpled drifts when he stopped, out of breath.

"It's awful slow going, m'Bright. If I mounted up with ye, we might make it back before daybreak. We can keep on this way, but we'll be slogging down C Street with every hungry miner and walk-shovelin' shopkeeper in Virginia. It's your call, lass."

She leaned forward, arms crossed against the horse's mane. The world didn't spin.

"Last night you didn't call me—"

His grin taunted her.

"You called me something else."

"Aye? What would that be?"

"'Vixen.'" Embarrassment snatched her breath.

"What?" He flattened his palm on the roan's shoulder, inches from her skirt.

"'Vixen.' Why that?"

His gaze traced her hair, and Molly thought it must be a rat's nest. His eyes circled her face before he squinted toward the horizon.

"Y'crossed over there, for a little, when you went and drew blood."

I bit him. That was no nightmare. Oh God, please erase it.

"You can get up on the horse." She offered the small concession, but couldn't look at his hand.

He didn't touch her. His right hand rested on his thigh and his rein arm spanned far out from her. It wasn't balance she sought, turning aside from the blue-white trail before them to fit her shoulder against his chest. Weariness wasn't what tipped her head to nestle beneath his chin. In searching for words to apologize, Molly stayed silent, offering her only bit of trust.

Riding through Chinatown, turning toward C Street, she broke their silence.

"Your dog, what happened to her?" Molly cursed herself when Day stiffened. She'd put things amiss once more.

All right, parting with hostility might be better. Better for Poppy and better for Rose Gallagher's girl, who carried her mother's hot blood. Better, but Molly couldn't watch Day as he continued his tale in a most casual, awful voice.

"Oh, she died. They caught her eating a dead baby."

"Merciful Heavens!" Worse, oh far worse, than she'd thought. Molly swayed forward on the horse's neck and he didn't stop her.

"There was a shipwreck, the worst that skeleton coast had ever seen, with shattered timbers and silk drawers and bodies, already bloated, long dead, strewn far along the shore."

"Maybe they just blamed her—"

"No. My beauty was eating it, right enough. I saw and that black minute told me how it must end. They hunted her with clubs, them not gathering goods of their own, but couldn't catch her.

"Kathleen told them I could call the Death Bitch to hand. They readied themselves to punish her. They jabbered of breaking her bones—ah, those bird-light bones—one by one, thinking I'd lure her out.

"I couldn't. Not that way." Molly twisted her fingers into his shirtfront. "Naw, don't try to stop me, now.

"This is what you wanted to hear, isn't it? I killed her. High in the rocks where she'd hidden, I whistled. She crawled to me on her belly, and I cut her throat with my knife."

Chapter
Seventeen

Snow cold and the scent of pine billowed from Molly's skirt as she strode through her mother's ghost.

Rose shuddered under the impact of Moll's body, thinking the girl gave new meaning to the word *headstrong*.

Cheeks painted apple-red by dawn's wind, Molly stared at a candle, pale and out of place on the board floor. Molly snatched it up and jammed it back into its copper holder. Next, she stormed into her bedroom, peered under the bedstead, then stood and slammed her clothes-closet doors before returning to the parlor. There, she kicked the love seat a foot out from the wall, stared behind it and frowned, arms cinched around her waist. Last, uppity and intent, mouth set like a do-gooder, she stomped toward the calico curtain that set off the kitchen.

Daytime work was taxing, but Rose knew she could be snatched away at any time. She'd wait no longer to make Moll listen. Their last meeting had been anything but civilized.

How, how, *how* to make this revelation less of an ordeal for sensible Molly? Suddenly, Rose knew. She'd taught herself a trick, time-honored by every spook she'd heard tell of. Not only would it be amusing, it would help Moll shake off some starch.

Before Molly parted the calico curtain between the two rooms, Rose dove under it. On the other side, she slithered upright and let the calico mold to what had once been her admired female form.

Molly stopped, one hand hovering before her. Rose saw right through the calico to her daughter's waxen face. Not exactly the reaction she'd hoped for. Rose returned to the parlor, to wait.

Moll's storming steps didn't take long to return. As soon as she entered, Rose layered her thoughts over her daughter's. *Easy, child.* Molly's mind revolted like a rearing horse. She flounced toward the calico curtain, back to the kitchen. Rose knew this was one footrace she could win. She needn't bother with feet!

Brat! Moll did it again. Her palm plunged past the curtain and her body followed, flinging Rose through the kitchen table, to the floor. Head set at a dubious angle, Moll stared at her.

"I'm sorry."

"Hallelujah. At least you've one shred of 'honor your mother' left. Now sit down, girl, and take your talking-to."

Molly smoothed her skirts and obediently sat. "I thought I'd scared you away."

"No such luck, darlin'. I was here when that awful Hans came for his reading and here when you lost your sister." Guilt bleached Molly pale as milk, and her mind swirled so that Rose barely kept up.

"No, don't explain. Yes, I know it's daylight, and no, you haven't lost your mind." Rose had no instant to spare for sentiment, or she would have lulled the girl. But showing herself was difficult, and daylight work leeched her strength exceedingly fast. First her illusory body vanished, then her ability to project words. Last, she returned to that most useless form, a dark shadow beneath the red love seat.

"If I haven't lost my mind, what are you? Demon or angel?" Molly placed both palms on the table, as if for balance.

"Neither. A ghost seems to be quite a separate thing. Just think of me as your mother, come to help you."

Didn't that twist her Molly's pretty lips into a scornful pout? The girl hadn't forgiven her in this incarnation or the last!

"Truth to tell, Moll, you're right. I didn't help you much, there at the end." How could she have allowed men and drink to muddy her mind and blot out her children? *"And I haven't helped you much since—whenever it was."* Time truly had become a burden. *"I was an inept mother. I might be an inept ghost, but I love you and I won't waste this chance to put things right."*

The dog scratched, then whuffled at the doorjamb and Molly's mind jumped back to the reality it knew best. She frowned, swiped at her skirts and started to stand.

Day!

Moll's mouth rounded and ah, didn't that ripple of desire feel like the Heaven Rose had always hoped for? Lust had been her downfall, but that thick intoxication that flowed only from men warmed her like burgundy wine.

Molly fought to move a step off.

Day! Moll stopped and Rose knew she'd found the magic Moll craved. She might just drive the girl crazy with it!

But human feelings had their price. Rose wavered and weakened. She must make Moll believe, at least long enough to give her the list. If Molly didn't trust her own eyes, how could she trust her heart?

Quick as the blink of a mortal eye, Rose had it. That night, when she'd rushed, shrieking like a banshee, into Moll's face, Rose had toppled the candlestick. It was the first object she'd moved, and she'd paid with dreadful weakness, but it had made Moll believe.

Rose considered the heavy pottery crock atop the stove. Cream-colored, old and filled, just now, with sourdough starter, the crock had crossed a continent. Rose gave it a shove.

"Mercy!" Molly's fingertips covered her lips and her green eyes went wide, showing bloodshot strain.

Rose butted the crock with her shoulder, then fell along with it, grateful the gummy batter couldn't cling.

"Molly, I've three things to tell you."

The girl shook her head, eyes closed.

"Willing or not, you must act. I know best, this time. Or if not best, I know more."

Molly looked down, then. They both watched Rose's transparent feet fade away. Next, it would be her hands, then legs, arms . . . She had no time for coaxing.

"Moll, you must keep that man about you. Yes, Day!"

Rose shivered. Even Heaven-sent lads could lead her astray.

"He'll save your pretty neck, Moll. Do what you must to keep him near. Feed him, touch him. Lord, how he loves it. Please him and please yourself. No back talk, girl!"

Once she understood the futility of covering her ears, Molly fought Rose's intruding words with her mind, pushing urgently as a cat resisting water.

"Moll, listen. I mustn't scare Poppy, and she's near. Just . . ."

No legs, arms, not much of her face left. She must hurry.

"Don't let any harm come to Ginger. She's an old puss and important to us, somehow, and come to think of it, a saucer of brandy wouldn't go amiss, these cold nights, to warm her old bones . . ." As her sight faded to black, Rose thought she saw Molly struggle to her feet and seek that brandy bottle for herself.

"The horse and mule live thirty years, not knowin' nothing of wine nor beer—"

Raucous barroom voices paused for the answering clamor.

"Cows and sheep at twenty die, and never tasted scotch or rye—"

Day preferred drinking alone. He wanted to get pure pickled and pass out, forgetting Red Molly, before surfacing at his bloody job. But these fools wanted a new chum.

Arthur Pendragon—the tall dark one—and Geordie—
bulldog-built and a lively devotee of "witch theater"—followed Day from one tent saloon to the next, determined to
cheer him with outrageous toasts and recitals.

Now the two miners sat on the sawdust floor of Daddy
Slim's, drumming their heels to punctuate each stanza's end.

"Your modest sober, bone-dry hen, lays eggs for nogs,
then dies at ten—"

"—All animals are strictly dry, they sinless live and
swiftly die!"

The two leaned their heads together, drawing other voices
to bellow along.

"But sinful, ginful, beer-soaked man, survives three score
years and ten. And some of us, though mighty few, stay soz-
zled 'til we're ninety-two!"

The airborne boot that followed an opaque drinking mug
made Day twitch half a smile.

From dawn, when he got shut of Moll Gallagher, till now,
he'd passed hours in ways most men would envy. The
green-eyed witch would find out, too. The prospect twisted
him in knots.

He'd made Shambles in time for a breakfast of Sacramento peaches, cinnamon rolls and conversation. Persia listened to his excuses, pitied his weariness and purred an
ultimatum. Tonight marked his last chance to work and hide
out at the Black Dog.

Day stashed his gear in the room Persia indicated. Spare
as a maiden aunt's, the chamber had pale curtains, a pitcher
and bowl, walls painted green and a soft, middle-sagged
bed.

Set on sleep, Day carried his gear up and judged it a sign
of fatigue that Robin ambushed him on his second trip.

"Hey, Mr. Day!"

Deborah's boy—or Persia's, he hadn't puzzled that out—
in knee pants and cap, waved, a few yards from the buckboard.

"Hey, Robin, how's the kitten?"

"Fine, sir." The boy leaned forward on his toes, clearly
obeying orders not to come near the joyhouse.

"Why aren't you in school today?"

Robin's cheer faded. "It's Saturday, sir, but I'll be going." He took a step, then turned back. "She's not deaf, Mr. Day."

"Just Day, son." He tousled the boy's hair, so silky; Deborah must wash it every night.

"Are you—do you think you'll come over any more?"

"I came this morning, but you were sound asleep."

"I wasn't! I heard you. I hurried, but when I'd dressed, you was riding away. Then you came here."

All told, breakfast with Persia had taken a good half hour. Robin had stood out here, waiting, that long.

"Saturday, is it? I'm dreadful tired, now, but would y'be available to play tomorrow?"

"Play, sir?"

"We could play ball, fly kites, shoot marbles. You decide." Day hefted his gun belt from the wagon, ignoring Robin's stare.

"Could we catch bats?"

"Bats?"

"You know." Robin pantomimed stealthy wings. "Sometimes the miners have contests, throwing them up and shooting them."

"Afraid I've missed that lively bit o'fun."

"It's disgusting, Mama says."

"I'd agree with your mam. Let's let them live, shall we?"

He watched Robin run, dodging and feinting at some mock foe. Then Day entered Shambles's tight foyer. Undaunted by the steep stairs, he slung on the empty gun belt like a bandolier, gripped his long rifle and climbed.

Courtesy for the sleeping hurdy girls made him set his boot heels soft, but he disturbed one, just the same.

"Here, kitty, kitty, cat man," a sleep-soaked voice beckoned. The parts of him that had nestled all night next to Moll alerted the rest.

A yawning blond leaned in her doorway. Fuzzy hair, sticking out and backlit by sun, made her look like a demented baby duck.

"My name's Georgia. I thought you were coming yesterday. I just knew we'd be best friends, by now."

Her pout ended in a pink yawn and Day laughed. This lady might make him a new man.

"Tell you what, Miss Georgia, come along with me, and we'll do some catching up. By tomorrow, we'll be talking about old times." He shifted the gun belt higher and extended a hand.

"Always did like a man who was well armed." Georgia slid her curled fingers up the barrel of the Sharps.

Day snaked his arm around a waist that bent willingly close. Screw Moll Gallagher. Better yet, screw pretty Georgia.

But he hadn't. Here in Daddy Slim's, ordering another beer, it was easy to say he'd given in to weariness, but it wasn't so.

He'd come up randy as a goat when Georgia collapsed backward into the quilts. When he'd loosened his buttons and heard her moan of appreciation, he'd shucked denim down his thighs fast. He remembered spread-eagling over her, but after that, nothing. Not till she woke him with a cup of coffee and mouthful of giggles.

An elbow spilled Day's beer.

"Livin' in the whorehouse now, are ye, me 'andsome?" Arthur flipped bangs back from eager pup eyes.

"Aye. Eatin' there, too, but that's all. I'm bartending at the Black Dog." Day wiped his lips with the back of his hand. "I've nothing to do with the girls." Best get rid of that black stubble, if he planned to stay on unrecognized.

"What about Red Molly? You're spending time w'her, ain't you, now?" Geordie stood and brushed sawdust from his breeches.

"Something about Virginia City has made a superstitious fool of me." Day displayed his palms. "And her dog went and bit me. She patched that."

Dubious, Geordie shook his head, squaring off as if he'd fight. Day entertained a fancy of drawing the Colt and snapping a shot into the little bulldog's head before finishing his beer.

"Settle yourself, man," Arthur advised. "We've all had a fair bit of drink."

Geordie shoved off from the spindly bar and lurched away. For all that he kept fixing Day with a hard look, the young miner couldn't serve up the fight Day had been spoiling for.

Lord, let me go home. He yearned to hear waves thunder, crash, then hiss and search over the sand. He'd run mad listening to that stamp mill, always booming in the background.

And Moll. What did she want of him? To curl against his neck, like she had this blue dawn? Or to mince up his heart with her coldness?

What did he want of her? Red hair running riot over creamy breasts? A night when he had her over and over, then swung into the saddle and left? Hell.

Arthur slammed his mug down and addressed Day.

"Now, you're a smart one, ain't you, Day?" Arthur asked.

"Oh, aye, the smartest."

"Tell me, then, what d'you think about them cuttin' off tribute minin'?"

Every Cornishman in town was supposed to be a blessed genius at hard-rock mining. "That's where ye rent diggings and work them on your own time?" Day asked. "For no pay but what you dig up?"

"Aye."

"Well, how are you doing with it? Are you finding any color?" Day thought he sounded sufficiently mine-wise.

"I'll tell you, it's like the Cornishman writin' home to tell his da about prospecting for gold in California—'Where 'tis, 'tis. Where 'tisn't, there am I.' "

Arthur gave a rueful laugh, then glared past Day again. "I'm not sure I like the looks of that, now."

Day followed Arthur's stare. Ten paces off, Geordie glowered and gestured. Day grinned, baiting him, and turned back to Arthur. "What's gained by shuttin' you off from tribute mining?"

"Bosses don't be telling us why. If we want to work alone, we have to go off to Gold Hill, Silver City, someplace there's still unclaimed ground," Arthur said.

A hand gripped Day's shoulder. "Did you keep Moll Gallagher out all night?" Geordie snarled.

Well, now.

Day's core closed, silent and dark. Still as stone. His vision narrowed until Virginia City held nothing but a lucky man who couldn't know Day's Navy Colt lay under Persia's bed.

Day vibrated with the tension that presaged drawing. It sluiced through him, as heady as wine. God, how he'd missed it!

Settle yourself. Look past that hand on your shoulder. He's a kid, reeking with liquor and self-righteous wrath.

Day shrugged from under the hand.

"Just a minute, now, cousin."

Geordie stood with his leg cocked funny. It was a fair guess he had a knife in that boot.

Trust Moll not to forge a proper lie. They hadn't concocted a tale to tell folks, because, riding down the silent street, they believed no one had seen.

Moll might tell the truth, but he wouldn't. If men thought she'd fallen, her black magic wouldn't protect her. They'd be panting around her porch like dogs after a bitch.

Something ripped inside his chest.

"No. I wouldn't hurt any lady. Let alone a fine healer like Miss Gallagher."

Call me a liar. He stared into Geordie's face. *Go ahead, I'd like to fight ye.*

Geordie looked away, still lecturing. "She's a fine girl, for all folks say. Just . . . not for us rough men. Got it?"

"I hear ye." Day tugged the brim of his hat and scooped two bits from the bar. "Come down to the Black Dog, later, and I'll stand you a shot of redeye."

Geordie wasn't the only one wanting to give Day hell. The starched-ruffle gambler, Richard Griffin, waited at the Black Dog.

"You'll have to wait in line, Griffin." Day tried to concentrate as the bartender going off shift muttered instructions. "I've had my ass chewed all day long. It belongs to Persia and the Black Dog until closing time."

Griffin, aligning the white cuff of his shirt below the gray coat, made Day feel crude. Light from the brass chandelier glittered on Griffin's jeweled cuff links.

"I can wait." Griffin slipped into a chair facing the bar.

Persia's saloon boasted a carved mahogany bar, sailed around the Horn from Boston. Plain pine shelves hung behind it, displaying a range of bottles holding two kinds of liquor.

If a man asked for lager or ale, he got beer. If he asked for redeye, tarantula juice or snake head, he got whiskey. The customers—or fancy girls carrying their orders—came to him. All Day need do was draw drinks and take money— "One bit per glass. See the man in the corner if you're usin' dust."

A German named Weiner, pince-nez hanging on a ribbon around his neck, waited in the corner. Before him sat a gold-dust scale and paper markers that he issued for credit.

Beneath the bar were two boxes—one for dust markers, one for coin—and a buffalo gun named Pete.

Pete made Day's mouth go dry. A ball from Pete could blow a hole in the back wall that a man could jump through.

Persia admitted the gun was more useful for effect than enforcement. Responding to a beer-brave miner with a mumbled offer to "Go see Pete about it" was enough to make every man in the place hit the floor.

All the same, Persia wanted Day to wear his Colt, too. He told her to choose between the Colt and the white apron that she insisted gave the Black Dog "tone."

"Why wear a gun I can't get to?" He'd demonstrated how the apron muffled his holster, before arguing that a quick draw was impossible from behind the bar anyway.

"Your outlaw could go down the street and have a bath by the time I cleared the bar top. It must be a good foot from here"—Day had clapped his hand on his holster—"to here." He'd raised his index finger, pointed like a gun, above the bar.

Persia discounted his arguments and stroked the polished

wood. "Put a scratch on my bar, and you're a dead man, Day."

Then she'd turned in a huff of gypsy purple and descended the back stairs.

Still and all, if it came down to shooting, he'd blast a hole through the bar and worry about Persia later.

"Thanks for taking care of Molly."

At last check, it was one o'clock in the morning. Raised voices, clanking coins and the piano had ebbed to a murmur.

Seated across from Griffin, Day held his peace. Smoke from lamps and cigars swirled in the rafters, making Day grateful for the saloon's broken window.

Griffin looked ungodly neat. He'd sat in a saloon all night—a saloon from which Day had actually ejected a man on horseback—yet his full sideburns curled to perfection and his side-parted hair lay smooth as the mahogany bar.

"Molly told me you happened on her, before the snow-storm."

"Aye?"

"I suggested you might have gone looking for her, like you did when she had trouble in Chinatown, but she shot me down with those . . . rather direct eyes of hers." In another man, Griffin's tone would have accompanied a smile.

Day swallowed a belt of the Truckee River water Persia deemed the only drink suitable for vigilant bartenders.

If he never saw Moll Gallagher again, he'd remember her smoky emerald eyes and her auburn lashes, spiked with tears because she'd hurt him.

"She said you built a shelter and kept her from freezing."

Day shrugged.

"She said you tried to get her back before anyone noticed she'd been out all night." Griffin idled with a pack of cards, cutting, stacking, shuffling. "I appreciate that. I didn't get up the hill until the storm broke. I heard about Poppy, but talk said Moll was at Mrs. Green's." Griffin spread the cards with a light-fingered sweep of his left hand, then closed them together.

"Save your breath, man. I've done me good deed for the month. That's all."

"That gives you away, too, flying into Cockney parlance when you're emotional."

"Aye, you Mississippi men bein' experts on dialect—"

"Kentucky." Griffin tapped each corner of his card pack. "Funny, I would've guessed you for a poor gambler, Day, but you've done well here, so far."

Day's heartbeat picked up. He swirled the glass of water, pretending he had only Moll—not a hemp-toting sheriff—on his mind.

"Cards aren't the safest means of employment. If anything happens to me, there's things you should know. About Molly."

"About her and Persia?" Day's words tumbled out before he could claim disinterest.

"Persia, and Favor and Poppy and everything else you should know before you get into this."

"The only thing that wants getting into—"

"Listen, damn you—" Griffin's fist hit the table. "I'll put up with your pride and posturing, but utter one profane word against Moll Gallagher, and I'll plug you under the table."

The gambler wasn't left-handed. Day remembered it the same instant he heard the derringer's rolling click.

"I'm not a man who makes plans, Griffin." Day gave up bluffing. "Moll couldn't depend on me. Hell-bent Washoe zephyrs blew me up to Virginia City. I'll only be here 'til they buffet me somewhere else."

Pleased with the poetry of the sentence, Day took a breath as the saloon's doors admitted a wind scented with bitterbrush.

"My only plan," Day added, "is to make that girl wear some color. I've a yearning to see that, before I go."

Griffin's frame didn't move, but Day saw agreement ripple through him, as if someone'd strummed a harp.

"She's worn black since her mother died. She thinks it keeps folks at a distance."

Day nodded. Hadn't he thought her a pretty widow, until Eleanor VanBrunt told him different?

"Rosie died vomiting blood."

Only practice kept Day from flinching at the gambler's bluntness. His finger traced a scuff in the table's finish.

"Rose said a string of broken hearts killed her. Persia said liquor finally burned through Rosie's genteel belly lining.

"At the end, Moll was the only one there, toting basins, scrubbing sheets, tending Poppy." Griffin used a knuckle to smooth each side of his mustache. "Can you blame the men? They wanted loving and readings, but when it came to dying, they left Rosie to her kin." Griffin shook his head.

"Persia says she offered to take them in, feeling sentimental, since she was expecting her own young one."

"Robin?"

Griffin nodded. "When Persia visited, Rosie reared up in bed, half-gone with pain, screaming that she'd only sinned for love. Swore she'd never been a gold-grubbing whore and claimed she'd use a butcher knife on her wrists before letting herself be tended by one."

Griffin's matter-of-fact tone didn't blur the picture that flashed through Day's mind.

"And how old was Moll?" Day asked.

"Twelve or thirteen. I was making my prodigal's return to Kentucky, about then." Griffin's short laugh was bitter. "But the fatted calf came with too many conditions. I would have done more good here."

Blood and butcher knives in the name of love.

"Small wonder Moll's not so friendly toward men." Day opened fists gone numb with gripping. He rubbed blood back into his white knuckles and his heart slowed its lurching gallop. Then he caught Griffin's side glance.

"What else, damn ye!" Day's hand clamped Griffin's forearm. "Let's have it all."

"Molly and Poppy moved into Persia's house, the ground floor of what's Shambles." Griffin stopped, then forced the words to march in hammering precision.

"Remember Favor? The bastard I told you about? He couldn't content himself with Persia's whores."

Cold claws of dread grabbed Day by the nape, but he listened.

"One morning he came downstairs from an all-night orgy and saw Moll eating breakfast. He cozied up to her, asked her to sit on his lap. All very avuncular, until he began haggling with Persia. Molly escaped when Luba Washington spilled coffee on him, but Moll didn't make it out the front door."

Day couldn't remember four words harder to dredge from his throat. "Did he do it?"

"Persia says not. Moll bit him and Luba brained him with a black iron frying pan." Griffin's lips pulled back in a skeleton's grimace.

She bit him. *Bit* him, oh Molly!

"Luba hustled the girls back to Rosie's shack, got them the dog and a rifle, taught Moll to shoot and Poppy to bake. Moll had already started reading hands."

"Did he have a gun? A knife? Why didn't someone stop him?"

Griffin shook his head.

"And Persia let him come *back*?"

"Favor's rich, and he hasn't done anything the sheriff could arrest him for. A girl sitting in a whorehouse . . ." Griffin shrugged stiffly. "Still, when he comes to Virginia, he goes to Daddy Slim's and his cribs. He's one man deserves shooting in the back. And he knows it.

"Persia didn't sell him her place when he wanted it." Griffin offered the information without judgment.

"The woman's a blamed humanitarian, now, isn't she?"

Day hated the patience required, but he'd landed in a prime position for ambushing Favor. Day slept in the whorehouse and worked in the bar Favor wanted. And the man had never met him. He had the perfect setup for . . .

Another murder? Day looked at the wallowing clouds of smoke above him. What was that old saw? *Might as well be hung for a sheep as a lamb.* The law sought him for murder; he might as well run from one he could justify.

"Favor's due in for the Louse Town races. Rumor says his black filly will run the legs off any colt in the territory. I'd have to watch for Favor's man, Cock-Eyed Tony, take care of him in the crowd, then I'd go after Favor." Griffin leaned his chair back, savoring the idea. "Or we could team up."

"Griffin, leave the killing. It's already too late for me."

Griffin made no sign he understood, only tossed back the rest of his whiskey. "Moll would miss you more than me. It's the gospel truth, so shut up."

Day almost choked on the irony. He couldn't tell Griffin that Moll had bitten him. Knowing what that meant, he'd never get another chance with her.

Blood and butcher knives. He'd seen her confront both in Chinatown, seen her kneel in the streets, using bare hands to stem gore spurting from a drunkard's leg. She squared off with her demons daily. All but one.

Day stood up from the table. "Madam Persia ordered me to clear the place by two o'clock, since they'll be in settin' up for worship." Day's muscles cramped with inactivity. His legs wanted to run.

"I know." Griffin surveyed the saloon. "Things get powerful quiet about this time of the evening."

Openly, the gambler slid the derringer from his palm to his vest pocket, gave a civilized nod and strode into the night.

Day polished the mahogany bar as he would fine saddle leather. What if he took Moll from this tawdry town to Ireland or Cornwall? What if he dressed her in gloves and a little bird-wing hat, escorted her to high tea served amid velvet cushions?

Day arranged the bottles in even ranks. He couldn't give Moll Ireland, nor tea and velvet. But he knew how to finish off the one fear Moll hadn't beaten.

Nobility was hard to swallow. It grated his throat like sand, but he'd choke it down just the same. Sure, he'd leave Molly. But he'd leave without taking his hero's reward, riding out of the high Sierra before the next snowfall, after he'd hunted down and killed the monster called Favor.

Chapter Eighteen

Molly grabbed Deborah's doorjamb to slow her momentum. She'd thrown open the boardinghouse door to welcome Margaret Bride for after-church coffee and nearly collided with Day's chest.

"You're not Miss Bride!" Molly blamed the fresh-washed morning sky—not the man outlined against it—for dazzling her.

"I daresay you're not Robin, either."

Devilish blue eyes beguiled her from his tanned face. A faint herbal incense hinted he'd cajoled a Chinese merchant out of a cake of Dragon soap. With his head cocked to one side, the sun sparked russet glints from his black hair.

"Robin's changing from his church clothes." How would a proper lady act now?

He'd held her like a husband, during the snowstorm. He'd tolerated her lunacy and saved her life. Good sense dictated a truce. And yet the instant her eyes flowed over his loose

183

white shirt, she recalled her mother's assessment of Day, and worried that the feelings weren't her own.

He met her stare, as if he could read it, and Molly knew the fluttering pulse for her own. She gestured vaguely toward the stairs and Robin.

Day shifted, hefting an armload of newspapers and sticks. A ball of string tumbled from atop it all, attracting Soapy, with Robin in pursuit.

"Day!" The boy's small hand caught the doorframe below Molly's. "Not bats, right?" Robin touched the sheaf of newspapers.

"Not bats. Guess again." Day stepped inside, reminding Molly she'd impolitely kept him waiting outside. Their shoulders brushed and the smile Day shot over the child's head warmed her, though she had no inkling what he meant.

"Kites!" Robin somersaulted from between them, battling the kitten for the ball of string. "We're going to fly kites!"

Drawn by Robin's shouts, Poppy appeared, drying her hands. She dropped the flour-sack towel to tag after.

In a minute, she'd snatch up the towel, but now Molly lingered on the porch, facing inward, letting the autumn sun warm the black silk between her shoulder blades. She watched Day set the papers in a stack, squaring their edges with large sure hands, pinning the recaptured string between an elbow and his ribs, out of reach of the kitten's claws. Day caught her eye, then looked away.

"See if you can't make a terrible big pot of paste, dovey." He dispatched Poppy to the kitchen. "Mind you, pick up the towel."

"Excuse me." Margaret Bride hesitated behind Molly, hand raised to the cameo at her throat.

"Miss Margaret!" As Molly guided the teacher past Day to Deborah's kitchen, she felt almost relieved.

"Hello!" Deborah blew a swatch of hair from her eyes as she used both hands to lift an iron skillet. "Tell me you won't mind if I keep cooking. I cook no Sunday supper, so I'll have a full table for dinner."

"Oh, the aromas led me down the street." Margaret plucked off white gloves. "I don't know how you keep house, tend a child and conduct business while cooking for so many!" The schoolteacher unpinned her hat and placed it aside before touching the china teacup Molly had delivered.

"Stay for dinner." Deborah drained spitting grease into a tin.

"Oh!" Margaret's face marbled red and pink. "I certainly did not mean to invite myself."

"It's our pleasure." Deborah ignored Margaret's distress. "What a nice change to have educated conversation at our tables."

Deborah presented a platter of doughnuts. As she opened the kitchen window, Deb darted Molly a pointed look, though she knew the Gallagher sisters had only visitors of the paying variety.

"We'd welcome you." Molly managed. "Any time. Tomorrow night?"

Molly hardly noticed Margaret's response. The open window allowed Day's voice into the kitchen. It mixed with the cheep of sparrows and creak of starlings, tempting Molly out of doors.

"No, me 'andsome. Give over the knife. I'll notch those sticks."

Deborah and Margaret exchanged smiles at the sound of Day's patience. Molly broke her doughnut in halves, then quarters. She looked up only as Margaret covered her lips, stifling a cough.

"I've had it forever." Beyond Margaret's troublesome cough, Molly caught the purl of Day's voice amid the children's.

". . . Hold the sticks crossed . . ." Day's hands would instruct, not insist. ". . . Aye, that's got it . . ." Those dark male hands had held her gently captive.

"The wheezing has improved since I swept the dear little cottage free of sawdust." Timid Margaret sat waiting, so Molly reached for her ever-present bag.

"We'll start with candlewick tea." Molly considered the bag's interior, as if her preoccupation stemmed from medicinal choices. "But a mining town breeds breathing complaints. I've a dozen treatments if you don't take to this one."

Molly uncorked the bottle of fuzzy leaf and flower fragments. "We can brew the tea right now, if you've a mind to drink it."

"Water's already on the boil." Deborah lifted her kettle.

"I'll grind it finer, next time." Molly shook the bottle at eye level. "It's bitter, so we'll need a drop of Deb's honey." Molly had just decided duty muffled Day's distraction quite nicely, when he spoke again.

"She'll fly like an eagle, darlin', once we get a bit of arch in her back. Just tighten the string . . ."

When the man painted such pictures with his words, he was far more conjurer than she.

"If this weren't my only bottle, I'd give you some to take at bedtime. Poppy will bring more, tomorrow."

"Of course. Though, if you didn't mind, might I accompany you to VanBrunts' to buy a bottle for it?" Margaret sipped the tea without a grimace. "And might you pour me a little, there? I do have a time breathing, at night."

"Besides, it's a glorious azure day." Brash as brass, Day invaded the kitchen. "And you ladies are required to applaud our grand launching!"

Knees smudged with porch dust, shirt sleeves rolled up from brown forearms, Day looked proud as the kite-brandishing youngsters as he extended the diamond-shaped newspaper offering to Deborah.

"For your forbearance, ma'am."

He bowed and Deborah clutched the kite to her breast. For Molly, the scene fell far short of charming.

"Will it fly?" Deborah held it at arm's length for inspection.

Day considered the flock around him. It had grown to six.

"It better." Humility drowned beneath soprano cheers and stamping feet. He renewed the smile meant to coax the women outdoors.

"I've sliced a ham." Deborah surveyed her cluttered kitchen. She glanced at Day, blushed and hurried on. "I've boiled potatoes, onions and greens and fried doughnuts.

That's food enough, isn't it?" She turned a defiant smile on Molly. "Couldn't I steal away for an hour?"

He'd tempted them both, offering nothing more than play. It would be cutting off her nose to spite her face to refuse him. Still, running after a pack of children, sitting in an October meadow, watching him—what would he think?

Birdsong and wood smoke rode a soft breeze through the window. Dying summer's gift called to her, tempted her to heed feelings that might not belong to her ghostly mother.

"I think perhaps I can harvest my yarrow later." Molly lifted her chin, joining Deborah's small rebellion.

"Oh, d-dear," Margaret stammered. "I suppose my lessons might be planned by lantern light, since you've declared a holiday!"

They trailed behind, surrounded by Day's entourage of scampering children, who dragged their kites on skittering stick spines or cradled them like infants.

When a gust flared and flagged, Day jammed down his black hat and fell into step beside her. "What d'y'think? The field up Union Street? Would that give room enough?"

He turned to her for advice, a Pied Piper not quite sure of himself. Beneath the children's chatter, above her own thudding heart, Molly's voice came in breathless snatches she blamed on the pace.

"There's a better field, and closer, behind VanBrunts'."

"Thanks, m'Bright." He didn't touch, but his smile, flashing over her, felt as if he had.

"This way, troops!" Day drew stares and chuckles as he vaulted off the boardwalk and turned uphill, with children scampering behind.

Deborah wagged her head after Day as she linked her arm through Molly's.

"Sigh." Deborah pretended to shiver.

"'Sigh'? What on earth do you mean?" In case Deborah was determined to embarrass them both, Molly glanced over her shoulder.

"What if we drop in at VanBrunts', first?" Margaret caught up, wheezing. "To get the bottle for my medicine?"

The women swept inside the mercantile. Squinting in the

dimness, they made out Eleanor at the counter, sorting crackers into a jar.

Molly moved to a corner where odd bottles, scrap leather and metal fittings lay jumbled into bins.

"What are they up to?" Eleanor nodded to the crowd, out-side.

"Mr. Day helped the children make kites." Margaret's voice held an invitation.

Molly looked up from an amber bottle to see a flicker of longing cross Eleanor's face. Then she glanced toward the back room.

"A travesty on the Sabbath," Hans VanBrunt's voice boomed.

Though she didn't ask, Molly wondered why laboring on the Sabbath was any less a travesty than kite-flying.

"Pardon me, ma'am." A young miner collided with Deb-orah. "Excuse me." He bowed past and addressed Eleanor. "Could I buy me some twine, real quick-like?"

"And sticks!" added a heavy-booted laborer.

"Sticks? I don't sell sticks! Look in the hills for sticks."

"Oh Jake, you know there ain't hardly a bit of wood for pickin' up. How about these?"

"Those are knitting needles, young man." Eleanor stiff-ened as Hans lumbered to a stop behind her.

"I have barrel staves, but they'll cost you fifty cents each."

The miners plunked down their combined wealth of coin and dust and departed, but before Margaret had paid for her bottle, four more miners rushed in, begging newspapers, sticks and string.

"Sticks are a dollar."

When Margaret's jaw fell agape, jolted by VanBrunt's greed, Molly distracted her.

"Let's pour some candlewick tincture off for you." Molly hurried Margaret toward the counter. "I'll distill more as you need it, but don't try to make it yourself."

Eleanor settled a lid on the cracker barrel, turning atten-tive. Slightly abashed, Molly continued her explanation.

"That's important. You might mistakenly use seeds. Now, the flowers, roots and leaves—"

"Heaven forbid you'd get for free, what the witch could charge you for." Eleanor peered at the amber bottle. "Six cents, please."

Speechless, Margaret plucked the coin from her reticule.

"Nevertheless, the seeds are poisonous." Molly took a short breath, considered the teacher's blush and thought they might both benefit by flinging open the door to this stuffy structure.

As the prickling constriction worsened, Molly used a discreet index finger to ease her collar away from her throat. Deborah and Margaret pressed near and a strange man crowded her other arm.

Danger. The word jolted before her as if splashed on the wall with red paint. Molly cast a quick look at the man. The stranger's hat slanted so low she wondered how he could see.

Flee. Red splatters like sparks obscured her vision. Molly took the bottle from Eleanor and shoved it into Margaret's hand.

"I'll wait outside."

She backed away as Margaret fumbled with her change. Before Molly could escape, Poppy opened the door. Light glared behind her.

"Moll, I can hardly see you." Poppy edged down the cramped aisle. "Deborah, Day says to bring your kite before we lose the breeze."

"You are flying kites?" Hans leaned across the counter. "Big girl like you?" He gave Poppy's cheek a flat-palmed pat and Molly's revulsion overcame her fear.

"Poppy, come here."

Deborah and Margaret started at Molly's sharp order, but all three joined her brisk retreat.

Outside, clouds scudded white against the sky. As they hiked the side street toward the kite-spiked horizon, Molly consoled her skittering mind. She'd imagined Hans's lechery and the stranger's menace. Yesterday's ghostly delusion and her confusion over Day were to blame.

Sheep had once grazed in the meadow, but now it swarmed with a kite-flying throng. Robin's kite dove in spirals as a dozen miners, dirty and clean, off shift or ready to go on, creased newspapers, spread paste and battled teasing winds.

"Did y'get it?" Day ran before a child's tumbling kite, coaxing it to mount the breeze.

"I forgot!" Poppy clapped a hand over her mouth. "I was supposed to get cloth for tails!" She showed Molly a coin.

"No matter!" Day tugged a kite string in short jerks as the little girl beside him chortled and reached for his hand. Poppy ran with them and Margaret paused to speak with one of her students, as Deborah and Molly seated themselves on the grass.

"He's not the son of a bitch you called him, is he?" Deborah stood close enough to whisper.

"I never did, and I'm shocked at such language, Mrs. Green." Molly let the sunlight paint her closed eyelids.

"It takes no witch to see it. You can't keep your eyes off him, Molly."

"He makes me—" Happy, scared, crazy? "Look at my hands." She laughed at her silly tremors.

"You like him."

"I want him around." It wasn't the same as saying she liked the man.

"Molly!" Deborah intentionally bumped their shoulders. "You are the strongest woman I know, immune to disease, blood and snippy neighbors, yet you're afraid of him. Aren't you?"

"He's a fake. He's not at all what he pretends to be!"

"Who is?" Deborah started to speak, closed her lips, then began again. "Anyone would say I'm a good wife to Michael. Even though he's a wandering, gold-besotted fool, I'm faithful, modest, all that. You won't find a soul in town who'll say different." Deborah slanted a glance after Day. "But this morning, when Day gave me that kite, I wanted to forget I'd ever had a husband. And I still love Michael more than breath."

More fuddled than informed, Molly crossed her arms in a tight tangle. "It's not your fault he tempts you. And it proves I'm right. I'm no more to him than anyone else."

"Molly, close your mouth and look. Over there. Look at him, right now."

Robin flew his kite from Day's shoulders. Day smiled and moved his hand in a vague wave.

"It's you he's watching. You he rescued in the snowstorm. He was with you all night and never laid a hand on you. Am I right? I'll wager he's never been that chaste before."

Fire and snow. Madness and peace. What had happened in the white heart of that storm? Unshed tears grated Molly's voice down to a whisper.

"He'll leave me."

"He might." Deborah gave a sensible nod. "Michael does it each time he gets the itch, but he comes back."

Molly sniffed and the meadow smeared orange, gold and green.

"You might as well get it out! Are you afraid he'll hurt you? Because he will." Deborah dismissed her worry like dirty laundry. "I've hurt you, Poppy has, but it's worth it. Will you stop being my friend because I admitted he intrigues me?"

"Of course not. Now, take your kite back. This twine's about to amputate my fingers." Molly unwound the string, handed it back to Deborah, then flexed some color into her fingers. "Deb, what if I started to love him?"

"I think you do already." Her only concession to Molly's fear was a lowered voice and a smile. "Molly, what do you want? No man is perfect, but Day might be the handsomest man who ever rode into this sorry town. He's crazy about you, and watch him with the children. Moll, it could be wonderful."

It. A warm ribbon of feeling unfurled and Molly knew Deborah wasn't speaking of romance, but of sexual congress.

"If you fight"—Deborah uttered a cynical laugh as she stepped back to save her shuddering kite from falling— "over unwashed socks or burned beef or the tone of your voice, you won't die from it. Nobody does."

Deborah's intensity proved her kite's undoing. Both women jumped up, but not before the kite somersaulted, weaving a crazy spider web of neighboring kite strings. Deborah winced, called apologies and ran to help the children relaunch their crafts.

Standing alone, Moll realized Deborah had been right about one thing. She couldn't help scanning the crowd for Day. At the meadow's edge, he applauded a yellow-haired prostitute as she held her skirt hem between her teeth and wriggled free of a red petticoat.

"Whoooeee!" A man in farmer's overalls, possessor of a tin of paint, waved hands and arms smeared green.

"Just hold your horses, honey." The blond spread her petticoat on the grass, then knelt and ripped it into strips. "Paint me a pretty picture on my kite and I might trade you a piece of my petticoat."

The farmer rolled backward on his spine, howling as if she'd offered more than a rag of red flannel.

"I have a confession, since Mrs. Green is occupied." Margaret Bride, her face pink, sidled up to Molly.

She regarded the teacher's guilty face. Molly thought herself jaded by small-town secrets, but she couldn't imagine the teacher pregnant, addicted to drink or snuff. Perhaps she was a devotee of lusty novels.

"I want you to read my palm."

Laughing with relief, Molly drew Margaret to a tree-sheltered niche and read. A lively mind, a level head, too much concern for the opinions of others, but a strong and sympathetic heart.

"And marriage, within the year!" Molly looked up for confirmation, surprised by what she read.

"No!" Margaret clutched her throat. When she removed her spectacles for polishing, tears crowded her hazel eyes.

"Now how can that be a surprise, ma'am?"

Boots braced as wide as his shoulders, Day stood before them. A green-daubed kite showed from behind his back.

Molly imagined they looked like fawning subjects, with their heads snapping up in awe. Lord have mercy, the man was handsome!

"Do you know, a drifter was looking for you last night, Miss Margaret?"

Molly watched the schoolteacher's discomfort, knowing it would be short-lived. She recognized the cadence of Day's storytelling. Molly leaned back on her arms. She wondered how he'd decorated that kite behind his back and wondered if it might be for her.

"Looking for me? You're teasing, Mr. Day."

"No, ma'am. He asked for the schoolteacher, but bein' as we had this conversation in the Black Dog saloon, and as I, myself, have a small skill at reading, I served his needs, best I could.

"He had a receipt for a gravestone, y'see, and wanted to be sure it was made out just right."

"How sad." Margaret tucked her legs under her skirts, and held her glasses in her lap.

"The party eulogized, it turned out, was still among the livin'," Day explained. "But I read out the inscription, like he asked, to the entire gathering of gentlemen." Day sat cross-legged on the grass. "Would you like to hear what it said?"

Just then, Molly saw the kite. Within a wreath of vines glared a pointy-nosed animal. The lettering read—

Margaret glanced at Molly, questioning the propriety of Day's story.

"Oh, tell us!" Molly spoke for the reluctant teacher.

Day stretched, rolling his shoulders like a tomcat, eyes lazy as he nodded. Molly snatched the chance to glance at the kite. The lettering read "Vixen."

"I warn you, ladies, there wasn't a dry eye when I'd done the reading. But I see you're game.

" 'To Tar Baby,' it read, 'who had the eyes of an eagle, the spirit of a tiger, the temper of a lamb, the body of a horse and the eternal devotion of this sinful man. Amen.' "

In the meadow, a magpie squawked.

" 'The body of a horse'?" Molly asked.

"Aye, a beautiful inscription, don't you think?"

"This was—" Margaret Bride actually giggled. "A grave marker for his horse?"

"Oh, aye. He brought the sainted Tar Baby right through the saloon's batwing doors and up to the bar for a taste, and though the Black Dog's patrons weren't averse to drinking elbow by fetlock with such a paragon, the proprietress had Tar Baby removed."

Molly yearned for more. More of Day's tales and teasing, more of his deft gestures and irresistible grin. Could he be the same man who'd drawn a gun on Stag? Who'd shaken with hatred toward Hans VanBrunt? Who'd stolen the only kiss a man had taken from her lips?

Day was as unpredictable as the Sierra skies, and that should be warning enough for anyone, even Rose Gallagher's girl.

"Have Molly read your palm, Mr. Day. It's a most interesting process." Margaret's face turned as dark as a plum at her boldness, just as Deborah hailed her from the crowd of kite flyers.

Margaret's eyes lingered on Day's painted kite as she stood, cleared her throat and repositioned her glasses.

"Mr. Day, I h-have some watercolor paints of my own. If you would be kind enough to stop by school someday, I feel—I mean, I trust, we could turn kite-building into a mathematics lesson, and follow up with a touch of art appreciation."

Smitten and stumbling, Margaret moved off with as much speed as her hampering skirts allowed.

Molly's knuckles grazed denim as she took Day's hand from where it lay on his thigh. Her heart pounded louder than the wind slashing the newspaper kites.

"Shall I read your palm, Day? And see if I can find a tale as wild as one of yours?" His hand's weight vibrated up the veins in her wrist. Traces of white paste clung to the ridge of muscle beneath his smallest finger. She touched it. "You have a unique plain of Mars."

"Molly. Stop it." His hand closed like a trap. "Look at me, Molly, not my goddamned plain of Mars. Look at *me*."

His voice was urgent, his hold relentless. The muscles in that brown forearm didn't bulge, didn't brutalize, but he wouldn't let go until she obeyed.

All the same, Molly wished she hadn't looked.

"Do you see a man who wants to hurt you?" His eyes

searched her face. "Do you see anything to be afraid of? Tell the truth, Moll."

"No, I don't think you—"

A kite crashed between them, holding them silent as the farmer bowed and apologized.

"Day, the men who beat down my mother didn't need to use their fists. They used hope and promises to damage her beyond saving. Now, please let go." She made her hand fall limp, prey in a predator's jaws, but he didn't give in.

"Why? I know, sometimes, you like it." His brows arched high and confidence surged in his voice before he glanced back at the field. No intruders wandered near, but still he lowered his voice.

"Tell me you don't like it when I touch you." His thumb skimmed the skin inside her wrist. "Tell the truth."

Memory recreated the pressure of Favor's palms against Molly's temples. She almost gagged, though she knew it wasn't the same.

"I don't like it when you touch me."

His fingers loosened, but he swallowed and shook his head in disbelief. "I'm just not buyin' it, sweetheart. I'm not."

A disbelieving laugh claimed her. "You are an arrogant son of a gun, Day. I'll give you that."

"No, Moll, it's not that simple." His thumb stroked the thrumming blue veins once more. "I understand about the closeness, about being forced."

Her stomach clenched and panic fluttered like a bird in her chest. Who had told him, and what?

"I know, Moll, but sometimes—" Confusion clouded Day's face until Robin, backing at a trot, eyes fixed on his kite, stumbled over them, then continued backing across the meadow.

The impact appeared to clear Day's mind. He cocked his head to one side, struck by a revelation.

Clearly, as if she viewed his brain's pictures, Molly knew he'd remembered the dog bite and the afternoon in her kitchen, when she'd grown drunk on the feel of his skin.

Still controlling her hand, he moved it, stroking her fingers, light as moths, over his forearm.

"Do you like it, when—*you* touch *me*?" Day faltered and his embarrassment made the truth easier.

"Yes," she whispered.

Past the white of his shirt, the meadow swarmed with people who didn't know she'd lost her mind.

"That is a starting place, m'Bright."

He pulled her up, plopped a twine ball into the hand he'd possessed and said nothing about the attached fox-faced kite.

That was all? Molly twitched the wrinkles from her new black gown. Did one engage in the most intimate conversation of her life and then go fly a kite?

Blast the man! She wanted to stay. She wanted to listen. She refused to plunge into a meadow full of shrill children!

He closed the string more firmly inside her hand.

"I'll stand here and hold your kite up. Wait for the wind, Moll, then run into it, fast as you can. I'll be right behind you. I won't let go until it's safe. Understand?"

"If Robin can do it, I think I can manage."

The breeze freshened, blowing a lock of hair across her cheek. Summer had ended, autumn was almost gone, but one treetop blazed defiance, shaking bright limbs at winter.

Molly bit her lip. The chill wind was truly invigorating, a little exciting. She grabbed a handful of skirt, started to move off, but Day's fingertips tapped her waist.

"Moll, about touching—"

"Hush! I want to get this kite up!"

"Now, I'll be good as I can be—"

"I'm determined to make this kite fly!"

"—but if you feel like touching me—What I mean is, if you're feeling froggish, just jump right ahead. I sure won't stop you." Because his laughing face begged for a kiss, she turned away from him.

Molly ran into the wind. Day was crazy, a dream weaver, a charlatan, but this time he'd caught her. Her heart felt decidedly "froggish," as if it had every intention of leaping right out of her breast.

Chapter Nineteen

Faded lilac silk draped the dead woman sprawled near Molly's porch. Stiffened in a barely raised crouch, the corpse climbed the earth as if it were the wall of a cage.

Instinct kept Molly on the porch. If the dead woman had thrashed and moaned, Molly would have rushed to her. Had she bled, Molly would have pressed the wound, then bound it; but she had nothing to offer this rigid corpse.

Dawn hadn't yet melted frost from the sage, and chill air wrapped Molly's breath around her like a shawl. Cinder circled and whined, seeking scents that had worried him before daybreak.

As always, Poppy had departed through the back door. She hadn't seen this carnage. The cow lowed, and Glory bolted and neighed as Poppy passed the corral. Basket over her arm, blue skirts flowing, Poppy walked on, oblivious to the dead woman and what appeared to be a second body near the corral. Molly let her go.

Like spilled ink, the dead woman's hair covered her.

Molly didn't have to turn her faceup to know she was a girl from the cribs of Chinatown.

She wasn't Lin. This girl was taller. Perhaps she'd come, seeking help in the night. Logic nosed through Molly's mind. No blood pooled around the body. No last reflexive scratching marked the dirt near claw-set fingers. The girl had been dumped.

Molly stared past the body, past the porch rail, the rain barrel and the woodpile, wondering if the sheriff would investigate a dead prostitute dumped at Red Molly's shack.

"Come on, Cinder." She clucked her tongue for the dog to follow. "Cinder!"

Panting, rolling his brown eyes white, the dog obeyed. Poppy had passed the farthest end of the corral, passed the second body and not noticed. She'd almost reached the road.

"Poppy! Honey, stop in at Sheriff Merrick's." Poppy cupped her hand to her ear. "The *sheriff*. Tell him there's been an accident and I need him."

Poppy waved and walked on at a brisker pace. Molly's knees softened.

"Just let me catch my breath a minute, boy." She sat in the dirt, holding Cinder's head as he rolled his rheumy eyes.

Glory's skittering hooves made her look toward the corral. The other "body" climbed stiffly to its feet.

"I don't know what's happened." Molly swallowed to moisten her throat. "But apparently my voice can raise the dead."

Day swore he'd been wet down, tied in a knot and hung on the fence to dry. His knees creaked. His spine threatened to shear off in pieces. No fisherman's child should sleep on the ground. A heap of nets would feel a treat, next to this dusty horse pen.

Molly's filly pawed the ground, tossing her mane and snorting. She'd issued her protests all night, except once, when she snuffled his face and drooled on him.

Leaving the Black Dog, he'd blamed moon madness for his misdirected steps. Instead of retiring to his room at Shambles, he'd headed for Moll's, then spent the best part of an hour staring at her cottage. Finally, with the excuse of getting an early start at gentling her filly, he'd fallen asleep.

Stag, limping off in miner's garb at daybreak, had wakened Day with curses and a plea not to tell Moll where he'd gone.

Now Day regarded the cottage again. For a minute he didn't grasp what he saw.

"Sweet Jesus." *Don't run, man. An easy trot will do it. Don't provoke the dog, on top of it.*

Cinder snarled. Moll crouched beside the woman she'd rescued over a week ago. Someone had saved the Chinese lass a second try.

"I think her neck is broken." Molly squatted, her fingers laced over the skirt covering her knees. "Cinder, stop it!"

Abashed, the dog circled two times and dropped down with a grunt, facing away from both of them.

A sleep-raveled braid hung over Moll's shoulder. Her face shone moist and pale as milk.

"You doin' all right, Moll?"

"Compared to her?" Molly's laugh held no humor.

"I can't do anything for her. I'm asking what *you* need."

She looked up, with a face peaked as a child's, and that's when Day knew it would never work. He couldn't wait for her to touch him. Here they squatted, a body between them, and his brain insisted that kissing would help.

"Could you get your wagon, and we'll take her—home?"

Damn. In place of yesterday's kite-flyin', hair-streamin', laughing Moll, he had this somber woman. As they stood, her shoulders faltered against his and Day wasn't a bit ashamed for wishing the tart had chosen somewhere else to die.

"Aye, I'll go back to town and get the wagon."

Before he could, Richard Griffin charged up on a steel-dust mare. She would have trampled them, if Griffin hadn't hauled her into an open-mouthed rear. Behind him loped a white horse, carrying Sheriff Merrick.

If they'd come to arrest him, Day figured he was lost.

"I was in Merrick's office when Poppy came." Griffin

sympathized in bare words, without laying a hand on her. Day kicked a rock as big as his head.

Her bleak moment gone, Moll confronted the sheriff.

"I'll tell you how I know it wasn't an accident."

Day hung his thumbs in his pockets, wondering how he'd teach the lass not to bait lawmen with her low expectations.

"See the bruises on her cheek, and where her eye's swollen?"

"Mighta happened in the fall, walking up here in that long thing coulda tripped her." Merrick fingered his drooping gray mustache, attempting to reason.

"What about her arms?" Molly demanded.

Day settled on his boot heels to study the corpse. Best if he avoided staring Merrick in the face, anyhow.

The purplish sleeves had fallen back to the dead girl's elbows. From there to her wrists, bruises clustered like grapes.

Day turned back to confirm Moll's claim and ended up setting his teeth over a lovesick groan. Even here at her ankles, the scent of lavender soap flowered through Molly's dress.

What an ass was he. The law stood ready to jerk a loop around his throat, but Mark Owen Daywell only imagined Moll's skin.

"—anyone could see she was holding her arms up like this, trying to protect herself." Sarcasm battled the anxiety shaking Moll's voice. Day rose and stood beside her.

"Miss Gallagher." Merrick tipped up his hat brim. "I'm not accusing you of a thing. You're coming at me, fractious as a she-wolf, and all I want is to get this girl back to her people."

Moll grimaced as Merrick dismounted and grappled with the corpse. His gelding sidestepped the grisly burden.

"Hold my reins, will you, Griffin?"

Moll's silence lasted until the body seesawed, diamond-hitched, across the horse's withers. She studied the dirt where the girl had lain, then Molly's voice rose, triumphant.

"All right, then—" She brandished a pointing finger and Day wondered if there'd ever been such a woman for calling down trouble on her own head. "Where's the urine?"

Molly surveyed their faces, then tossed up her hands as if the men were just short of morons. Day's lips trapped a bubble of morbid laughter. His Moll was a piece of work.

"If she was coming up to my house and fell and broke her neck in the dark, where's the urine?"

"Miss Gallagher, my patience is 'bout run down."

"Sheriff, if I'm understanding the lass right—" Day smeared on the heavy brogue. "She's sayin' that when folks die—" *Hee-haw like a jackass, Daywell, if you don't want him comparing you to that poster.* "—they, well, they piss, sir."

"I know that!" Merrick roared with frustration. "But what in creation would scare her into falling and breaking her neck? There's not much these girls ain't seen, and dying folks don't lose their ur-reen unless they're scared!"

"Sheriff, I think Miss Gallagher is right. I think the dead always do it." Griffin regarded the ends of his reins, shrinking from a topic so obviously beneath him.

"The hell you say." Merrick braced for another voice to challenge him. None did. "Reckon I *do* know enough not to ride in and accuse a bunch of Chinamen of murdering one of their own." Merrick swung aboard and rode out the gelding's objection to its double burden.

"Been down there lately, Sheriff?" Griffin's molasses-sweet question made Merrick check his rifle boot.

Day flushed. Griffin and Merrick were riding into action. He wasn't. He was afoot among horsemen, with his Colt out of reach, hidden in a whorehouse.

"I'll ride along." Griffin almost yawned with nonchalance. "And I'll take Miss Gallagher. She has a way with those people."

What had Moll bristling now? The gambler had asked her to ride with him into ambush. It seemed just her cup of tea!

Day's fingers searched the side seam of his denims and he realized that he was truly itching for a gun.

Molly didn't spare him a glance, only approached Griffin's horse. As she bent, passed the front of her skirt hem between her legs and tucked it into the back of her waistband, Day forgot his revolver. She stuck her toe into Griffin's stirrup and used the gambler's thigh as a boost to pull herself up behind him.

Griffin's mustache cocked up at one corner. "Keep an eye on Moll's place. Just in case something's up, can you, Day?" Griffin wheeled his horse after Merrick's.

"Aye, boss. Nothin' I'd like better." Even in the tan flurry of dust, he saw Moll twist around for another glimpse of him. But then her silhouette merged with Griffin's and all Day saw of Molly was the flick of her cinnamon braid, beating time between her shoulders.

Day sidestepped the marmalade cat and let himself into Poppy's kitchen. He opened the pie safe. Empty. Melancholy closed around him in the cottage's stillness.

"Not a pan left to lick." He commiserated with Cinder, who'd nosed the unlatched door open and let in the cat.

"Even hired hands are due biscuits"—he pitched one to the gray-muzzled cur and watched him snap it into crumbs—"and coffee, aren't they, m'handsome?"

Cinder rolled his eyes in reproach and licked the floor.

. . . wedding night . . .
Day shifted without opening his eyes. The words were just a fairy's dream-meddling. Curling back in the chair, he sought the sunbeam that had warmed him as he dozed in the girls' kitchen.
Be spinning thoughts of your wedding night.
There was nothing for it, but to talk back to the damnably persistent nightmare.

"I fancy myself more of a despoiler of virgins." The muffled words amused him in the sodden way a drunkard finds himself downright hilarious.

Cinder, drowsing nearby, scrambled up with a yelp and Day gasped beneath a drowning wave of soul-swallowing cold.

"You'll wed any girl you have in my house!"
Day's eyes stared at the bone-white cleavage of a woman whose shriek scored the inside of his skull like captive lightning. Worse than that, he could see straight through her, to the wall.

"Aw, no, now." Day blinked and tried to fashion words that could soothe the vengeful spirit. "Easy, love." He wiped his hand across his lids before looking again.

Cinder quaked against Day's outthrust hand, and it wasn't the orange cat that had frightened him. The specter remained, insubstantial and colorless. Unfettered by feet, she floated.

Impossible, but his mam had raised no fleering fool. She'd called it unwise to deny the existence of fairies, pixies or ghosts. Weak humans shouldn't be insulting such as them.

The phantom's eyes—smudged grass-green against the pale—fixed him with coquettish confidence.

"I've been 'easy, now, love'd by men who'd make your smooth Cornish tongue sound like a bucketful of rocks. The name is Rose and if you can't keep your behavior proper, I'll be takin' your soul with me when I go!"

"Truth to tell, uh, Rose—" Day broke off. Moll had called her mother by that name. With all the trouble *living* mums caused a lad, he sure wouldn't cross a maternal ghost. "—ma'am, I've never had a virgin." There. He'd bared his soul in a confession no one else had heard. "That was only the sort of bluster a man says to have on the fellows."

"I'll tell you, lad, the first time's not the best." For an instant her green eyes vanished, as if closing to savor a memory.

"Aye?" Day gripped the underside of Moll's table. It felt real enough. Rough-hewn, hammered together quickly. Nothing dreamy about that bent nail cutting the pad of his thumb. Damn, but it felt real. And the creature looked real.

When her eyes opened again, filled with a sultry light that made his guts grab, Day wished Methodists crossed themselves for protection. He did it anyway, just to be safe, and she smiled.

"It's the second time you come together . . . the girl knows the worst he'll do to her is nothing compared to the love . . . the lad's rod is like an axe handle, and, he's convinced he knows the way of it. . . ."

She was a lusty one, this ghost. His knees wobbled from her talk. In life she must have been—

"I was, but my Moll's not. Do you have that?"

"Aye." Moll's mother. She'd said it out. The ghost *was* Moll's mother!

"Swear to me now. You'll marry my girl before you have her."

Day swallowed as if his throat had swollen from gulping thistles. He held his word dear. Yet what would it matter, making a vow to a nightmare?

"Swear to me, lad, and no changing your mind."

"I swear that if I have Molly, I'll marry her."

The words' echo woke him. That or the tap of paws as the marmalade puss vaulted down to the floor. Either way, the specter vanished in a swirl of smug laughter, and that just couldn't have been real.

Molly crossed her arms on the top fence rail and perched her chin atop then, watching Day ignore her.

She'd slid down from Richard's gray half an hour ago. She'd told him nothing, and told herself she wanted to walk the rest of the way home to sort out her thoughts. In fact, she wanted to be alone with Day. But he was enthralled by her horse.

Day petted Glory, coaxed her, fed her tidbits from his pocket and spared Molly nothing but a frown and a stifling hand gesture when her return startled the filly. So much for taking the measure of a man. She'd been foolish enough to imagine she'd finding him brooding over the dangers of Chinatown.

His shirt fluttered back from his tanned throat as he strolled, humming, toward Molly. Whenever she'd seen him in town, his stride had verged on a run. Energy had packed his muscles, as if he strained against leisure. Now he sauntered and Glory trailed him, like a pup.

Molly pushed her sleeves down and his eyes swung her way.

"I see McCabe came." She waved toward the avalanche of goods on the porch.

Day nodded as he drew near. Glory followed, hooves stuttering in uneasiness as her ears flicked toward Molly.

"McCabe's not much for conversation, is he?" She prodded him for a response, but none came. "Deborah's husband Michael always said McCabe didn't need to talk. McCabe likes fighting and he's too big to be beaten by any man in town."

She might have been humming a tune, rather than doubting his skill as a pugilist. Day looked unruffled as he drew abreast of her, then walked past. Enough. She couldn't resist taunting him.

"Don't you want to know what happened?"

Glory shied and snorted. Bolting for the wooded end of the corral, she left Day in a shower of grit. Day snatched off his black hat as if it had offended him. He studied it before storming her way, his usual stride restored.

"Aye, I'd just love to know."

Day's voice quaked, explosive in a way she'd never heard. His blue eyes glared from a face dark with exertion and dust. When he leaned on the rail, hands bracketing her elbows, he smelled of horse.

"I'm crazy to know, dying to know."

To Molly, Day looked unduly flushed.

"I'm not soothed by fancying you in a place where knives and broken necks are the order of things."

Though experience with human bodies told Molly it was quite impossible for angry heat to radiate from Day, it seemed to.

She must hold her ground, raise her chin from her arms and keep her feet planted, even though her breastbone curled away from the threat of him.

His intensity made no sense. A daintier sort of female might have swooned. She refused to give him an inch; she'd faced angrier men and stared them down. She concentrated on the smell of the sage that Glory had crushed. She listened to the scrape of Day's fingers on the underside of the rail. And, since their noses weren't a rolling pin's width apart, she stared at clusters of gray, starbursts of light, centered in his blue eyes.

Day looked away first. He pushed off the rail and matched his fingertips together, as if praying.

"I want every detail, Molly." His hands shifted to the top of the rail. "But I'm trying to gentle this filly of yours. That trailing she was doing? Following after me? That's what I've worked toward, for—"

"Why are you angry? I don't want to fight with you."

Day paused. The weather lines at his eyes tightened. He squinted at the sun and ignored her question.

"—for three hours. Now, keep your voice lamby soft, and explain why the hell it took you so long." He recommenced walking.

In Chinatown, a shutter hanging on one hinge had creaked in the breeze and chickens had scratched as she called out for Kee. "But no one came."

Day sat in the middle of the corral, feigning interest in his boot heel. Glory stood a dozen feet off, ears pricked toward the chirr of a cicada.

"I don't even know her name, but the waste of it, Day."

Except for the cribs, Chinatown was her favorite part of Virginia City. The houses were neat and people kept to themselves. Women cut pork into drying strips, while old men smoked long-stemmed pipes in the sunshine, setting children to swish away flies.

Molly rubbed her neck at a sudden cascade of chills. Day watched, impatient for her to go on. "The girl with the knife—China Mary—Kee said her son would gather wood for me.

"Two donkey loads of wood, he said, and whoever left her brought it. I can't imagine we didn't hear it."

Day shook his head. If he'd slept in her corral, he would have heard. Had the wood been there yesterday, when she'd meandered home in a lovesick haze from kite-flying?

"It's the sort of thing Kee would do, keeping the promise, but sending some kind of message."

Molly explained how she'd argued with Merrick, then given in. Only Molly's black shawl, which she'd spread to separate China Mary from the ground, marked Molly's protest at the lack of investigation and arrest.

Now Molly slammed her fist against her thigh, furious at her confusion. She looked to Day. For all his joking bluster, Day was a canny reader of people. Did he think the woman had been murdered? By Favor's order? Was this the encore to Poppy's "accident"?

Mercy, what made her stand here, wondering? She should be making Margaret's tincture, gathering willow slips or weeding those pitiful pumpkins. Instead she watched Day, slumped and lazy, but intent as a predator. With nothing but his will, he was reeling in that filly, just as he was reeling in her heart.

Oh, fiddle. Poppy would be home soon enough. Molly should paw through McCabe's delivery and plan dinner.

Day's low voice ran like a brook as he stood close to the filly, leaning against her shoulder, like another horse.

Molly smiled at the two of them, drowsily cocked together, eyelids drooping: the handsomest man in the West, playing bedfellow to a sleepy horse.

Before she could lose her nerve, Molly hurried across the yard, scooped a dipperful of cold water and returned. She stood on the bottom fence rail and reached over the top, offering the water. Day wasn't asleep.

His hand slid lazily along Glory's withers, down her back and ended with a pat on her rump.

If Day came to her, she'd touch him. He'd said she could.

She saw him take the first step her way, and missed the rest. Suddenly he was there. She didn't release the dipper as his hand surrounded the cup of it, drinking, his eyes shaded black by his hat. When he stopped drinking, the dipper dangled in her fingers.

She dropped it. Daring herself, she touched a water bead on his sun-rough lip. As she did, his tongue licked out to collect that last drop. They both laughed, then stopped.

He stood so near, his shirt might snag on the log rails. She'd do it. What'd she'd wanted to do for weeks. He'd said she could.

As if she wore a lead bracelet, she lifted her hand and let her thumb move along the red-brown line of his jaw.

"I'm dirty." His chest swelled fuller with each breath. "I've been sleeping in the corral, working your horse."

He'd shaved while she was gone, and his skin felt smooth against the hard bone of his jaw. How intimate to have a man shave in your house and then worry that he was dirty.

"I don't care."

She could hardly believe she'd said the words, but she felt their impact, saw him tense, alert. Molly took her hand from his face and said it again. "I don't care, Day."

In the shade of his black hat, his eyes moved, scouring her face. He kept his promise. He didn't climb over the fence to her, didn't grab her wrist, didn't reach through to touch her waist.

Molly leaned forward, measuring, though embarrassment dragged at her. "Day?"

"Aye?" Teasing danced in his words, though he kept a sober face.

"Can I kiss you?"

"Aye." He took off the hat and held it behind his back.

"But I can't reach."

He stepped closer, pressing his shirtfront against the top rail, just as she'd imagined. He loomed above her. "Better?"

"You're not going to make this easy, are you?"

"What would be the fun in that?"

Her lips reached his, butted against them unsteadily, then held as her hands clung to the fence.

She pursed her lips, kissing him as she kissed the crown of Poppy's head each night. It felt wrong.

Mind whirling, thoughts shooting off like sparks, she tried to assemble what she knew of kissing. Nothing. She pressed forward, matching her mouth to his.

When Day's lips opened, *opened*, then pressed back, she uttered a rising sound of understanding and would have fallen if she hadn't grabbed the top rail tighter. He kept his promise, but Day's mouth . . . What he was doing transfixed her.

His tongue touched her top lip, inside, and the fence rail groaned under Day's grip and Molly heard her own gasp.

He murmured, "Molly," against her lips, and the wonder in his voice made her keep kissing. "Molly, girl."

Beneath her fingers, she felt his jaw muscle bulge as if he were in pain. Molly pulled back to look at him. His half-lidded eyes were dark and heavy with something like anger. It quickly turned to fear—as real as if he'd seen a ghost.

Molly settled on her feet. "You said I could touch you."

"Aye. Anytime. It's all right. *Anytime*, Moll."

"You're angry." All her joyous churning stopped.

"Mad, perhaps, Not angry." His voice shook, as it might with laughter, but no way on earth was the man was joking.

He lunged at the fence and climbed over. "Shall I cut that wood for you?" His voice was matter-of-fact as he strode to the woodpile. "Look down the hill. Poppy and Margaret, isn't it? You'll need wood for the stove."

"Oh no! I invited her for dinner! I forgot." Molly squinted down the hillside and saw nothing. Pray God he was hallucinating.

Day tore off his shirt. A button caught. Blue cotton ripped, but he let it fall as he took up the ax. For a moment, he stared at it, as if it were a snake, then he gripped. The ax's head glittered in a murderous arc as he struck off five rounds of the largest log.

"Those are too big."

"You'll get your bloody wood, and it will bloody well fit your stove."

So, Day wanted to fight. Perhaps food would settle him. She felt a raging hunger herself. "Do you want to stay for dinner?"

Already Day's shoulders and ribs gleamed with sweat. It slicked the contours of his torso, and she didn't find the effect offensive. He looked like an Indian brave, bare-chested, his black hair pasted on his forehead and curled wet against his neck.

He stopped chopping, shoulders canted toward the arm with the ax. His expression was not kind.

"I think I'll pass up the invitation, m'Bright."

He fell to hacking as Poppy crested the hill. Margaret came along just behind, her hat held tight with one hand.

Molly looked back at Day, saw wind picking at his hair and hoped it cooled him.

Turning to the canned goods, she selected tinned beef and peaches to serve with Poppy's biscuits and Deborah's honey.

"Day?" Molly caught the doorframe before bolting inside. Considering his aggressive state of mind, it might be unwise to speak. "I told Lin—since Kee lets her go to the Black Dog for customers—I said she could pass messages to me, through you."

Day grimaced before hefting the ax again.

"Wonderful, m'Bright." The ax crashed hard enough to split the maul as well as the wood.

"Tanglin' with the Chines tongs, is it? Ah, Moll, you're a girl who always leaves me somethin' to look forward to."

Chapter
Twenty

Day yawned as he left Shambles. He hadn't slept one peaceful hour since that nightmare. He'd just swallowed a sip of scalding coffee from the tin cup when he beheld a sight nearly as worrisome as the she-ghost in Molly's kitchen.

"You're not set on turning me in and collecting the reward, are you, Abby?"

His old sweetheart, in an ice-blue gown and fashionably puffed hair, sent him a smirk that said he'd become a poor excuse for a desperado when she could track him down.

Shaking his head and grinning, Day settled on the big gray rock he'd come to think of as his. Stiff brocade belled out as Abby perched beside him. With the ease of old intimacy, she took his cup, drank, and watched him over the rim.

"You wore shiny spurs when you were Lightfoot." She kicked a slipper at his naked boots. "I used to hear them ringing down the hallway to my room and I remember thinking there was at least one good thing about being a whore."

Pride, pity or some other feeling a man on the run ought not to indulge made Day kiss her. Abby let him, then pulled the poster from her reticule and tapped it on his chest.

"The reward's not big enough to interest me, Lightfoot. I'm here to save your silly ass."

But first she accused him of breaking his own rule.

"Do you remember, about this time last year, I asked where I could find you if I felt the desire for a late supper, some night? Remember what you said?" She raised her eyebrows and mimicked his response in a strained baritone. " 'Ma'am, in my line of work, it's not smart to have habits.' "

"I didn't say 'ma'am.' "

"Maybe it was 'love.' You always were my sweetest man." She tipped her moon-blond hair against his shoulder and followed his gaze toward Chinatown.

Day could blame this habit on Moll. He'd started taking breakfast on this rock overlooking Chinatown, watching for Favor. So far, he'd witnessed nothing but twists of smoke and far foreign voices reminding him of fishermen shoving off on the early tide. But he liked daybreak in the red-light district. The street's earliest visitor was Poppy, making deliveries. Today, with luck, she'd run out of bread and go home, instead of showing up to trudge beside him as he set off to school Moll's filly.

He'd spent a week gentling Glory, skimming his hands over her back, down her legs, sighing his breath in her nostrils so she'd know him even in the dark. A hastier man would have snubbed her to a post and broke her to saddle in a day.

He'd gentled Molly the same way. He had but one chance to get it right, so he'd let her come to him, talk to him, touch him quick as fairy wings as she offered a midday sandwich. There'd been no kisses since that day at the fence rail, but he felt them brewing. How could he explain Abby?

Then again, she might understand better than he had. Maybe he wasn't staying for Molly alone. Maybe he was

Lightfoot O'Deigh, a violent man waiting for the showdown to come to him.

"You want me to read that to you?" Abby bumped her shoulder against Day's, reminding him he sat staring at the poster.

It resembled the one he'd had from Persia. Only luck had kept him free; the likeness was that close.

"You rode the stage from Carson to save me, Abby?" Her loyalty humbled him, while her taunting smile made something rise up in him. Abby gloried in courting trouble. She knew him as a dangerous man. Not a cat salesman.

"I came to warn you, and not about that bounty." She dismissed the manhunter with a wrinkled nose. "Rankin's hired Pinkerton's agency to find you. Keep an eye cocked for 'Detective E. V. Bragg.'" Abby strung out the name to mock it, and Day pictured a bespectacled beanpole of a man.

"Bragg has a list of every gun you've worn, every horse you've ridden, every man you've tracked, and every woman you've been with—as Lightfoot. Luckily everyone mentions that red stallion and black beard." Abby stroked his cheek, lamenting its clean-shaven state with her gesture.

"Rankin's set on seeing you swing. And even skittish as you are about plans, I think you'd better make one."

Before he could make excuses, Abby frowned past his shoulder.

"Hell, honey, we've just run out of time." Abby waved at a woman who marched toward them as if she were leading a regiment.

Abby snatched the poster and fanned herself with it. Day rubbed his forehead, trying to fathom Abby's giddy performance.

"—better accommodations than that canvas-walled boarding house. Shambles is at least clean. Miss Claret thinks much of you, and Georgia would rather kiss your elbow than the Pope's ring!"

The girl spared Abby an unblinking stare. Who in hell was she?

"I fear the same can't be said for Mr. Day's landlady, Elizabeth Thomas." She faced him, then. "Though you paid quick enough, she finds your manners wanting, Mr. Day."

"Detective Bragg," Abby seemed to address the young woman. How could that be? "As you've guessed, this is Mr. Day."

For a little girl dressed in a grown woman's clothing, she had a nasty tongue. From a distance, he'd thought her tall, but she didn't reach his armpit. In a mannish suit the color of coffee grounds, she studied his face as if preparing to mark it off in inches. Only the spill of white lace below her chin kept him from taking her for a boy.

Abby squeezed Day's arm.

"Detective—?" Day's incredulity winced under Abby's pinch.

"E. V. Bragg." She extended a gloved hand to take his, but her fingers' tough grip couldn't reach halfway around his.

Fear flowed out of Day. Muddling her shouldn't take long, and her departure would assure his safety in Virginia City. He felt indulgent as Miss Bragg took paper and a pencil from her reticule. If she represented Pinkerton's high-flown detectives, the agency would be the flash in the pan most had predicted.

"I need to ask some questions, due to your striking resemblance to the murderer Lightfoot O'Deigh."

When the lurch of surprise receded, Day answered.

"We could step into the parlor." His arm swept toward Shambles, before noting her horrified expression. "Of course, Mrs. Green has a restaurant down the street. That might be better."

"I'm quite comfortable interviewing you here. If you feel too much the object of public scrutiny, you might tell folks I'm a reporter for the *Territorial Enterprise*."

Miss Bragg didn't seem to be joking. He nodded for her to continue.

She asked where he'd lived before Virginia City, how he'd earned his living and how long he'd been employed. Her fingers tightened on the pencil as she asked if he had personal knowledge of a prostitute named Shawnee Sue and where he'd been the afternoon of August 10, 1861. She sighed when he swore there were citizens of good character who'd verify his whereabouts and moral uprightness.

Wordy as she was, little Miss Bragg could not coax truth from a practiced liar. Still, she appeared pleased with her inquisition, as she closed pencil and paper inside her battered velvet reticule.

"I think that will be all, Mr. Day. I'll be in Virginia City until tomorrow. If I require more answers, may I ask for you at the Black Dog saloon?"

"Aye, miss. But since you're a lady—"

"In my occupation, I expect no concessions for gender." Flushing, she tugged up her gloves and turned to go. "Oh, Mr. Day?"

The little thing blinked her auburn eyelashes and he figured she was fixing to ask where she could get a glass of fresh milk. Day restrained his urge to pat her frail shoulder.

"Yes, Miss Bragg?"

"Can you think why someone would contact our Sacramento City office, refuse all rewards and suggest you as a murderer?"

Day's amusement froze, not at her words, but at the stiff precision with which Miss Bragg aimed her reticule.

"Pardon me, Detective. Would you be carryin' a *gun* in your bag, there?"

It could only be a derringer. A sneaky cardsharp's weapon. Still and all, it punched a nasty hole.

"Please answer my question, Mr. Day. It's unnecessary to involve Sheriff Merrick, don't you agree?"

"Aye." He cast about for an answer. Who? Persia's girls would want the money, as would Persia herself. Griffin, for all that he was a gambler, wasn't underhanded. Deborah Green had no call to want him arrested and Brown Bess wasn't so imaginative.

He should have been looking over his shoulder, all along.

"I couldn't say *why*, miss, unless I knew *who*. And I'm sure you wouldn't be telling me."

"No, I wouldn't." She shrugged. "Good morning, Mr. Day, ma'am." She nodded her flat brown hat and left Day speechless.

"Know what my doorman Jeb said about her?" Abby asked. "Jeb, mind you, is a man with considerable *legal* experience. He said he wasn't a bit surprised to find out what she was, because she had the eyes of a hangin' judge—'cold as Billy Blue Hell.' "

Day agreed and thanked the Lord that Miss Bragg was too green to know she'd run him to ground. *Best sharpen up, Daywell. For a man who doesn't like surprises, you're fair inviting them.*

Day didn't *think* he'd kill anyone tonight, but he might. He'd suffered enough aggravation to make six men run amok.

The Black Dog swarmed with customers. A couple of mine bosses stood free drinks for anyone who could prove injury from a mine accident, and half the town's population stood about pulling up pant legs and opening shirtfronts to show burns and scars of varying age and gruesomeness.

"It's all about impressing Deideshomer—" explained Geordie. The short Cornishman had apparently swallowed the worst of his jealousy over Moll.

"Deidsheimer," corrected Arthur.

Day slammed two beer mugs down. If *he* were bloody Deidsheimer, he'd be rich and gone. The German was sharing his cross-timbering plan to make mines safer, teaching it to all and not taking a penny. Instead of making himself rich, he'd signed on as manager at the Ophir. Hence the celebration. Day flat wasn't up to it.

Hacking Moll's wood into a hundred stove lengths hadn't defused Day's fury. Abby had left him feeling like a eunuch. She'd meant no harm, coming to "save" him, then remarking on his lack of spurs and his predictability and stroking his bare boy's face. Nor could he blame Glory for refusing the bit and kicking him in the kneecap when his attention wandered after Moll as she passed by, silent as a swan. And since this dry desert had no wee folk to chide—he wondered whose tiny voice had been nagging him to do right by Molly when he hadn't had a chance to do her wrong!

Day twisted the bar towel tight enough for a garrote. He'd

never been one for pumping his troubles into a woman's body, but he should have taken Georgia's offer and done just that before washing up for work. His juices were by God on the boil.

In this bar alone, he saw half-a-dozen men who wanted a beating. McCabe, that lumbering pig-eyed freighter, was foremost among them. He stared, stood too close, spilled a drink and motioned Day to mop up. There was Sheriff Merrick, too, and Richard Griffin, sitting in the corner, sporting a lazy grin.

Griffin and Merrick had faced Moll's enemies. Day wrung out a rag as if wringing their necks. If he was half the man he'd been before laying eyes on Moll, he'd flog them all senseless, then castrate leering VanBrunt and throw Cuttin' Jack's maiming into the bargain, just because the barber was drunk.

"Now, I know"—Cuttin' Jack addressed VanBrunt, who nodded until his yellow hair flapped—"that the witch is after my customers. I don't like it, but I know." He waited for his eyes to roll back into position. "Brown Bess, though, I wish the witch'd take *her* off my hands, 'cause that cow ain't never gettin' well."

Jack must be a pure comfort to his patients. Day kicked an empty beer barrel out of his path. Stag, who'd sat drinking with single-minded devotion, his back propped against the wall, upended the barrel and used it for a stool.

Day longed for the sea, the range, anyplace beyond this smoky town where the stamp mill pounded out every minute lost.

"Cousin, can you disappear for a quarter hour?" Arthur stroked his burgeoning mustache with affection.

"No chance, cousin," Day answered.

"We're heading up hill to take in a bit o' witch theater." Geordie nodded at the men gathered near the saloon doors.

"I've gone, myself, but I'm ashamed of it." Day felt guilt twist in him. "Give the girl a bit of privacy. Quit spyin' on her!"

"That's not it at all—" At Geordie's injured bawl, Mc-

Cabe sensed a fight and lumbered closer. "We're just watching—"

"Stay away from the witch, pup." McCabe thumped Geordie's breastbone with the heel of one meaty hand. "She's my property."

Day's fists clenched at his sides. "McCabe, I was raised believin' whiskey made fools, not liars, but I'm thinkin' I've somethin' to write home about, seein' I've met a man who proves it's not true."

"Why, I thought you was deef and dumb!" McCabe shouldered past Geordie. "You're just one of them fancy-talkin' Irish fellas."

Day felt his neck swell as the freighter pounded his mug on the bar.

"Not Irish—" Geordie's voice soared, and he tried to elbow back to his space at the bar.

"Shut up." McCabe backhanded Geordie to his knees.

VanBrunt and Cuttin' Jack jostled closer, eager to watch punches fly as long as they flew in another's direction.

"I'm talking to *him*." Seeing he had an audience, McCabe stabbed a finger into Day's chest.

Before he withdrew it, Day felt the dark calm descend. His focus centered as if he still wore a gun belt. "Stag, step back here, will you, lad? Tend bar a moment?"

Day didn't look to see if Stag obeyed. He watched space open around McCabe.

"Miss Persia's not likin' a lot of rough play in her saloon." Day gave McCabe an excuse to back down. He wouldn't. There was blood in his eye and Day was spoiling for a splash of it. But McCabe was big. Broad as the giant of Carn Galva, but not near as sweet. The trick would be to get in, stick him and get out.

"Next you'll be threatin' me with Pete." McCabe jeered and nodded toward the buffalo gun before forcing Arthur and a stomach-clutching Geordie onto his side. "You know why he won't go with you, up to the witch's, don't you, boys?"

"Don't listen." Day knew what the sot was trying.

"He doesn't peek at her from up on the hill, now. He's the young stud horse the witch picked out to service her—"

Day's arm snapped a twisting punch to McCabe's belly. His slamming fist made the freighter's head snap back, opening up the jaw. Jesus! A jaw like a rock! First Day's knuckles went numb, then his arm and his shoulder. The mistake and a slippery puddle of beer let McCabe catch him in a bear hug.

What had happened to bloody Lightfoot? His hot lungs couldn't suck a breath. He turned toward the crook of Mc-Cabe's arm to breathe, then jabbed with his left, since it was all he had loose. Merciful God, there went a rib.

Day levered a thumb into McCabe's eye and dug deep. The freighter reared back, roaring. He didn't let go, but loosened enough that Day's breath returned with an explosive rush. That gave Day air enough to slam his forehead against the giant's vulnerable nose. Shouts dinned around them, cowardly VanBrunt's loudest of all. As blood rained from McCabe, the freighter let go to grab his own face.

Stick and move. Day punched the hands covering Mc-Cabe's bleeding nose. The freighter tossed his head like a wounded bull.

"Stand and fight like a man." McCabe's shout was muffled by the forearm clearing his blood-wet mouth.

McCabe wheeled after Day, countering with a rush that would have snapped Day's spine against the bar if he hadn't sidestepped. Persia's bar shuddered beneath McCabe's bulk.

"Stand still. I didn't come here to dance." McCabe cradled the hand he'd crushed with his own weight.

As if she'd felt the assault on her prized mahogany, Persia appeared at the head of the stairs leading down to Shambles.

"Hell to pay." The voice might have been Griffin's.

"Why didn't you use Pete?" Swaths of gypsy purple slashed behind Persia. Her hands smoothed over the bar top. She bent, her fingers searching for scratches. "Huh? Why didn't you shoot him?"

Day sniffed. He hadn't taken one in the nose, but he felt

each breath in his ribs. Maybe McCabe had only bruised him.

"Why?" Persia's teeth showed as she snapped the question.

Abashed by Persia's fury, McCabe ducked his head and wiped his nose in a move that smeared his cheek red. "I didn't break any windows." McCabe coughed and spat.

"Out!"

The freighter's final crudeness, paired with VanBrunt's guffaw, pushed her over the edge, but Day noticed Persia included him in her banishing gesture.

"Out! You. You can serve drinks." She pointed out befuddled Deidsheimer, who settled his spectacles and wet his lips. "Get behind the bar and use Pete if you have to!" Then she wheeled on Day. "I thought you—"

Day clamped his hand around the wrist behind Persia's accusing finger. He lowered it to her side.

"Am I fired?" Cold dark calm washed back over him. "Because if I'm fired, there's a bit more business I'm attendin' to."

Feet scuffled as men scattered. Did so many wager they'd be part of his unfinished business? With McCabe gone, he turned to VanBrunt. Day's blood was up and he was by God ready to punish VanBrunt for his evil leering after Poppy.

"Take it outside!" Persia railed. "No pay tonight and— just talk to me tomorrow!"

Day caught VanBrunt at the swinging doors and rushed him along with a shove. It hurled him past the boardwalk and landed him in a sprawl on the torchlit street. "I'll thank you to leave that little girl alone!"

The vile coward wouldn't even stand. Instead, VanBrunt kicked at Day's feet from where he'd landed, panting. "I haven't done anything!"

"I've seen y'fondlin' her in the street." Day pointed toward VanBrunt's store.

Since a pack of men had followed the fight outside, Day stopped talking. He could finish this without sharing Poppy's shame with the whole town. He stepped closer, knocking VanBrunt's shoulder with his knee, begging him to fight.

VanBrunt lurched up, tossing the hair from his eyes. "I can do whatever I want." Saliva slicked VanBrunt's lips. "She's mine."

Day grabbed each side of VanBrunt's collar, shaking until the man's teeth cracked together. "Poppy's not"—Day shook again—"bloody *yours*, so keep your hands off her!" He sent VanBrunt spinning.

Back in the dust, VanBrunt rose on his elbow and Stag closed in, arm cocked. There'd be no shortage of men to ram VanBrunt's teeth down his throat, but Day couldn't walk away. He had poised to fall on VanBrunt and beat his thick skull into the ground, when Griffin stopped him.

"Save it." Griffin released Day's elbow when he jerked against the restraint. "Save it for Rankin." Griffin's voice fell to a whisper. "He'll be here Friday."

"Rankin?" Day steadied himself on the gambler's shoulder.

"Favor, you know. Rankin's his real name." Griffin edged Day away from the men circling VanBrunt. In their beer-soaked numbers they were brave.

"Friday for the race, he'll be here. I overheard *him*"— Griffin's head jerked toward VanBrunt—"talking it up, like it was a personal coup."

Favor, who'd hurt Molly. Rankin, who'd framed him. They were the same man. What could he do?

Day fingered his damaged ribs, hoping it would hurt. After this brawl, Merrick and the Pinkerton would know "Day" for who he was. Time to run. No time to tell Moll to be careful.

VanBrunt scuttled away, as if his burly carcass were invisible. Stag grabbed him—back of the collar and seat of the pants—and swung VanBrunt's head into the watering trough. Whatever the action cost Stag's mending leg seemed to be worth it. The young miner gloated, shaking his fist.

Wind kicked up, tearing the words out of VanBrunt's whimpering as he fled.

Favor. If he wanted to fight Molly's monster, he must be

here Friday. Rankin had respectable credentials. He'd impress Merrick. If Day wanted to live, he'd be long gone by Friday.

Molly. Day walked toward Shambles. He'd get his guns and go. He snagged the reins of a buckskin horse freed during the commotion. It didn't matter whose horse. He'd get his guns and ride up to Moll's. Day swung onto the buckskin. He touched it into a gallop.

Every bit of the darkness and fight had settled low in him. *Molly*.

Chapter
Twenty-one

Fountains of flame cracked the black sky, spewing molten fragments of wood as Molly let fly another armload.

So, Day wanted to buy her with his labor. He thought to strike a bargain with sweet consideration instead of coin. Molly shaded her eyes against the fire's yellow glare. How, when every minute of her life had warned against him, had she still come so close to falling?

For days he'd worked with Glory. For hours he'd cut, chopped and split this dear-bought wood, which might have warmed her through the winter. Instead, it lit the autumn night and sprays of sparks cascaded about her wind-wild hair. Let it burn!

Hot sap popped and spat, sending Cinder into snarls, but Poppy slept on. No matter that Poppy had set the match to Molly's fury, had innocently revealed Day was just what Molly had feared. Worse than a charlatan, worse than a liar.

She picked up a branch and slung it into the blaze. Flames reached above her head now. She gazed up to their towering radiance, holding back her hair as the wind blew, heedless of the skirts she offered to the fire.

At dawn, Poppy had seen Day sitting outside Shambles with a silver-haired lady in his arms. Poppy had confided it as they walked to the river to do laundry. Could Molly picture that?

Only as well as she pictured that traitor's kiss. Pain grabbed her heart and twisted, now as it had then. *Lady*. Molly knew only one silver-haired lady, that regal creature from Carson City, the soiled dove whose gaze had combed over Day with the look of a lover. As Molly imagined them together, she'd knelt side-by-side with Poppy, scrubbing a tablecloth cleaner than it had been in years.

At Shambles. In the morning. Oh, she'd begged Poppy for more misery while she hung her clothes and concentrated on the hot October wind skimming her belly, where her mismatched laundry-day basque gapped above her skirt.

Didn't Moll know Day lived there now, at Shambles? Oh, he'd left Brown Bess's a long, long time ago.

Making dinner, Molly tried to excuse Day's lodging as a condition of his employment. Later, brushing out Poppy's hair and loosing her own, she'd told herself it was possible that Day remained chaste, keeping shyly to himself in Persia's brothel . . .

Oh, *yes*! A man like Day, living innocently among whores. A man who turned pallid Margaret Bride flush with desire. A man who made loyal Deborah consider adultery. A man who took untouchable Molly Gallagher and made her feel lust. Oh, certainly.

And what if that cold-eyed detective had actually been a cast-off mistress? That would explain her improper question, asking if Molly had *consorted* with the man!

Cinder's growls escalated into harsh barking. Stiff-legged, he stared behind her.

Fire illuminated Day's leg, swinging free of a horse's back. It gilded the jut of a spur on his boot and painted his face devil red.

"What in hell are you doing?" His voice cracked with the same impersonal heat as the blaze.

Molly struggled to lift the biggest log above her head. She launched it into the fire, stumbling back in a shower of sparks. He steadied her against falling, standing so near she felt the leather and metal, the gun on his hip. Guns, spurs, prostitutes!

"The scarcity of wood and my five days of work aside—"

His lilting tone was to blame, a voice that had cajoled her into friendship. Almost, trust.

"—this fire is way too big, m'Bright. It could jump to your little cottage—"

"Get out of here!" He should be riding away instead of playing at concern. Murder, the detective had said. They'd hang him if they found him, and Molly would be damned if she'd load his death on her conscience! "Isn't it bad enough you haunt me all day?" She shouted over the flames. "Night brings the only privacy I get!"

Using that trick of tilting his head forward, so his hat shaded his face, Day tried to hide, but his eyelashes lowered with pity. If it hadn't meant touching his face, taking the chance her fingers would linger instead of punish, she would have slapped him.

Did he think her selfish, vanishing each night into the cool, unjudging darkness? Why shouldn't she crave relief from sickness, from the critical stares of Eleanor and Brown Bess? Why shouldn't she try to escape from predatory men who waited, watching her on the street, licking their lips, watching for her to slip into the hellish morass where her mother had floundered? And she would not feel guilty for taking an hour's peace from her sister's simple questions and unwitting hurtfulness.

"Where's Poppy?" Day raised his voice over the hot wind that seemed to speak from the fire.

"Inside, asleep—"

He didn't let her finish before he pushed. "Step around here."

Day's hand nudged her waist. He didn't wear gloves and his bare thumb touched skin as he nodded her around the back of the house. Glory's nicker floated down at the sound of his voice. He'd been seducing them both.

"Is this it, then?" Molly grabbed Day's wrist, holding his hand there, against her flesh, so he couldn't deny the touch. "My noble cat man. 'I won't touch you, Molly!' Now, I'm finally invited to step around back and sample what you've being lavishing on Persia's girls! That's it, is it?"

"Molly, I've given you no reason to say that." Day frowned.

She hesitated, wanting to swallow her venomous words. Oh, he was good at this, just as good as he was at weaving lies to hoodwink unwary miners. And she was weak, following that pressure on her skin. As if she hoped it was true.

"Molly, they watch you."

As if the fire's rushing wind obeyed him, it hushed.

"When you let down your hair and walk with the cats, at night, they sit over there." He gestured toward the hillside across the road, and she knew he'd joined them. "They sit still as if they were at a play, at *church*, and they call it witch theater." He waited.

"So, you won't leave me a thing, when you go." Molly felt her face tug into a grim smile. He heard the trap in her words and watched her as he would something wild. "How amusing it must have been! Me on display, singin' to the cats, as if Crazy Rose had come back to Virginia City." She spread her arms and bowed to the dancing fire. "Only this time it's Mad Molly! Well, I'd best give the boys something to watch."

Should she unbutton her blouse and dance? Lift her skirts and kick her toes at the stars? Damn them all! Molly searched for something else to burn, refusing to give tears for his betrayal.

"Molly, don't do this." His hands moved as if he'd stop her from flinging handfuls of kindling into the fire. "They're not watching, not tonight."

He'd soured the best of her memories. Molly stared into the flames, reliving the night she'd delivered her first baby. She'd pirouetted, spinning her skirts wide as they'd go, bowing to the moon, blessing her own glorious skill, singing until her throat was sore. Had they watched? Breathless with humiliation, she knew.

"Well, what a shame they'll miss the grand bonfire!" Molly wrenched her gaze from the flames. Day's hands hovered inches above her shoulders. She moved toward him, nudging her body against his. "And the seduction of Red Molly?" The throaty taunt couldn't be hers. "Will they miss that, too?"

Was she staging a fight to the death? Was she driving him away forever or trying to make him stay? Molly stood, the front of her body grazing his, when what she wanted was to wring her hands, rip her hair, fall on her knees.

"Molly, I don't know what to do about you." His eyes scanned her from eyebrows to lips. "I don't want you feeling like this!"

"Like what?" She denied her loss, wishing tears could turn her voice to acid. "Feeling like what, Day?"

"Sweet Molly." His hand caught her first tear as he smoothed her hair back from her face. "Tell me what I can do."

He was stubborn, leading her toward the back of the house. Just in case he was wrong, in case someone was watching. And she followed.

She stopped when they stood beyond view.

"Tell me." Molly fought her voice level and stood facing him, taking both his hands in hers. If he lied, she'd feel it through his hands. "Tell me Poppy was wrong about seeing you—with that woman from Carson City."

The shadow of her house couldn't hide the shake of his head.

"Then tell me that detective is wrong." She gripped harder as his hands closed around her fingers. "Tell me you're not a murderer. That the man with the black beard isn't you."

He opened his hands and let her go.

Molly backed toward the door. A killer, he wouldn't even deny being a killer!

"And you're living in that place." She came back to shove him in the chest, pleading for him to hurt her in a way she could salve and bandage. "With those women!" Molly grabbed his shirt. "Kissing them? Like you kiss me?"

"Never, Moll. Never, like you." He closed in darkness, covering her against the wall of the house. Day pulled her arms around his waist, then pressed against her. The gun creaked in its leather holster as her shoulder blades flattened against the wall. He kissed her hard, taking her mouth without gentle preliminaries.

Dizzied, she felt him whirl her away from the wall, pulling her against the front of him. *God, he knows, knows what it's like when I'm trapped.*

His hand was in her hair, winding full of it, pulling her head back to kiss her neck above the high black collar. So savage, except that she wasn't scared. She molded to him, lifting her lips to kiss him. Then she held her mouth quiet against his and he began a gentle invasion.

He slanted his mouth over hers. With each stroke of his tongue, his hands feathered her waist, touching skin where her basque gapped away. He hesitated—to think? To breathe?

She pulled back, drawing breath of her own. As if air gave her bravery, she twisted her shoulders apart from Day's. But then his hands smoothed back and forth, memorizing the skin he could reach beneath the tight garment, and she didn't go.

"Moll." His lips brushed the hair over her ear. "I don't know what's right and what's wrong, with you."

Warmth hammered through her arms and legs. He lifted her hair away from her ear and she trembled.

"I'm having a hard time believing I know what you want from me."

"You know," she whispered, afraid he'd heard. Afraid he hadn't.

"Someone could be coming." His fingers worked at loosening the laces at the back of the basque.

His gentleness made her trust. "You said they wouldn't," she said.

"Last chance, Moll." He punctuated his words with kisses. "All this week—Hell, since I saw you walking down the street, the wind carrying your skirts like a queen's train, I've wanted this." His hands flowed inside the black material. "You asked the truth from me, Moll, and the truth is this: I'm a man, and I'll do whatever you let me."

Be scared. Back away. The voice came from all around her. *He's given you fair warning and it's too soon, too soon.*

"Moll, do you know what you do to me? What it's been like, waiting to touch you?" His fingers, secret beneath her basque, tightened as he pulled her roughly against him.

"Let go! Day, no."

His arms lifted. Molly rolled away from him, pressing her back against the house, so that she stood beside him. Fearful he'd bolt off into the night, she trapped one of his hands, forking her fingers through his.

She'd missed her last chance to stop five minutes ago. Day had warned her. He was a man. A man denied . . . what might he do?

He gave her humor, dark and sweet as his hands. Melodramatically, he rapped his skull against the house.

"Bloody hell, Molly. I'm a bit old for breakin' it off like that. But I gave y'my word."

She heard his teeth grind together. "I'm sorry."

"Some bloody stupid promise, don't you think?" As Day moved to stand in front of her, she heard the unfamiliar ring of his spurs. Was it the wind that painted her with gooseflesh as his hands smoothed the black linen basque down to meet her skirt? "I'll wait." He slung his arms loosely around her waist and rested his cheek on hers.

Cinder paced somewhere, toenails clicking rock. The bonfire's glare had faded to an amber stain on the night. Glory trotted up and down the fence, came to a pawing stop, and Molly felt Day's face move in a smile.

If they stood like this forever . . . the wind gusting past her house, held warm in his arms. Safe. Poppy inside, asleep . . . But one question still nibbled at her mind's edge.

"Why are you living there?" Molly thought he might pull away. He didn't.

"Why shouldn't I?"

She'd expected a taunt, not a question. She did her best to answer. "Because a man shouldn't live with a group of women. Especially women of low repute."

"Ask me not to, Moll. Jerk up that chin—as I've seen you do times enough to give me pause—and tell me not to."

"You're teasing me." She breathed a plea at his ear and felt him shiver. "Please don't live there, Day."

"Aye, I like that." He tugged her hips near, then put her away from him. "Now, *tell* me I'm not to live there."

"I j-just did!"

"No, m'Bright, y'merely asked."

"Day," she whispered urgently. "Do not live there, any more. Move into that palatial shack with Stag. Tomorrow."

"Good girl. I believe you're learning the way of it. Now, absolutely forbid me to live in that place."

Molly placed a palm on each side of his face, certain he was *doing* something here. She'd watched him make Glory beg for the bridle. Molly rubbed her lips over his.

"I surrender." He turned away, uttering an almost-inaudible, tuneless whistle. "You win. I'll move my gear tomorrow."

As if he'd recalled each of her demands for truth, he turned sober. "I don't know how long I'll stay, Moll. There are things you need to know."

"I don't want to hear."

"Aye, but the poster and all—"

"Day." She set three fingers against his lips.

Day kissed them and pulled away. "You'd have a right to be curious."

"Day, shut up."

He uttered a long-suffering sigh. "I'm afraid there's but one way to shut up a man like me, Molly girl, and you might be after practicin', because I feel a long, talkative spell comin' on, else."

Chapter
Twenty-two

Hair like hellfire and eyes like emerald smoke, he'd thought on that first day. Moll by firelight was more beautiful. And Molly in his arms, turning feverish sweet—for that Molly, Day knew he'd march into flames and call it Paradise.

Pummeled by McCabe's fists, Day had ached when he arrived at Moll's last night. But holding Moll had hurt better than anything he'd ever felt. So had pulling her against ribs he'd feared were broken and winding his battered hand in her hair.

This morning, his skull felt as if the stamp mill might've lodged inside. Day balanced his clothes parcel and rifle, barely smirking at the caterwauling beyond wine-haired Claret's door.

Day descended Shambles's stairs with clatter enough to rouse Persia. Given the uproar at the Black Dog, the "borrowed" horse and the wanted poster, he had no reason to be free or employed.

"You're lucky." In a flurry of paisley, Persia flapped a

current of musk and an unsealed letter in his face. She dismissed Day's excuses. "Take this and go. I'll expect you at sundown."

He took the page penned with flourishes, closed Shambles's door behind him and paused to read Abby's letter.

"'No man in hiding would make such a spectacle of himself,' quoth young Det. Bragg of your brawl, and so we are off to Carson, once more.

"Yours (you ever-lucky rogue), Abigail Fletcher."

Day hefted his belongings and trudged toward Moll's.

"I would venture to say"—Rose reclined on the red velvet love seat and gazed up at the marmalade cat perching on the curved backrest, ignoring her—*"that is, I would venture to say if anyone were listening, Ginger, that I've been patient long enough."*

Dawn hung just below the horizon and five long hours had passed since Molly had entered the cottage, her fingers touching her lips, to sigh her way toward bed. Perhaps a few more minutes. The girl truly didn't allow herself enough sleep.

Rose pointed her ghostly toes, extended them from beneath the hem of her white gown—a garment she roundly despised, by now—and skimmed her foot above the cat's fur. Bristling, Ginger pounced to the floor, settled under the love seat and recommenced her toilette with great forbearance.

She floated in to hover over the bed, taking care to direct her thoughts only at Moll. *Tell me.*

Rose took it as a measure of Moll's growing belief that her eyes stared wide only for an instant. Then she cuddled down into her quilts.

"Tell me!" When Poppy thrashed as if coming awake, Moll tossed her legs over the bedside, glared and staggered into the parlor. She collapsed on the love seat and let her head loll against the wall as if she'd drowse once more.

"When I saw that conflagration, I thought you meant to burn this house and me along with it!"

"Could that happen?" Molly swept one hand across her eyes.

"*I don't know.*" Rose studied her daughter's surly expression. "*And I'm sure you don't need to. All I've done is wake you, Moll. Sleep when you're old, and make the most of this lifetime!*"

That had the pretty child's eyes open. Though philosophizing didn't come natural to Rose, it guaranteed Moll's attention, and made a good deal less noise than shattering dishes.

"*Now, tell me, after you vanished around the edge of the cottage . . .*"

Moll stared with raised eyebrows.

"*. . . was he just the loveliest man for kissing?*"

"Mother!" Moll's stare jiggled into a gawk.

To give the girl time for the sputtering she seemed compelled to utter each time her mother broached the subject of romance, Rose floated down for a nose-to-nose study of Ginger. The old puss uttered a short meow and batted Rose's cheek.

"*Ginger could carry me about, if I knew the way of it, I'm certain. What do you think it would take, Moll?*"

"What I think is that you should quit spying on me!"

"*True.*" Rose wondered what it would take to stop her wavering between selfish desires and her children's welfare. "*I suppose if you're to entice the lad, you need a bit of privacy.*"

"Do you insist that I lie with him, Mother?" Molly stormed into the kitchen, drew a basin of water, quietly so she wouldn't wake Poppy, and took down a bar of soap. "Is that it?"

"*Only after you marry him.*" Rose vowed not to let this encounter rage beyond her control. "*Day'll protect you, Moll, like I can't. He'll keep you from working so hard. He'll—*"

"—be in jail!" Molly splashed handfuls of water into her face. "At best!"

"*What? What did you say?*"

"Or dead and buried, after they hang him." Water dripped off Molly's chin.

Rose tamped down her first evil thought. She would *not* accompany the dead desperado to his next wild range. She would *not* consider how to console him.

Molly's hands rubbed the soap with angry energy, building up lather before she glanced up and caught Rose's flicker of guilt.

"Oh, you'd like that, wouldn't you!" Molly's eyes blazed with enough jealousy to consume her good sense.

Rose moved away. She dearly hoped Moll wouldn't ram her through the table again. It had jarred her particles into tiny puzzle pieces which had taken days to reassemble.

"Enough, Molly."

"It wouldn't matter to you that I love him!" Her eyes glinted like green poison.

Rose's sigh shook the little cabin. The child had worked herself into such a state that she hadn't even heard the words she shouted. She needed a shock to set her right again.

"I never resorted to this before." Rose circled behind her dripping daughter. *"But then you were such an obedient child."*

"Mmmph!"

The bar of soap jammed slightly going past Moll's teeth, but Rose found that if she concentrated her energy on her hands, leaving the rest of her form to fade, she could build a satisfactory amount of suds in Molly's mouth.

When Molly wrenched away, she grabbed up a cloth and sprinted back to the parlor. Was the child laughing or crying?

Both. Molly slid down to the floor, still scrubbing the cloth at her lips as she leaned her head against the love seat.

"That was terrible." Molly sniffed. Daylight crept through the parlor window and Rose saw Moll's eyes were red as her lips.

"Does it sting something awful?" Far back, Rose remembered her own mother inflicting such punishment. Molly gulped and nodded.

"Mama, why didn't you ever hug me?"

"I did, Moll!"

"Not enough."

"Why, I did all the time, love, till you grew sick of it!"

"I didn't know—" Moll's voice broke. "—I should have been storing them up."

"Moll." Tenderness should have fled with heartbeat and blood flow, but it hadn't. *"Molly, that's what Day can give you that I can't. This time, you'll know to store up. Live folks are so blind to fleeing hours, so everlasting blind. They think love goes on forever, and it does . . . just not that way . . ."*

As if she recognized the exhaustion left behind outbursts, Moll sat silent, lavishing her mother with dove-mild looks. Then she looked toward the curtained front window, lightening with the dawn.

"It's getting light, isn't it? Mama, are you going?"

Rose wondered if Moll's face had blurred with tears, or if daybreak and all this had sapped her strength.

"You could be different, Moll." Rose felt her edges diminish and her pale hues ebb. *"If you can only trust him, you'll be different."*

Rose dwindled to pink mist, watching Molly cry. In a moment, though, the sound of hooves brought Molly to her feet. Day. Molly stepped to the window, drew back a corner of curtain. Tears for her ghostly mother were forgotten, as Molly watched for her man.

As she should.

If freckled Detective Bragg posed no threat, Day feared that Sheriff Merrick did. Dust from hauling his gear to Moll's shack had hardly settled when Merrick rode in.

"Saw McCabe this morning." Merrick used his broad saddle horn as a table for rolling a smoke. "Skinned up so bad his mama couldn't tell him from a fresh hide. Then there's VanBrunt. Couldn't hardly see him in that hole-dark store, but Miz VanBrunt tried to file charges. Hans refused to let her. Soon's he finds something to use for a backbone, I expect he'll settle with you.

"You know anything about that gal detective?" Merrick

squinted past a haze of smoke, watching Day slip a bridle over Glory's lowered head.

"She asked about a gunslinger who got in a scrape down by Lake's Crossing." Day smoothed Glory's mane back from the headstall. "I'm not the man."

Merrick nodded and shortened his reins. As soon as his eyes dipped, Day cursed his laxness.

"One more thing, mister. You've taken to toting guns. Been my experience that a man wearin' his holster tied down like you got, don't spend much time talkin' to folks that piss him off. I'd count it downright courteous if you kept out of trouble."

Persia waylaid Molly before she reached Deborah's. If pressed, Molly couldn't have said whether she'd been going to confess, or brag. Neither mattered, once she reached Shambles.

Molly had sworn never to reenter Persia's brothel, but the madam's sagging petticoats and humility had broken Molly's resistance. Now, childish memories darkened Shambles's entrance with shadows. One step inside the foyer, her nerves jerked as if grazed by a hair-raising warning of lightning.

"Claret's been bleeding since first light." Persia gestured toward the stairs.

Molly let her eyelids droop, conjuring a flash of last night's security to armor her against old fear.

Day and Rose both loved her. The jagged stabs of terror faded and Moll followed Persia up the stairs.

Claret had lost too much blood ever to leave her bed alive.

"By all that's holy, why didn't you get help sooner?" Habit controlled Molly's voice, but her eyes fixed on the scarlet bed and her mind wailed a dirge.

"If you hadn't been so reluctant—" Persia began.

Molly didn't spare the excuse a word. She went to Claret.

"Darlin', it's Molly Gallagher, remember me? From that silly trip to Carson." Molly stroked Claret's brow, clammy beneath wine-colored bangs. "What's this, you fallin' into such a state?"

By accident, someone had done right. Trying to raise the girl free of the bloody pool underneath, they'd elevated her legs. It hadn't been enough.

"Get me clean cloth," Moll said. "Lots of it."

"I'm dizzy," Claret whispered.

"I should say so, but I'm here now, and I'll help you."

Cheeks pale, shoulders shivering, Claret frowned in confusion. "Isn't it stupid? Someone like me, dying from this?"

"Hush, now. Who said a thing about dying? I know a few tricks Madam Persia's never heard of." A board creaked and Molly glared over her shoulder, snatching a fresh sheet from Georgia, who searched the room anxiously, then left.

"Could you take a little tea?" Blackberry wouldn't help, when she'd bled so long. At best, the drink might warm her.

Claret choked at the suggestion, then shook her head, gagging as she tried to speak. "Can you tell Velvet . . ."

Claret's voice sank under the sound of ripping sheet. Molly folded a neat pad and pressed it to the bleeding.

"Your sister?"

"Do you know Velvet?"

"Of course, we met in Carson. Remember what a warm evening it was? And Velvet wearing that candy-pink gown?"

Claret's board-rigid belly told Molly's fingers that the girl was bleeding inside. Too late to hope it would stop. Too late to care what caused it.

"Is it a babe you're losing, Claret?" Delicate probing said no, but if it *were*, she'd grab that breath of a chance to save it.

"No." Claret's eyes widened. "I can't believe I could get hurt so bad. A girl like me."

"What are you going to do?"

At the madam's voice, Molly tightened from scalp to fists. "I'm praying, Persia. You might give that a try."

But it was almost over. Claret knew. Molly knew. Holding a pad to the flow of blood with one hand, Molly gripped her temples with the other.

Claret shifted, frowned. Molly thought they both caught the stench at the same time. Mother of God, she'd like to strangle whoever fouled the girl's last breaths with that cigar.

"Velvet's to have my things. That little silver bangle from San Francisco. You'll tell her?"

Molly wiped her hands and sat by Claret's head. "You want me to write it down, darlin'? The silver bangle, and you've got a little canary, didn't you say?"

Claret's lips, tinged blue, twitched a smile. "Dickey. Dickey bird. And you, take that belled sash . . . I bet you've nothing like that at home!" Claret wrenched sideways on a cry.

"And your nice dresses?" Molly forced herself to go on. "Velvet would like them. That pink gown she wore in Carson was beautiful. Like the sunset. Do you remember that sunset?"

Molly babbled, knowing Persia deemed it surrender. But Molly had learned death should come with gentle words and quiet. Frantic measures merely sent folks screaming to the end.

Claret reached toward the ceiling, sighed and was gone.

At first Molly thought she heard Georgia patting Persia's back, but both women had gone. Squinting into the bedroom's dim corner, Molly saw a man, applauding.

Favor.

She fought the strangling grip of fear. Trance shimmered out of reach. Dream terrors blossomed like smoke, pulling her lips into a soundless scream. She'd hide in Claret's bloody bedclothes rather than face Favor.

"An outstanding performance, Molly. The first I've witnessed, though your reputation is legendary. The Witch of Six Mile Canyon, grown from my favorite girl."

She didn't speak, afraid she'd quaver like the child he recalled.

"Surprising you'd go to such trouble for a whore." He chuckled. "Blood tells, they say."

She didn't move, didn't tremble as she had when he'd held her head between his hands.

He looked the same, with dark hair trimmed short, mustache neat. His flat-planed cheeks angled below satyr's eyes and his mouth was just as big, his hands huge.

He lounged in the chair, crossing a polished shoe over his knee. He sucked the cigar until its tip glowed hot. "People in this town are interested in you and your little sister."

Above all, she'd protect Poppy. Molly stood. She locked her hands behind her back.

"Are you responsible for this?" She indicated the crimson lumps of bedding.

"Of course not."

His suit and linen were impeccable. And it meant nothing.

"Nicely matured." Favor regarded his cigar's tip, but she knew he didn't speak of tobacco. "I would have sought you out if you hadn't come to me."

She tried to sharpen anger into a weapon, but Molly knew if he'd sent for her, she would have come. He knew how to remake her into a frightened child.

Molly crossed her arms and raised one brow, praying he'd believe her scorn.

"I wanted to assure myself you'd received my message." He studied her confusion. "Mary, Mary, quite contrary? And Poppy's 'accident' with Mr. Skinner?"

She could not breathe, dared not run. The room tightened around her. A vise compressed her temples.

She hadn't imagined it. He'd killed China Mary. He'd stalked Poppy with someone called Skinner. "I received them."

"Fine. Just keep your mouth shut. We'll take things no further." The angle of his head shifted. His shoulders sagged, languorous. "Why don't you come over and see me, Molly?"

She moved one foot, telling herself he had no power to make her cross this room, thick with the scent of blood. No power to stop her before him, clamping the cigar between his teeth, indolently fingering a fold of her skirt.

"Why don't you do me a favor, honeybunch?"

Favor. The whore's nightmare. Even then she'd known that his "favors" were awful.

"We have an old debt between us, little Molly. By now you might know how to settle it."

She slapped his hand free of her skirt and Favor shook his fingers as if he'd burned them. "Still running, little girl?"

Her knees ratcheted into movement, but they no longer seemed hinged. If he had cackled maniacally, everyone would know what he was, but Favor's laugh flowed good-natured and rich. She must reach the door.

"Just keep your mouth shut." Favor's voice swirled after her. She stumbled on the first step. "Because, Molly? If you don't keep your pretty mouth shut, I know how to close it for you. Remember?"

Molly ran until her ribs heaved, then bowed, hands on knees, trying to breathe. This time Evil would win. She wouldn't question Mary's death, or Claret's. She wouldn't seek out a man named Skinner, who'd set a team of horses to trample Poppy.

Battling Favor, she'd gain nothing and lose everything. Respectability, earned by obeying prudish rules, would go first. If she told Day—the flicker of hope, planted by Rose, died. Favor had never trespassed into Rose's cotton-wool world. Telling Day meant offering him as a sacrifice and she wouldn't. Even if Day were the murderer she'd accused him of being.

Molly walked home. Day would be there and she should make him leave. If Favor ruined her, he'd guarantee that everyone knew, flaunting, bragging, ambushing, until suicide beckoned. It was a summons Molly knew she'd never answer, not while Poppy lived. And if Favor hurt Poppy, she'd kill him.

Molly looked down on her house and the noon-bright corral where Day worked. Blood echoed in her ears, pounding in concert with the stamp mill.

She'd kill Favor if he hurt Poppy. Crystalline in its purity and sharpness, the revelation carved its truth on her mind.

Healing was her calling, but it ranked second to Poppy. Favor could force her to forget her vow to heal.

Chapter
Twenty-three

Day kept Glory cantering in circles at the end of a rope, but his eyes tracked Molly as she picked her way down the hill. She looked harshly respectable, dressed in black, with her intricately woven red plaits pinned down tight, but she ignited a pounding in his core.

When she stopped a few yards from the corral, her eyes filled with him, thinking of shadows and firelight, before they darted away. *No regrets, love. We've no time.*

He nodded, but kept the filly cantering through a golden haze of dust. Moll set her bag on the step and leaned her shoulder against a porch post, clinging with fingers that spread carefully amid the barbed splay of firethorn.

Today was Tuesday. What right did he have to Molly, when he'd be gone Friday?

She looked weary. If stiff underpinnings hadn't prevented it, Moll would have perched on the step. At her gentle smile, he pondered how he'd feel if she sat there, watching him work, always. Day set his jaw against such romantic foolery.

Always wasn't about to happen. And if he couldn't have her always, he'd have her now.

He squinted past the horse, watching Moll turn at a scrub jay's call. Day reeled Glory in, set on showing off Glory's progress. Before he could, Moll approached. Sweet quarry coming straight to him, she flicked her skirts through the gate and latched it behind.

Did Moll feel a thrumming through her veins? Did a dry mouth have her swallowing over and over? Motionless but for a lock of hair blowing over her cheek, Moll stopped. Day freed Glory and raised an arm, telling the filly to move off.

"M'Bright?" Day's hands were still busy coiling the rope. He hadn't even opened his arms when her black sleeves closed around him.

Once, he'd thought Moll cowed by his size. That first day in her parlor, she'd snapped her head back, frowning as if he were a beast she'd shoo outside. Now her wrists snugged under his arms, making a big safe wall of him. Plummeting through space, she'd caught him to stop her fall. Day practiced feeling solid.

"You know that Dragon soap?" Cheek pressed against his chest, Moll mentioned a transaction he'd thought secret, a fair swap for harness brasses too grand for Abner.

"How did you know about that?" His chin rubbed her hair.

"It's like incense." Her face burrowed into his chest. "I could . . . I . . . smell it on you, Day."

He wanted to pull her against him, to raise her up on her toes and kiss her, but he let her take the lead.

Stag gone. Poppy gone. Alone. *A fisherman's patience, Lord, allow me what I was born to and I'll make her honest after.*

No grappling in a bonfire's smoke and glare. This time, he'd bathe her, sliding the Dragon soap over her pink shoulders and down the bumpy beads of her spine. They'd bask in sun from the cabin's single window, and let the wind that hunted between the wall's mismatched boards chill them and drive them closer together. Now, wind bound them together with Moll's long skirts.

Creaking and clanking levered them apart. Moll slipped away as Cinder barked and iron-wrapped wheels slid out of control. Curse the driver for bad timing and clumsiness. Armed, Day would have shot the dolt and called it public service.

"Mine accident!" Arthur, a faint beard fuzzing his chin, drove the rig. "Geordie, Stag and another lad—one's holding timber off the others. Stag called up, told me to get you, miss." Arthur's hand shook with reaction as it passed over his face.

Moll had shaken her head throughout the whole recital.

"Bring them up. I don't enter mines. Cinder, hush!" Molly jerked Cinder's collar, then bustled into the house.

"Do something, man." Beseeching, Arthur looked after her.

Hell. Day added Moll's crossed-arm resolve to her panic in the snow shelter. The lass wasn't overfond of confined spaces.

"Stop thinking of a way to ask what I will not do." Molly emerged with an armload of sticks and cloth. "They could bleed to death while y'fret."

She plucked her bag from the porch and climbed into the wagon bed, exposing black stocking up to her calf.

Arthur slapped the reins and Day hurdled in beside her. With their backs to Arthur, Day caught Moll's shoulders against his own. Minutes ago she'd melted against him. Now, she poked upright as a post. Day took her hand to kiss and found fingers like icicles. He pictured Stag spurting gore, China Mary's hypnotic slashing and Moll tending them. For all her fear, he knew such a healer wouldn't stay topside.

Day rubbed his thumb across her knuckles. He had no fondness of mines, himself. Open sky, open waters and broad moors were bred into his bones. Hard-rock miners were a separate breed of Cornishman.

He looked at Moll, blinking against the dust roiling up to coat her face. Dust tears marked crooked streams down her cheeks. If not for a miner's error, Moll wouldn't be weeping.

No, they'd be wound together in that snug cabin, making love till the only thing Moll cried for was pure joy.

Half the town had gathered above the Empty Pockets mine.

"Mr. Day, thank Heaven you've come." Margaret Bride awarded Day a smile fit for a hero. "And Miss Gallagher. Perhaps *you* can do something for those poor men."

A frown veed Moll's forehead as she jumped from the wagon. "Why aren't they up yet? I can't work on anyone stuck in the bottom of a mine shaft."

"Moll, it's Stag! Did you know it's Stag?" Her pink cheeks drained white, Poppy crushed against her sister. Moll patted her back as a miner approached.

"We was just trying on that square timbering, ma'am. No harm to it, we thought. Worked well enough for the Ophir."

"I don't care." Moll drew a ragged breath. "If there are injuries, set them before me and I'll do my best."

"Mol-ly!" Stag's voice echoed up from the mine.

Day watched every set of eyes, save his and Moll's, fix on the shaft's opening. Moll stared at the cage above it.

Could such a rickety affair, little more than a box with pulley and crank, carry twenty or thirty stone into the bowels of the earth? Day sucked in his breath at his mind's suggestion. Moll might go, if he went with her.

Moll moved to the shaft's lip, unsteady as she looked down the black tunnel. Her hands gripped her hips. "Stag, let them bring you up. I can't—Tell me what's happened."

Moll seemed intent, her world shrunk to the yawning darkness at her feet. He bloody hoped so. Smatterings of criticism and slurs of cowardice ran through the crowd. She shouldn't hear.

Day heard. Next time he ran amok, there'd be a few "respectable" folks stanching blood from their noses.

"I'm holding . . . timber . . . Geordie's back. He's . . . legs—" Stag's voice rose in snatches. Moll shook her head, trying to understand. They all caught the next part, clear enough.

" . . . down here, when the son of a bitch blows!"

His wounded leg? *That* son of a bitch? Or was Stag speaking of some underground steam pocket? Or some pre-placed explosive?

"Just go down there! Molly, you have to!" Poppy begged.

Moll started to shake Poppy loose, then Day saw her stop. Without turning, she felt the burden of the town's accusing eyes. They'd decide if Poppy remained with her. And if Moll let three men die, down below, they'd add murder to her sins.

"You know she lost Claret this morning? Persia's little curly-haired gal? Damn near lost a babe, coupla weeks back."

"Sounds like to me, she's lost her nerve."

No. He saw the word form on her lips, as she raised forest-dark eyes to his.

"I'll go with you, Moll. If there's shiftin' around to be done, I can help." A chorus of voices seconded his offer. "Thanks, lads, but I think we'll be a bit crowded as it is."

Since Day entered the cage first, only he saw Moll brace, stiff-armed, in its doorway. Then she came on, shuddering as if she passed through a veil of spider webs.

The cage rocked below the surface, leaving daylight and onlookers behind, then hung tapping against the rock wall. Day drew breath and dedicated himself to distracting her.

"Before your fire last night, I beat the daylights out of McCabe." The cage lurched down a few feet. Day hoped that bragging cured nausea. "Don't you want to know why?"

"Yes," she whispered.

Dark as the inside of a cow, the shaft walls vanished as the cage hovered and dropped, hesitated and plunged.

"McCabe announced that you were my mistress." That was prettying it up a bit, but it should snag her attention.

"And you hit him." She managed a nervous laugh. "For saying what you want to be true."

If the concealing blackness made her brazen, then God bless the dark.

"Not, 'want,' m'Bright. It's what I plan. The first plan I've made past my next meal, mind you, and there'll be no escape."

The cage plummeted. What the hell, had the bloody rope snapped? He grabbed Moll as the cage jerked like a hanged man stopped short by a noose. The rope held, slamming the cage against the side of the shaft, throwing them to the floor.

She gasped and he grabbed for her, maddened to encounter sticks before her ankle. Finally he touched her hair and tugged her head against his shoulder. "My brave Moll."

Her shuddering breath tangled with a choked laugh. "Your plan didn't include this, did it?"

"There's a lot it didn't include, Bright. Ask yourself why I'm here, riding down a mine shaft that's makin' me sick, set on rescuin' a man I hardly know, in a town where I'm not safe."

Stag's unintelligible shout interrupted.

"We're coming." Moll sounded stronger. A good thing, since confession or lack of air made Day light-headed and wobbly.

Watery light wavered below the cage. Why didn't they just let the blessed thing down and have done?

"You're doing all this to bed me?"

Torture. Moll's bluntness in the dark was lovely torture.

"It can't all be lust, can it, Moll? With us the way we are, suspended between Heaven and Hell?"

Gliding now, the cage passed erratically lighted levels of the mine. Blink and you missed flashes of huge timbers, rock, miners laboring by candlelight. Their words came in snatches.

"—accident—"

"—below—"

"—witch!"

Weird lighting, wet-torsoed men and heat made the descent a preview of Hades.

"Woman in the mine!" called one superstitious idiot.

Moll didn't notice. "Is it very, very hot?"

"Aye. It's said lads drink prodigious amounts down here."

"Stop!"

The rope yanked tight at Stag's scream. Day's head slammed against the cage. He judged it a measure of his anxiety that he checked the cage for damage before exploring a jaw still sore from McCabe's fists.

By a wavering candle flame, Day fumbled with the door. Moll gathered her doctoring tools, and then they were out.

He smelled wax and fresh-cut pine. Heat and wet combined in the airless quiet. The oppressive dark made his eyes strain wider.

A profane prayer rasped from a pile of flesh and wood, but it took Moll and the candle to bring sense to the tableau.

Stag formed one side of a triangle. A timber formed another, and the last few feet of the timber pinned Geordie—the triangle's base—across the knees. Only Stag's shoulder, wedged underneath the crushing weight, protected Geordie.

Geordie's hand was raised above his head, jammed against Stag's thigh. Why in blazes—?

"Is it bleeding?"

"Don't know, Molly." Stag grunted. "Think it's sweat I feel, but just in case . . ."

"I see. Save your breath."

Geordie, suffering under the wooden pillar, applied pressure to Stag's healing wound, that spurting horror from the day they'd met. Moll crouched between the men: Geordie, moaning, but motionless, and Stag, trembling under the timber's weight, now that help was near. Day stood as if he were watching a play, trying to ask something useful.

"Where's the other lad?"

"No other."

"They said three miners," Day insisted.

"Sorry."

"This piece of wood you're holding up, Stag, what does it do?" Molly studied the tunnel's ceiling.

"Supports the others. Not a load-bearing piece, yet."

"You could let it go—"

A groan protested, and Moll's hand soothed Geordie's brow. "—once we have this fellow out, of course. You could release it and the roof wouldn't collapse, right?"

"Shouldn't."

Though Stag's lack of conviction chilled him, Day considered the precision-cut wood. "Let's get after it, then. I'll

replace you, Stag. Likely I'll be able to lift it off Geordie,
bein' as I've no bum leg."

But he *did* have a slow-healing shoulder and he'd gone
and reminded Moll of Cinder's bite. Her eyes narrowed in
disapproval.

"Moll, can you pull him out when I've got the timber
up?"

"Do it."

The plan took one straining second to execute. Day
slipped into place. Stag scrambled clear and Moll dragged
Geordie aside.

"I'm lettin' her down!"

Though the crashing report of wood on dirt seemed to
stretch for an hour, nothing else fell save dust.

Moll took over. "Day, help Stag shuck off his trousers."
She raised the candle and sighed at his surprise. "If he's
burst that wound, I'll stitch him first." She indicated
Geordie. "Don't gape like a maiden aunt. Drop his trousers,
will you, Day?"

Who'd've pictured Lightfoot O'Deigh, showing another
man's privates? He did as she ordered.

"Fine." She made a quick study of Stag's thigh. "No further injury, but extra support won't hurt. In a minute, Stag.
Now for you, sir." As Moll turned back to Geordie, Day
pushed at Stag's trousers, urging the fellow to cover himself.

Day found more candles. He jerked back at the scuttling
movement of a rat, then lit the cave for Moll's operations.
Scissors flashed from her bag and glittered as she snipped
Geordie's trousers. With painstaking slowness, she cleaned
the jagged wound.

"Lord have mercy, Moll, he's not goin' out for tea!"

"I can clean it now, or he can lose the entire leg to putrification next week." Geordie's gasp made her bend closer.
"Don't worry. I never give patients over to Cuttin' Jack."

First she glared at Day, then her lips parted as she considered the tight darkness. Her breath came short and Day
knew that his interruption had cost Moll concentration and
control.

Like a mother animal, she crouched over Geordie. Day

steadied her shoulder and she startled, as if waking, then tended Geordie as she spoke.

"Day, must you sit, doing nothing? T-take some cloth. Fold it into a pad as big as the palm of your hand, then tie it on Stag—snug, but not tight—with a strip." She glanced at Day's handiwork. "Not there! Where it's bulging!"

Molly frowned, her eyes comparing the size of the cage to her splints' length. She broke them into shorter pieces, snapping them over her knee. Still dissatisfied, she discarded them and wadded cloth behind Geordie's broken knee before tethering it criss-cross.

Rising from her squatting position to stretch, Moll insisted Day go up first, with Stag. "None of your nonsense, man."

He complied, but warily, and his every muscle slacked with relief when the cage rocked to the surface, bearing Moll and Geordie squinting into the sunlight. Day waited for cheering to break out. It didn't, though the girl was a bloody heroine.

There came a collective sigh, Poppy's laughter and Arthur, bowing over Moll's hand, saying, "Thanks, oh, thank you, miss," but no burst of thanksgiving.

Moll pulled away from Arthur with a smile, but Day heard exhaustion in her sigh. Damn them. She'd risked her life to save one of them and they still scorned her.

Day locked eyes with Margaret Bride, then began applauding. The schoolteacher spared a quick glance at frowning Eleanor VanBrunt, then Margaret, too, began to clap. Her students joined in. Stag whooped feebly and the miners who'd rallied to hold him merged, crowing agreement.

Bruised jaw set, Day stared the good people of Virginia City into mending their shameful behavior. When he helped Moll back into the buckboard, her bravery had by God been recognized.

Chapter
Twenty-four

On Wednesday Molly resorted to her mother's brand of magic. Invisibly, Rose floated as close as the girl's shadow, just to make sure she got things right.

Uneasiness had shackled Moll since she'd come off that hillside, her mind filled with death. Whenever Moll reached for a trance, she failed; Rose could not help. Still drained by her wrestling and preaching with Molly, she barely flickered after her daughter.

Tonight, Moll waited until Poppy slept, then crept into the kitchen, where she stood staring into the cupboard.

"What am I doing wrong, Mama?"

If she'd had eyes, or tears to fill them, Rose would have wept. Instead, she did her best to reply.

"You're not wanting to see what's there, Molly girl. In a trance, you must look and accept. It's not always pleasant, but it's our gift." Rose might have saved her energy. Only Ginger glanced her way.

Molly snatched the white dish from its shelf, ladled in two dippers of water, and carried it outside.

No! If Moll conducted her business outside, Rose feared she'd get it wrong. Molly couldn't remember the ritual of catching the full moon in a reflecting pool.

Returning for the candles, Molly paused.

"No. Bring that bowl back inside. Catch the reflection through the window. It works, child." Molly faltered. *"Molly! Molly, let me help you."*

"What do you want?" Moll's whisper faltered between despair and irritation. "I know you're here, but are you speaking?"

"Look at me! Here, beside the table." Memory struck Rose like a fist in her belly. A little red-haired child stood beside a ragged harridan slumped over a glass of brandy. "Mama," the child begged, "I'm right here. Look at me."

Molly's eyes strained wide, seeking Rose, but after ten minutes, it was the simple lapping of a dog that took Molly outside, away from her mother's pleading.

"Shoo, you vile animal!" Molly watched as unrepentant Cinder wagged his tail before stepping off a pace. When she sat, he settled beside her. The old dog respected neither seer nor reflecting pool. Small wonder, when Rosie's pool, toward the end, had been a glass of brandy.

Molly arranged the candles so that the water reflected no flame, only the cool disk of moon. She crossed her legs inside her skirts, letting her hands rest atop her knees.

She willed her neck and shoulders to relax—then hoped Day wouldn't return early from the Black Dog. She concentrated on breathing, on filling and flushing her lungs—then listened for bootfalls. Her mind refused to float. It recalled Geordie's knee, golden wine and Day.

After leaving the Empty Pockets mine, she'd played reluctant hostess to a celebration. Philipp Deidsheimer had arranged delivery of ham and champagne, "for averting tragedy which would have cast suspicion upon the safest of mine constructions." Day had produced a bottle of burgundy wine, then stashed it behind the firewood "for another night." Stag danced to test his leg and Poppy baked a cake. Before Day departed for work, they'd eaten every crumb.

Day's kiss, as he left, quaked with a special intensity. Drat! How far off lagged scandal, when a mere memory made her knee jerk, turning the moon into a wobbling oblong?

Night wind carried the scent of charred wood. As an old woman in a rocker, would she breathe that smell with longing?

Since her vengeful bonfire, Day had drawn her in ways she'd never imagined. "I'm a man, and I'll do whatever you let me," he'd warned, but he'd made no move to seduce her.

Day slept only steps away. Day ate half his meals in her presence. Day raised his eyes to hers each time he drank from the dipper. Without asking why, Day knew she needed him. He'd followed her into that death-trap mine. He'd joined in her gleeful victory over fear.

That champagne night, as she'd recounted Stag's bravery for Geordie, Molly saw pride shine from Poppy's face. Stag had intercepted the look, and their sudden link was almost audible. Sickened by what she'd allowed to happen, Molly had felt the lantern-bright room dim. Then, over Poppy's flaxen head, Day offered the gentlest of smiles, and Molly felt comforted.

And, despite misgivings, his body beckoned hers. Yesterday, watching from the window, Molly saw Day return from bathing in the stream. Crossing toward his cabin, Day had stopped, considering the dwindling woodpile. Bare to the waist, hair slick and wet, he'd hefted the ax. Broad bands of muscle crossed his wide shoulders, and other bunching muscles paired between his ribs, then tempted her eyes downward to where his denims hung from his hipbones. Hotter than a blush, blood had flooded her. Molly turned away.

He'd even befriended her dog. Cinder now paced at Day's side, resting his nose in the man's cupped hand. Often, she spotted Cinder's gray muzzle in the shack's shade, and he remained long after she'd finished weeding the vegetable patch.

Devotion ran both ways. She'd seen Day help Cinder

climb the porch. "There now, old lad," Day comforted, when the dog moved slow with rheumatism.

Just as naturally, Day had sensed Favor's threat. He'd oiled her rifle and drilled her on loading and firing.

"In case you're caught here, alone." And then he'd looked away, reluctant as she to say when that might be.

Handling the weapon with awkward dislike, Molly insisted she was a healer, sworn to restore life, not take it. Day nodded, loaded, warned her against the recoil and helped her aim for the white stone on the fence post.

Focusing on the captured moon as if it were that white stone, Molly slipped away. Her eyelids drooped and the moon spread, welcoming her to its milky embrace.

Firethorn, as green and red as that on her porch, twined dense and verdant. Within the labyrinth pulsed a serpent, bronze and thick. Molly held back the image, tried to slow its mutation from snake to dragon. The dream would not obey.

Snow dappled the reptilian hide as it throbbed brown, then black. A few flakes, at first, like ice on midnight waters, then more, until a dragon, limned in snow, reared against sheets of fire.

She recognized the flakes, frenzied as gnats in a glass. She knew what came next. And who. Molly tried to look away, tried to comfort Cinder's whining. Her hand would not lift.

His visor raised, the knight galloped, shivering the water's surface.

Molly leaned back on her palms, almost breaking the trance.

Real as the white china seabed beneath him, Day struck down the dragon. Wide-shouldered in armor, he spurred the plunging stallion forward.

Molly felt the sting of hair whipping her face as she shook her head. *No.* Lance leveled, Day rode on, cold and deadly, tilting at her breast.

"No!" Stiff-necked, Molly peered around her. No heartsblood. No scarlet-stained snow. No death. Only an old dog, snoring in leg-churning sleep. Only pain where the thin bones on the back of her hand had struck. Only a broken bowl, and a shard of china, rocking in the moonlight.

Inside, a frosty rose-scented breeze, like ice on flower petals, greeted her. The night outside was calm. Rose had returned.

When Cinder refused to follow, Molly left the kitchen door open. Not for Cinder's rescue or her own retreat. She wanted to see Rose again. The trance had merely left her edgy.

Rose looked more ghostly than ever before.

"Since my death, you mean. I look better than that, now, don't I?" Rose soared into the middle of the parlor, brushing her gown into even folds.

"Of course. Bridal white from top to—"

"Toes, if I had them?"

"I tired you out, last time. I'm sorry."

"Molly Maureen, wipe that tragic frown from your face." If dark smears of eyes could twinkle, Rose's did. Casting off recrimination, Rose whirled like a fairy, and did what she'd always done best: looked on the bright side.

"You've snagged yourself a fine man in Day."

"If only I knew what to do with him." Molly wondered whether her heart or stomach lurched.

"Your heart, love, and don't be interrupting, or I'll 'magnify' old Ginger's yen to plop yesterday's mice on your pillow."

"Whatever you say, Mama." Molly's laughter flashed back at her, reflected in Rose's eyes. What a simple measure of love.

"Now, the lad's itching something fierce, but I've worked a deal with him."

"With Day? You've worked a bargain with Day?"

Anything was possible, she supposed. After all, level-headed Moll Gallagher stood here in her bare feet, having a conversation with a ghost.

"He's not sure quite why he's got himself on a head-tossin' short rein, but it's because I—when you went off one morn and he dozed here by my stove—I told him he might'nt make love to you, without repeating marriage vows, first!"

The image of Rose meddling in Day's mind delighted Molly.

"True, it's a nice bit of fun to tamper with him, but Day's a man about to bolt free." Rose shook a warning finger. *"Hear him whisper a proposal and you'd best brace yourself!*

"Ah there, I've got you laughing straightaway at everything. Molly dear, I'd give up hope of Heaven to feel you hug me."

Rose's form faded to the silver of late-spring ice. Seeing her mother's weariness, Molly curbed her questions about Rose's bargain with Day. Rose always came back.

"The best I could do was this . . . "

"Did he promise—?"

"He did, after a fashion. Though it took a curse, pure and simple." A laugh, too vivid for the shade that remained, trilled like a silver whistle. *"I've no doubt it's a weak thing, my curse, since I've come up short on other ghostly powers. But a mother's curse? To protect her daughter's virtue? Faith, Eve left Eden with that one token, don't you think?"*

"A curse?" For all Day's bluster, he was a sweet man . . .

"'Twon't hurt him a bit. He's not sure what put the idea in his mind, just knows he's craving a honeymoon."

Only a glimmer of white, so faint it might have been candlelight, showed above the love seat, but Rose's voice rang smug and laced with giggles.

"I cursed him with one jinx no man dares test, and here it is: If handsome Day wields that manly part of himself without a proposal of marriage, he'd best enjoy it." Rose's outline vanished, but her laughter lingered. *"Because that will be the last time he'll have the use of it—ever."*

Flustered by her mother's ingenuity, Molly lost sight of Rose's position. She'd gone. The tension that Rose vibrated through the air had dissipated.

Then a thready voice whispered from underneath the love seat.

"Men may be the weaker clay, Molly mine, but oh so much fun to sink your fingers into . . . "

*   *   *

Candlewick root and stalks of horsetail lay strewn over Moll's kitchen table. Unable to sleep after the visitation, she'd stayed up all night, working. She'd put in a full day's labor, and Poppy had just returned from her bread rounds.

"I'm back." Poppy brought the cold in on her skirts. "You should have said 'take a wrap,' Moll. It's chilly outside."

"Sorry." Still afraid that her sister would notice something odd—a lingering whiff of brimstone?—Molly kept her eyes lowered as Poppy rattled off morning gossip.

"Everyone's talking of tomorrow's horse race. Did we ever go to one?" Poppy moved into the other room, accepting her sister's distraction, readying herself for school. "Molly?"

Poppy's tone made Molly's fingers go stiff and cold. Poppy stood in the doorway, brushing her hair. "I saw Mama at the window this morning."

No. Rose wouldn't do that. Unless she had to sneak a peek.

"That's nonsense, honey." Molly brushed loose seeds from her palms.

"I know." Poppy divided her hair into three sections. "Probably it was sun on the glass, but she looked so young and pretty. Was she, Molly? How I can miss her, when I barely remember how she looked?" Poppy cleared her throat when Molly didn't answer. Then, she considered her sister's spare breakfast, set among the herbs. "Your coffee is cold. And your scone. Shall I fix you something else?"

"No, run along, honey. Just run along." By the time Molly looked up again, Poppy had closed the warped door behind her.

Molly wished weariness hadn't distracted her. She might have sent along the potions for Margaret Bride. Herbal infusions were a small reward for the teacher's diligence.

Without asking an extra penny, Margaret tutored Poppy after school. During these sessions, the schoolteacher had made a shocking discovery. Although Poppy trailed behind her classmates in reading and writing, she loved mathematics. The more complex, the better.

"She'd rather work fractions than join the others for recess. The quickest way to make Poppy finish a page in her primer is reward her with a sheet of equations. She'll move beyond my skills, soon." Margaret had tapped a finger against her lips. "I'd send for more textbooks, but they cost dearly."

Molly didn't ask the value of Poppy's number-juggling, or inquire about employment for a mathematical genius too simple to remember her shawl. It was enough that Poppy was learning.

Molly patted out a layer of root on her drying sheet. If only money—*always* money—weren't an issue. Could she convince big-city publishers to swap books for tinctures? Not likely. Perhaps Rose could magnify Hans VanBrunt's generosity next time he came for a palm reading.

Voices ... not from the parlor, but the porch, drew Molly's attention. Walking past the red velvet love seat, she shivered, then opened the front door.

Stag's boot cocked on the lowest step of their porch as he bit into a fresh scone. His crumb-dusted shirt witnessed that it wasn't the first. Poppy, her braid untidy, gazed up at him.

"I thought you'd left for school." Molly pressed Poppy for a reaction. "Your hair's a rat's nest!"

"You didn't say! When I came in, you didn't say!"

Of course not. She'd hardly glanced up.

Poppy's distress made Molly assail Stag. "And why aren't *you* at the mine?"

"Just going." Stag tipped his hat and left with no apology.

Jerking in breaths so deep they burned, Molly fussed with Poppy's hair. "You're going to be late." She fastened Poppy's combs with careless speed. Poppy winced, then pulled away and balanced her books on one hip.

"Poppy." Molly extended the battered tin lunch pail. "After all the rules, all the times you've recited them— honey, what good is knowing algebra, when you won't understand about men?"

Poppy's expression fell far short of contrite.

"Don't you have anything to say?" Molly felt perilously close to tears.

"I saw you kiss Day."

"Poppy, I—" Molly's throat narrowed. *Oh thank you, Mother, for turning friendship into something tawdry.* No excuse squeezed past her lips.

In seconds, it didn't matter. Poppy kissed her on the cheek and left for school.

The leggy Kentucky filly would be Moll's salvation. Day tightened the cinch, watching Glory's ears flick back for his voice.

"There now, lass. You're sweatin' up just thinkin' about it. Calm yourself, Glory." Beneath the palm he placed on her side, Glory quaked with anticipation, but never blew up her belly to foil saddling, never swung her head around to bite, only regarded Day from beneath the gold forelock shading her eyes. Not a mean bone in Glory's body, and she flew like bloody Pegasus!

Day touched his left foot to the stirrup and swung up quick. Not quick enough. Showing her one bad habit, Glory lurched as she felt weight. He'd fallen on his arse the first time, but the filly waited for him to stand.

Tending bar, he'd tried thinking like a horse. Glory veered left when he mounted left, right when he mounted right. He might try a flying leap over her rump to the saddle, if he fancied spending his last days with Moll, healing. No, Glory's vice could be cured with schooling. Until then, he counted her thief-proof. And though Glory was green, she'd win tomorrow's race.

At worst, the two-hundred-dollar purse would be his farewell gift. At best, it would be Poppy's scholarship, paying room and board with Margaret Bride while Molly rode away with him.

He didn't pray for boons. Oh, once, sinking beneath green glassy waves for the last time, he'd prayed for help. Then, Da had grabbed him. Together they'd choked and clutched the keel of the capsized boat until help arrived. This time, only Moll could save him. Tonight he'd seduce her; tomorrow he'd propose marriage.

Just then the ginger cat, eyes glinting like hard brass coins, yowled from the fence post.

"*Or* t'other way around!" The blasted feline sniffed, and Day knew for certain that he only imagined phantom laughter tinkling weightless on the air.

"Favor's been at Persia's all week." Richard Griffin's uncharacteristic snarl froze Molly outside her back door.

"Y'knew he was comin' for the race." Day said.

He and Richard stood at the corner of her house, Day sounding quite matter-of-fact as he unsaddled Glory. What did he know of Favor? Why had Richard told him, when she'd been so careful not to?

"His black filly's stabled two stalls down from your mule."

"Hope she doesn't scare easy." Day released Glory and she sprinted away before Richard spoke again.

"Some commotion's going on down at his Chinatown joyhouse. A couple of girls tried to take off and all Hell broke loose."

"Better not tell Moll. She'll be down patching up heads and stirring up trouble."

Better not tell Moll! She was one step from rounding the corner when Richard's voice stopped her.

"I should've married that green-eyed witch, way back. She needs a level head and a strong hand."

Molly didn't wait for Day's response. "Does she now?" It was worth ten dollars apiece to see their shock. Her anger evaporated as she stood, tapping her toe, arms crossed.

"A pity you're enjoying this so much." Day's rascal smile sent her smugness plummeting straight to the pit of her stomach.

"Is it?"

"Aye. I had a lovely surprise, but with you bein' so ired, Moll, what's the use?" Day mimed despair, but the look he shot Griffin was too sharp for conspiracy. "We'd best call off the whole business."

Griffin crossed his arms, taking no part in Day's teasing, but Molly's anger still simmered.

"Tell me your surprise." Despite her flat voice, when Day tilted his head to the right, Molly noticed the soft channel beneath his ear, above his blue collar. Moll shivered at the thought of placing a kiss there.

"This is the truth of it, Bright." Day ignored the look Richard shot him. "If you'll allow it, I'm runnin' your filly in the race tomorrow. It's a surprise, I know, but Margaret tells me Poppy could do with more books."

Margaret. Not even *Miss* Margaret. The man wove charms no female could resist!

"A two-hundred-dollar purse wouldn't go to waste."

"Two hundred dollars?" After books, it would buy a new roof and a new porch.

Day nodded. The sun danced rainbow glints along hair he'd pulled back with a strip of leather. A decent woman would offer to cut it for him.

Then she remembered Poppy. *I saw you kiss Day,* Poppy had said, excusing her own runaway heart.

"Is she fast?" Molly narrowed her eyes toward the filly.

"Faster than any horse I ever rode."

Glory whuffled her lips along the ground, looking for fodder more interesting than sagebrush. She didn't have the look of a champion. "Can I ride her?"

"No!"

"Not yet." Day shouted down Richard's objection and gave him a quelling look. Then, in spite of Richard, Day took her hand. "I'd consider it an honor to ride for you, Moll. I'm not small as a lot of the riders will be, but I've better experience."

Secretly, Day's thumb stroked the center of her palm. Molly shuddered and jerked free.

"I don't need your credentials. If you're sure she won't be hurt . . ." Glory returned to the fence, stretching her thin-skinned muzzle toward Day. "I don't know horse doctoring."

"I'll take care of her, Moll." Day swallowed, as sincere as if he were taking priest's vows.

"Can she beat Favor's horse?"

Day's face went still, his eyes' light flattened, and she recalled his stillness the night she'd almost shot Stag. *There.* Day's hand hovered near his pistol.

"I haven't seen his horse run, but Glory's fast, and I can't believe that these territorial riders know tricks I haven't tried."

Molly knew Day was wrong. His were the tricks of a good man. Favor kept slaves, hurt women, liked pain.

"Speaking of tricks, McCabe is still in town, sleeping in his wagon, behind the livery." With military briskness, Richard mounted his gray.

"I'm not desiring another meetin' with the freighter McCabe." Day rubbed his rib cage and winced.

"Just mentioning it." Richard's tone, so stilted and curt, begged Molly to respond.

"Richard, I'm not angry. I'm honored, in a way." Molly studied the toes of her black boots. "Who'd guess a Southern gentleman would pretend to—"

"It's not how I would have asked you, Molly. And there's no pretending about it. I'll marry you any time you say." Responding to his spurs, Richard's gray mare bolted from the yard.

Day flung his hat into the dirt.

Before Molly could unravel Richard's words, Day loomed beside her, his body clouding out anything less substantial.

"What do you want, Day?"

His hands reared up, gripping and releasing the air, as if he'd grab her shoulders. Then, as if a knife slashed the tension binding him, Day took her hand.

"I'm leaving the Black Dog a mite early tonight, to rest up for the race. I'm coming to see you before I turn in." His statement sounded awfully like a dare and Day must have seen her reaction. "Settle, m'Bright. You can tell me no."

Moll took a shuddering breath and moved back. He didn't release her hand, though she moved to arm's length. "I'm telling you 'no,' now."

He held her fingers to his lips and kissed each knuckle. *Mercy, they must be rough and bitter with herbs!*

"Tell me tonight, love. Tell me tonight."

Chapter
Twenty-five

"You can sit for a minute, but I'll give you nothing more than a cup of tea." Hands folded in her lap, Molly sat on an upright chair she'd hauled from her kitchen to the porch.

Prim? Oh yes, Day's flame-haired vixen sat stiff as a vicar's wife. He lamented the lost dreams that had sustained him as he worked, then trudged up the hill. In fancy, Moll had awaited him here in a thin white nightdress.

Between drawing beer and mopping the bar top, he'd planned to lure her away from the cottage; down to the stream he'd take her, to the grassy flat where he basked, alone, after bathing.

Flesh-and-blood Molly sat on the porch, tapping a toe and extending a cup for him to balance once he took the other chair. Day sat. He claimed the teacup from Moll's too-steady hand. No table stood between them, but a frayed-wick lantern sat on the porch, throwing tawny light to outline Moll's shoulders, braced tight with irritation.

"Now, you know I prefer coffee, m'Bright—"

"*You* insisted on coming back. *I* didn't invite you."

"Aye." Startled by Moll's vehemence, Day slopped a drop of tea on his cuff. Had waiting soured her? Had shame curbed her craving? He hadn't *imagined* her eyes on him, all week.

He swallowed the tea with difficulty. Though it took no more than Moll's glances to keep him hot and restless, the lass needed schooling on how to brew bracing brown tea. This stuff was weak as water.

"It smells flowerish." Day gestured a half-toast with the cup. "Nice."

"It's jasmine. McCabe brought it from San Francisco."

He hadn't made time to pull on clothes that didn't reek of saloon smoke and beer, but Moll had steeped blossoms of exotic Oriental jasmine. Faith, he felt like an ass.

A cat yowled inside the house, sounding for all the world as if it warned Moll to have naught to do with him.

"Nice," he repeated. "For tea."

"I've served it, because I'm not encouraging you." But she was, with that quick green glance. "You have me quite aggravated."

A devilish sweet whisper tempted him to aggravate Moll in ways she'd never forget.

"I know little bits about you, Day, but they don't add up. Each snip of information contradicts the others!" Her index fingers dove toward each other and missed.

Molly stifled her outburst with the back of her hand. She bent to adjust the lantern wick, though it burned clear and steady. Her hair fell forward to blanket her shoulder, and the light fired some strands bright gold and left others dark as burgundy wine. Moll might not have donned a nightdress in welcome, but she'd loosed her hair for none but him.

"Let's have it, then. What's got you spitting like a cat?"

"You don't like cats." She sat erect to face him. "That's one. You like dogs. You don't like mules; you like horses. Yet you have neither horse nor dog, and you arrived with a wagonload of cats, drawn by a mule." Moll sat back, *ah-ha!* etched in every line of her body.

Day gave a low whistle. "Damning stuff, I agree, but I do like *you*."

"That doesn't matter!" Moll was breathless with anger. Day resolved to take advantage.

"If you're looking for a showdown, Molly girl, we'll start with a kiss." She didn't move fast enough to avoid his hands. He leaned to catch her, and chair legs skittered on the porch boards.

Moll's lips opened before he coaxed them, and her eagerness made him moan till he realized the girl was straining like Hell to talk.

"See?" Molly's accusation whispered against his cheek and she didn't pull away half as far as he gave her leave. Day held on, hands raining inducement down her spine, until her sharp wrench warned him to stop. If their chairs tipped over, it would quite ruin the mood.

"That 'showdown' remark? You've done something with guns. You're an outlaw!" Molly bolted to her feet and flung a hand toward the cottage. "I kept that poster, Day. How dumb, how *blind* are they not to see beyond that beard?"

Day stood, edging after her before she fled into her house. "Y'kept the poster?" Likely he couldn't needle her out of this fury, but he tried. "Y'been studyin' my face?"

"You are the most infernally maddening man!" Moll's hand reared back to slap him, but her voice was a plea, and by the time her hand reached him, the slap had become a caress. Molly's thumb traced his cheekbone. "I *don't* like you."

Day captured her wrist. His fingers dusted endless circles on the tiny bumps of bone, memorizing their delicacy. He moved her hand to his mouth, remembering her sweet shudder when he'd touched the rise beneath her thumb. He tested it with his teeth and Moll closed her eyes. He increased the pressure, and her head tilted, ever so slightly, backward.

She fought to open eyes that looked, even by lamplight, unfocused and languorous. Oh, yes, he remembered how to do this.

"Let me kiss you, again, Moll. One kiss and I'll be off to me own bed," he lied.

"I'm not doing that anymore." Eyes open, her arm stayed doubled against his chest and he still possessed her hand.

"A good decision." He kissed the center of her palm and forced back her tight black sleeve.

"It's not smart," she sighed.

"You're right." His lips feathered over her wrist, then, before she anticipated it, he raised her chin to kiss its underside as he eased a finger inside her collar.

"I can't."

Day pressed his lips to the corner of her mouth. Patience. Don't insist. Moll surrendered, kissing him with a sigh. Aye, patience had lovely rewards. She smelled of pine and roses. Day's own smile brought their lips apart, but he rejoined them, trailing his hand over her skirts, kissing and talking, never trusting her resistance.

"No. You said you'd stop . . ." She moved to him, not away.

"I will, love, I will." *Gentle, gentle and slow. Pay attention to her, not the traitor nerves screaming to pound on.*

"I don't even know your real name." Her lips nuzzled into the cove of his neck, but her voice simmered with shame.

"It wouldn't be safe to tell you, Moll."

"And, would it—" She whispered so low that Day held his breath for fear he'd miss a word. "—would it be safe to make love to you?"

Yes, yes, yes! Wild blood clamored the only answer. "Aye. I wouldn't hurt you, Moll."

"You don't make any sense." Her voice quavered between laughter and tears. "*I* don't make any sense." And then she wept in earnest, and he could only hold her.

Hellfire. Beshrew him for the slime-soft son of a sea slug.

"Moll, don't cry. Why are you crying?"

Her tears unmanned him more surely than a kick between the legs. Mark Owen Daywell would not take a woman in tears.

Day judged it past midnight. Crickets chirred in the sagebrush. The Big Dipper spilled a shooting star, and he'd stroked Moll's hair until it sparked.

Neither felt the cold until a rock slipped beneath a foot, then rattled down the hillside. Lifting his arm from Moll, he palmed the Colt. Moll shivered.

"A deer?"

With a silencing gesture, he shook his head and set her away from him. A veteran of too many stalking nights, he knew the slide of a careful foot put wrong.

"Here dog. Nice dog." Thin as a ribbon, the voice floated. "Song Lin."

If Moll was right, Day wagered Favor had cast the Chinatown trollop as bait. A grassy-tar smell rippled from the girl. Moll's audible sniff said she not only smelled it, she disapproved. Then she saw Lin's injuries.

"Merciful heavens, what've they done! Day, hold the light if you please."

His Moll was gone as quick as that.

Lin shrank from the swaying swath of light, but Day saw the left side of her face, deformed with swelling, streaked with branching flows of blood.

"You can trust him." Moll spoke over Lin's fearful words. They both kept talking, in fact. How could they understand each other at all?

"Opium, Lin? I smelled it before I—you're twitchy—"

"I tell you everything, but he has to go." Slurred by her split and swollen lip, Lin's voice was still intelligible.

"No, I'll have to do some stitching. He could keep you steady, hold your hand."

Lin spat into the dirt, declining his aid. Nevertheless, he held his hand between Moll's shoulder blades, fragile wings, too light for human bones.

"If you need me, Bright, I'll stay." She settled against him and her pale temple rested on his shoulder.

"I'd better do it alone." Her fingers drummed softly on his arm. "Unless you can tell me how opium will affect her bleeding."

"Not my vice, lady."

"I guessed as much."

The echo of Moll's teasing accompanied the crunch of his boots as Day crossed the yard to his shack. Why did Song

Lin's hammered face and bruises, even the pall of opium, trigger Moll's exhilaration? His passion, on the contrary, reduced her to tears and confusion. He hadn't the first clue what to do about it.

Ordinarily, Molly woke as Poppy returned from her morning rounds. Today, Molly's gritty eyes opened as Poppy's feet touched the cabin floor. She heard her sister's chattering teeth, heard her jumble kindling into the firebox and slide the wooden lid from the crock of sourdough starter.

Moll pressed her cheek against her pillow, listening for her mother's presence, willing herself to block the memory of Day's hand against her breast.

Ice cracked on the water barrel and splashed into the kettle. Poppy's habit was to sip mint tea as she formed dough she'd left rising overnight. This morning, Molly heard the clunk of the iron skillet, the hiss of frying meat, smelled pungent onion and garlic. Poppy planned to sell pasties at the race.

None of that pried Molly's mind free of the facts: Day had touched her bodice and she'd allowed it! Allowed it? Merciful Heavens, she'd loved it!

Ashamed and excited, Molly wondered if Rose had fibbed. Could her mother's powers extend outside the house? It was a more satisfactory explanation than her own lust.

Far off, the shack door slammed. It would be Stag, not Day. Stag moved into the predawn dark to the mine, leaving Day alone.

Last night, when Lin insisted on returning to the cribs, Molly had chosen a path both Rose and Day would forbid. If they'd known. Molly didn't intend to share her plan.

"Take care of yourself, Molly." Lin had denounced Molly's idea. "Nobody else going to do it."

Although her scheme was dangerous, Molly knew the timely distraction of the Louse Town horse races wouldn't come again. Something in that peril even sharpened her feelings for Day.

"Desire, Molly girl. You picture the maleness of him, brown shoulders against cream-colored sheets. What would you like to be calling it, friendship?"

"Mama?" Censure filled Molly's whisper, but the puff of rose sweetness vanished as the back door opened.

"I couldn't go off without seeing you." Stag's voice came from the rear of the house.

"I wish you wouldn't go. It's not safe." Poppy sounded like a sweetheart.

"Once I strike it rich, I'll stay home with you."

Kissing and nuzzling came next. There were no secrets in this little house. Molly pressed her face into her pillow. Could Rose have meddled with Poppy's feelings as well?

As the door closed, Molly walked barefoot into the kitchen. She doused her face before addressing her surprised sister.

"I want you to take Cinder today."

"I will." Poppy flipped sizzling meat and vegetables. "Why, though?"

Molly pulled on a fresh chemise and told the truth. "There's a bad man in town, and Cinder will bite him if he tries to bother you." Favor would shoot the old hound without blinking, but such an attack wouldn't go unnoticed.

"All right."

Molly tied her bloomers and stared at her dress. She did not want to wear her corset, nor her crinoline. In twenty years, she hadn't given undergarments ten minutes of thought; in the last week, they'd been constantly on her mind.

Outside, Hannah mooed a protest and Poppy passed a hand over her forehead.

"How could I forget?" Poppy snatched up the pail and banged out the back door, without settling the door in its frame, without pulling the skillet off the fire.

Molly did both, then dashed for the front door. Poppy wouldn't guess where Molly had gone, and Rose couldn't follow.

After the first prick, Molly's bare feet felt neither stones nor stickers. She picked up her skirts and ran, set on reaching Day's arms before something stopped her.

Molly fidgeted at the shack door, hidden by a stand of head-high cornstalks. Should she knock? With what excuse? She should have brought coffee.

Her heart had thundered out of her chest into her throat. An impossibility, but she felt it. No blood vessels struck with such impact.

She'd just peek in, not wake him this early on race day.

Opening the door, she heard a metallic click in the dim, windowless shack. She'd swung the door fully open before she recognized the sound of a gun's hammer, cocking.

Naked except for the sheet draping his lap, Day sat on the bunk, one arm extended and ending with a silver revolver. The other arm braced his forearm from beneath. Day sighted down the gun as if he didn't recognize her, bare legs tight, toes gripping the wood floor. Quite, completely, naked.

Abruptly, his face drained white, as if he'd faint.

"By all that's holy, I might have shot you, Moll."

In slow motion, he pointed the gun to the ceiling and eased the hammer down, before slipping the gun between the mattress and the bed frame. Day moved to the head of the bed, leaned his back against the wall and pulled the sheet to his waist. He tilted his head as if regarding the rafters, but he barricaded sight with his forearm.

Molly noticed his hand's tremor, his pallor and stiff limbs. She could help.

She crossed the room, skirts rippling and billowing without the crinoline. She sat beside him. "Well, then." She cleared the hair from his panic-wet brow as well as she could, without moving the arm over his eyes.

"Well then, yourself." A plume of breath shivered in the cold air. "Y'almost met your Maker, Moll Gallagher. Did you see angels? Did your life flash before ye?"

"It wasn't as close as all that. You knew it was me."

"You'd be sick to your stomach if you knew how close."

You're a healer. Help him. She moved the arm barring his eyes. They remained closed, black lashes above violet-shad-

owed hollows. She extended his strong forearm, revealing
its delicate underside, coursing with veins.

Helpless to stop, Molly touched that skin, softer than her
own. Her fingers wandered higher than his elbow. He trembled. When she looked back to his eyes, Molly caught her
breath.

A healer wouldn't fix what ailed him. She'd opened his
eyes, fair enough, but Day no longer looked vulnerable. He
was a predator lying in wait. His eyes, smoke-blue in the
dim shack, and his beard-peppered jaw, hardening at her
touch, gave him away.

Molly wanted to be his prey: stupid, careless, oblivious to
danger, but caution remained. She cupped her hand over the
muscle of his far shoulder and he watched her. When he
didn't pursue her, she leaned over his chest, skimming her
hand up the sinews to his neck. Although he still watched,
she felt safe, hypnotized by his gaze, by the shack's darkness, where none but Day knew what she did. Molly settled
beside him, ready to flee. When he remained still, she
walked her fingers down his collarbone, to the center, before
placing a kiss in the hollow of his throat.

He took her under the sheet to a soft flannel nest, filled
with the male scent of him. And though her ankles twined
over his legs and his chest felt hard beneath her searching
hands, they only kissed. Relentless kisses that wouldn't let
her think.

Too close. Too breath-snatching, cornering close. She
fisted her hands to keep from touching him, pushed away so
a space opened between them in the warm bed.

He waited, eyes adoring her, and Moll's alarm faded
under her body's chant that he should come closer, that he
couldn't get close enough. Again, her hands sought the rasp
of his morning beard, then the separate glory of each rib. But
when her knuckles grazed his hipbone and he bucked
against her, Molly flinched.

"No, Bright." Day sounded as if he'd been running, and
he spoke through gritted teeth. "Moll, this is it. No further,
if that's what you want."

"Day—" Even she couldn't say whether she meant *stop,*

but then his hands were everywhere, stroking, molding, in-flaming. No choice, no control, no way to escape, to breathe . . .

"No," she whispered. "No, Day, please."

His hands stiffened, withdrew, and her regret was instant.

"Molly, open your eyes."

"I didn't mean *stop*." She never wanted to look at him again.

"Yes, you did." He took a shuddering breath. "And I stopped."

Humiliation gulped her will to stir, to speak, but when he placed one meek kiss on her cheekbone, she looked. She tried to think past the gray starbursts around his pupils, past his eyes' dark centers that widened to take her in.

"When you say yes, Bright, it's forever. You'll be mine and I'll take you with me. I can't stay, and I won't leave you."

She wanted to trust his words. She wanted to believe that Rose had failed again, that he'd stopped because of her fear and not Mad Rose's curse. It wasn't that Day wouldn't risk his manhood for a quick tumble. He'd stopped because he loved her.

"I'm sorry." She forced her fingernails into the palms of her hands, trying not to cry.

He stayed beside her, rose on his elbow with his head in his hand and refused to let her escape.

"Sorry?" He cleared his throat. "When you gave me such a gift? When you changed your mind, saying you didn't mean *stop,* I knew I could make you want me." He traced her lower lip with one finger. "*That,* Bright, is the feeling a man lives for."

When she still didn't speak, he wove his fingers through hers and squeezed. "Believe me, Molly."

He looked bereft, adrift, and she knew how to keep him from floating out of reach.

I love you. The words formed in Molly's heart, but twenty years of silence kept her from speaking.

Chapter
Twenty-six

Molly sat at Deborah's breakfast table, deliberately chewing buckwheat cakes and bacon. Over the water-slicked heads of miners, she saw Deborah blow her breath toward heat-damp wisps of hair. When she raised her brows, Molly nodded, unable to gather a smile. Later, she might confess her veer toward ruin. Not now.

With her hot face turned downward, Molly prodded a wedge of sorghum-sodden dough, then glanced around the table. With even syrup scraped from their plates, the miners waited for her to finish. Molly folded her napkin and slid from the table.

Boot traffic clomped the boardwalk outside. Shouts brayed from one side of the street to the other. She must find McCabe. His failure to appear at Deb's table meant a race of her own against the effects of holiday whiskey.

"Hear you've a horse running, Miss Molly, fit to beat every colt in the territory!" A miner blocked her path to the door.

"Yes, I do."

"I'm bettin' every cent I ha', 'cause, God's truth, y'saved Geordie's life down the mine, and I've a feelin' that filly will do me the same!" Another miner crowded between her and the door.

"Thank you." Molly edged past, fighting the desire to fan away a cloud of parlor potpourri, stirred by the men.

"Why, I saw Day ridin' her—"

"—always knew him to be more'n a peddler—"

Four men tightened the noose of their bodies as Molly pushed her cuffs up. The open door admitted the dead still-ness that presaged a thunderstorm. She reached to unbutton her collar as the men's excitement jostled them closer.

"—up Gold Hill way—"

"—lit out like a cat with her tail afire!"

She must have air. She'd die without it.

"So blamed fast, I'll be puttin' my dollar on her!"

The back door promised air and water.

"Excuse me, gentleman, I need—" She gestured and fled.

The pipe gushed cool water and Molly welcomed it with hands and face. When the spout gurgled its last, she chafed the drops over her wrists. She tipped her head back to regard a sullen sky, as heavy as a cast-iron lid.

The door slammed. Deborah untied her apron, shook it, and three red hens scratched and worried for crumbs.

"Are you going to tell me, or bust with it?" Deb slung the apron over her shoulder.

A confession would scorch her tongue. "Sorry. Not yet."

Deborah flinched at the rebuff.

Raucous lyrics, a tin flute and the neighs of tethered horses bombarded C Street. Each minute Molly indulged her melancholy, McCabe's sobriety and usefulness dwindled. The revelry wouldn't wait for the race to begin at two.

"You're not pregnant, are you?"

"What?" Molly had heard the accusation, but far worse was Deb's voice, vibrating with bitter acceptance.

Stepping around Deborah, Molly opened the boarding-house door. She longed for scathing words. Thick breakfast smells closed around her, smothering flippant remarks on loyalty.

"Moll, come back!"

Molly lifted her black wool cloak from the coatrack, but she didn't drape it over her shoulders. Humidity tilted her stomach with queasiness as she closed Deb's door behind her. Perversely, she longed for the chill that flowed from Rose.

As Molly bustled away, she wondered for the first time whether part of Rose's reputation had sprung not from truth, but slander.

Molly hated to enter the saloon, but recognition of McCabe's bellowing halted her. She paced past the swinging doors, then turned back. A bead of sweat stung her eye. What did she fear? That someone would think her a loose woman?

She blotted her brow. If Deborah believed it, who did not? Molly had tied the enveloping cloak over her breasts, preparing to enter, when fingers tugged at her skirt.

"Mama said—" Robin panted, "to *please* come back!"

"She did?" Molly kissed his exertion-red cheek, then opened her reticule. "Robin, what if I give you a penny to go in and tell the bartender a lady has business with Mr. McCabe?"

The reticule hung lightly from Molly's wrist. Her medical bag sat at home, deeding any race-day tramplings to Cutting Jack. She flattened her guilt with the greater good of the deed McCabe would help her accomplish.

Framed between the swinging doors, Robin turned. "Can I spend it on anything I want?"

"Anything. Bring him back with you, and there'll be more. I'm going to be a rich woman come nightfall."

"How's that?" Wiping beer foam from his jowls, McCabe pushed aside the saloon's batwing doors. Robin jumped back.

"I have a fast horse, Mr. McCabe. I also have a business proposal."

"Yeah, yeah. You got my attention."

"Can you haul some cargo to Mormon Station?"

Day must have battered the freighter's brain, because Mc-Cabe offered his arm. To her further astonishment, she accepted, and revealed her plan, as they walked toward the livery stable.

"Ain't she just showin' her belly like she's proud of it!"

Day threw his weight on Glory's withers, forcing her down from a sky-pawing rear. Sweated shiny as glass, Moll's filly drew applause in the impromptu parade to the post.

Where in bloody Hell was Moll? He was in no condition, no *damned* condition to ride Glory to a win.

First, Poppy'd run home, demanding permission to see the race. With Moll gone, what could he say but yes? Next, Griffin had pranced up on his steeldust, not to apologize for his bleedin' marriage proposal, but to ask if Day planned to shoot Favor, or should he, Griffin, take the chore?

Now, Day searched the hillside slanting above the buildings. A cicada's silver wing flickered. Thunder muttered across a bruise-colored sky and Day cursed these inland storms that scraped every nerve raw with waiting. He'd welcome the slashing honesty of an ocean blow.

A whistle shrilled and Glory bucked. Strolling banjo players strummed and a fool tossed firecrackers. Day straightened his leather vest to cover the Colt and searched for Moll's red hair.

He'd insulted her, right enough. But which had sent her running? His trespass or *not* taking her? He'd played the gentleman and even that might be a mistake! When a lass offered herself up like that, it was hardly gentlemanly . . .

His heart jammed high in his chest, thudding like the God-awful drum up front of this mad jubilee. In black top hat and silver beard, an itinerant rainmaker beat Hell out of a drum and burned torches on his red-and-gilt wagon, swearing heat and concussion could leech rain from the clouds. For a price. Though folks knew rain meant misery in a mining town, the crowd applauded his showmanship.

Deborah, in a crown of burnished braids, clutched

Robin's hand and scanned the crowd. Nearby, Poppy and
Stag whispered together like children.

Horses broke stride, threatening to race before they got out
of town. Dust-blinded, Day lost sight of anyone he knew.

One black—Favor's?—refused to bolt. She wore the look
of Ireland's heavy hunters, cold-blooded stock that wore
down the competition. Stirrups short, quirt on his wrist, a
blond boy perched atop her.

A slab-sided bay careened into Glory. She only tossed her
flaxen forelock and whickered.

"That's a good lass. Where's Molly, now? She wouldn't
miss your maiden run."

Maiden. Did it all turn on that? Had she run off, with no
one to come after her? *Molly, girl, what do you want of me?*

Then, Day saw him.

Horses and humans swirled on the descent to Louse
Town, but he saw only Rankin, the man blaming him for
Shawnee Sue's murder.

Randall Rankin reined a palomino against the black filly.
Unhampered by the cigar clamped in his teeth, Rankin addressed the black's rider.

Day touched his clean-shaven jaw. If Abby and Persia
recognized him, if Moll had, too, Rankin might.

He did. Yanking the palomino on its heels, Rankin glared
across the parade.

Like the Colt's hammer coming down on an empty chamber, Day felt their connection.

"He's seen you. I'll drop back and get on the other side of
him." Griffin slowed his horse and edged across traffic.
"Watch out for Tony."

Cock-Eyed Tony. The bad man's accomplice had to be Antonio, Rankin's handsome, flawed lieutenant.

Rankin was Favor. Ruthless Favor, the whore's night-
mare. And he'd—set hands on Molly. What had he done?
The question exploded like a bomb inside Day's chest.
What?

Rankin kneed the palomino across the stream of riders.
Restraint had never been Rankin's style. He'd forgotten it
wasn't Lightfoot's, either.

Come ahead, you bastard. Day gripped his gun. Glory sidestepped away from Rankin's approach. "Settle, beauty. Save it."

Rankin squinted, making sure, before he jerked the palomino into step with Glory. "It *is* you."

"Bloody right."

Reveling in Rankin's shock, Day straightened his fingers, then gripped the reins. No gunplay here and no murder. Not with hundreds of witnesses, including Poppy, Deborah, maybe even Moll.

Better to goad Rankin into shooting. And if Rankin stayed cool now, so much the better. Day'd lead Rankin away from Moll, finish him and heave his dandified carcass down a mine shaft.

"Shove that smile back down your murdering throat, O'Deigh."

"Ah, now, imagine a fine swell like you, bein' seen with a gunslick like me." The words rolled like whiskey on his tongue.

"They know—?" Rankin cast a quick glance over the crowd, then corrected himself. "They *don't* know what you are."

"They're not after carin', are they, *Senator* Rankin. Or Governor, is that how you'll have it? What a cryin' shame if the good voters of Virginia City knew what you are."

"Some know and don't care." Rankin fingered the silver studding on his black saddle. "Those who don't know, won't find out. Think they're going to believe you?

"You've grown." Rankin measured him. "You were developing polish. That's what Sue said. Told me I should use you in Frisco. But you're the same ignorant trash you were when I found you."

As the crowd thinned for the start, Day locked his temper down. "Sure, and they know about the cribs, these folk. They talk of the whores y'hurt so bad." Day swallowed bile dredged up by images of Favor reaching for wee Molly. "And the opium."

"There's no law against it."

Day turned his eyes skyward. Lead gray with molten

edges, the clouds blocked the sun. He willed the heavens to rupture.

"No law against forcin' a child, either, but there's common decency. That's something even this ragtag lot knows."

"Fine words coming from a killer—"

Careful.

"—who can speak the language just a little better than my Chinks. But I've heard enough. Try your elocution on Merrick."

Sheriff Merrick flaunted a red flag and an upraised revolver, threatening to start the race, though few horses had lined up. Many were besieged by luck-seekers who plucked mane or tail hair from the animals they'd bet upon.

A gunshot couldn't disrupt chaos. Day wished for that little pepperbox pistol of Abby's to press against Rankin's ribs.

"Merrick's seen the poster." Day shrugged at Rankin's threat. "He's not believin' it's me."

"I'll tell him."

"Y'don't scare me, Rankin."

"Now that I have you, I can kill you whenever I like."

Day smiled. *Go for the gun, big man. Jerk it out and squeeze it off. C'mon, you're foamin' for satisfaction.*

"You left a woman, blood-drenched. A dead woman—"

Day's anger spewed. "*You* told me Shawnee Sue was swappin' stolen cattle for lovin'. *You* said the cattle were yours—"

Geordie, limping along on his crutches, broke through the crowd and led an entourage of miners to Glory's side.

"Only one way to mark a horse for luck. Right, Day?" Oblivious to tension and poised trigger fingers, Geordie beamed up, spat in the middle of his palm and smacked spittle on Glory's shoulder. His cronies crowed their delight.

"There! Now there's no chance Miss Molly's horse will lose! Good wishes to ye, cousin!"

"Molly?" Gratification curled a corner of Rankin's mouth.

Damn him to hell! What had possessed Geordie to speak Moll's name? He couldn't ask. The miner lurched off into the crowd, oblivious to Day's fury and Rankin's low chuckle.

Molly coughed against the dust raised by McCabe's wagon and reveled in victory. Bent on rescue, she'd invaded Favor's "village" of damned females. Only Lin had come along, but that was one. One slap to Favor's smug face.

Satisfaction came at a dear price. She hadn't agreed to nurse McCabe free for a year, hadn't risked Favor's retaliation and Day's rage for one woman's freedom, but it must be enough. She prayed McCabe, Lin and that single stranger stayed silent about who'd done the deed. If Favor knew she'd crossed him, he'd crush her.

Arriving, she'd had to push past Lin to enter what she'd mistaken for a joss house. Opium vapors had parted, showing women arranged like random lengths of kindling. A few gazed up, hollow-cheeked from greedy sucking.

In the room's center, a brazier's fire had gilded a young boy's frown. No older than Robin, he'd transferred a gummy brown bead of opium to the bowl of a pipe. Her begging changed nothing. The women lay clotted together, complacent as the dead.

A clash of falling brass marked the boy's agitation. Face sheened with sweat, the child's fingers flew to prepare another pipe. The smoky space compressed as if the walls cinched closer.

A gust of wind, heavy with rain, tempted her to go.

"All right." At least Lin sat in the wagon, ready to flee.

"You're all right yourself, *signorina*. Tell me you're looking for a way to pay for your pleasures."

Blood-red gouts . . . Molly blocked her eyes, and the unsought vision. He thought her a opium addict; sinking into a trance would make her vulnerable.

As his hand gripped her shoulder, she recognized a touch she'd never felt. The man with the damaged face had triggered the same scarlet horror in VanBrunts' store. He wore clean linen, black vest and a luxuriant mustache, but confirmation simmered in his eyes.

Molly had never experienced such a blinding mental connection. She didn't want it. Peril would come from surrender. Survival meant a display of strength, showing no reaction when his fingers burrowed into her flesh, seeking the shoulder joint.

Molly leaned into the pain, sifting the mind behind the burn-smeared face.

"It must have been a terrible fire." The words, a healer's words, not a victim's, came before she thought.

"Gun, not a fire." His grip wrenched her a step nearer.

"Please release my arm."

He did. Relief said to fall back a step; instinct told her to stand firm. The outlaw loomed closer, boots stirring her skirts, but she didn't move away.

"Thank you." She crossed her arms. "My name is Moll Gallagher."

"I know who you are." His voice shimmered with carnal undertones and Molly thought again how handsome he'd been.

"And you? Might I ask your name?"

He battled the flicker of courtesy that had survived Favor's influence. "You could ask."

He turned his back, breaking their link, then strode to a horse cropping rabbit brush and mounted.

He wouldn't tell Favor. Molly knew that as strongly as she knew he'd purposely broken free of her thoughts, letting them fall into the dust of his departure.

Now, sheets of dust slanted behind McCabe's wagon. McCabe handed Molly down at the turnoff to Dutch Nick's, the nearest he dared come to the racetrack before continuing on with Lin.

Molly waved. Her disappointment at Lin's silence faded as shouts signaled that the race was about to begin.

Wind rose and rain fell as Molly rushed toward the Louse Town racetrack. With each step into the gale, she cheered for Glory and Day. She imagined Glory's streaming mane licking around Day's face as he urged her faster and faster. Running into the wind as if she matched them stride for stride, Molly felt the last barriers to trust fall.

Pistols fired and horses neighed. Molly hadn't run fast enough. Cheers proclaimed a winner before she began the descent to the track. Day. It had to be Day and Glory.

Breathless, she paused at the pound of approaching hooves. Grunts wrenched from the chest of a laboring horse as a rider made away from the track at racing speed. Molly flattened herself against the cliffside, out of its path. She crossed her arms over her head to form a canopy against smacking, fat raindrops.

"That's got it, lovey." The rider's voice soared over the slamming hooves. "Good girl."

Day! Before Molly could call to him, the horse was upon her. Glory hugged the road's edge for maximum speed, brushing Moll back even farther. With a stutter of hooves and flashing gold tail, Glory swept past.

Molly stared after the lathered horse, the clamped-down black hat, the rider's broad-shouldered litheness.

"Day! Day, it's me."

The horse stopped, hooves dancing in place. Through the rain's gray curtain, she saw the rider's back stiffen, but he didn't turn. The filly plunged, fighting the tightened reins.

"Day!"

Then he loosed his reins and set his heels to the filly's ribs. Glory leapt forward, answering her master's command.

Chapter
Twenty-seven

What's the use of feeling huffy as a wet biddy when they can't hear a word you say? That's what you should be asking yourself, Rose Gallagher! Wait till nightfall, though Moll won't listen then. Oh! It surpassed every infuriation known to have Moll walk through me! And now, when my two blessed daughters should be banding together, they're having these carryings-on!

"Molly, I'm not afraid of him." Poppy sat behind a barricade of sugared doughnuts. Pretty thing, with her brow smooth beneath a blue ribbon. The window behind her ran with rain, and though she'd have to fight the downpour to reach school, Poppy looked downright serene.

"You should be afraid!" Molly's pestle stabbed at a bowl of dried catnip.

Who has the fever? Or is it colic, Moll? Catnip's good for colic. Is it that new Happy Days babe?

"Why should I be afraid? Stag's not going to hurt me."

"You don't know that!" Molly's rueful laugh must've burned her throat.

Maybe Moll had taken to chewing catnip herself. Raw catnip turned a docile dolly into a shrew . . . but no, it was him. She'd been in his arms, given him half her heart and he'd gone.

"They say they won't hurt you, honey. And if you refuse them, they leave." Molly's lips pursed like an old maid's. "Even if I'd given in, he would have gone. Though he might not have stolen my horse!" Molly stopped, fearful she'd shocked Poppy.

"You need to get more sleep," her sister diagnosed. "Why did you start getting up with me? Your eyes were always closed when I came home from delivering bread. I liked waking you."

Molly shook her head, and Rose knew the Cornishman haunted Moll more than her ghostly mother. Every minute since she'd watched him ride away, she'd ached as if her heart had been dragged out through her breastbone. Rose knew the pain too well.

"Stag's not to come calling, do you understand? You may not have him in this house—"

"If you're here, Moll—"

"Not even if I'm here. Cross me in this, Poppy, and I'll evict him from the shack! I probably should anyway!"

"It's all Day's fault, not mine." Poppy pouted.

Moll's trust had been shaken. For a few weeks, Rose had watched the girl believe. With kind words and patience, pasties, chopped onions and scratches behind the old dog's ears, Day had purchased her daughter's heart. *Ah, men. I miss your lively lovin', but not your faithless wandering.*

Now, even the weather had turned bad. Virginia's dirt roads ran with mud. Yesterday, from behind the curtain, Rose had watched a horse slip to his knees, then slide, pulling an ore wagon atop him. Leaving the beast in agony, the driver had jumped loose and run to pound the door for Moll's Remington.

The barrel was still hot when the driver returned and begged a cup of coffee while bemoaning the storm. He claimed dozens of miners with staggered shifts, who took turns sleeping in shacks, had fallen sick and lay crammed in together, crowded and surly.

Rain provided one reward. Folks stayed home, unable to embellish Red Molly's latest scandal, featuring a faithless desperado, lost gold and stolen horseflesh.

More exciting talk than they splattered on me, girl.

"Why don't you go see Deborah?" Poppy tucked two fat doughnuts into her lunch bucket.

"She can walk up here as easily as I can go to her."

Something amiss, there. Rose's interest quickened at the prospect of gossip.

Molly looked up in time to see Poppy hazard a guilty glance before slipping outside.

Sneaking, pretty girl? It takes no ghostly powers to guess why. Young Stag's waiting on the front porch while you slip out the back. Is that it?

Candlelight silvered rain creeping beneath the door. Molly slammed down her herb bowl and wedged the door tight in its warped frame. She wiped up the gritty sugar Poppy had spilled all over the table and glared at the primer Poppy had left behind.

Molly closed her eyes, fighting tears.

Sweet lass, you'll bear anything for Poppy, won't you? Even bickering. Faith, she's the only one you trust with your love. Now she's developed a mind of her own. That's all it is, dear. Don't make her pull away.

Cinder barked and dragged himself, poor old thing, from under the table. He stalked on painful joints toward the front door, though the knock had rapped at the back.

Let it be Day. I could do with a rainy-day tale and a kitchen full of kissing!

"Molly!" Muffled and accompanied by the sound of feet stamping off mud, the voice was a woman's.

"Deb?"

Deborah entered on a gust of wind, mixing the smell of cinnamon with damp wool. "If this keeps up, we'll wish we'd grown fins instead of feet!"

A spate of cats—gray, yellow and brown—burst in

around Deborah's ankles, then bolted past Rose. Only Ginger vaulted up on a chair and feinted a front paw as if Rose could pick her up.

"I can't keep them out!" Molly watched the cats vanish under table and bed, then dart for the parlor.

"Why would you want to—?" Deborah shook out her cloak and hung it next to Molly's.

"Customers don't like cat hair—"

"—poor things."

Their words collided and neither woman continued. Deborah pushed back a soaked lock of hair. She filled her cheeks full of air and expelled it with a *whoosh*.

"I'd hug you if I didn't think it would make you angrier."

A good friend indeed if she knew Molly scorned touching.

"That's the look that makes folks believe you're a witch," Deborah pointed out as Molly set a cup of lemongrass tea and a doughnut before her. "Otherworldly, cold, stretching your neck up and looking down your nose—Umm! These are good—in case you want to cultivate it. The look."

"I think I've mastered it."

Deborah's laugh sputtered through a shower of crumbs. "I think you have! Oh, Moll, don't hate me, please? I didn't mean what I said. Remember when we were talking about Day, in the meadow, with the kites? You were afraid he'd hurt you?"

Molly nodded.

"I told you it would be worth it. Something like that"— Deborah's hand fluttered impatiently—"and asked if you'd still be *my* friend if I were stupid and hurt your feelings. Remember?"

Molly polished a finger around the lip of her cup. "What did I say?"

"Nothing, but you must know why I said what I did, by the pump?"

"Because I'm the kind—"

"No. Stop it!" Deborah slammed her palm on the table. "You haven't got the sense God gave a goose when it comes to yourself, Moll Gallagher! I said it, because—" Deborah scrubbed her nose with a white handkerchief. "Because I thought I'd pushed you into it—with Day."

Molly examined the buttonless cuff of her sleeve, folded it under and leaned it closed on the table.

"It was stupid, but it had nothing to do with you or your mother. Besides, I think we would've gotten on fine, Rosie and me. She did what she had to do." Deborah drew an even louder sniff, and Rose thought what a perceptive friend Moll had.

Deborah turned Molly's arm to display the neglected sleeve. "It seems unlikely she had it in her to be a seamstress!"

As if I could! I'll tell you, young woman, when I came to Virginia City, it was wivin' or washin'. No jobs in between. Except what I choose. And it was always done with affection, not money-grubbing coldness.

Molly returned Deb's squeeze, then blinked at Rose as if clearing her vision.

Deborah insisted on an official end to the fight. "Are *we* all right?"

Moll struggled as if she'd swallowed a chicken bone, then managed, "We're all right."

"Good." Deborah fumbled in her reticule. "Because I couldn't bring myself to give two hundred dollars to an enemy."

"Two hundred—"

Deborah tossed a leather pouch into Molly's hands. Gold coins and curled currency packed the chamois pouch.

"It's the horse-race purse. Not a complete villain, is he?"

The handsome Cornishman has smitten more than one heart, passing through town!

"He stole my horse, Deborah."

"And left you two hundred dollars."

"Two hundred dollars won by my horse—"

"A horse that would still be standing out there, as little use as that cow, except she didn't give milk." Deborah sat back, arms crossed and smug.

"True." Molly pulled the drawstrings and moved the sack against her breast.

"And you'd give every penny to have him back."

"Half, maybe."

Hooves splattered the mud outside and passed by as Deborah explained. "He tossed me the bag as he rode off. Someone might have been after him, the way he kept glancing over his shoulder. In that crowd, who could tell? He shouted something like, he'd be back as soon as he could."

Molly closed her eyes, refusing that futile hope as Deborah prattled on. "Now you can order those books Margaret says Poppy needs."

"They're ordered. This means we won't have to eat them."

After Deborah's departure, Rose trailed Molly when she picked up her childhood journal. Rose settled to read over her daughter's shoulder. If she'd had the power to turn pages, she would have read it herself, long since.

"I hop he dint mak me deef." Molly gripped the journal, though her hand jerked up, as if she'd cup and protect her left ear. *"I feel all watery in my ear wher he grabd my head and pushd me down and my nees hurt from hiting the flor so hard—"*

Rose felt moaning, like wild wind, rising within her.

"I know we'r fine with the black dog and gun Luba gave us, but I'm scard of the gun and scared Favor will come here when thers nobody and I sit up and wach Poppy and sleep and wake up and sleep again I'm real afraid."

Powerless rage rumbled through Rose. Who would hurt a motherless child? What had he done that Moll had been too innocent to record? *Angels above, bless me with one hour of retribution!*

Molly slammed the book closed and dropped it before stroking Cinder's head. "Mother? I can feel you vibrating. Are you incensed? Didn't you guess we had to stay with Persia?"

Her girls had gone to Persia! Madam of a whorehouse!

"Mother?"

With all her perception, Rose couldn't read Moll's voice. Did her soft stepping from word to word signal anger?

Molly shrugged, left her bedroom and sat in the parlor chair, Cinder on one side, the Remington angled across her lap. Rare drops plopped from the eaves, promising a clear evening. The sky shone rose-gold through the curtains. A breeze coaxed wet sage indoors and Rose ached for the powers of a real woman.

When Cinder's growl broke into a snarl, Molly knew she'd made the right decision. She'd sent word for Poppy to stay after school with Margaret.

Favor was coming, just as she'd known he would. And he came without Antonio and the man he'd called Skinner. His shadow moved alone, beyond the curtains.

"Come in." Molly didn't wait for his knock.

Favor hesitated, perhaps fearful of ambush, but pride spurred him on. As he opened the door, firethorn twisted red and green behind him. His dry hat and mud-free boots made him look as if he'd come courting.

"I see you're expecting someone." He nodded at the rifle.

"I was."

Favor closed the door. He placed his hands on his hips, drawing back his coat to show he wore no gun. Bullets had never been his worst weapon.

"I got to thinking about our conversation at Persia's." Favor began a majestic pacing. "Upset by Claret dying on you, you might have misunderstand what I said."

"Your orders seemed pretty straightforward to me."

"I do love the daring, grown-up Moll Gallagher." Favor stroked his bottom lip with the knuckle of one finger. When he stepped toward her, Cinder bolted up with an explosion of staccato barks. Molly grabbed his collar.

"Put that dog out or I'll kill him."

She didn't want it to be this way. She could call his bluff and dare him to cut Cinder's satiny black throat. No. Favor threatened and she obeyed.

Clumsy with the tall rifle, she shoved Cinder outside.

"You've commandeered my parlor, now what do you want?" Molly raised her voice to be heard over Cinder's barking.

Favor seated himself on the love seat and pulled his hunter-green suitcoat closer. "Perhaps a palm reading."

"No." Molly levered a bullet into the chamber.

He laughed. Because he knew she wouldn't shoot? Or because he'd remembered a more effective way to strike?

"So you've taken up with Lightfoot O'Deigh. Don't deny it, Molly. It's the talk of the town, though he called himself Day, didn't he, while he was with you? Not a terribly original variation, but I doubt O'Deigh's *mind* was what attracted you."

"He trained my horse and did some chores." Molly watched Rose stalk around the man, trying to discern the threat he posed.

"Molly, dear." Favor leaned forward, forearms on thighs. "As a young man I made mistakes. Succumbing to your beauty was one."

Fingers curved in rigid claws, Rose hunched over Favor. Maybe she'd figured him out. Hope gave Molly a thrill of power.

"Take your hat off inside my house," she told him.

He complied, without losing the thread of his lie.

"I'm taking steps to remedy my mistakes. Supporting your intention to keep Poppy, for instance, in spite of that accident, which might have been so serious." He beamed with false sincerity. "I've discouraged the VanBrunts from removing Poppy to a proper home. They're eager to take her in. Hans, especially, is quite fond of your little sister."

Molly remembered Day's fury. He'd glared at her, burning his suspicions into her brain. And he'd been right.

"Nor have I made much of Claret's unexplained death. What's one whore, more or less?"

"What is it you want?" Impatience pushed aside Molly's resolve to stay calm. Why didn't Rose do something besides hunch there, like a vulture? "Do you expect me to go to Carson and tell someone you're not fit to run the government?"

"Damn, you keep this place cold as a tomb." Favor chafed his forearms, then nodded her way. "But that's very good, Molly. You have no one and nothing to tell. Remember that."

"Leave." With that, Molly saw Rose fade away completely.

"Not before I offer you a little advice about Lightfoot. He murdered a whore in Lake's Crossing and I hear he beat up McCabe and VanBrunt pretty badly. It's how he settles things." Favor bit the end off a cigar and picked a flake of tobacco from his tongue. Then he winked.

"The Pinkertons and my people are tracking him—" His unconscious grimace made her heart vault up. "—but he'll be back. It's one of the things he does best, hiding behind women's skirts. I'll be watching for him, Molly."

Smoke wreathed Favor's head as he eyed her rafters. "I did want to clarify your peculiar friendship with my Chink girl, Song Lin. It's just as well you couldn't lure the rest of them off."

So the outlaw, the flawed man whose mind communed with hers, had lied even to himself.

Favor chuckled at her surprise. The Remington felt slippery in her hands.

"The boy told me, Molly! You are such an innocent." He leered. He didn't say it. He never had to. It was understood: he'd ravage that innocence if he could. "And McCabe will make a double profit on his transaction."

Favor knew everything. Molly's finger caressed the trigger's cool half moon.

"McCabe already had my shipment of opium packed in his wagon. I hired him to drive it down to Sacramento. It won't be difficult to find Song Lin."

Favor jumped up from the couch. His expression, curved around the jutting cigar, was that of a joyous father, watching his babe take its first step.

Mama, I need you.

"I do find your naïveté delightful! So childlike, after the life you've led." He walked closer, taking the cigar from his mouth as his eyes roamed her.

Oh, please, no. She wanted to scream. She wanted to shoot. She thought of him taking Poppy, and did nothing.

"You're just like that gun, Molly, fine and dangerous . . ." He pushed the gun barrel aside. The wave of cigar smoke made her stomach lurch. ". . . but completely harmless in the hands of someone who knows how to handle you."

He grabbed her chin and kissed her. Molly's mind howled in outrage, for Favor's kiss hadn't been punishing and cruel. It hadn't been gross. It had been a parody of chasteness, a kiss paternal in its purity. He'd kissed Molly Gallagher to prove he could. His power reigned absolute. He could do whatever he wanted, even when she held a loaded rifle.

And then he was choking. Both Favor's hands grappled at his throat as Rose spun herself like a long icy muffler around his neck.

"Mama, no! He'll—"

Twisting, twining, tighter and tighter, Rose protected Molly as best she could. Rose vanished as Favor bolted out the door.

Molly heard him slip on the rain-wet porch, heard him splash into a puddle, muddying his pristine trousers.

Molly closed her eyes. She wondered why Cinder wasn't barking and she wondered if Rose had any notion how absolutely she'd convinced Favor to wreak revenge.

The first Empty Pockets miner died that night. When two of his shackmates took sick, the others called for help. Blackie, seventeen years old and so scared his teeth chattered, called for Cutting Jack. Arthur Pendragon summoned Molly.

"Jack." Molly met the barber on the shack's muddy footpath.

"You know what we got here?" Jack's eyes lingered on the hem she lifted clear of the mud. Molly mulled over Arthur's description of the dead man's symptoms and relayed them to Jack.

First, a miner named Mac had fallen foggy-headed. Nothing of consequence, they'd thought, blaming it on a pocket of bad air. A couple of days later Mac had grabbed at a pain in his gut and turned hot and thirsty. They gave him water, worried as he babbled, grew quiet and, while they slept, died.

"I hope they haven't buried him." Molly slowed as they reached the shack.

"I don't take that for bloodthirstiness, but I hate corpses." Jack glanced at her, askance. "You say a thing like that, Molly, and if I had bristles, you wouldn't know me from a porky-pine." He shuddered and bowed her in ahead of him.

Gray and windowless, the dwelling backed so far into the hillside brown slugs of mud oozed between the boards. Five men slept in the one-room shack.

Mac lay twined in a sheet. Blackie fell weeping on Jack's neck, though Molly couldn't guess what he expected of the barber. Joe Potter lay on his side in the other bunk. He raised one hand as Arthur made introductions, then swallowed painfully and closed his eyes. Geordie leaned his back against the wall.

"Sorry t'trouble y'again, so soon."

One dead, two sick, two scared to death.

"Perhaps you could step outside with Mr. Slocum, Geordie, while I prepare your friend for the funeral. Arthur? Bring me a bit of water, if you could."

Her inch-by-inch examination of Mac found only advanced stiffness. He'd died long before dawn. He had a miner's muscular torso and ragged hands, a nasty scar on his thigh, a number of well-scratched insect bites and a bloated belly.

Mouth metallic and lips numb, Molly chafed her hands together as Arthur returned with water. "How're you feeling, lad?" She washed her hands before touching the dead boy.

"Best o' the lot." Arthur's mustache twitched, underlining his guilt. "I'm worried about Geordie."

"Did you all eat together, last night?"

"Aye. Except for Mac. And Joe. He ate down to Brown Bess's with his partner, Sean."

Bad food would be too simple. Death without blood was rarely easy to figure.

"Where do you fetch your water? And where's your outhouse? Has any of that changed?"

None of Arthur's answers suggested cause or cure, but

she'd ordered water from another well, just as a precaution, when Blackie interrupted.

"One thing we got in common, we work Empty Pockets mine."

"I see." Molly waited, but he said no more.

She worked all afternoon, urging water and yarrow on Joe, coaxing him to chew willow bark as his fever climbed. She didn't notice Jack's departure, but marked his return.

"Mrs. Green told me to take this rig." Jack gestured to the mule and wagon as Arthur and Blackie loaded Mac's corpse.

"It's Day's." A dream without a nightmare! "Tell him—"

"Mrs. Green said it was yours, traded for the filly."

Molly tapped the dented tin cup she'd carried from the bedside. In reflection, her hands loomed clownish and pink.

" . . . at Bess's."

"Pardon me?" Even in this pest house, Day clouded her mind.

"Sean, I said. That talk-your-leg-off Irishman. He's complaining of a sore head, pain in his gut and dysentery.

"He works in the Empty Pockets, too, but Bess don't want you coming down. I'll tend him."

"I've plenty to keep me busy here. I hope no one breaks a leg in this mud. Arthur?" What kept her turning to the young Cornishman for help? "On the way to the cemetery, could you stop at Miss Margaret's school and tell Poppy where I am?"

Molly sat alone with Joe Potter, until Jack returned from the funeral. He off-loaded feverish Geordie, who'd collapsed during the burial text. Jack spat as he announced that Brown Bess had taken to her bed.

"Bein' as she's more comfortable with me—"

"Go." Molly waved him off, too weary for manners. Jack held the mule in place. "For mercy's sake, what?"

"Everyone of 'em's from the Empty Pockets mine."

"Not Bess."

"Aw—" Jack flipped his hand in dismissal. "Bess's been sick a long time. Should've had a doctor. This'll finish her."

"Are you keeping some secret about the mine?"

"It's pure superstition." Jack's cheek bulged as his tongue

sought a wad of tobacco. "Geordie and Arthur don't believe, but Blackie can't help hisself."

Pure superstition. Blackie stood kicking at rocks until she approached, then he vaulted into the wagon beside Jack, who slapped the reins and rumbled away.

"Miss Poppy sent some pasties." Arthur broke Molly's musing some hours later. He extended a cloth-wrapped parcel redolent of potatoes and pepper.

"You eat them. I'm not hungry."

"No, they're for you. And Miss Molly, y'must know, the mine . . . There's been a *woman* in the mine."

"So, that's the superstition—" Molly's lips clamped shut. "Of course. And not just any woman."

"Aye."

"A witch."

"So they say." Arthur followed her inside. It seemed to comfort him to pat her back as she fashioned a rest for Geordie's leg. So she allowed it.

Chapter
Twenty-eight

"Then why don't I turn them into toads, Stag?" Molly's whisper cracked. Sage water, destined to soothe Geordie's brow, slopped from the bowl and onto her dress. "Merciful Heavens, I'd save myself a lot of trouble and a fair amount of sleep!"

"Didn't say I believe them, Molly. I don't."

When had Stag stopped calling her *miss*? Uppity pup!

She gazed around the shack. She'd burned every garment, glove and blanket, then requested all new things from Van-Brunts'. In the time it took to scrub the walls and shovel a fresh dirt floor, the supplies arrived. Eleanor's terse note waved off payment. "Since we now have a benefactor, we can afford charity."

Favor, no doubt.

Molly had folded the note into her pocket, keeping it as a talisman against flagging energy. Pure spite held off the disease and defiance kept her from dying.

Confused by her lapse in attention, Stag forced a laugh.

"I'm drifting, Stag, sorry. No new cases, you say?"

He shook his head. Several days—she wasn't sure how many—had passed with no new victims. How many had there been in all? Eight?

"Just keep Poppy away, will you? Don't go near her. I've a few books you can read in the shack. Is it still raining?"

"Miss Margaret loaned me books and I filled some time shimming up that back door and, uh, the rain's turned to hail."

That's what it had been. She'd daydreamed kite sticks, nose-diving against the wooden walls.

"And you're showing no bug bites? No fever, dysentery—"

"For decency's sake, don't ask again!" Stag grinned, but Molly found nothing amusing.

The dead included Bess, a man named Grady and Joe Potter. Molly's eyes continued checking for Joe, and her breastbone kinked as she remembered his dying cries.

Each day she fought harder for Geordie, whose coughs threatened to burst his swollen belly. After Joe's nightmarish end she'd taken to tying a kerchief over her face.

She quarantined the sick, forced cool rose-hip water and controlled fever with yarrow, willow and cool baths.

"What's the date?" Molly frowned at a glimmering spider web, survivor of her cleaning frenzy. "Stag?"

He'd gone and the date didn't really matter.

Molly grabbed a broom and approached the web. A thimble-sized spider balanced on liquid silver threads that quivered with her testing.

"It only looks like magic." Molly commiserated with the silent spinner. "It comes right from your guts, doesn't it?"

Relinquishing the broom for a wet cloth, she saw to Geordie.

"How's your leg, sweetheart?"

Geordie's eyes opened. She could tell before he spoke that the bulldog Cornishman would insist that it was still the day of the mine accident.

"Better. 'Fore long I'll be watchin' your witch theater."

"Shh." She dampened Geordie's hair and broomstraw mustache.

"Y'wouldn't hold it against me? Day, he near beat me for it, and him as sweet on ye as me . . ."

From the other cot, Arthur watched with dull eyes. Molly yawned and pressed her spine hard against the ladder-back chair. She'd best splash her own face with water before she nodded off.

"Hell! Dead asleep that girl packs a punch like a she-ass!"

Cutting Jack's gaping mouth tilted before her. Richard's blurred features floated beyond.

Molly blinked and stood up, weaving. Jack was already done for if susceptible to the disease, but *Richard*—

"Richard Griffin, you're a fool if you don't get out, now!"

Black coat askew on his shoulders, Richard pressed his hand to his jaw, propping up one side of a bemused smile. "Promise not to hit me again, and we'll discuss it."

"Don't be ridiculous." Molly's head swam and her legs threatened to collapse. "Geordie—"

Molly whipped her head around so quickly that she felt nauseated. *Please, let him be all right.* She'd fallen asleep and left him.

"Accounted for, miss." Geordie slumped against the wall, his chin smeared with foam, a tin mug dangling from his hand.

Arthur sat cross-legged on the floor beside Blackie. A bucket sat between them.

"You brought these men beer? Are you mad?" She grabbed both sides of her head and sank back into her chair. So weak a stalk as her neck could hardly support it.

"Will you get out, Richard? This is suicide." Molly bit the inside of her cheek. Pain kept the ready tears from thwarting her.

"Are you sick or just tired?" Richard sank to his knees and searched her face with tenderness past bearing.

"Please go." She struggled to stand, but he held her in her seat. Molly clawed her hands through the hair at her temples. "Don't make me fall to pieces. I'll be no good to anyone."

"I think it's over, Moll. These boys can nursemaid themselves. It's been near a week since anyone came sick."

"Is Empty Pockets still closed? I think it was the water, here, but—"

"Closed for good." Richard's assurance barely beat Arthur's skeptical snort.

"They'll stay out for a while." Arthur wiped his lips. "Until folks forget, but that mine was showing good color, and the cross-timbers are set. 'For good' will last six months."

Geordie snored, slack-jawed. When Moll leaned forward to ease his mouth closed, Richard shrank from her.

"I didn't really hit you, did I?"

"I'm sure it was reflex." The miners were purely tickled by the gambler's discomfort.

Molly scrubbed her face with both hands. Her skin felt greasy, and dizziness washed over her again.

"I'll go home for a while." It was a good idea, except she found she couldn't stand. "And I'm going to spend my new-found wealth on bath salts—lilac-scented bath salts." Molly's head lolled back. Was that a snowflake sifting through the cabin ceiling? "And a copper tub, big as a horse trough, and I'll hire a covey of starch-aproned girls to fill it, over and over, so it will never cool."

"Your two hundred dollars won't last long at that rate," Jack snickered.

It *was* a snowflake, with attendants. That sieve of a roof had as much chance of keeping out weather as she had of privacy in this town, when even the barber kept her accounts.

"Maybe Griffin'd take your winnin's and parlay 'em into some real money!" Blackie suggested.

"Griffin wouldn't touch it." Richard glared. "That money belongs in a Sacramento bank, where it can earn interest."

"No, Poppy needs books." Molly yawned. "A new roof . . ."

"You're a good girl, Molly." Richard helped her stand and

wrapped her cloak around her. He slung her arm over his shoulders when she staggered. "You've done your best; now I'm going to take you home."

Three days later, Molly opened her door to a morning of glaring brilliance and a copper bathtub. A blue-shadowed trough led down the snowy hill behind it, back toward town. Cinder had barked its approach for half an hour.

"Don't ask where we got it." Arthur and Blackie, directed by Geordie, maneuvered the tub into her parlor.

Molly clutched Cinder's collar and waved them toward the kitchen. Mercy, there'd be room for nothing else, but what could be more luxurious!

"Poppy will have kittens if you block the oven. Where *did* this come from? I know it wasn't in VanBrunts'!"

"I said don't ask, nor about this either." Arthur levered a wooden screen from the inside of the tub and worked with Blackie to erect it.

"It's a gift, and it ain't polite, y'see?" Geordie made excuses. "Careful, lads, it's got that bad place where y'must prop it up with kindlin', she said."

Snow stars shimmered, then melted on the garish screen. Inexpertly painted magenta and gilt, the piece left no question of its origin. It took little imagination to picture it in Shambles, draped with the tawdry garments of Persia's girls.

"These *are* from VanBrunts'." Geordie leaned on a crutch to pull a brown paper package from inside his coat. "They had no lilac bath salts, but this soap is—"

"Otter of roses," Blackie pronounced, solemnly.

"Don't think that's it, me 'andsome."

"Lavender!" Molly caught the scent before ripping the paper.

"No more than y'deserve for slavin' over us." Geordie hung his thumbs in his suspenders, in spite of the crutches.

"Thank you." She folded the paper back around the cakes of soap and held the package to her chest. "Arthur, let's see your cheek."

His hand flew to it, as though fearful of what he'd find.

"Oh, she's going to punch you, sure."

In fact, Molly surprised all three miners and herself by kissing their proffered cheeks.

Within hours, Poppy presented Molly with the ideal opportunity to christen the copper tub.

While Molly nursed the miners, Poppy had missed two days of school. Molly looked no further than Stag for an explanation, so when Poppy explained her teacher's proposal, Molly agreed.

"Miss Margaret asked me to spend the night at her house. The snow's getting deep and she's afraid I won't be able to get down in the morning. She doesn't want me to miss more lessons, since you paid for all those books! She said we can do figures until midnight!" Poppy's palms came together in a prayerful gesture.

Molly walked with Poppy back to Margaret's. After the dark days just past, Poppy's chatter was a delight.

"Did you know Richard told everyone you needed a rest and they were to leave you alone?" Poppy crab-stepped down a slick incline above the schoolhouse. "He told Clara's father that if his lumbago pained him too bad, he should come see him, Richard, and he would put him out of his misery, personally."

After tea and tinned English biscuits with Margaret, Molly walked home against a gale, determined to push her breath back into her lungs. She resisted the temptation to haul her snow-caked skirts above her knees to ease her passage.

Enthralled by wind-sculpted snowbanks shaded by twilight into whales and blanketed bears, Molly planted one foot in the thin snow over a sagebrush. By the time she'd disentangled her limb, she was soaked, but smiling. Every container she owned was warming water for her bath. And, thanks to Richard and Margaret, she'd have her cottage to herself until tomorrow afternoon.

Even Rose could be discouraged. If her mother insisted on interference, Molly simply walked right through her and Rose vanished, leaving a cold spot that was easily avoided.

Molly squinted up at the snowflakes, pelting down in tangled twists of white, and thought of dinner. Since she planned to enjoy her own company, she'd cook the basil-and-butter concoction that made Poppy pinch her nose and shudder. After brandy and a bath, she'd dine, then sort through the armload of Eastern newspapers and the book Margaret had loaned her.

Molly juggled the newspapers to read the headlines. War, slaughter and discord at a place called Manassas. She resolved to ask Richard, a Southerner, to explain the chess-board maneuvering of the war, but tonight she'd read the book.

Snow squeaking underfoot, her underskirts soaked, Molly regarded a low spot in her yard. She'd find a black stain beneath the white if she dug. A spot of scorched earth, where nothing grew but regret. Molly shook off the hood of her cloak. Wind blasted her cheeks. A vee of wild geese rushed overhead.

Damn him. Day, Lightfoot, whatever the hell his name was, damn him and his blood-thrumming memory.

She stomped her feet, shook her skirts, and stormed into the house to pour a glass of brandy.

Chapter
Twenty-nine

If a man could go blind staring at the sun, Day believed the same thing could happen watching Moll Gallagher doff her clothes.

He hadn't meant to spy, but his worry that she'd come home with Poppy, who couldn't keep a secret, kept him hidden behind the couch. Cinder snuffled and wagged Moll's approach, but stayed curled by Day, lifting dark eyes in thanks for another warm body.

Day heard the door slam, watched her snowy skirt pass, heard the clink of glass on glass, water sputtering on iron and a stream of poorly delivered profanity.

He should quit skulking, stand up and apologize for this invasion. Aye, they'd had that one out already! In truth, their fight, the night of Moll's bonfire, hadn't ended so badly.

Water deluged the tub wedged between the kitchen table and the God-awful screen. High time to stand forth and announce himself.

Wait a little, now. Wait or she'll turn you back into the

snow, out of pride. Wait. She can't do that bare-bottomed now, can she?

Day saw no phantom, this time, but he felt the flirtatious presence from before. She held both his shoulders from behind, kneading his flesh till he shivered with the cold.

Day wished for Mam's Catholic comfort of crossing herself, then did it anyway.

Cinder heaved himself up, shook and sniffed. Day waited, three minutes, five, then stood. Two strides away from the curtain dividing the parlor and kitchen, he stopped to listen. A man alone dreamed such sounds: the soft clutter of falling garments, the satisfied *mmm* and swish of skin meeting bath water.

Now what? When the answer came, Day all but choked.

A bit longer. You're no buck in rut, are you? You're a gentleman remembering his manners . . . and his vow.

He heard a splash, the splatter of wet hair on shoulders and rubbing soap. Moll's heat-flushed face would have droplets clinging to cheekbones and lashes. Her red hair would be lathered in crests of white. An herbal scent flowered and glass clunked down. A swallow, then silence.

He tried not to think that the new tub could hold two.

Poppy. Sweet Lord, where was she? The closing storm made it difficult to judge, but shouldn't she have come home, by now?

Cinder nudged Day's knee, sore from saddle abuse, and he grimaced.

"Cinder?" Moll called to the old dog, who danced in place, toenails clicking the wooden floor, eyes urging Day to reveal himself. "Cinder, what is it, boy?"

Go on, he gestured the dog. Day twisted his face into a menacing pantomime. Cinder gave a waggish woof and nudged harder.

"Suit yourself, Cinder, but I'm staying here till the water ices over. Come in or keep quiet."

Moll sighed again, and Day heard a metallic ping as her toes hit the far end of the tub. Then she blew bubbles.

Lip-deep in warm water. Long white body submerged,

except for her breasts, which might bob on the surface. . . . That finished it, ghost or not!

Need had dragged him back here, against all logic, and any minute, Poppy could come bounding through the door. What a pretty picture that would be: the three of them, with Moll naked. Much better, if it were the two of them. With Moll naked.

"Sweetheart, it's Day."

A strangled gasp and massive slops of water preceded Moll's furious "Where?"

"On the other side of the curtain, love—" Day doubted that she'd heard through her helpless swearing. "As I'm acting the gentleman, it'd be fittin' for you to talk like a lady."

"Damn your—'gentleman'! I'm bathing!"

His mind told his mouth to shut, but his tongue seemed to be taking no orders. "Moll, I've been gone two weeks and we have a great deal to talk about, but just now I'm comin' to kiss you."

"You can't! I'm not dressed."

"All the same, I am." His regret was genuine. He'd suffer for this intrusion, but he had to hold her. He could not stop.

Water's *whoosh,* a flash of hip and thigh, then a white nightgown fluttered from a hook. He saw its hem, floating on wild rocking bath water, before he let himself look up.

Ropes of red hair framed eyes wild as Medusa's, then twisted and dripped over her shoulders, wetting transparent patches over Molly's breasts.

Before she climbed out, he caught her. Moll fought for a minute, her outraged squeaks vibrating his lips. He cared that he'd made her unhappy, but she wasn't frightened, just mad. He didn't stop. Soaked through, the little gown made it easy for his hands to devour her back and hold her against him.

Hands shoving his shoulders weakened to a feathery patter, then slipped down. Moll's fingers curved around his upper arms, smoothed to his elbows, then circled his ribs and clung. Sweet Lord, how far to the bed?

"Where—?"

He sealed Moll's mouth with his before she finished asking and felt a gloating pride that she'd stopped fighting.

"I'm back," he said against her lips. "That's all that matters."

Her head's tilt offered a white curve of throat and he kissed it. Dear Lord, she *wanted* his touch, invited it!

The nightdress gaped open. His lips touched the hollow of her throat, brushed back and forth over her collarbone. She pressed forward so suddenly a wave of bath water drenched his trousers.

"I'm going to lift you." He cradled her shoulders and scooped her knees. The sodden gown stuck to everything.

The screen's splintering crash didn't slow him, and Molly spared it only a finger-spread gesture before grabbing his shirt to slow her descent to the bed.

Bloody boots! The wet denims bound him like shackles and the soggy dress tangled them together. His fingers locked with hers, wide-flung on the bed, as her lips opened with a groan that belonged to both of them.

As if wakened, Molly tore her mouth away. Fear glinted dark in her green eyes, but she stayed, molded to him by bath water and desire.

"I'm glad you're back. All my best resolve—"

Five kisses lined her lips, corner to corner, before he let her breathe. "Intentions and good sense don't matter between us, Moll. Haven't from the first."

Day steadied his breathing. He closed his eyes so lust wouldn't glare out and scare her.

Moll caught his hand. When he opened his eyes, hers focused on him, speculating. "You stole my horse."

"No, now. I paid two hundred dollars for the loan of her."

"She wasn't for rent."

"No?" Day tried to think. Too many questions loomed. He'd just have to erase them with matters more demanding.

"Where's Poppy?" He kept Moll spread beneath him.

"Margaret's." Her hesitation made him watchful. The black pupils of her eyes pooled wide as she added, "Until tomorrow."

"Sweet witch." He sighed, rolled beside her and lifted her hand to kiss. "Until *tomorrow*?"

Moll Gallagher was as good as his.

She wriggled up the bed, breaking the match of their shoulders, chests and legs. She sat up, eyes skittering everywhere. What was she searching for?

She stayed on the bed, sitting on her heels, knees nudging his shirtfront. A damned uncomfortable position. Although, he ought to be able to reach out and caress her ankle.

"Day, you're going to tell me everything, first."

First! Joyous hallelujahs rang off the walls of his skull. "I'd have it no different." Except if talking came second.

"Will you give your explanations over dinner?"

Day swung his legs off the bedside opposite her. Molly's expression turned dubious as he unbuttoned his shirt and she babbled on about dinner.

"—probably won't like it. No meat—"

"Hush. I'll like it, and I'll make my explanations from the bath." He shrugged off the shirt and looked over his shoulder. Moll's eyes widened when he caught her staring.

Pretending she hadn't, Moll drew her fingers along the bath's surface. "It's pretty cold."

"Fair enough." He hung his shirt from her bedpost. "I'm pretty dirty."

He righted the screen and it stood solid, if askew. *Why delay the shucking of breeches, Daywell? Makin' love to the girl, she's bound to see a fair amount, don't y'think?* Still, he felt shy as Moll's eyes outlined his every rib and muscle.

"I should put a gown on, over this shift."

"Is that what it is? And me thinking you'd gotten a white dress." He hadn't really. Day recognized it for an undergarment. It triggered a faint worry that his saddlebags, stashed behind the couch, had crushed the dress he'd brought her.

She reached toward a wall hook, where her dress hung like a dead crow.

"Here now, if I'm to bare me soul, let's not you be puttin' barriers between us. That's fair enough, isn't it?"

Moll uttered an unladylike *humph* and turned her back on him. Without dressing.

"I was a dumb kid, right off the boat, set on finding a horse-riding job." He hurdled the side of the tub, banging his bad knee. "I'd heard the Barbary Coast was a wicked place, so I naturally figured there'd be racing."

"I can boil more water, if we're going to have your life story," Moll offered, without turning.

"Don't give it a thought, Bright." Blazes! If beer were this cool, he'd call it a treat. "Y've already had the first half of me life, now I've got to the interesting part."

"All I want to know . . ." She crumbled dried leaves into a bowl. ". . . is why you—"

She wouldn't let on she cared that he'd left without a word of explanation—after that sweet grappling on the cot. God, what she must have believed! He'd tortured himself with a dozen versions of it.

"Left?" He let the word hang, wanting just a pinch of commitment from her.

She shrugged, and when he stayed quiet, she glanced back, miffed. "Yes!"

"It all leads up to that, I promise."

He told how he'd been working as a bootblack for money enough to eat, when two bearing-reined carriage horses bolted down a street steep as a sledding hill. Day had stopped them. Rankin had been the nabob riding inside the coach.

"Just like you did the first day, here." A wood-handled knife jutted from the fist perched on Moll's hip.

A hip not decently clothed. A hip he would know, by this time tomorrow. "Just like. Have y'got soap that doesn't smell so fancy?"

Moll tried not to look as she flipped him a cake of oat-meal-colored soap, and Day's modesty turned to pleasure as she considered his exposed chest. Curiosity made a good start.

"So I began workin' for this rich rancher, as a 'range rider.' That's what he called it."

"And what's your real name?" Moll spoke quietly, giving him a choice to hear or pretend he hadn't. Day scrubbed his hair with scalp-searing vigor.

"I chased off squatters, unless they agreed to raise corn for Rankin. I drove off cattle thieves and rounded up maverick steers for branding.

"Corn and beef would be better than gold, said the boss, because a great war was brewing. He guessed right on that."

The water lapped stone-cold around him. Why had he thought himself ready to tell her that Rankin and her monster, Favor, were the same? Could he admit that he was accused of murder, when he couldn't even speak his proper name?

Wind screamed around the corners of Moll's cottage. Cats sitting body to body like books on a shelf watched her cook. A shy, untouched girl, cooking in her underwear, for him. Lord knows his mother would beat him for such behavior.

"Ever kiss a man in a bathtub, Molly girl?"

She dropped something into a hot skillet and pivoted to face him. "Only a tart would do something like that!" She took several irritated strides forward.

"Pity." Their eyes held so long he found it hard to breathe. "Y'keep starin'. Is it m'beard?" He rubbed his jaw. "Shavin' hasn't been the first thing on my mind. D'you hate it?"

"It's not for me to like or dislike how you look." Moll moved her lips like a sleepwalker.

"Who better, Moll?" Day held out both hands. She stepped close enough to clasp them, and the beseeching look on her face fairly split him down the breastbone!

"I love you," he whispered.

Her brows rose so high they disappeared in her fiery hair.

"I do. I, Mark Owen Daywell—for whatever it's worth— love you, forever."

Molly closed her eyes, and when he pulled her hands, she came closer, joining in a kiss that made her hands tremble. Or maybe the shaking was his.

"I'm going to drown us both." He searched her face for what it meant to her, this fool declaration that lurched his belly high into his chest.

"Not before dinner."

He couldn't fathom that, not quite, as she backed away, leaving him to dry, dress and approach a silent table.

He stared down at two china plates and an arm-thick white candle. No lantern to create a pool of warmth in the storm-wrapped house, with snow clumps so big they thumped the windows. No giddy girl wrapped around him in delight at his confession.

She turned to him and Day's bare toes curled against the wood floor when he saw the platter wobble in her hand.

"Tell me the rest after you eat." With a shaky smile, she added. "I have coffee."

Starved, he fell on the food with barely enough manners to use a fork. Gold-fried delicacies were sprinkled with green flecks and something melting and pungent.

"It's wonderful! What is it?"

"You're joking. I know you'd rather have meat."

His wordless, full-mouthed protest made her laugh. Lucky thing, too. Day would have stood on his head or painted himself blue to earn her mirth.

"Jerusalem artichokes—those sunflower-looking things— have tubers like potatoes." She waited, eyebrows raised, but he only chewed. "With basil, butter and some dried cheese. The bread and rose-hip jelly you recognize, right?"

He growled, nodded and stuffed more of Poppy's brown bread into his mouth. Moll giggled. For that silver tittering he'd be her jester all night.

Coffee had been poured and they both watched snowflakes sift through the ceiling, toward the candle. The teardrop flame dodged and sank into ivory shoulders of wax, then nosed forth again. Finally, Day moved it from the weather's path.

"I'll tell y'the worst of it, Moll." He sipped the black brew and swallowed. "But first I'll tell y'the best. It won't make any sense till y've heard the worst. Still—"

She raised a quelling hand and Day nodded. "Right. The best is, I've killed but one human in my life, a man who would've shot me in the back if I hadn't heard the hammer rise. I never killed a woman. Not the one on the poster, nor any woman.

"The second good thing's something I discovered last

week. The man who's saying I killed her—Rankin? He's not gone to the territorial police. He'd told the Pinkertons— remember that little Bragg woman?—*they* put out the poster. If I satisfy them, and do for Rankin, it's over."

Molly nodded, rose to let Cinder into the house and waited.

"All right. She's a woman named Shawnee Sue, a working woman, you understand?" His neck hardened to granite. It was that difficult to look up at Moll. "Sue's dead. That much is true." Day tightened both hands around his cup.

"Sue was Rankin's partner. They worked together, and she was nearly as low. Sue was taking cattle—rustled, mostly—in payment for her girls' services, then she'd sell them to Rankin. He was that cattle-hungry, didn't give a hang where she got them.

"Sue got crafty and hired a man who was a fair hand with a running iron. He changed one brand to look like another. Then some of Sue's sportin' gents stole Rankin's cattle, re-branded the lot and ended by selling his own back to him. Faith, he never knew the difference.

"Or wouldn't have, except I told him." Day leaned an elbow on the table and covered his mouth with that hand. "That was my fault. I can't ever change that."

Molly might have said a word of comfort; instead she took the hand still on the table, gripping so tight it hurt.

"Rankin ordered Tony to kill Sue. That woke me in a hurry. I was no 'range rider' and my employer was no decent man.

"I rode to warn Sue, but they were just behind me. I dodged to one side of the corral full of Sue's bawlin' acquisitions. I stayed dead across from them, mounted, but leaning down, thinking I'd ride in and grab Sue."

He pulled his hand away from Molly, gesturing in illustration. "Picture it, now. Me over here, leaned down with me face as low as my stirrups, then all manner of cattle and fence and whatnot between me and Sue. And her a little thing, hardly tall as the stock. I couldn't make that shot! No one could.

"She never had a chance to explain. Tony rode around the

corral, slow in all the noise. I saw—" Day stared as if the image lived before him. "It was a damned buffalo rifle, a Sharps, comin' up from his scabbard, comin' down level . . . *That* shot I tried to make, to hit him first.

"He says I got Sue in the crossfire. At the race, Rankin said the bullet was mine."

"At the race? *My* race? Glory's race?"

"Rankin was there, Moll." He wanted to hold her as he spoke, but he let her huddle across the table, with only their hands connected. "Rankin is the man you call Favor."

She drew two denying breaths.

"Favor. No." She shook her head so violently he feared the candle flame would catch her hair. He remembered Moll's reckless fear in that other snowstorm.

"Favor can't be. He . . ." Cinder whined, his muzzle lifting her elbow until she touched him. Her dazed stare vanished as she put the facts together with what she knew of Rankin. "Favor killed that prostitute, then blamed you for it. And now he's threatening you, so you won't tell."

"Aye. And a bit worse, Bright, he's got a price on me."

Moll stood, opened the stove and stuffed it with kindling. She left the door open, transfixed by the hungry flames. "Do you believe in the Devil? A personal devil who hunts you, making you so weak that you'll do whatever he wants, just so he won't harm the people you love? Do you believe that, Day?"

"I don't believe Favor's him. The Devil's infallible, and Favor doesn't know where I am. The Devil's everywhere, and Favor's not in this room, Moll. And the Devil can't die."

She didn't hear, only stared, transfixed by the flames. When she trembled, he wrapped her in his arms, pulling her away from the stove and latching it closed before sitting her on the bed.

Moll's sobs were the worst thing he'd ever heard. Tearless, sucking gasps that had one awful twin.

Hungry and lost in the cream-thick fogs of Kilkenny, he'd poached a doe, missed a killing shot and pierced her through the lung. Floundering and groping in that nightmare blindness, he'd heard the doe draw a hundred rasping breaths before tripping against her. Straddle-legged and staring, she'd begged for a bullet.

It had taught him never to pull the trigger till he was sure. A lesson learned, he'd thought. But now Molly's indrawn breaths ripped her apart. She wasn't ready. And there could be no quick bullet for Moll.

"Bright, I know he hurt you." He held her, when she would have struggled away. "You have to tell me."

It broke, the grip of fear fractured, and she swung reproachful eyes to his face. "If you knew, you wouldn't have said—what you did."

"That I love you? Y'think it would matter?" He wanted to shake her. "Y'think I'd blame you for whatever he did, after he's hounded me? After I saw him order a woman cut down as coldly as you'd slice meat?"

She shrank in his arms, her knees up under her gown, rubbing her face against his chest. Her singsong voice questioned at every breath and Day had the eerie feeling that he held a child.

"I was finishing my breakfast? And he came down from Celia's room? She hung back, but he had her wrist. He let go. He was doing up his shirt."

Molly's hand fumbled at the front of her dress and Day recognized the moves of a swell placing studs through an evening shirt. It was still that real to her.

"He saw me and picked up one of my braids." Molly pressed her hand to her cheek, still feeling the silken brushing of one tasseled end. "He said, 'Honeybunch, why don't you do me a favor?'"

Molly shuddered, wedging more tightly into Day's arms, hiding. "And after I ran, he caught me? And he pushed me on my knees and he squeezed my ears harder and harder until I screamed and threw up my breakfast and he yelled— 'That's not going to work! Being sick won't—'" She stopped repeating words that must have played in her head ten thousand times. "That's when Luba hit him with something."

Day rocked her, wishing she would cry, afraid to urge it,

SHADOWS IN THE FLAME

afraid to interrupt, because he never wanted her to go back to this nightmare. He wanted to help her kill it.

"Luba hid us and she gave us Cinder and the gun and she said not to be scared." For a minute Day heard grown-up Moll Gallagher, not Favor's victim. "But, Day?"

"Yes, m'Bright."

"I never stopped being scared!" A final sob tore her control and her tears soaked his shirt. "Every night I have to go out and make sure he's not there. Every night, I remember. He said he'd come for Poppy and me. Every night!"

An awful screaming, a banshee's lament, howled in the chimney. Chaotic wind moaned around the house, causing the walls to shudder. And then came stillness.

Chapter Thirty

Molly let Day wrap her close, making a stronghold of his arms. The room spun around her. Only Day felt solid.

"What can I do, Bright? Tell me. Let me help you."

"What *would* you do?" Molly knew what he wanted. A blood-dark need inside her reveled in the asking. "Would you kill him?"

"Aye." He held her so tight, she could barely breathe. "If a bear galloped after you, would I shoot it? If you were walkin' toward a rock slide, would I stop you? Molly, I *love* you."

Her face buried in his blue flannel shirtfront, she breathed him. Day, who loved her. Mark Owen Daywell, who loved her forever.

With a flash of impatience, he rolled her atop him, as if it were the only way he could see her face.

"Sit up. There, like you were astride a horse. Now look at me." He judged her with a stare, and saw her suspicion. "Have a bit of faith, Moll. I want you to marry me!"

Marriage! None of Rose's lovers had ever—Rose was gone. Molly felt it in her fingertips, in the roots of her hair, on her skin. Her mother's ghost had left them alone.

And Day loved her.

"What did you think, I loved you just for tonight? I want you to come with me, marry me! I've nothing to offer you. A decent man wouldn't ask it, but I want you more than it's decent to want a woman."

As his hands steadied her, Molly wondered if he felt her thighs tremble. He seemed not to notice. He regarded her with great seriousness, as if her response were valuable and very important.

"I'm not noble enough to ask you to wait until I have money and a house, 'til I'm not on the run! Pride's a weak thing against *this*, Moll. I can't wait for you."

She collapsed against his chest, then slipped over beside him, before he could stop her. Her lips moved against his warm neck. "I love you, Day."

She might have set a match to both of them.

His kiss took her with force, nearly knocking her back from him. Their mouths rushed to lock, heads turning side to side, and the closeness wasn't fearful, it was glorious.

Her hands cradled each side of his jaw, rough with beard, while her index fingers stroked the smoothness of his temples. He opened sky-colored eyes and she touched the sun lines marking their corners. Then, he closed over her with another kiss.

Molly arched against him, a mad slamming of thoughts, crashing one over the other. She'd waited a lifetime for this. She'd never wanted this. Never known it would take her like this. Like the rock slide, the avalanche he said he'd protect her from. This insistence was far more dangerous.

Clumsy, she tugged at his shirt and he welcomed her fingers, working at his buttons. "God, Moll. For so long . . ."

She stared at the tanned width of his shoulders, narrowing to the copper button holding his breeches.

"Should I take off my gown?" Even as she asked, Moll felt helpless and numb-fingered.

Day caught her against him, his arms crossed behind her back.

"Molly, I'm not going to stop. If you take that off, I cannot stop." A feeble flare of intelligence said Day was testing her.

"Then tell me," she began, and wondered if he'd muttered "bloody Hell" beneath his breath. No, she'd been mistaken.

"What, love?" he asked.

"Are you going to leave?"

"I'll stay if you tell me to."

She wouldn't, not if Favor knew he'd come back to her. And the thought of Favor's evil made her ask one last awful question. "If I don't make love with you, will it hurt less if—"

He held her, staring into her eyes as if he could reel the words from her. "I won't leave ye, Bright. You decide when we go."

"Not that." She shook her head. "If something happens. If Favor—"

"If I *die*?"

She nodded, hating the tears, hating the heat that grew even as she waited for this most horrible answer. He sighed as if she'd hurt him, then spoke with deliberation.

"Molly, I could tell ye it would be worse, because ye'd know me better. Or because, if there was another man, you'd have lost this first time to me."

"No!" She circled his ribs with a silencing embrace, but he kept on, his face buried in her neck.

"But if I were dead and we'd been together, you'd know how much I love you, because I'm going to make you sing with it, Bright."

She shivered and his tone changed to his wheedling merchant's charm. "And it *would* be my last regret and my eternal torment, my everlasting, burn-in-Hell regret, Bright, if I missed this, but don't let that be influencing your decision."

"You are a shameless swindler." She kissed his grin once, then again. "I knew it from the first."

Candlelight gilded his face, flickered off the black meanderings of his hair, glinted off his eyes and showed the smile that questioned, one last time.

Molly answered with open arms and open eyes and trust. And she wasn't afraid, even though she could never truly be safe, again.

Too many nights on the trail spent listening for renegades told Day when she woke. Sunlight glaring off a hard freeze slipped between his lashes, but he pretended to sleep because sweet Molly, so afraid of touching, had her hands all over him.

"Is that gouge from a bullet?" Moll struggled from under his arm, and he gave her room enough to rise on her elbow.

Only then did Day open his eyes. Lush as he'd imagined, all copper and ivory and haunting green eyes. His Moll.

"Good morning." He touched the back of her head and leaned her into his kiss.

"You didn't answer me."

He wouldn't, either.

Growing shy under his stare, she filled the silence. "I've planned your way out."

"You've been admirin' me fine young hide, and don't be denyin' it." He kissed her lower lip as her mouth fell agape.

"Shameless *and* arrogant," she diagnosed.

And though most women would be devising sticky questions about other females, Molly probably *had* devised his escape.

Boards creaked out front. Probably just firethorn, shifting in the wind, taking the porch timbers with it. Still, Day dropped his hand off the bedside, grabbed the leather of his gun belt and draped it on her bedpost, over his shirt.

"You had a gun under my bed!" If a girl could flounce lying down, Moll did.

"Aye."

"When did you put that there?" She shoved away his caressing hands. "I've been with you every minute!"

"In case of trouble, I wanted it close."

"I understand why. I'm asking *when*."

"Yesterday, before you came in from the storm."

"You put it under my bed." She did seem to be repeating

herself. He nodded and Moll pounced. "You were so sure you'd be *in* my bed?"

"Walked into ambush again, did I?"

"You planned it?" She wore the look of a woman impatiently tapping her foot.

"All the time. Didn't you?" He waited for her answer, but settled for her blush. "I had hopes, Bright."

"Disgraceful." Moll watched his lips.

"I think you'll survive the disgrace," he said. "In fact, I'm sure of it."

The next time they woke, Cinder was scratching to get out. Cats were yowling to come in. Abner brayed like something demented.

"They all need to be fed, is that it?"

Moll lay flat on her back, a smile on her lips. Down the hill, a rooster crowed. Day lifted her wrist and watched her arm plummet to the bed. "Go back to sleep, I'll tend them."

Tucking the blanket around her shoulders, he felt as mated, as bound, as if they'd sworn vows in a church.

Except they hadn't. He spent a peculiar moment, waiting for a ghostly claw to snatch his soul. Just as he'd thought. The figment must have bloomed from a bad bit o' mutton.

Moll wasn't in bed when he stamped off the snow, slammed the door and blew warm breath on his hands.

"Why do you keep animals like this?" He watched Ginger sniff the doorway, lick her shoulder and mew, before deigning to step in.

Moll didn't answer. He found her, hastily dressed, in the parlor, holding the Remington.

"Someone's coming."

Cinder barked fit to split his skin. Day reached for the gun.

"Oh, that makes sense, now, doesn't it?" Molly jerked the rifle out of reach.

"Pardon me, miss, for thinking to protect you!" His hands fell back on his hips.

"Hide behind that screen and don't breathe." She pointed.

"It's someone on foot. It won't be Favor. I don't need this."
She drew a deep breath, regarding the rifle as if it had materialized in her hands.

"Better safe, sweetheart." Day snatched the rifle, cham-
bered a bullet and crouched behind the screen, just as he'd
been told.

No slip on the ice had wrenched Eleanor's arm from its
socket, but Molly didn't argue. Sweating and pain-blanched,
Eleanor sat on the red velvet couch, supporting the limb.

Molly unfastened Eleanor's gown and verified her diagnosis.

"I'm going to have to pull hard." Molly demonstrated,
using a cupped hand and fist to show Eleanor how she'd
treat the dislocation.

"Just be done." Eleanor looked toward the wall.

Praise be, she was strong enough to do it the first time.
Molly raised and hooked the robin's-egg gown before
Eleanor's shock-numb nerves wakened. Wiping her hands,
Molly watched Eleanor huddle with pain, still cradling the
arm.

"I'll get some tea." Molly stood. The sliding of the bone
head into place had made her queasy. Besides, a delay might
allow Eleanor time to gather the truth. That might be worth
the minutes lost with Day.

"Tea'll be just a moment." Molly hugged her arms around
herself, staring at the stove, not the garish screen protecting
Day. The VanBrunts' benefactor was Favor. Rankin. Eleanor
must not learn Day had returned.

Water hissed inside the kettle, fixing to boil. She glanced
back. Beneath the crooked screen she spied the toe of his
boot and a frayed denim cuff. She gathered the tea things
and rejoined Eleanor.

"I want you to do away with him!" Eleanor's outburst
pained her shoulder and she grabbed it.

"Your husband?"

Eleanor nodded. "I was only passing through and heard
him mention things that are private between a husband and
wife. He wasn't talking about me."

Eleanor's head bowed, but her eyes gazed up, like a beaten dog's. Moll's cup clattered on its saucer. *Did* she mean Poppy?

"Who was he telling?" Molly knew. Only one man would encourage Hans's sickness.

"Mr. Rankin. I hardly believed it. Hans wasn't telling exactly, more—hinting. And Mr. Rankin said—I can't repeat it." Eleanor convulsed as if she'd retch.

Molly heard a boot scrape on wood and glanced back, fully expecting Day's eruption through the curtain.

"Eleanor." The woman wept harder. "Eleanor! He knows you found out, doesn't he? That's why he twisted your arm? To make you quiet?"

"How did you—?"

"And Rankin, does he know?"

Eleanor shook her head. "No, Mr. Rankin had gone. Can't you cast a spell or something?"

"Leave him. Today. Now! Get out of his house!"

"And go where?"

"Mother Mary, if I could make a spell, I'd give you some nerve. It doesn't *matter* where!"

"And live like you? A woman alone? I couldn't stand it."

Molly let Eleanor's words vibrate around her, making the woman wear her disgrace.

"That store is mine, too."

"Eleanor, stay with me. I have a dog and a rifle, and he's afraid of me."

Eleanor snorted. "It's true. If *you'd* warned him to stay away from your sister, he'd never have risked it."

"What do you mean?"

"And Mr. Rankin's awfully angry with you. He was going to 'ignore your interfering,' he said, until you did some mischief in Chinatown with that filthy freighter McNab."

"McCabe."

"He's had an accident, and Mr. Rankin said McCabe got his just desserts for helping you. Mr. Rankin says he's warned you, twice, now all he has to do is follow you to that cat man."

Lord have mercy, Favor would come here, after Day. It would be her fault.

" . . . just desserts!" Eleanor's laugh was crazed.

"Eleanor, have another cup of tea."

"No, you've done quite enough." Eleanor adjusted her skirt. "You'll take your fee in trade, of course."

"There's two needs killin'," Day had threatened, as soon as Eleanor left, and Molly needed two hours of reasoning, begging and promising, to convince Day he must go.

With their arms linked around each other's waists, they embraced inside the back door.

"You've broken your first promise already."

"I haven't. I'll be yours, always," Molly promised. Each time she spoke of love, Day looked smug, as though he'd taught her a foreign language. "But I can't leave Poppy. Not now."

"I'll be faithful forever, but y've made your choice, I guess."

"It's no choice! What would she think, coming home to an empty house. Again. And when would I be back?"

"In two weeks, just like I told you."

"Oh, Day." She slumped against his chest.

"We've had it out." Day kissed her hair. "And I'm thinkin' I shouldn't curse progress. Yesterday at this time, I'd never—"

"Mark Owen Daywell," she pronounced, stiffly. "I'll thank you to keep your roguish hands where they belong!"

His laugh challenged her, then faded to sober instruction.

"Two weeks, Moll. I'll take Abner and the buckskin, and leave Glory. I'll free the mule to make great heavin' tracks and hope they follow him. Now, you've got the map to Sandy Blind Canyon in case you need me?"

He tilted her chin up. "Yes," she said.

"I'll stay there just a few days, to see if Rankin's following. If I've lost him, I'll make peace with the Pinkertons, and tell the territorial police about Rankin, prayin' God they believe me." Day reached down to rumple Cinder's ears as the old dog nudged between them. "I still say it would be easier to shoot him."

"You'd be on the run for real."

"I know, I know."

Molly's chest jerked with the clutch of old tears when he parted from her. Blue flannel shirt and denims, and his gun belt slung low on his hips made Day look like a saddle tramp.

He hefted his saddlebag and withdrew a string-tied brown paper parcel, turning it, curiously.

"Now, what's this? A present?" He tilted back the brim of his black hat and frowned. "Aye! Now I remember! I seem to have purchased a dress about your size. Might even serve as a wedding dress for—what was it the seamstress said?— 'for an unconventional bride.'"

He took another step back from her, rubbing his fingers up and down her sleeves, a full arm's length away. "Open it later, when I'm gone, and imagine it's me holding you."

He opened the door. The wind's chill nearly stopped her heart.

"One last story, Bright, and no tears, now. Ridin' together with a Californio lad, a few months ago, we passed some hard days. Had a run-in with a grizzly, and one with the law. And when we parted trails—" Day stopped to clear his throat. "He said to me, '*Vaya con Dios.*' 'Go with God,' is what it means. Since y'can't go with me, I'm leaving you in His hands. And I'll owe Him one."

Chapter
Thirty-one

Snow shimmering on her golden hair, Poppy swept into the house before Day's buckskin horse crested the ridge and vanished. Singing the wonders of mathematics and Miss Margaret, Poppy seemed so dear that Molly jarred her with a hug. In spite of Day, she'd been right to remain with Poppy.

"I have to tell you," Poppy gasped, "Stag's sent home for money. He has some in a Sacramento City bank. Or his family does." Poppy worried her lower lip a minute, then tossed the troubling distinction aside. Her face clouded as too many thoughts crowded in and she started over.

"It's like this. Stag thought mining would be a lark, but it's not." Poppy held up one finger. "Brown Bess's boardinghouse is going to ruin with Bess dead." Another finger pointed up. "And, I'm the best baker in town." Poppy regarded the three fingers, then flicked all five in a joyous dance.

"So, Stag and I are buying the boardinghouse and getting married!"

Molly hoped Poppy, alone, had spun this web of day-dreams, but she said nothing, because she felt Rose's rest-less summons from the parlor. Molly feared she had explaining to do.

Poppy's rapture didn't last. By nightfall, melancholy had claimed her. Moll's remedy was to fill the copper bath with hot water, and leave Poppy to soak.

"Mama?" Molly heard only a floorboard, creaking under her feet. Perhaps that screaming disturbance last night had been Rose. Did ghostly constraints allow her to vanish in shame at what had happened in the wake of her death?

As Molly watched, a depression the size of her fists, side by side, appeared in the love seat. Suddenly, Rose filled it.

"Molly, love." Rose looked faint and frail as she patted the place beside her. She paid no mind to her hand passing through the velvet. *"You must sit beside me. I—I'll try not to be too cold."*

"I doubt you can help it, Mama. I brought a shawl." Moll settled beside her mother, and though Rose's pleasure lit a smile in them both, Moll had to steady herself. How extra-ordinary that comfort and terror mixed in one unearthly mo-ment.

"Molly, I heard what you said—was it last night?" Rose's hesitant expression recalled the aftermath of one of her mor-tal binges, but this disorientation was deeper.

"Where did you go?" Molly feared the answer.

"Ah well, it's difficult to say." Rose shook her head, and Molly saw through her to the wall. Why had Rose faded so? *"Once I started howling, I was yanked back to the dark."*

Molly yearned to grab her mother's arm and hold on. "Heaven?"

"No." Rose's chuckle darkened with rue. *"Whatever else it may be, it's not my idea of Heaven. Heaven was seeing you realize you're in love. Was he good to you, child?"*

Her blush must have confessed for her. Rose's bawdy chuckle quaked the air, soundlessly.

"But, to be clear, before Poppy's done bathing, that darkness is no Heaven. Limbo, perhaps? An afterlife slap on the hand for not learning quickly?"

"Which lesson, Mama?"

Rose tossed her flame-orange hair, brightening with a touch of pride and self-mockery.

"I've learned that guilt has no purpose, especially after all these years. Fear has a short season, too. Nothing can hurt me, now. Those are new lessons." Rose shook her head. "The old one, I think I've mastered. After all this vanishes, only love remains."

"That's what you said before." Molly decided not to hold her tongue. As Rose's color grew more vivid, she thought she might risk a touchy question. "Only, I've mulled it over, Mama, and it seems to me—I'm speaking plainly now—"

"You won't hurt me."

"—it seems all the harm you did us, came from loving those men." Molly covered her lips, but she couldn't call back the words.

"That's where we both went wrong! 'Twasn't love a bit. I was only salving the loneliness your da left behind." Hazy bliss dimmed Rose's eyes, then left them grassy green. "It's sweet to make men ache, but it wasn't worth hurting you. And Poppy.

"If common decency couldn't stop me from being a slattern, then love for you should have. There!" With that, Rose plucked up the corners of her skirt in a curtsy and tossed her hair in a bow to the rafters.

Then, like water covered with a sheen of moonlight, Rose paled to a disturbance on the air and disappeared.

Ensconced in the copper bath, Poppy soaped one arm and frowned. "I don't know why Stag went."

"Where did he go?" Molly turned from the dandelions she'd left simmering on the stove.

"I have dough rising." Poppy eyed the wisps of steam. "Don't let that make the stove too hot."

"Poppy, you haven't made bread all week. Now when I

want to brew something—" Molly took a breath. "Where did Stag go?"

"He didn't meet me in our place. His note said he was going to Blue Clay Mountain to cut lumber. I don't know why."

"Isn't your meeting place *here*, behind the house?"

"No. Miss Margaret lets us meet in the classroom." Poppy's lashes flared up, then she sank beneath the bath water.

Margaret was a traitor. Did she think Poppy a fairy-tale princess? But something else was awfully wrong.

"Wait, you *don't* meet behind our house? Ever?"

Who, then? Whose heavy form lurked at the herb-fringed back window as Molly walked the cats? Her flesh prickled and her scalp contacted. "Who sent Stag lumbering?"

"Sent?" Poppy's fingers drummed the tub side. "It was Hans. His new partner wants to sell wood at the store, so he hired Stag and Geordie and um, you know—"

Molly did. She knew just what Favor had done. Stag, Geordie and Blackie had appointed themselves her guardians, so Favor had sent them away.

Fear doesn't last, love. You can do this.

Molly fought her rapid breathing. Poppy mustn't worry.

Steady. Oh, yes, much better.

Molly stirred the dandelions one stout stroke. She'd protect Poppy and Day. Favor could do with her as he liked, because no pain, no revulsion, nothing on earth would hurt her worse than injury to one of them.

"I'm sure he'll be back before long." Molly rapped the spoon, then set it down. "Hop out of the tub, honey." Molly opened a warm towel. "I'll have a little soak before the water goes cold."

Hoping it truly kept senses alert, Molly poured peppermint oil into the bath water. Poppy crawled into bed straightaway, but Molly wouldn't sleep, not with Favor on the prowl. Cinder paced from kitchen to parlor, the curtain dragging his back like a costume for All Hallow's Eve. He whined with each battering gust of wind, ears lifted.

After a day without snow, ice crusted the yard and porch.

Footsteps, no matter how stealthy, should be audible. Still, the stimulant bath couldn't hurt.

Midnight came, cold and black, and Molly heard them. Boots struck the snow's crust, sank, and kept coming.

Red heat sluiced over her head and shoulders. Antonio, the burnt man Day had labeled "merciless," sent his aura before him. She wondered if he came with Favor and Skinner, because she heard footsteps of at least two more.

Molly shrugged off her cloak and snugged the Remington to her shoulder. She hadn't barred the front door. Determined men would merely burst through the back, frightening Poppy.

Even the lantern light glared crimson with Antonio's approach. The rifle's black eye would greet the first intruder. If he *were* Favor, she'd shoot.

The back door shuddered, splintered. *Poppy!* Molly wheeled toward the curtain as Cinder's growl exploded into a volley of barks. They ended in a yelp. The front door slammed the cottage wall. She turned again, training the rifle on a dark shirtfront. Then Poppy's scream extinguished every other thought.

Antonio had Poppy. A bloody tide flooded Molly's vision as the man strode into the parlor, gripping the tail of a noose. He towed Poppy behind, as if dragging a load of firewood. Poppy's mouth gaped. Her arms crossed the bodice of her nightgown. His eyes fixed on the Remington, Antonio jerked Poppy stumbling forward.

"Put the rifle down."

"Certainly, once Poppy's safe, outside."

Good, you've calmed crazy folk before, Moll. Look away from Poppy, from the appeal in her eyes. If you've ever had the Sight, use it now! That devil's reaching out to you. Keep him reaching.

"No chance." Antonio shook his head.

Molly took a step back, colliding with the velvet couch as she made herself the apex of a deadly triangle. Finally she glanced at the other man. He was Kee, whorelord of Favor's cribs.

Green-figured silk buttoned up the side of his neck. In spite of the whores, the opium and his invasion of her home, Kee offered a blade-thin chance of humanity.

"Antonio, what's the harm?" Kee's lips moved under a wispy mustache long as black guitar strings. "Let her go."

Antonio shrugged and tossed the end of the rope over Poppy's shoulder. Poppy worked at the noose, her gasps breaking the silence. Because Kee and Antonio watched her rifle, Moll tried not to follow her sister's frantic movements.

"Don't worry about it," she told Poppy. "Just run." *To Margaret*, Molly wanted to add, but this victory had been too simple. She wouldn't endanger the schoolteacher, as well.

Poppy tripped, then hauled her skirts above her knees to run. A brief scuffling outside probably meant she'd fallen.

Oh Poppy. Rose hovered near the window, despairing, and Molly felt her mother's urging. Molly must help them all, even if the odds were three to one.

"The gun." Kee nodded toward her hands.

"In a minute." Molly couldn't surrender it just yet. If that made her a liar, she was in good company for deceit, and suddenly she knew her strategy.

Antonio and Kee considered themselves professionals, and professionals received fees for their work.

"Gentlemen, I've come into a handsome sum of money from my filly's race. I'll gladly double the salary Rankin pays you, if you guarantee my sister's safety."

"And this we should believe because you broke the bargain you made with us two minutes ago?" Antonio's smile didn't touch the burned side of this face. "We know you don't have the money, but you're as good a gambler as the man who does."

"I *do* have the money." The day Deborah had given up the pouch, Molly had stuffed it beneath her compost bucket. "Let me show you."

"Don't move until you've given Kee that rifle."

Molly clutched the weapon tighter still. What, after all, did she have to lose? They'd hurt her either way.

"You're playing a good bluff." Antonio's eyes darted toward the front door. Could he sense Rose hovering there? "But Favor found out that Griffin's banking the cash in Sacramento, tomorrow."

"No." Molly stopped. Richard gone, too?

The door burst open.

"Skinner, weren't you watching the door?" Kee shouted as Poppy, propelled by a shove, staggered across the room.

Molly tried to aim the Remington, but the rifle wavered and Antonio stepped in, striking it from her hands with a backward smack of his revolver. Before Molly caught Poppy to her, Antonio snagged the end of the noose and yanked it tight.

"Did ya shoot the damned dog?" Poppy's captor was a stranger with a tobacco-streaked beard. Skinner. He bawled his query from the front door, then edged inside. "Told ya I ain't comin' in 'less you have."

He did, though, and Antonio's lips twitched in irritation. He spoke to Molly, not Skinner.

"The deal is this: Tell us where McCabe stashed Song Lin and the opium and you ride with us. Otherwise, we take her, alone." Poppy gagged as Antonio jerked the noose tighter. Molly felt panic choke her as well.

"I'd tell you anything. You must know that." Molly caught his gaze and fought to drown him with her thoughts. Antonio nodded. "But I don't know where Lin went and the only opium I know about's in Favor's village."

Antonio shrugged.

"Let me tell Favor, myself." Fulfilling any filthy pact would be better than watching Poppy's terror. "Please."

"Sorry. There's no other deal."

"Where in Jesse Hell's the Dutchman?" Skinner spat on her parlor floor, but Molly concentrated on Antonio. "I never signed to ride as far as Sandy Blind. Damned Pinkertons and that Bragg bitch are on to me. Outside this town, I'm bounty bait."

Sandy Blind Canyon. Day would be there. He'd help Poppy if he could. Molly shuttered her thoughts as Antonio stiffened, then strode toward the door.

*   *   *

"Molly, help me." Poppy clutched the doorframe, though the rope choked her. Rose rippled to her side, sending what comfort she could through the uncaring air.

Lord, and she might as well be saying "Mommy, help me." Rose fused her mind with Molly's, pulsing the strength she still possessed into her daughter. *That's it, girl, go after him.*

"Please, why would you do such a thing?" Molly moved after Antonio, though his handgun warned her back. "Poppy's innocent. She has nothing to do with Favor. It's me he's angry with."

Molly, don't let him go. Keep him here. Once they have her outside, we're lost. She's lost. Rose watched Molly direct her mental force at the outlaw. Closing her eyes, Moll pulled him.

Antonio took an unsteady step. "Cursed *bruja*, leave off!"

Molly grabbed his gun arm, meaning only to detain him, but Antonio turned. So smoothly that he might have been on runners, he pivoted and clubbed her temple with his gun butt.

Poppy screamed. Molly pretended to fall unconscious and Rose drifted to her side.

That's it, love. Pretend you're paralyzed. Let your mind nail your knees to the floor and freeze your hands in place. You hear no ribald jokes about your limbs, nor Poppy begging.

Grateful that Molly couldn't see Skinner turn back after Antonio left, Rose maneuvered between them. *Don't move, Moll. Feather your breath in and out, slow, now.* Moll couldn't see the villain shiver, but certain sure Moll felt his rifle barrel prod her ribs. Ugly ogre, offal-eating scavenger . . . *No, don't move until the door closes, Moll, not until horses crunch through the snow. He'll only hurt her worse. And you.*

Dead, you're no help, at all. Don't move.

Skinner was not assuring Moll was safely out of the way. He wasn't trying to revive her. *Bastard.* Rose wafted so close she could wave her fingers over his flesh. *Feel something cold blowing down your neck, do you? Satan'll have us both if you touch my girl. I'll take you to him myself, and count it a lovely bargain!*

Outside, Poppy moaned as they threw her over a horse. Just then, the bearded man squatted next to Molly. Molly never stirred an eyelid, but she must have smelled his fetid breath, because her mind whimpered as clear as any frightened child had ever cried.

And then Skinner reached for a handful of Molly's hair.

No! Rose poured her spirit into the word and lunged for him. *No!* Flaming and swirling, Rose soared above his matted hair, a firestorm of pure energy. She screamed with a banshee's fury and spun him with hot winds, warring for Skinner's very soul.

And when the doorway stood empty and the door flapped in a chaotic breeze of her own making, Rose ceased all movement, all thought, all feeling. Ash floated, but what had burned? Exhausted past revival, Rose's spirit fluttered, then fell to the floor in tatters.

Molly raised her palms from her ears.

"Mama?" She was alone. The cabin smelled of sulphur. A black scorch marked the wall beside the front door.

The crunch of hooves, moving over snow, faded. They couldn't be taking Poppy far. The Dutchman! It must be VanBrunt. They were taking Poppy to VanBrunts' mercantile, to Hans.

Molly shrank from a wet nudge. Concentrating on the sounds outside, she'd missed Cinder, limping up to her. The dog's head wound had turned sticky. He lay beside her, panting.

"Sorry, boy." Nausea spun and Molly's vision dappled as she scooped a dipper of water for Cinder and one for herself.

Minutes later, Molly knew a foretaste of Hell. Darkness reigned in the corral. A slit of silver moon showed Glory's complacent form, but Molly had never saddled her in daylight. By touch, the task was endless. When Glory raised her head out of range, Molly left the bit dangling, then mounted from a rock and hoped Glory would follow the tugging reins.

Molly pounded the mercantile door until Eleanor slid back the bolt.

"Where is she?" Molly dodged past Eleanor, snatched up a lantern and stormed through the dark store. "Poppy!" Molly rammed into a table. It fell, upsetting a rack of metal pans and a jar of marbles. The swinging lantern cast crazy shadows everywhere. Favor's henchmen weren't hiding in the store. Neither was Poppy.

Where had they taken her? *Where is my baby sister with her thin bare arms exposed to the night?*

"Eleanor!" Molly crashed through a prim parlor with vanilla walls and pink pillows.

"He's here." Eleanor spoke from the hallway's end.

He. Did she mean Favor or Hans?

Strong arm supporting the damaged one, Eleanor stood in a wash of amber light, attention darting between a dim bedroom and the hall clock.

"Where's Poppy?" Even if she had to shake it out of the shopkeeper, Molly knew she'd force Eleanor to tell.

Eleanor showed a skeletal grin. "Where he won't get her." Eleanor's head moved in time with the pendulum.

Molly glanced inside the bedroom. Hans's enormous stomach swelled beneath a quilt. He thrashed and groaned on a bedstead too spindly for his weight.

"He didn't care for his dessert." Eleanor's chuckle came breathy and faint. "I don't think it agreed with him."

"I didn't come to tend his cursed belly. For all I care you can dump him down the nearest mine shaft. Eleanor!" Molly jiggled the woman's shoulder. "Rankin's men took Poppy. They mentioned Hans. Does he know where they've taken her? Look at me!"

"Look at *him,* the fat swine. Enjoying your just desserts, Hans?" Eleanor slipped from Molly's grip. "He'd have taken Poppy for his foster child, but when they brought her and saw Hans's state, they took her away."

"Where! For the love of—"

"Control yourself." Eleanor's lip curled. "That Chinaman came into my house, will you believe it? They let a Celestial into my house." Eleanor's skin pulled against her skull. "He said if Hans recovered, he was to pick up Poppy in Sandy Gulch."

"Sandy Gulch. Do you mean Sandy Blind Canyon? Eleanor!"

Molly left the woman humming an alphabet song and gloating over her husband's indigestion.

I am in Hell, Molly thought, tripping among the store's black hulks. But Glory still stood tied outside, with Molly's medical bag strapped to her saddle. The night wind cleared away the store's stench as Molly struck a match to cast wavering light on Day's map to Sandy Blind.

Glory labored through the night, striking out with slim forelegs, pulling herself through the deep snow, following Molly's directions and floundering through belly-deep drifts.

When they passed the hotel, Molly noted it as a landmark, but banned a fantasy of clean feather beds sheltered by stout stone walls. Molly watched for the rock outcropping Day had sketched. Near here, she should turn east. Having turned, she would thread through a cluster of foothills to a hidden spit of sand. She stopped the filly, maneuvered her left leg over the saddle horn and pitched to the ground.

"I'm sorry, girl." Glory rubbed her head on Molly's skirt, hard and harder. "I never intended to ride horses."

Molly embraced the filly's head, blocked nightmarish thoughts of Poppy, and waited for the light.

At dawn, Molly tried her luck at tracking. Where the snow was frosted thin and pocked, she saw one divergent set of prints and took them as Abner's.

Glory sidestepped as Molly leaned to study the ground beneath her. "I don't know, Glory. It looks as if they've followed Day into his canyon."

"You don't know much about guarding your backside, either." The female voice made Glory shy, dumping Molly into the mud and soft snow, but Eustacia Bragg's hand snagged the filly's reins before she could bolt.

"That was a stupid thing to do!" Molly recognized the uppity detective who'd tracked Day to her door.

"Letting me ride up behind you, now *that* was stupid." The detective swayed to her horse's movements, still holding Glory's reins. "Or did you mean me catching your horse?"

"I'm sorry." Molly swiped at her skirts, smearing even more red mud. The detective's mannish hat and suit of cinnamon twill made Molly feel vilely unkempt.

"What if I'd been the bounty I've been circling for a week? The one who fancies Bowie knives and polecat-greased hair?" Miss Bragg sounded more like a coddling nanny than a detective.

"All for that handsome face on the poster. Disgusting, isn't it, that I had Lightfoot O'Deigh and let him amble away?" The detective allowed herself a dignified huff. "And I can't fathom why you'd endanger yourself, trailing after a man who did *that* to your face." She swallowed her incredulity and squinted toward the horizon in what she no doubt hoped was trail-toughened scorn.

"Day would never—" Trapped, with no energy left for outrage, Molly conceded. "Yes, it's him I'm following, but he didn't hurt me." Molly touched her temple, feeling the broken skin overlying the dull ache. "The men who're after him, who kidnapped my sister, one of them hit me."

"Your sister? The blond?"

Molly waited. Next Miss Bragg would mention how sad it was, because Poppy was simple. Aching with fatigue and worry, Molly wished for the remark, so she could resent something besides Eustacia Bragg's efficiency and welcome assistance.

Molly snatched Glory's reins from the Pinkerton's gloved hand. The filly shied at a far-off popping.

"They've been plinking away at something for an hour." Miss Bragg tilted the watch pinned to her jacket. "I was about to find out what, when you rode past. Now, I think it might be your man."

Her man. Gunshots. She pictured Day's lazy stance with a Colt revolver on his hip. He and Poppy must be in the midst of those gunshots. Molly's weary mind clicked over and over, like a tin of Deborah's straight pins, rolling down a staircase, step by step. Suddenly, she knew what to do.

"We need to switch horses. And clothes." Molly watched the self-satisfied female mull that over.

"Do we?" Miss Bragg didn't look shocked, merely wary of all that red mud. "And why's that?"

"You'll be the decoy and I'll crawl in there on my belly, like a snake amid those rocks." Molly explained how the detective's split skirt would lend her agility and camouflage. "You ride Glory out there, fluttering around like you're me, all distraught." Molly cursed the detective's superior smile. "You're a good rider, so you can put on a show and stay out of range."

"Good plan"—Miss Bragg's approval came with a nod— "for saving Lightfoot's hide. Lightfoot is my first priority," she mused. "And taking him in alive would be preferable."

Miss Bragg chewed the inside of her cheek, thinking.

"If you're considering what you'll get out of helping me—" Molly cast about for an irresistible lure. "I'll hold the real criminals for you."

"Would you?" Miss Bragg's eyebrows vanished beneath her forelock of auburn curls.

"Skepticism may be your trade, Miss Bragg, but I'm honest. To the best of my ability, yes, I'll hold the bad men for you."

"Even if it's O'Deigh?" For once, Miss Bragg grinned like a girl. "Of course, you'd hold him. With both arms. If we're separated, don't wait. I'll find you." She exhaled a dismissing breath and studied Molly's Remington. "Shall we switch weapons?" She displayed a tidy silver pistol. "This might be handier clambering over boulders."

"I'll try it." Molly handed over the rifle with cold fatalism. "Well, let's go."

"Right." Miss Bragg swung down from her horse. "Be quick, I'm not eager to stand around in my cammy, knee-deep in slush."

*   *   *

Day knew how Moll Gallagher treated horses: gingerly, after the fashion of someone affectionately inclined toward porcupines. The black-clad equestrienne astride Glory was not Moll.

No matter who in Heaven she was, he could use the distraction. He'd been pinned in a casket-sized tumble of boulders for an hour, while three men held target practice on him from behind Poppy's keening form. He'd grown damned sick of it.

The impostor put on quite a show, riding to the camp's margin, pulling Glory into a graceful curvet, then jerking the filly up on her haunches and galloping off in mock fright.

"Get her!" Rankin shouted.

Kee set his gelding running. Antonio stayed put, not quite taken in. Tony, curse his nerveless soul, made few mistakes.

Antonio aimed a look toward Day, pinned down and short on bullets, then glanced at Poppy, hog-tied and shivering outside the dugout. Antonio shook his head and set off in pursuit.

"Last chance to prove what you're made of, O'Deigh!" Hoarse from an hour of such taunts, Rankin's voice echoed in the canyon.

"Still the shanty trash I took off the streets, huh? How long will you let this girl lay crying for someone to help her?"

"Help her." Resounding off the rocks, the echo mocked Day. He assessed the canyon once more.

Out of practice and half drunk with dreams of Moll, he'd stumbled out of the dugout at daybreak to find his buckskin gone. Damning his inattention to hobbles, Day had set off after his sole source of transportation.

In minutes, Favor and his rout had slipped into the canyon and started shooting. When Day finally settled in a safe position, they'd taken off Poppy's gag and made her call him.

"This little girl's getting awfully tired and cold. It'll be hard telling Moll why you didn't help her simple sister."

Rankin strode back and forth, squinting. About the only thing Day's refuge provided was the sun smack behind him.

Blinded, Rankin guessed at Day's position. Clouds scuttled before the wind, though, and the advantage wouldn't last.

"Fine, O'Deigh. I'll amuse you with a few stories about your lady love."

The cocky bastard lit a cigar and puffed smoke. Out of range, damn him, and he *knew* it. Rankin dropped his match and Poppy flinched.

No more. Day's eyes traced the best path to Poppy. A flash of red-brown, some beast, showed in the rocks, then vanished. Keeping the sun behind him, Day planned to skitter over the boulders, taking occasional blasts at Rankin. With luck, he'd reach Poppy before Rankin drilled him.

He dearly hoped so. He'd hate missing Rankin's fury when he found that "Molly," wasn't.

Day almost made it. He vaulted, rolled, even got off a shot that nicked Rankin's arm. If not for Poppy, he'd have nailed Rankin for fair. Hunkered down, squinting past the grit in his eyes, Day took satisfaction in the blood blooming on Rankin's immaculate linen.

Something above Day started a shower of scree. Heart wrested into his throat, he listened. Nothing.

God willing, he'd snatch Poppy with one arm and punch Rankin with the other. Day clicked back the Colt's hammer. His last bullet rolled into position.

Eyes dazed and swollen, Poppy lifted her head and stared. Her wavering hand indicated a sound to her right.

Shit! One step out of the sheltering rocks, he knew she'd heard Antonio. The outlaw had only pretended to pursue the rider. He'd circled back to catch Day unaware.

Antonio's whining shot sheered off rock chips to peck Day's face. Both men bent their knees, braced their forearms and fired. Poppy screamed as Antonio fell to his knees beside her. Dying, the gunman's finger jerked once more. Poppy's screams rained down like knives as Antonio fell across her.

Ankles still bound, bare feet scuffing pasty snow, Poppy tried to come to him. Day lurched, got an arm around her waist and pulled her. He held the hot gun—empty and useless—wide of Poppy as he hunted for Rankin.

Day used his chin to push aside Poppy's dusty hair. Where was he? Rankin's revolver lay jammed among the rocks.

Rankin sprang up from hiding, stiff-arming Poppy's back, so that her weight and impact bowled them both over.

"Take her." Rankin stood close, but Day couldn't spare time to reload. "Why should I waste two bullets when I can put the same one through both? Fine, stand in front. It works just the same."

Should he throw the Colt at Rankin's head?

Day worked to get Poppy behind him, so he could see clear. Rankin had to be bluffing, since his revolver lay out of reach. Then he saw it. Rankin's arms cradled the Sharps buffalo rifle that'd killed Shawnee Sue. The bastard was dead right. He could blast a hole through them both.

"You've given me that superior look for the last time." Rankin balanced on a rock six feet away. Poppy's teeth chattered at his nearness. "I'd shoot her just to shut her up."

Day gave Poppy a push, but she couldn't run. Hell, she couldn't even walk.

Sweet Lord, Moll, I'm sorry.

Day squared his shoulders and tugged down his black hat. If the Sharps ball didn't catch him square in the chest, he might pounce close and strangle the man, but it was a bloody long leap.

"Let the girl go." If only he could get Rankin mad enough to err. "Unless you've a cravin' to shoot up another woman. Poor thing's mad with fright. Take me in or hang me, but y'might as well leave her here."

Poppy's keening wove primitive background for Day's last sales pitch, but Rankin wasn't buying.

Aw well, Moll, I'll bet you looked pretty in that dress.

"Tell you what, O'Deigh." Rankin rolled the cigar to the corner of his mouth. "Why don't you do me a favor? Why don't you beg? Why don't you just kneel down, right here—"

The bullet took Rankin in the shoulder. Before Rankin's body spun with the impact, Day launched, hitting him with a tackle that ended on sheer flat rock. Rankin's neck snapped like the lash of a whip.

The gunman. God bless him, had he aimed for Rankin? Day scrambled back to Poppy and stayed hunkered down, scanning the rocks. Where was the bloody shooter?

Poppy clung to Day's ankle as Rankin's last ululating cry battered the red stone walls. Then, as if Satan had clapped his hand over the screaming lips, the sound stopped and Rankin lay still.

Day crouched by Poppy, wringing her hand before he faced the footfalls scraping on the brow of earth behind him.

Feet planted wide on the snow-patched earth, long strands of hair licking like flames, stood Molly, a smoking revolver clutched in her outstretched hands.

Chapter
Thirty-two

With the detachment of a hawk sailing above, Moll watched Day pry her fingers off Miss Bragg's revolver. The gunshot had rocked Moll's insides. She'd never believed she'd hit Favor.

"Let go, Bright. Let it go, now."

Her fingers released, but stayed stiff as twigs. Day stuck the gray barrel in his holster, wincing at its heat. Molly shivered and her knees buckled, almost dragging him down.

"Sweet, dauntless girl."

Day draped his arms on her shoulders, staring into her eyes, and yet she felt a fog divided them.

"You did what had to be done, but you didn't kill Favor. He broke his neck."

Day lifted her into his arms and over the ankle-wrenching boulders. She twisted to look. Down below lay Favor. Blood smeared his white shirt. A trickle of red crossed his chin.

As they reached clearer footing, Day let Molly down. Hooves clacked on rock and they both turned.

"Nice beastie." Day snatched the reins of the riderless horse. "Didn't tie him, and he stayed by in all the commotion? You're no youngster, are y'lad? We're keeping this one, Moll."

Too weak to contradict him, Molly untied her medicine bag from Miss Bragg's horse and stepped carefully toward Poppy.

"Moll, Poppy's not injured." Day wasn't lying, but he meant to rush her, by hiding the truth. Molly wasn't fooled.

"Get on the bay and I'll take Poppy with me on Rankin's black. We need to get away from here. Now."

Molly saw Day hold the bay's head, expectantly. She heard Poppy panting and walked past Day to her sister.

"Take this." He pressed leather reins against her hand.

She let them drop and knelt, tucking her cloak around Poppy.

"Damn it all."

Day backed away long enough for Moll to check Poppy's eyes. The black centers pooled wide within a thin blue rim.

"Molly, I'm cold."

"I know, honey." Molly touched a vein in Poppy's rope-burned throat. Her pulse fluttered like a bird's heart.

Day returned, leading a big black horse. "Moll, y've one minute to dose her, then I'm throwing you both aboard. Give me every hard look y'have, sweetheart, I've had worse."

Day's boots stood near enough to touch. Day, handsome and commanding as a soldier, dark and rough-bearded and dear.

"I don't know if the laudanum will help her forget or push her into nightmares. She doesn't look good, Day."

His smile warmed her. He snatched the hand she'd flung toward Poppy and kissed its center. "Hello, there, Bright. You're looking a bit peaked, yourself. Let's get you someplace safe."

The black horse snorted, scenting something borne on the rain-heavy wind. Day clamped his hand over the vibrating nostrils before the black called. Molly grabbed the bay.

"Give her the medicine." Day jerked the black's cinch tight. "If we have to run, she can't be thrashing about."

Crooning and explaining, Molly measured the syrup and tipped it into Poppy's unresisting mouth. The rain had begun.

"Quick now, help me get her up before me on this big mare."

Between them, they managed. Day placed a quick kiss on Poppy's tangled hair. "Here we go, Pop." He swallowed hard enough that Molly saw. "That's me girl. Moll, mount up."

"He's not mine." Miss Bragg's bay stamped as Moll fumbled with her medicine bag.

"Fine, Bright, then I've no doubt his owner'll be along in plenty o'time to accuse us of thievin'."

Day tugged the brim of his hat to shade his eyes, gave the black a slap on the rump and didn't look back.

When they reached the Gold Hill hotel, Molly didn't hear Day's excuse for Poppy's lethargy. She only staggered under the burden of Poppy's weight toward the room Day indicated.

Mercy, what a world, when two tired women raised more eyebrows than Day, bristling with revolvers and rifles.

When Poppy slept, Molly edged from the darkened room into the hall. She collapsed with her back against the door, listening to the rain's lulling patter, recalling VanBrunts' dark hall. Had Eleanor poisoned Hans?

She raised a hand to her chest, monitoring her heartbeat. Hans and Favor. *Guilt doesn't last,* Rose had told her. Let it be true, because even now, where rue should lodge, she found only faint regret that she'd broken her code as a healer.

Favor had wanted Day down on his knees. Molly's revulsion uncoiled with a snap. She'd do it again. Draw back the hammer, lift the gun—Molly startled as Day materialized before her.

"Poppy's all right?"

"I think so, but she'd rest better at home. We're so close."

"We needed a lull before ridin' back to Virginia. It'll all be waitin' for us—kidnap, murder, stolen horses.

"All that"— He leaned and kissed her cheek—"just isn't the thing for a honeymoon, do you think?" Folding his fingers through hers, Day led the way to a dark, rock-walled saloon. Scarlet-faced from the roaring fireplace, a bartender slept with his head on one hand.

Day mixed hot cider with brandy and dragged chairs to the yawning hearth. He refused excuses and conversation.

"I'll only tolerate the sound of liquid, flowin' down your throat." He nudged her lip with the flagon. "And wearin' down your resistance."

Smiling, Molly drank.

Bitter wind moaned outside the hotel walls. A grandfather clock bonged inside. Just noon. Molly imagined crows hopping, pecking the wet and wind-flapped clothes of Favor and Antonio, dead on the Sandy Blind rocks.

"Here, now." Day pulled his chair closer, sheltering her with one arm, rubbing a finger between her brows. "None o' that."

A gust down the chimney made the logs spray feathers of sparks.

Day rubbed Molly's neck, kneading the taut muscles. When her head rested against his shoulder, he took the cider from her and set it on the hearth.

"Go upstairs with me, Moll?" His blue eyes engulfed her. How could he offer both haven and exhilaration?

Yes. Forever. Every night of my life. She wanted to concede everything she had, but the dozing bartender might hear. She stood and Day's hand steadied the small of her back as they climbed the stairs, legs moving together on each step.

The room was no wider than Day's outstretched arms, and when the saloon's patrons arrived at sundown, clanking coins and raw laughter would filter in. But for one dark afternoon, the whitewashed walls formed a bridal bower.

They stood silent. Without taking her eyes from his, Molly shrugged off Miss Bragg's brown jacket and shed the horror they'd locked outside. If he noticed she wore another woman's clothes, he said nothing, only let his hands move quickly from her nape to her waist, letting in slaps of cold.

His fingers felt warm and sure, but once, a tremble took his confidence. His hand splayed over her skin.

"Are we still all right, Moll? I'm not rushing you?"

Molly kissed Day with all the love she could fit into a minute or into eternity, but words were as out of reach as the stars.

"Eustacia Bragg!" The rap on their door attended a commanding whisper.

Molly started upright, but Day pushed her back to the bed's warmth. He wrapped one blanket around his waist, and patted the other over her. Muscles played across his shoulder as he hobbled to the door.

"I'd ask y'to take a chair—" The detective's boots clicked on the wooden floor as she entered.

Miss Bragg wore a wrinkled gray serge. She hung Molly's mudsmeared gown on a hook as she crossed to a window, refusing to look at either of them.

Day closed the door. "—but as y'see, we're short of amenities." Day yawned, stretching. The tucked blanket loosened and Molly thought she'd blind the female Pinkerton before allowing her to look.

When she finally spoke, Eustacia Bragg stuttered. "You h-have my horse."

"Women are always sayin' that to me." Day ruffled his hair into a rooster's comb. "What's the time, lass?"

Lass? Molly's jealousy clamped below her heart. She'd "lass" Day for flirting with this half-sized hussy!

"Just struck seven." The detective blushed. "I've been waiting since three o'clock yesterday."

Molly's fingers pressed the mattress, counting. For nineteen hours, she and Day had twined arms and legs and hearts. Straight through dinner and nearly breakfast. She smiled at the shocking truth of it, then gasped.

"I've got to go check Poppy!" Molly rose, with the blanket held beneath her arms.

"I met her on the stair and we had breakfast together." Miss Bragg slipped a paper from her reticule and focused on it, rather than on Day's resplendent form. Her eyelashes flicked up only once. "S-she helped me carry a meal to my prisoner."

Kee had swooped down on the detective, expecting to spar with Molly. Shortly thereafter, Miss Bragg had handcuffed and arrested him. "He's given credence to your story, Miss Gallagher." Eustacia consulted her notes. "After viewing the bodies, Kee confessed that Randall Rankin and Antonio Scarletti had conspired in a number of deaths.

"But that doesn't erase the murder of Shawnee Sue." The detective's level glance turned on Day. She expected no resistance. "I'll require you to come with me."

"It's better, Moll." Day stifled her protest with a hand that didn't reach her. Molly's legs trembled. She settled on the bed, certain she'd think of something. "No, now. I won't have it hangin' over us."

Miss Bragg bustled to the door, her back turned to them both. "We'll leave within the hour."

As soon as Day bolted the door, Molly collided with him, too eager to be coy.

"Only an hour?" Molly tripped over their fallen blankets.

"Not enough, Bright, when we have serious business to discuss." His sober expression stilled her. "Suppose you could deliver a letter to Richard Griffin?"

Molly nodded.

The room's writing table had no chair, so Day perched on the unmade bed to write. Instead of reading over his shoulder, she watched him, hand swooping and slashing over the paper.

Day looked up suddenly, his face tight as he snared her hand. "If something should happen—If I'm delayed, and you should find yourself—Step closer, Bright. There, now."

Day buried his face in the belly of her unlaced camisole, inhaling her. "If you should be carryin' our babe, is what I mean to say, then I'd want you to confide in Richard. Would you do that?"

"Aye," she mocked him, reaching for her dress, trying to crush his melancholy.

"Promise one more thing, Molly mine?"

She memorized him, naked and gesturing with a pen in a honeyed patch of morning sun.

"Promise you won't wear black again, till I'm dead?"

Throat constricted, she dropped the gown and used her index finger to mark a cross over her breast.

"Till the day we're married, then never again." She kissed his shoulder's peak, as the heel of his hand sealed the letter.

Day snared Molly's wrist and lounged back against the rumpled, sunstruck sheets.

"Three quarters of an hour left." Her heart lurched at his dare-the-Devil smile. "Forty-five sweet minutes. What kind of a man turns down the challenge of such a lovely little slip of time?"

Gray-bottomed clouds mounded over Sun Mountain, shadowing Molly's first glimpse of home. It hunched bleak and silent, until Cinder erupted barking from under the porch, and Stag, dressed for travel, ran to meet them.

"God, honey—" Stag dragged Poppy down from the saddle, where she rode double with Molly.

Before Glory could make good her threats to buck, Molly slid off and walked the distance to the corral.

She tried to ignore Poppy and Stag, but his emotion-choked voice made Molly falter.

"Don't *ever* do that again. I didn't know where you were, I wanted to come after you, but I didn't know where to look!"

Molly peered over her shoulder as Stag stroked her sister's hair. Stag's fierce gaze made Molly turn away.

"Molly, don't go." Stag sheltered Poppy under one arm. "Poppy and I are getting married. I have money from home and I'm going to buy Brown Bess's. We want your blessing. You can live with us, if you like."

Are you sure? When you can't guess what's happened in two days? When your bride's been kidnapped and manhandled? When each day you'll be reminding Poppy of things she knew the day before?

Watching Stag's hand soothe up and down Poppy's back,

Molly couldn't ask one of the questions. "You have my permission."

"Dauntless," was she? Then why did she long for her mother? Molly moved like a sleepwalker, righting furniture disturbed by Antonio's invasion. An amber-colored bottle, holding a spear of hardy lavender, sat untouched. Vivid purple and fragrant, it had been a token from Day, the last time he'd wangled his way into her parlor.

Two nights ago, three men had stormed her parlor and her mother had driven them away. The scorch on the cottage wall would probably never scrub off.

Two nights. Had it been so little? Just this morning she'd held Day for the last time. Folded together like hands in prayer, they'd blended far more than bodies. Then he'd ridden off with Eustacia Bragg. He could be hanged for murder.

Molly blinked, clearing her vision to examine Cinder's wound. No inflammation, just dark rheumy eyes happy to see her.

Last times hurt too much for contemplation. But maybe they weren't always final.

"Come back." Molly whispered into the stillness, meaning both Day and her mother. "Come back to me."

Rose had erased years of selfish decline, prodded Molly into Day's arms, where she belonged, and then spent herself in a last explosion of love.

How unfair. *Most* girls probably learned trust and forgiveness from their mothers. But most probably learned more quickly. Still, the delay had come with a bonus. Rose had proven the warm clasp of love would last forever, if it must.

Stag and Poppy sat on the porch, snug in a cove of firethorn. Molly had never known her sister to hold such a long conversation. Marriage to a kind man surpassed Molly's best dreams for Poppy.

Molly opened the back door to a torrent of twining cats. She squatted among them, awarding pats to every back, scratches behind all ears. Their breaths floated into hers, hanging white on the frosty air. Purring rose to cacophony.

"Who are you?" A sleek black tomcat, too feral to accept her touch, skidded two steps and batted a piece of paper.

Summonses slipped beneath her door were rare. Molly hoped it heralded a very minor illness, for tonight she balked at healing.

"Come for breakfast. Deborah."

Molly shook her head, chafed her hands together and built a fire to warm her as she slept. She mounded kindling in the stove and added the note on top. It curled, blackened, then burst bright. Even tomorrow she'd be terrible company.

She could listen, though. Nothing happened in Virginia City that didn't pass around Deborah's table.

Molly wouldn't burden Deb with her troubles. Still, she might flaunt the gown.

Molly latched the stove and retrieved the brown-wrapped parcel from under her bed. Day had pouted over her failure to open it. Even now, she hesitated, wanting a proper audience before ripping the paper. Molly stashed the box, still wrapped, next to her medicine bag.

Baby Happy Days's croup dragged Molly from bed an hour after midnight, so she arrived early at Deb's. For hours, she'd held the babe's cheek next to her own, both heads draped to catch vapor from a pot of boiling water. Happy Days's parents dozed while Molly and the baby battled. Finally they'd won.

When the little girl lay sleeping, her thumb falling moistly from her mouth, Molly wound her limp hair into a tidy knot, then crept outside.

The pewter sky behind Sun Mountain mumbled thunder, but Deborah's parlor glowed with lamplight. Deb sat on the hearthrug pawing through a wooden box. She bounded up as Molly eased into the hall.

"I would have knocked if I'd thought—"

Still in her nightclothes, her brown hair in plaits, Deb untangled her legs and stood, her arms wrapped around her ribs.

"I've been going through Christmas decorations. Stag told me about the splintered door, the blood and I—Oh, Molly, I said the danger with Favor was all *over*." Deborah wrung the words out. "I didn't tell anyone else what I thought." Her hands made banishing movements in the air. "But I made a deal with God. If you came back safe, I'd really celebrate Christmas, this year!"

Molly wrinkled her nose against an absurd tingling. Silly tears. For the first time, she and her friend embraced.

"You bought my safety with Christmas decorations?"

"Any complaints?" Deborah pulled back, holding both of Molly's hands.

"None."

"Good." Deborah moved toward the kitchen. Soon, hungry miners would pack the boardinghouse.

Molly blurted out her secret. "Day and I are getting married."

"What?" An avalanche of potatoes rumbled from the bucket Deborah had been draining out the back door. She stood with hands on her hips. "Lucky, lucky girl." Deborah crushed her in a second, wet-handed hug. "I suppose I'll have to reform, and try thinking of Day as a brother. Impossible. Perhaps a very handsome cousin."

Blushing and smug, Molly drank coffee while Deborah ran upstairs to rouse Robin.

"Molly!" Margaret Bride, dressed in brown-and-white stripes and an out-of-season straw hat, entered the kitchen. "I've been invited for breakfast, too."

Lowering herself into a chair, Margaret discarded small talk and grabbed Molly's hand. "What about Hans?"

"What *about* him?"

"Since Hans disappeared . . . You knew he'd—disappeared?"

Margaret pulled Molly's hand to bring her nearer. "Eleanor told me she put candlewick seeds in his blackberry pie. Candlewick. Remember, kite day? You told me never to use the seeds."

Twice guilty, Molly closed her eyes.

"She told me, after school yesterday, that once he 'quit

twitching'—she said it just like that!—she rolled him down a mine shaft!"

Molly buried her head in her hands until Deb returned.

"You told her."

As Molly looked up, Deborah's eyes met Margaret's.

"You both know? Eleanor told you both?" Molly shook her head. "That woman *wants* to be caught!"

"Actually, Margaret told me." Deborah drew herself up like a judge. "And I'm certainly not going to the sheriff. What with his scheming to adopt Poppy!"

Molly's chest labored to draw breath. The room spun around her as a maelstrom of noise, blood and guilt crested. Margaret's cold hand smoothed Molly's brow and she looked up.

"Favor is dead, too." Molly waited for horror and reproach. Neither came. By Margaret's grim-set lips, Molly concluded Deb had confided Molly's past, as well. Resentment flared, then faded, and Molly considered the three of them: a conspiracy of women, holding silent because justice hadn't fallen within the law.

"Lucky thing he's dead, because McCabe's scalped him. Not literally of course, but I heard McCabe took Favor's opium clear to Leadville, Colorado, and made himself a fortune."

Molly laughed with gaiety verging on hysteria. She tried drowning it with coffee. "I can't believe this gossip!"

"The talk's been here all along, Moll." Deborah wagged a finger. "But even when you weren't the subject, you wouldn't listen!"

"Or contribute." Margaret sipped her coffee as if it were champagne.

"Those days are over." Deborah held her cup to the middle of the table, proposing a toast. "Here's to Moll Gallagher. With a husband like Day, she'll have plenty to gossip about." Their cups clinked. "Now, what's hidden inside that box, Moll?"

Chapter
Thirty-three

Two weeks later, Molly missed a rung on the ladder to her rafters, and knew she carried Day's child. She could blame the weariness and lines around her eyes on worry over her mother's sudden disappearance.

"Not so sudden." Molly muttered as she wobbled back down the ladder. "She's been dead ten years, dunce."

Worry didn't explain her painful breasts or tight bodice, though, and she'd never been awkward. Yesterday, she'd tripped over the wild black tomcat determined to plague Ginger. Now, she'd nearly broken her neck reaching for a sheaf of cornhusks.

Distracted and plotting, Molly managed to deliver the husks to the Chinese woman who tied them into dolls. She didn't stop at Deb's. Instead, walking home, Molly decided to dose herself with raspberry tea, reputed to bring on reluctant flux. It failed.

A somber visit with Sheriff Merrick brought no news of Day's capture, trial or release.

"I know you'll be anxious to hear, Miss Molly, although it looks like you got your filly back." Merrick leaned against the doorframe of his office and nodded toward Glory, tethered outside. "How'd you go about that?"

"It's a long story, Sheriff. Actually I'm satisfied with the outcome of that one of Mr. Day's offenses." Molly gave up trying to rebutton her black mitts. Could even her hands be swelling? "It's more a matter of notifying him of something he left behind."

Bite your tongue, Moll Gallagher. It takes no mind reader to sort through that. What it did take was another woman. Miss Eustacia Bragg responded to Molly's letter of inquiry with astounding promptness.

"I regret to tell you," Miss Bragg's letter began, "that I have been discharged from my post with Mr. Pinkerton's agency, due in part to my handling of the Shawnee Sue case. Mr. O'Deigh's whereabouts are, once more, a mystery to me. With apologies and fervent good wishes for your future, E. V. Bragg."

Outside the mercantile, Molly folded the missive into her reticule, and Poppy's attempt at comfort only deepened her gloom.

"He'll be back, Molly." Poppy squeezed her sister's arm. "Some morning you'll open the back door and Day will come shining in."

By the time the two reached home, Molly had decided patience was her best course. Poppy lingered outside with Stag and Molly went indoors alone.

"I've done all I can do." She addressed Cinder as she refilled the water in the amber bottle holding Day's lavender. "It's probably nothing but nerves." When her hand bumped the lavender, shattering it into faded violet kernels, Molly scolded herself. Only superstition made it feel like an omen.

Day didn't return, nor did he write, so when Molly's dizzy spells ended and she didn't suffer from morning sickness, she pretended to forget. In late November, as she trimmed back splayed canes of firethorn running riot over her porch, Day's baby reminded her. A ripple like a fish's tail swept through her belly. Her hand went to it, protective and sure, and Molly knew. Like his father, this child refused to be ignored.

At noon, Molly set out to deliver Day's sealed letter to Richard. The autumn scent of burning leaves and fried sausage lured her to the campfire of two Irish miners who offered to share their roadside meal. For an instant, the greasy scent tilted Molly toward nausea. Then she turned ravenous, and shared a stand-up dinner with them, promising a reading in exchange.

Two hours later, Richard Griffin, glinting with sterling shirt studs and the pride of a winning streak, met Molly outside the Black Dog saloon.

He skimmed the letter, then looked up, one brow crooked. "Have you read this?" An ore wagon rumbled past. Blaming her lack of response on the noise, he repeated his question.

"I don't *want* to read it, Richard!" A street mongrel shied and scuttled away at her tone. Molly lowered her voice. "He wrote it because—He said if something happened to him . . . Can't you just take care of it?" Molly's clenched fist struck her skirts in frustration. "For once in my life can't someone else take over? I am so weary of being in charge."

Richard's poker face deserted him. His features sharpened, as if assessing a stranger. Then, he cupped her elbow.

"Let's walk down to Mrs. Green's, shall we?" His touch was gentle but determined.

"I won't have Deb knowing." Moll crossed her shawl ends more tightly around her. Deb was a careful observer.

"She won't. And she won't mind lending her parlor for an hour. I'll take care of everything, Molly. I just think it's best that you know what's coming."

Sitting on Deb's green settee, Molly read Day's letter. She sipped her tea down to a few scattered leaves and smirked at the symbol left behind. A cane, a sure sign she needed assistance. If she could concentrate enough to read that, why didn't Day's letter make sense to her? Richard sat with folded hands, waiting.

"Not yet, Richard. Please." She couldn't banish the memory of Day on that last morning, his long muscled body covered with sunlight. "Can we wait? Can I let you know when?"

Richard lifted her hand, kissed it and escorted her all the way home.

The next morning Molly surrendered propriety to comfort and left her corset folded in a drawer, atop Day's letter. She'd wait until Christmas. Day would return by then. If he hadn't, she'd do what had to be done.

He'd praised her for that, there on the wet, blood-spattered hillside. *Sweet dauntless girl. You did what had to be done.* Would he feel the same now?

That time, she'd defended Day. This time she'd protect his child. No matter what she wanted. Or didn't want.

Rose's self-indulgent life and selfless second death had shown Molly the truth: love asked for more than small sacrifices.

Poppy and Stag married on Christmas Eve in Deborah's parlor. Beautiful in red plaid taffeta and corkscrew curls two days setting in rags, Poppy held Stag's arm beneath a piñon pine cluttered with popcorn strands, beads and candles.

Then Molly was truly alone.

Two weeks into January, Molly moved the button on the waist of her newest black skirt. That day she asked Deb to iron the wrinkles out of the lovely peach-colored wedding dress and sent Robin with a message for Richard Griffin.

Christmas cheer left no joyful hangover in Virginia City, Day decided as he stalked the town's boardwalks in search of Moll.

Her cottage stood silent, firethorn guarding the porch, and though Cinder licked his hand, the cats scattered, humpbacked and shy. Glory galloped to the fence, then backed snorting as if she'd never allowed him astride. And no one would say where he might find Moll.

Not that they didn't know. Every man Jack of them, miners, soiled doves and bartenders, knew.

Day's heart hammered against his breastbone. Nothing

could be wrong. Not now. Not when he'd finally sweet-talked old Pinkerton himself into believing. Day needed only Moll, running into his arms, to prove life perfect.

He wanted to marry her. Today.

Virginia's snow had been lavished on fall. January's rock-hard streets smelled like summer. Raw gusts mixed wind and sand in a notorious Washoe zephyr. The cantankerous wind grated a man's nerves along with his hide.

Ringing buckles, galloping hooves and a cracking lash took an ore wagon past. In its dusty wake, he saw a familiar face.

"Persia!" Gypsy purpled and feathered, the tawny-maned madam sashayed up a side street, arrogant and busy. Until she recognized him.

"Jesus Christ. What are you doing back? *Today?*"

"Glad to see y'too, Madam Persia."

Her cleavage heaved. The pulse in her neck beat so hard that he counted the pounding.

"I'm looking for Moll Gallagher."

Persia sawed a brass bangle back and forth on her wrist. "I couldn't say where she is. You might try her cottage."

"I did."

"Listen, Day, I'm late going to stay with Robin while Deborah—I've got to go."

Moll wasn't dead. That much, at least, was clear. The next Virginian who denied him might not be so lucky.

Geordie. The little bulldog miner Day had helped pull out of the mine limped into view. If Geordie planned to keep on healin', he'd best confess what was going on.

"Geordie." Day blocked the boardwalk. By Heaven, the pup couldn't pass unless he wanted to duck between Day's legs.

"Day! Cousin! Great to—oh Holy Mother."

"I seem to be inspirin' a fair amount of prayer today, *cousin.* Now, tell me where I might find Moll, and no non-sense, either. If I take it in my head to bounce you off that wall, they'll be searching for you *next* Christmas. Let's have it." Day's roar made his own ears ring.

"I'll tell, but I'm warnin', you'll not like it. Moll's at the wedding."

Wedding. Poppy and Stag had done it. Moll'd worried

over that, but she'd seen fire flash between the two, the night after the mine accident.

"Poppy's wedding." Fair enough. Why all the secrecy?

"Uh—no." Geordie strangled out the word. "Man, you're going to hate this." He gripped Day's arm. "Moll's wedding. The party bit, afterward, actually. She married Richard Griffin this morning."

The wind held its breath while the street's silence played Day's head like a bellows. "Where?"

"Persia's given over the Black Dog—"

"Christ." Now *he'd* done it, takin' the Lord's name. But he knew how well Moll loved him. In truth, he wasn't swearing, but praying. *Oh, Molly mine, why would you do such a thing?*

Then he remembered the letter.

Geordie took Day's paralysis as consent to escape. Day's chaps slapped leather applause for his menacing performance. His spurs urged his boots toward the Black Dog Saloon.

It hadn't been two months, had it? Well, ten weeks? Bloody hell. *He'd* be to blame for forcing Moll, who couldn't stand any man's touch but his, to give herself to Griffin. But not yet.

Persia'd gotten herself a new rinky-tink piano and a banjo player, too. Just outside, Day heard loud guffaws and a splash of clean laughter he took for Deborah Green's.

He struck the swinging doors with the heel of his hand and paused inside. Sand spit in around his boots and the fiddle faded to silence. Moll's spooky orange cat lay dozing under a table. Something odd in that. Dogs, not cats, frequented saloons. Green eyes wide, the ginger puss bounced up, spitting and hissing. Likely she found his presence just as weird.

And then Day smelled Moll's lavender soap.

Beautiful as flame, as sunrise, as any sight a man could see and die happy, Moll wore the gown he'd bought for their wedding. Her hair was drawn up at the sides with ribbons and curled into pipe curls as tight as a schoolgirl's. One wayward lock squirmed past her collarbone, then hid inside her neckline.

And then he smelled roses. Overpowering, throat-clogging roses. A blast of cold slapped his back, rippled down his collar, flittered around his behind. That Godforsaken ghost was back, mad as the Devil—Lord, let *that* be a lie!—that he hadn't kept his vow.

"I meant to, Rosie. I meant to."

At his voice, Molly turned. She blanched, swaying in the protective curve of Griffin's arm.

Day strode toward her and men parted in his path. Cold billowed behind him, driving him on. Moll's lips moved with the shape of his name and then Griffin was setting her apart, reaching for his cowardly little derringer.

A handful of cards flicked off a table and onto the floor. The orange cat scampered through, scattering them as she headed toward the bar, but no one else seemed to notice.

"Richard, no!" Moll caught the gambler's sleeve.

Griffin replaced the derringer in his vest. His face wore a look like piracy, and Day didn't care for its implication. Griffin wasn't protecting Moll, he wanted her. He'd loved her all along and taken that letter as license. Might've waited till Day was dead, but no.

Bloodlust and a yen for hot gunpowder crashed over Day. He'd kill Griffin, but first he had to cut him off from Moll. Mark Owen Daywell would take no chance on crossfire, this time.

"Hellfire, Richard, you wouldn't shoot a wedding guest." Day figured that a gallon of beer might have goaded the gambler into a more daring swagger, but it couldn't have painted a falser smile. "I didn't come for trouble."

Griffin gave a short disbelieving laugh, and the mirth in it told Day that the danger was feigned. As usual, the gambler had something up his sleeve.

"Honest." Day's dark fear vanished. "I only came to drink a wedding toast to my best girl!" But then he didn't.

Moll's cheeks, flaring red, were a sight more intoxicating than drink, and the pale ivory satin, inset down the back of the paneled gown, tempted his hand.

"God, Molly, I can't help touching you." Day grabbed her—bridal gown, ribbons and all—and bent her back for his kiss. Moll's arms slid through his, her fingers gripping so hard that he felt her nails through his vest. His senses whirled, awash with her.

"I did it, Moll. They're not after me. I did it, and it's by God about time."

"What's this, then?"

Day opened his eyes enough to see a man dressed as a preacher hopping about like a terrier. Day ignored him and deepened his kiss, shamelessly.

"My bride, sir, seems to be having trouble breathing." Richard's narrow face, lurking just over Moll's shoulder, had never looked so foxlike. "I think you'd better release her and have a look at this."

The document flapping before his nose looked official. A warrant? Nothing else, short of an avalanche, could have torn him from Molly's arms.

"This better be good, Griffin." Day kissed Moll once more. He'd already left her lips swollen, but she clung to his hand. "I'll be back, Bright, even if I have to shoot my way out."

Griffin propelled Day into a corner. Everyone watched, missing the orange cat's leap onto the bar. Day might've scratched his head at the puss's perusal of the spirits, except that Griffin hauled Day's ear right alongside his lips and whispered loud enough to deafen a stone.

"Congratulations, you lucky bastard." Griffin pumped Day's hand. "You've been married today, and didn't even have to dress for it." Above his diamond stickpin and starched linen, Griffin disdained Day's leather and denim. "By proxy." Griffin presented the parchment certificate. It was no warrant.

Day considered the document, puzzling out the verbose legal language, portions of which he actually understood.

Wed this day . . . Mark Owen Daywell . . . Molly Maureen Gallagher . . . "Since there's no provision for such legal fripperies in this uncivilized territory, we told the good pastor I was you."

"But why so soon?" Day stared back at Moll, who seemed oblivious to the cat batting at her elbow.

"I should think even a simple Cornishman might puzzle that out." Instead of going for his gun to drive home the point, Griffin passed his hand, discreetly, over the drape of his watch chain. Over his belly.

Moll? Could Molly be carrying his babe? Day walked away from Griffin's further explanations.

"You understand, now?" Moll gripped the mahogany bar, whispering, carving out privacy in the midst of none. She reached for him.

"Aye, Bright, I understand." Day took her hand in both of his and called back over his shoulder, unable to look away from her. "Mr. Griffin, y'said I might kiss the bride?"

"Has a lack of permission ever stopped you?" Griffin glowered, but it was the bar-strolling cat that caught Day's attention.

The creature stalked down the bar to Moll's elbow, fixed its grass-green eyes on Day's and yowled. It took a few hearty laps of spilled brandy, shook itself, then looked up and yowled again.

"Aye, Mr. Griffin. Once or twice a lack of permission has slowed me down, for fair."

The cat purred, flicked its tail in a dismissing wave and leaped from the bar. Day would have sworn its eyes used to be gold.

Day swept Molly off her feet, the long silk skirts draping his arm and brushing the floor.

"Here now!" the little preacher insisted, again.

"Ah, don't be worryin' yourself, Reverend." Day winked at the man in black. "It's all right and proper. The bride's mum has seen to that."

Day jammed his back against the saloon doors. They swung wide, a threshold to the street. As Day carried Moll across, into the noise and sunlight, her laughter tickled his neck.

Down the street, unseen, a marmalade puss collided with a sleek black tomcat. Together, they spun toward the grave-yard in a wild capering dance.

Presenting all-new romances — featuring ghostly
heroes and heroines and the passions they inspire.

♥ *Haunting Hearts* ♥

__*A SPIRITED SEDUCTION*
by Casey Claybourne   0-515-12066-9/$5.99
A prim and proper lady learns the art of seduction — from a ghost.

__*STARDUST OF YESTERDAY*
by Lynn Kurland   0-515-11839-7/$5.99
A young woman inherits a castle — along with a ghost who tries to
scare her away. Her biggest fear, however, is falling in love with
him...

__*SPRING ENCHANTMENT*
by Christina Cordaire   0-515-11876-1/$5.99
A castle spirit must convince two mortals to believe in love — for only
then will he be reunited with his own ghostly beloved...

__*A GHOST OF A CHANCE*
by Casey Claybourne   0-515-11857-5/$5.99
Life can be a challenge for young newlyweds — especially when the
family estate is haunted by a meddling mother-in-law...

__*ETERNAL VOWS*
by Alice Alfonsi   0-515-12002-2/$5.99
After inheriting a French Quarter mansion, complete with
beautiful antiques and a lovely garden, Tori Avalon also
inherits a pair of ghosts...

Payable in U.S. funds. No cash accepted. Postage & handling: $1.75 for one book, 75¢ for each additional
Maximum postage $5.50. Prices, postage and handling charges may change without notice. Visa,
Amex, MasterCard call 1-800-788-6262, ext. 1, or fax 1-201-933-2316; refer to ad # 636b

Or, check above books   Bill my: ☐ Visa ☐ MasterCard ☐ Amex _____ (expires)
and send this order form to:
The Berkley Publishing Group   Card#_____

P.O. Box 12289, Dept. B   Daytime Phone #_____ ($10 minimum)
Newark, NJ 07101-5289   Signature_____

Please allow 4-6 weeks for delivery.   Or enclosed is my: ☐ check ☐ money order
Foreign and Canadian delivery 8-12 weeks.

Ship to:

Name_____   Book Total $_____
Address_____   Applicable Sales Tax $_____
                                         (NY, NJ, PA, CA, GST Can.)
City_____   Postage & Handling $_____
State/ZIP_____   Total Amount Due $_____

Bill to: Name_____

Address_____ City_____
State/ZIP_____

Time Passages

_LOST YESTERDAY
Jenny Lykins
0-515-12013-8/$5.99

Marin Alexander has given up on romance. But when she awakens from a car accident 120 years before her time, she must get used to a different society and a new life—and the fact that she is falling in love...

_A DANCE THROUGH TIME
Lynn Kurland
0-515-11927-X/$5.99

A romance writer falls asleep in Gramercy Park, and wakes up in 14th century Scotland—in the arms of the man of her dreams...

_REMEMBER LOVE
Susan Plunkett
0-515-11980-6/$5.99

A bolt of lightning transports the soul of a scientist to 1866 Alaska, where she is married to a maddeningly arrogant and irresistibly seductive man...

_THIS TIME TOGETHER
Susan Leslie Liepitz
0-515-11981-4/$5.99

An entertainment lawyer dreams of a simpler life—and finds herself in an 1890s cabin, with a handsome mountain man...

_SILVER TOMORROWS
Susan Plunkett
0-515-12047-2/$5.99

Colorado, 1996. A wealthy socialite, Emily Fergeson never felt like she fit in. But when an earthquake thrust her back in time, she knew she'd landed right where she belonged...

_ECHOES OF TOMORROW
Jenny Lykins
0-515-12079-0/$5.99

A woman follows her true love 150 years into the past—and has to win his love all over again...

VISIT THE PUTNAM BERKLEY BOOKSTORE CAFÉ ON THE INTERNET:
http://www.berkley.com

Payable in U.S. funds. No cash accepted. Postage & handling: $1.75 for one book, 75¢ for each additional. Maximum postage $5.50. Prices, postage and handling charges may change without notice. Visa, Amex, MasterCard call 1-800-788-6262, ext. 1, or fax 1-201-933-2316; refer to ad # 680

Or, check above books and send this order form to:	Bill my: ☐ Visa ☐ MasterCard ☐ Amex _____ (expires)
The Berkley Publishing Group	Card#_____
P.O. Box 12289, Dept. B	Daytime Phone #_____ ($10 minimum)
Newark, NJ 07101-5289	Signature_____

Please allow 4-6 weeks for delivery. **Or enclosed is my:** ☐ check ☐ money order
Foreign and Canadian delivery 8-12 weeks.

Ship to:

Name_____	Book Total	$_____
Address_____	Applicable Sales Tax (NY, NJ, PA, CA, GST Can.)	$_____
City_____	Postage & Handling	$_____
State/ZIP_____	Total Amount Due	$_____

Bill to: Name_____

Address_____City_____
State/ZIP_____

Our Town

...where love is always right around the corner!

■■■■■■■■■■■■■■■■■■■■■■■■

__ *Harbor Lights* by Linda Kreisel   0-515-11899-0/$5.99

__ *Humble Pie* by Deborah Lawrence   0-515-11900-8/$5.99

__ *Candy Kiss* by Ginny Aiken   0-515-11941-5/$5.99

__ *Cedar Creek* by Willa Hix   0-515-11958-X/$5.99

__ *Sugar and Spice* by DeWanna Pace   0-515-11970-9/$5.99

__ *Cross Roads* by Carol Card Otten   0-515-11985-7/$5.99

__ *Blue Ribbon* by Jessie Gray   0-515-12003-0/$5.99

__ *The Lighthouse* by Linda Eberhardt   0-515-12020-0/$5.99

__ *The Hat Box* by Deborah Lawrence   0-515-12033-2/$5.99

__ *Country Comforts* by Virginia Lee   0-515-12064-2/$5.99

__ *Grand River* by Kathryn Kent   0-515-12067-7/$5.99

__ *Beckoning Shore* by DeWanna Pace   0-515-12101-0/$5.99

__ *Whistle Stop* by Lisa Higdon   0-515-12085-5/$5.99

__ *Still Sweet* by Debra Marshall   0-515-12130-4/$5.99

__ *Dream Weaver* by Carol Card Otten   0-515-12141-X/$5.99

__ *Raspberry Island* by Willa Hix (10/97)   0-515-12160-6/$5.99

Payable in U.S. funds. No cash accepted. Postage & handling: $1.75 for one book, 75¢ for each additional. Maximum postage $5.50. Prices, postage and handling charges may change without notice. Visa, Amex, MasterCard call 1-800-788-6262, ext. 1, or fax 1-201-933-2316; refer to ad # 637b

Or, check above books   Bill my: ☐ Visa ☐ MasterCard ☐ Amex _____ (expires)
and send this order form to:
The Berkley Publishing Group   Card#_____

P.O. Box 12289, Dept. B   Daytime Phone #_____ ($10 minimum)
Newark, NJ 07101-5289   Signature_____

Please allow 4-6 weeks for delivery.   Or enclosed is my: ☐ check   ☐ money order
Foreign and Canadian delivery 8-12 weeks.

Ship to:

Name_____   Book Total $_____

Address_____   Applicable Sales Tax $_____
                                         (NY, NJ, PA, CA, GST Can.)
City_____   Postage & Handling $_____

State/ZIP_____   Total Amount Due $_____

Bill to: Name_____

Address_____City_____

State/ZIP_____